NADIR

The Rite of Kings

Book Three

NADIR

G.A. Renteria

To my mother Norma,

for without giving me books as a boy,

I would not write these tales as a man.

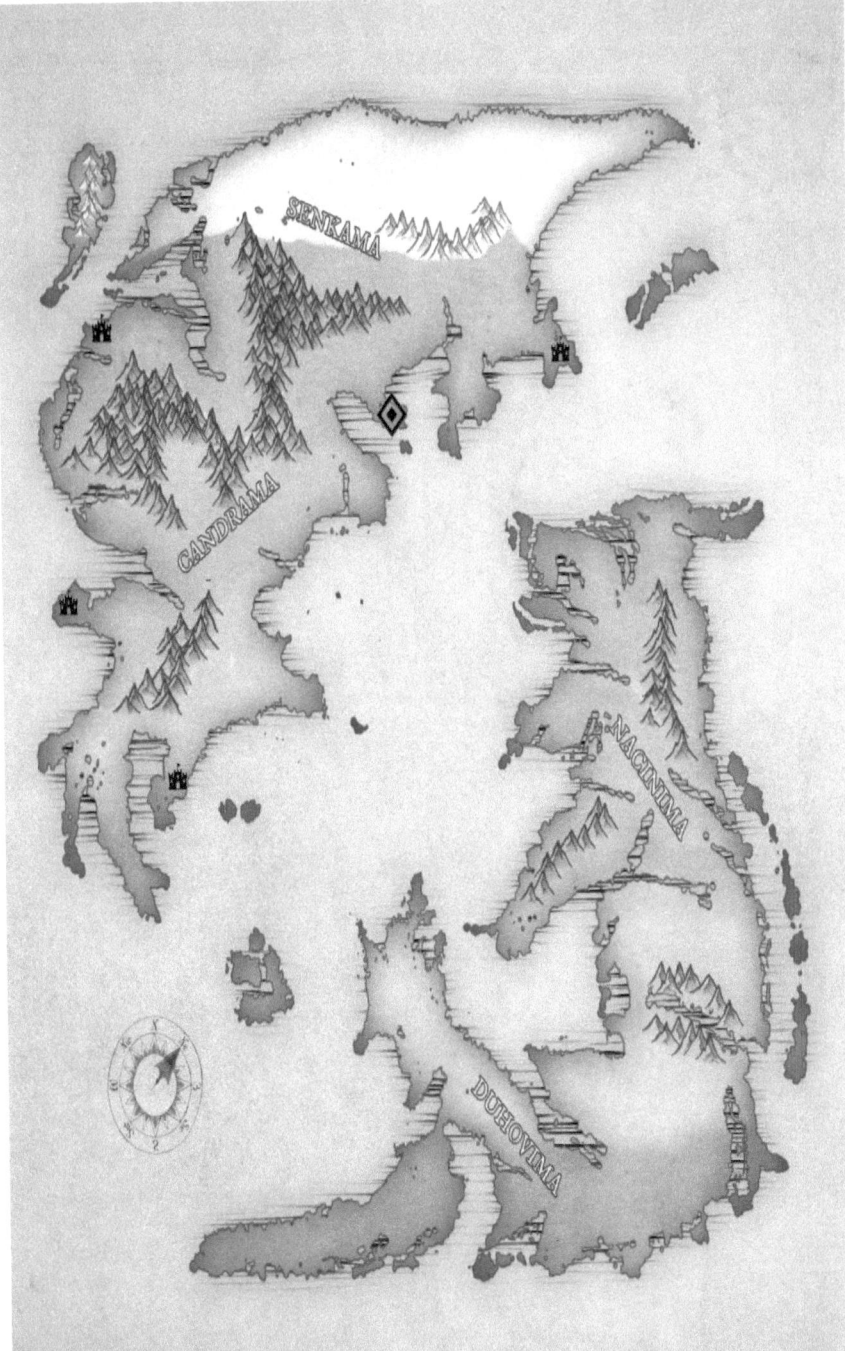

PROLOGUE.

Karja stepped into the outskirts of the nearby village. With anxious hands, he pushed the ebony locks from his face, sweeping them behind his ear. Each step took him past the nestled shacks and homes where he heard the people getting ready for the day.

His people.

The chattering of children filled the air as they wandered around. He saw some of them rushing towards the village center. Remembering what day it was, Karja followed their trail and a few of them looked back with bright smiles and inquisitive eyes. He rested his hand on his blade, twitching as he contemplated.

In the village center sat a gathering of worn stones around a large pit. Within the pit burned a bonfire and several members of his people stood beside it with offerings in hand. These were the heads of the different clans, convened this day in solemn remembrance. Today was their day to remember the losses of their people. Several of them bowed their heads with deference towards Karja, knowing he was a *krusho* for the Chuyara tribe. He stood beside his chief, Haljn, as they waited their turn for the offering.

"Where is the *cesogez?*" he whispered into his chief's ear.

"Talking with the half-blood. Their meeting went long."

1

An icy spike shot through Karja as he considered that information, "He is here today?"

Haljn nodded, "She invited him to the remembrance, it seems. He, too, lost much during those dark days."

Karja fell silent. He watched as the other chiefs turned to the sound of marching, bowing their heads respectfully. A tall woman with braided silver hair led a procession of her people. Her own *krusho* followed close behind, but Karja noted that they were farther back than usual. A lightly-tanned man with raven-colored hair trailed behind her instead. He stopped outside the gathering before he bowed his head respectfully to the other chiefs.

Karja noted the way they bowed their heads in response. He was still astonished by the fact that this southern half-blood had garnered their courtesy and respect. Grinding his teeth, he fought to suppress the feeling of the bile rising up in his throat.

The woman approached the bonfire with her offering in her hands. She held five long claws of a *davoarth*, their midnight-black hue striated by the flickering flames of the bonfire. She threw them into the conflagration. Flames licked at them, causing them to crack with a snap before they burned away into ash within the raging flames.

She cleared her throat before speaking, her gaze still on the dwindling ash. "The spring has come and gone, with another winter past behind that. Another winter that we thrived and grew as a people." Her gaze left the ash as she looked over the others, their faces filled with indulgent delight. "Yet, that was not always true. It has been many years since the dark winter that claimed much of our own," she said, drawing somber gazes from all around. "There is little that I can say that can comfort those that bore witness to it. We almost lost ourselves beneath the marching tide of the dogs of the southlands. Thankfully, with insight from our elders and the unity of our people, we found a place to stay safe while the wild men of the south ran amok through the lands."

Grumblings emanated through the crowd, but Karja noted they were in general agreement.

"We thought ourselves lost for a moment, fighting against the wills of the land itself to reclaim what was ours. What is *ours*." She marched around the bonfire, her words stirring with each step. Even the children, normally rambunctious and filled with fidgeting energy, sat still as they watched her with awe and respect. "And in time, we did. Even though more fell during the harshest years, we took back the lands and regained the pride we once held as a people"

In spite of his own feelings, a smile spread across Karja's face, an action reflected in many others at the gathering.

"The dark winter was thought to have stolen away a line of our people. A family as ancient as the blood that runs through my veins. Many believe the cruel blades of the duplicitous king's men and the frigid winter had ended the Ombroj line forever." said the woman. The procession quieted, with even the children becoming glum at the woman's shift in tone.

"However, today, I ask of the other chiefs who stand with me to remember our fallen, to recognize that the Ombroj line lives," she stated. There were several sounds of disbelief from the group, with even Haljn voicing his discontent. Karja felt a lump in his throat.

"Many of you know the man I speak of," continued the woman, walking around the bonfire to meet with each of the chief's gazes. Her silver eyes never faltered from their piercing gazes, and eventually they would nod and she would move on. She stopped before Haljn, and the man met her gaze before nodding.

"He will not fit, Nyeth," said Olwynn, the chieftain of the Varjud clan.

Nyeth drew before him, "I would hear your concern."

"He is not of our people. He profited from the kingdom's invasion, living amongst them in their wealth and splendor. He knows nothing of the suffering his kin caused."

Nyeth nodded, "It is true. Only recently has he come to learn of the depth of the kingdom's deceit against us. But for years, he has lived away from everyone and all, rejecting the ways of the southerners to better find a place for himself. He treads not into our lands uninvited and has shown the utmost respect for all of our people."

Several of the other chiefs murmured in agreement. Aida, the chieftainess of the Kabrea clan, spoke however.

3

"He walks with the southerner," she stated simply. Her disdain was evident in her voice.

Nyeth nodded once more, "He does. They rely on one another for protection and company. Would you allow someone to suffer alone in the wilds of the *otedien?* They care for one another as you care for the members of your clan."

Again, the sounds of agreement sounded through the gathering.

"It is an odd thing I ask, I know," stated Nyeth. "To accept him, half-blooded, as the surviving member of the Ombroj is much to ask. But, I do so for the future of our people."

"What does he feel?" asked Aida.

"Ask him yourself," replied Nyeth. She beckoned to the man, who worked his way to her side. Garbed in simple fur-lined leathers, the only proof of his southern heritage was the tan of his face compared to the pale skin of Nyeth. He stood tall, his shoulders unbowed, and he was unafraid.

Calmly, he stated, "I wish to be honest with this: I did not ask Nyeth for this. Regardless, she told me she wished to put it forth and to let you all decide."

"Do you feel you are deserving of the name?" asked Aida.

"I feel that whether or not I am recognized by the clans does not change the fact that I bear the same blood as you all," replied the man. "My mother bestowed little to me regarding her people. The only lessons she did give me were to help me thrive."

Karja eyed the man with distaste. He knew that Nyeth regularly met with him over the years, and at first it was to ward him away from the people. He'd proven to be respectful, however, and never asked anything of Nyeth or the others. Before long, he offered up pelts and furs of animals he and his companion had killed in exchange for more plentiful foods, while still refraining to cross into their lands. Nyeth had slowly introduced him into the villages, showing him the traditions of their people. It had unnerved many of the survivors of the *javeaf,* but upon learning that he too had survived the winter alone, they bestowed him grudging tolerance.

"I am aware of the concerns regarding her request, and I would not put this forth myself," said the man. "I had no expectation of being allowed to even talk with your kin, and my appreciation for the acceptance you have shown me is boundless."

His mastery of their language had grown as well. When Karja first met him, he used simple words and sometimes stuttered as he spoke. Now, however, their language flowed effortlessly from his lips, and he spoke with clarity and intent.

Olwynn drew up to him, "I can see the same steadiness in your eyes that your grandfather had. That same serenity that never marred the grey. But I must ask: why the southerner?"

Without hesitation, he replied, "It is as Nyeth said before. She is my companion. We rely on each other, and I would never forsake her."

"If we asked you to abandon her for Nyeth's claim?"

"Then I will refuse it," he stated staunchly. "Never have I sought laurels or titles. My name is my own. I need little else for my happiness."

Olwynn grinned, "As expected."

Nyeth was smirking, "I ask of the clans, will you recognize him as the line of Ombroj?"

Karja saw the other chiefs take a few moments to speak with their *krusho* before offering their own tributes to the bonfire and returning to their positions. Aida passed the man and gave him a wink before depositing hers into the flames.

Nyeth said, "Very well. If you would," she beckoned for his offering, which the man picked up from the ground. He opened the bundle and revealed five more claws of a *davoarth*, his voice quiet as he deposited them into the flames. He watched them burn, the flickering orange in his grey eyes before moving to Nyeth's side.

Nyeth gazed over her people, "All in is accord?"

The chieftains spoke their accord. Karja saw they were convinced, but his keen eye spotted the discontent in several of them.

Nyeth turned to the man, her face softening as she said, "Welcome then, to the clans of our people, Sehren Ombroj."

Sehren bowed, "I thank you all. Recognizing me as one of your own fills me with a deep gratitude that I feel I will never repay. I will not let it fade, and in time, hope to prove your belief in me."

Nyeth said, "There is little you can do for that Sehren. None have lived in *otedien* or tamed it as you have. You, with little doubt, have the blood of your kin in your veins. I believe few could stand to the same expectations."

She gazed around, and Karja saw that the chiefs were already nodding in agreement. With a wide smile, she said, "Welcome back to the people, Sehren."

The declaration made the bile rise in Karja's throat.

ASTORIA.

Astoria's breathing was steady as she pulled the litter behind her. Upon it was the remnants of a cleaned kill, wrapped carefully to prevent debris and insects from landing upon the meat. Each step she took was accompanied by a scratching sliding noise, and to the experienced woman, it was music to her ears.

We will have meat for a good while.

She leaned forward as she pulled the litter. Two roughspun cords were tied around her shoulders. Even though the ground was uneven, she managed to pull the haul easily.

As she glanced over her shoulder at the trailing litter, she smirked when she saw the bundled fur stacked atop one another. The *davoarth* had proven too large to take in its entirety back to camp, but Astoria's experience with the beasts had helped her sort out the choicest bits. The fur would provide them more to trade with their neighbors, and once Sehren returned, they could sort out what they would keep and what they would trade.

Her tracking had initially led her to a buck, but after wounding the creature, Astoria had found the beast at the end of its trail. Not that she minded; *davoarths* were not common around their home, and if she felled one now, it meant they wouldn't have to worry about one sneaking up on them in the night, trying to pilfer their stores.

With a steady stride, Astoria dragged the litter through the winding lands, following the familiar path home. Even with puffing breaths, her senses were still on high, and she stayed vigilant for any other creature that could come in the wake of the freshly butchered meat.

As usual, however, nothing intercepted her path. Astoria felt a surge of pride through her. This was their land; their territory to control. While she knew that none of the creatures understood that notion, she was confident that her presence and Sehren's presence had set an expectation for any wild beasts that entered their lands.

Shaking her head, she swept the tangled locks of her wild mane over her shoulders, letting them rest upon her back. She idly considered having Sehren trim her hair once he returned but recalled when he had done so before. With a smirk, she reconsidered. For all his precision, there were still things about him that lacked his normal edge.

The sun was quickly approaching the horizon as Astoria came upon the grove they had come to call home. In the few short years, more saplings had sprouted outwards from the copse, the tips of their woody bodies finally sweeping over her and Sehren. She dragged the litter, continuing towards the center, until she saw the familiar grouping of hides and tents.

Rimmed around a closely grouped set of trees was several lengths of thick leather, forming a large tent that dominated the center of their home. The top of it was offset, consisting of another piece held up by a long pole that rested over the opening, allowing smoke to escape. The tent was drawn closed, and Astoria was relieved that it remained how she left it. She walked past the low fencing they had made and opened the makeshift gate that Sehren had constructed. The lands had not been shy of wood, and after a particularly blustery winter, Sehren had taken many days and many trips to bring back wood that they used to put up a small fence around their home.

Astoria shut the gate behind her before continuing to drag the litter to another small tent supported by other logs. The creek, now widened to a small river, was covered in one spot by the tent. She finished dragging the litter to it, dropped the straps, and wrung out her arms before opening it.

Several long ropes affixed with mesh nets dangled into the flowing water below. The air was humid here, with the tent keeping in the flush of the river that flowed beneath it. With practiced strokes, Astoria cleaned the fat and meat from the bear, separating both from one another as she rested the cleaned hides beside her. She wiped her carving blade on the side of a rough wooden bowl, scraping the fat from it into it. The beasts were always thick with fat, even in the early months of the year, but it still amazed her how much she would clean from their hides when she cleaned them.

Astoria pulled one of the ropes, trying to find a mesh that was free. When she did, she packed the meat she had butchered into the mesh. Making sure that the meat was secure, she lowered it into the flowing stream. She nodded to herself once she saw that the mesh would hold and released the rope.

At least that's done.

She left the tent, dipping the litter into the stream downstream from the tent, washing away the remaining blood that was on it. Once finished, she loaded it with the hide and pulled the strap over her left shoulder before grabbing the bowl of fat and heading back to the center tent. She entered, setting aside the litter and bowl beside the entrance.

A waist-high stone pit sat in the center, about three feet in diameter, and Astoria approached it. She pulled the crude metal grate from the mouth of the pit before reaching down and clearing away the old refuse and ash. After she finished, she walked over to a set of splintered wood, breaking it into small pieces and setting it within the pit. Once she was confident there was enough, she shaved off flecks and chips from a remaining log, making enough to build a small, soft pile of tinder. Astoria retrieved an old, worn dagger from a wrapped bundle beside the pit, and with practiced strikes, skipped sparks onto the small pile until the telltale wisps of smoke and embers caught in the middle. Cupping the tinder carefully, she set it atop the bundled wood, blowing on it lightly to let the embers grow. They eagerly ate away at the chips before catching on the wood, and before long, a small fire was crackling in the center of the pit.

Pleased with herself, Astoria let the flames continue as she pulled the leather jerkin from her body. While warm, she found it too snug for wearing around camp. Retrieving a worn, threadbare coat, she wrapped herself in it as she tended the fire pit, adding more fuel to the flames until it crackled merrily. Once the flames licked the mouth of the pit, she set the grate back atop it.

She rested beside the pit, rubbing out the tingling feeling in her arms from the long trek home. Her lean muscles were tense but thankfully not sore. As she felt the stones growing hot from the flames, she leaned back against a fallen log that rested beside the pit inside the tent. Normally she sat atop it, but after the long hike, she was content to lean against it and let the warmth wash over her.

Her eyes trailed over to the notches in the log. She took the dagger and with some difficulty, added three more marks to the side of it. She glanced down the length of it and saw more similar marks, with different variations. She grinned as she counted, thinking that spring must soon be coming to an end and that from there things would be the warmest they would be all year.

Rising up with a stretch, Astoria grabbed a dented pail and walked outside to fill it in the stream. The bottom of it was black with soot, and as she filled it, she watched several birds digging through the soil for small critters. Once the pail was filled, she went back into the tent and set it atop the grate, sizzling and sputtering accompanying it. The flames licked the bottom of it for a while as Astoria idly kept count in her head. She stuck the tip of her finger into the water. It was tepid. Shivering in anticipation for what came ahead, she drew the pail from the grate and walked to a more sheltered area within their camp. Astoria divested herself of her clothing. With a deep breath to steady herself, she upended the pail and poured the water over her. It washed away the grime that had accumulated from the hunt as it rushed down her body. Shuddering, she dropped the pail and wiped away the remaining water, letting out short, sharp breaths. Even though she had let it warm up, the slight breeze that cut through the air still stung her skin with chills.

While she was pulling her clothes back on, Astoria paused as she considered the scars that ran along her arms. The slender ones that had accumulated over the years were each a poignant reminder from her training. Many missteps were carved in her skin, but with Sehren's instruction and care, even those had diminished over the years, showing only through the tan she sported from her time in the sun. She traced her fingertips over them before she pulled her shirt on and covered herself with the coat.

10

As she returned to the tent, Astoria tossed several more pieces of wood into the fire pit. Their tent held in much of the heat, and together, they had cleared most of the brush from the ground before laying down the rough skins they had gotten from Nyeth, making the ground even throughout most of the tent. Soft furs were tucked away in a nook by packs, and clothes were bundled together on top of makeshift tables and shelves. The cooking implements had survived the years, and with the meat they hunted and the crops, albeit sparse, that they grew, they had a decent source of food. Sehren would occasionally follow the stream until it reached an ice-lake, and would return with freshly caught fish tucked away inside a waterproof sack.

It was comfortable, which was something that Astoria never truly believed they would have accomplished. Not when they first had gotten there. When they had first set up their camp, it had seemed a temporary thing with each night uncertain of what the morning would bring. Sehren had constantly reassured her that they would survive, but that seemed a paltry thing in the face of the hardships they had to endure.

After the first winter, and several more hunting trips by Sehren, they had things that Sehren believed would be fit to trade with the Senkamans. Their first meetings had been rough, usually held with open contempt, but Sehren didn't let them stymie his attempts. Eventually he had returned with bundled bones and hides and subsequent trades became easier and more profitable for them.

The camp had grown, with Astoria coming to believe in Sehren's idea that they would tame a portion of the land for themselves. She experienced first hand the depth of Sehren's resolve. Even when she had given up and all seemed grim, he continued on, his mind set onto their goal.

Astoria squirmed. She had called him many things in the first year, and most of their meals had been filled with pointed, angry silence. Twice, she had raged against him, uttering insults and slurs she had learned at her time in the Friar's Reprieve, each one a stinging barb that soothed the festering hate that had built within her. But when his serene grey eyes had simply watched her as she screamed at him, neither judging nor condescending but rather with the air of expectation, the moment of peace she had felt had passed and all that had remained was guilt.

I was such a child...

Sehren had forgiven her immediately, had even told her that he had expected much worse from her, but Astoria had never forgiven herself. There was a pit in her stomach from the incidents, one that she remembered not while she contemplated alone, but when she shared a meal with him or when they lied down to sleep, huddling for warmth.

Astoria took a small twig, lighting the tip of it from the pit before walking to the shelves and picking up a roughly-made candle. Touching the flame to the wick, she watched it sputter and catch, before setting it inside a lantern, shutting it as she made her way from the tent. She grabbed the pail once more and filled it with water.

Following a familiar path, Astoria came to their small plot of tilled soil, the sprouts of many crops poking their small leaves through the surface. She smiled, glad that the crops had taken this year, and thankful that Sehren had taken the strides he did for them.

He should be back tomorrow, thought Astoria as a fluttering feeling filled her stomach. He was visiting the Senkamans, and from what he told her, he should have good news when he did return.

Astoria set the lantern upon the ground, taking the pail in both hands and carefully watering the crops. Sehren told her it was important to keep the soil from drying out, but not to drown them. She poured precisely, the pail emptying exactly where it always had for the past three years.

She retrieved the lantern, letting out a small sigh of contentment as she turned from the plot and headed back to the tent.

NYETH.

Nyeth sat as she watched the ceremony ending with the other members of her tribe giving their offerings to the bonfire. Each member moved with purpose. Nyeth could see that the wounds of the past were long healed, and each offering was instead a reminder of how far they had come as a people.

She swept a stray strand of her silver hair from her face, watching with appreciation. She had led them since her own father had pushed southward, guided by the words and wisdom of her grandmother. When she heard that many of their people had fallen fighting to maintain their borders, it was Nyeth that knew the only solution was to retreat farther north, to let the wild winter weaken and dissuade their foes. Only once the snows had finally broken, and the sun was able to grace them with its warmth once more did Nyeth feel it was time to return to the southern parts of their lands, to pick up from where their people had once stood.

That had been long ago, with over twenty winters having come and gone since then. The children that had been left behind during the war were now the ones that nurtured the growth of their people, each of their own ways not forgotten. Almost twenty three hundred of their people walked the lands of the north, with those able to travel to the remembrance here today. Her own clan's village could stand to host them all, but Nyeth knew that the living elders of their people sought not a reminder of the days long past, and she didn't blame them. It was a remnant of a terrible time, and despite the desire to ease the pain of loss with the passing years, time had done little to cause the pain to fade.

The Ombroj clan had faded away, its forebears injected with a somberness so profound that it had stolen away their vigor and reason.

Except now their heart beat again.

Her silver eyes landed upon Sehren. As expected, he was waiting for moments to talk with the different chieftains to thank them, as she had instructed him. It would take more than just her declaration and his honest word to sway the anger and resentment that was nestled within the hearts of their people. He was living proof of the times before, when things had been shaped with gilded lies of cooperation and unity between their people and the south. His survival after those times and apparent adaptation made most of them suspicious of him. It was apparent that he was strong of arm and sharp of mind when he went north, and that called into question his past. He never spoke of it, not even to Nyeth, and while others believed him to be hiding something, Nyeth could only presume that he was running away from something.

To this day, Korrenth, her personal handmaiden, believed him to be a spy or double agent, but even when the woman had tracked his movements through their lands, he never went further south than necessary for their trading. And when confronted by their people, he always stood calm with determined but peaceful words.

Today though, he seemed relaxed for the first time since she'd met the man. He was polite and respectful, greeting each chieftain with a bow of his head. Some of them must have been within a few years of him, but no matter their stature or apparent age, he gave them the deference and respect they deserved.

None shirked from him, instead watching him with tempered curiosity. Aida halted his departure, and Nyeth watched as the woman seemingly interrogated him, but he again answered with a calm, even voice.

"You placed your faith correctly, it seems," said Olwynn, the older man coming to sit beside Nyeth. His dark eyes met Nyeth's silver ones and his brow was furrowed. His face sported many small scars and wrinkles danced at the edges of his eyes and mouth.

"He has shown deserving of it," replied Nyeth.

"I do not deny that, nor do I think any other here would," continued Olwynn. He too watched Aida continue her conversation with the man. "However, it will take more than just naming him for him to truly become the successor of Ombroj."

"He knows," said Nyeth. "It was not something I considered lightly."

Olwynn nodded. "Me and mine believe you made the right choice."

Nyeth laid her gaze upon him.

"The decisions you have made have kept our people strong, fed, and warm. We are still small compared to the days long past, but there is no doubt that we will once again roam these lands freely."

"I thank you for your confidence," replied Nyeth. "But I believe you have more to say about this matter rather than simply voicing your support."

Olwynn chuckled, "I do not, but I know that many others will. I tell you this to let you know that the Varjud back you and your decision. Others will try to find the flaws in your plan, but I wholeheartedly believe in your choice."

Nyeth gave him a smile, "I am prepared."

"As I know you are." His eyes trailed back to Aida, who had extended one finger and poked it into Sehren's chest, drawing looks of concern. "Is that wise?"

"He can handle himself," said Nyeth, watching on curiously.

Sehren slowly tilted his head down to Aida's outstretched hand, before meeting her gaze. Slowly, he lifted his own, causing her *krusho* to twitch nervously, but he simply left his palm open, his hand offered before him. Aida trailed from his chest across his shoulder and down his arm, eventually stopping at his wrist. She drew a blade from her side, swiftly placing the edge against Sehren's wrist. Sehren never broke eye contact with her, and she tested the edge against his skin.

People watched on nervously, with several looking to Nyeth for guidance, but she remained seated.

She extended the rest of her hand into his, clutching onto his with a cheshire grin spreading across her face. She returned the blade to her side as Sehren clutched onto her hand, an amused look coming onto his face.

Nyeth let out a small breath.

"Reminds me of when you first met him," called a gruff voice. Heavy footsteps brought a giant of a man beside Nyeth, his corded arms crossing over his chest as he drew up beside them.

"Ghorun," said Olwynn with a respectful bow of his head.

"I recall our encounter being much more violent than that," commented Nyeth as she met the man's gaze.

Standing well over six feet, Ghorun was a rarity in the northern people. While they were certainly strong of arm, most of Nyeth's people were lithe, with frames of lean, compacted muscle. Ghorun, however, was a veritable juggernaut, his torso framed with rippling muscle. Amber eyes carefully watched the scene, filled with an inquisitive light.

"You believe Aida would not turn it violent if he responded in kind?" asked Ghorun, his tone revealing his answer. Olwynn chuckled and Nyeth gave a wry grin.

"I would hope with the ceremony she would spare us her tumultuous behavior," replied Olwynn, "but the Kabrea are ever known for their shifting tempers."

Small rushing footsteps drew Nyeth's attention to a small child that had tucked his head onto her thigh, his little eyes sparkling at her.

Nyeth felt her tension melt away as she met his gaze, "What is it, Mikja?"

"Can I go see the new chief?" he asked, his eyes filled with innocent curiosity. "Papa said a new tribe was made today!"

Nyeth turned her head to Ghorun, who was smirking, "He finished lessons early today."

"Mikja, you know what today is, yes?"

16

Tentatively, he nodded his head.

"Then you should know that it would be improper. He is not some spectacle."

Chastened, the boy said, "Okay, mama. Can I see him another time then?"

She gave a steady nod. "When the time is proper, you will greet him as you have learned."

"Yes, mama."

Nyeth reached down and gave Mikja a hug, rubbing his back as his small arms wrapped around her, "Go now and find the other children. They are doing things more appropriate for you."

Nodding, Mikja started running off, before stopping and bowing before Olwynn and looking to Ghorun. Ghorun gave him a short nod of his head, and with that the boy ran off.

"He is spirited," said Olwynn.

"He gets that from his father," replied Nyeth as she rose from her seat.

"I believe that is the Katski blood in him," countered Ghorun, "never have I known such enthusiasm in my people."

Nyeth gave him a withering stare, "Sometimes I wonder about the soundness of my decisions."

Ghorun laughed. "As long as you find insight from it, then there is not a problem."

Nyeth gave him a short laugh. Truly, she would have had a hard time finding a better consort than Ghorun. The man's prowess could not be understated and having a good bond with the Thunzi tribe made things much easier.

Nyeth returned her gaze to the ceremony, her surprise evident when she saw Korrenth walking alongside Sehren as he spoke with her. They were in deep conversation as they made their way over to Nyeth. As they stopped before her, Korrenth went into a low bow as Sehren respectfully bowed his head. Olwynn rose, giving a short nod of his head to the pair of them before returning to his people.

"I see that you managed Aida," said Nyeth.

"It is as you said it would be. She is almost something of a tigress," replied Sehren.

"Perhaps you should take that into account," noted Korrenth. "Rarely does she treat people with such open—"

"Disdain?" offered Sehren.

"I was going to say affection," said Korrenth.

"I admit I must have missed something in the interaction then," replied Sehren.

Korrenth laughed, "Aida is the only other female chieftain within our people. She has a strong front because much is expected from her."

"I thought the tribes preferred it that way," said Sehren, looking at Nyeth.

"They do. But unlike myself, Aida is still adjusting to her own chief taking an elder place within their people. Her people respect her, but others outside her tribe do not believe she has the fortitude to lead."

"They think she is unfit," surmised Sehren. "What do you believe?"

"She is well and capable of becoming a great chief, if she can keep herself under control."

"I see."

"And with you becoming the newest chief, she will feel threatened if others give you more respect," added Korrenth. "Your clan name alone already elevates you above most, and coupled with your feat of staying alive so long in *otedien*, you have already accomplished something of a reputation."

"I still do not see the affection you mentioned," mused Sehren. He looked to Ghorun for advice but the man shrugged.

"Aida is testing you to see if you are worth the effort," said Korrenth.

Sehren blinked. "Ah. I see."

"It would be a good match," said Nyeth. "Aida would feel less threatened if your people were to be joined in alliance, and you should start to look towards the future of your clan."

"So many things to plan for," said Sehren. "I knew much was expected, but it has not even passed the first day."

"We are giving you advice," said Korrenth. "The sooner you become more integrated, the easier things will be."

"I thought all the clans were allied with one another," said Sehren.

"They are now," commented Ghorun. "We could ill afford to be fighting amongst ourselves. But, with the clans rounding out, old enmities are being unburied, and it would be wise to seek out other bonds."

Sehren looked back over his shoulder, letting out a sigh before turning back. "I shall give it some thought. Aside from what you have told me before, is there anything else I need to worry about?"

"You are a chief now," said Nyeth. "Do not forget that. Your territory is your own, but you also are allowed to claim the old lands of your blood. None reside there as of now. They are still for you to take, if you wish."

"Without Astoria," commented Sehren.

Silence crossed between them all. Sehren's gaze trailed over to the other people at the ceremony, watching them for a second.

"That will never change, will it?"

"You knew that coming here," said Nyeth.

"I also knew I would never be welcomed into your lands, on the pain of death," responded Sehren, facing them once more, "yet here I stand, sharing a solemn ceremony with you all."

"Time moves forward, but she is not us."

"She is part of me. And I am part of her."

Korrenth cleared her throat, "That may be true, but then you will have to stay in the lands north. None here would suffer a southerner in our lands, present company included."

"Seems then I will have to pause any plans with the other tribes then," said Sehren.

"Is that wise?" asked Korrenth.

"It is what it is," said Sehren. "Perhaps we will revisit this in another five years."

Korrenth sought Nyeth's gaze for guidance.

She was conflicted. Sehren had asked only once before if there would ever be a possibility that Astoria could travel through their lands. She had denied him. When he asked if there was a way to sway her, she stated that if he ever asked again, she would force another *kruparu* with him. He had never asked again. Even with Nyeth's idea of reinstating him as the head of his clan, he had not bothered to ask her.

"I have always known that the hatred runs deep," said Sehren, drawing Nyeth from her thoughts. "When you first received me all those years ago and told me you were willing to trade with me, I was surprised."

"No one had survived, let alone had things to offer," said Nyeth.

"I thought it a sign of things that could come," continued Sehren. "But, I often underestimate the depth of our natures. I do understand it, though. I would no sooner return to the southlands than you would allow someone from there to cross into your lands."

Sehren looked to the small children that were running around the bonfire, his gaze softening, "That still, however, did not prevent me from hoping."

Sehren gave Nyeth a bow, before turning and walking with Korrenth as she continued discussing other matters.

"Ombroj blood truly flows through him," said Ghorun quietly.

"That it does," agreed Nyeth. She watched as Mikja gave Sehren respectful distance before running to his side and calling for his attention. Sehren looked at the lad, kneeling down as Mikja chattered away. "That it does indeed."

KARJA.

Karja walked around as the ceremony was breaking for the day. He saw the children coming out more and more to play around the bonfire, their innocent eyes watching the great conflagration with awe. Several of the older children bowed respectfully towards him as he passed, nudging the others to do the same. As he walked away, they turned back to the bonfire, chattering away with one another.

Feeling bolstered, Karja strode through the people, greeting others calmly as he passed. He was recognized as he walked by and in turn given much deference. Being the *krusho* of the third most populous tribe, Karja had earned the respect of his people many years ago. He scanned around as he walked, keeping an eye out for any sources of trouble, but he couldn't help but find his gaze drawn back to the southernblood.

He spotted Sehren speaking with Nyeth's son, the lad chattering with him as Sehren listened intently. A burning feeling crawled up Karja's throat.

The elders must be turning in their graves.

Stymying his frustration with a sigh, he continued walking, until he found Haljn seated with his other *krusho*, sharing a meal with

21

them as they talked. Karja bowed deeply when he arrived, "Pardon me for my absence, chief."

"It is no bother," replied Haljin. "Here in remembrance, I doubt any would be foolish enough to strike out against another."

"Karja," called Beluk to the pacing man, "The meal is done. You should eat before the meeting."

"I find have no appetite," replied Karja, his tone grim. "I merely wish to be done with this."

"Even still, we have a long march after this. You should put something in your stomach," said Sejun.

Karja conceded the point with a short chuckle, "You are right." He ceased his pacing and retrieved some of the roasted meat, stripping away pieces with his teeth before swallowing.

"It is odd to see a new clan made," said Beluk. He was round-faced, his dark eyes seated with always a tell-tale hint of whimsy. Like Karja, he sported dark hair, but whereas Karja kept his hair cut shorter, Beluk let it flow freely down his shoulders, tied back only in the front so it would not hang in his face

"You mean an old clan reborn," countered Sejun. He sported a long face and eyes of deep brown. He was wiry, and always attributed that to the Thunzi blood that shared his veins."It is not a new clan."

"Even still, it has been decades since anything of the sort has happened. Even before—" Beluk paused for a moment as he regarded Haljn. He cleared his throat and said, "before *Javeaf.* When was the last time another clan was officially named?"

"It was the Itzalak," chimed in Haljin. "As for when they officially became part of our people, that has been lost with the years."

"There were more of us as well, back then," said Karja. "Far more. Names forgotten to the bleak winters and illnesses that claimed their spirits."

The conversation quieted for a moment, before Beluk said, "But here we are."

"Indeed. Our people have always been strong, even after everything. And we have grown stronger. United together, I feel the clans have a true chance at being rebuilt again."

"So you think it wise to name the southernblood as such?" asked Karja, looking to Haljn for his opinion.

"It is too soon to say," replied Haljn. "However I find I trust Nyeth's judgment on the matter. Without her guidance, our people would have long ago died out."

"You mean without her conviction," said Karja. "The elders gave her the advice and guidance. She merely had the will to carry it out."

"And leads us still to this day," said Haljn, concerned. He considered Karja for a moment as the man ate. "You find him ill-suited."

"I do not trust him," stated Karja staunchly. "There is no proof of his lineage other than the blade that Nyeth has claimed he wears. Yet, none of us have seen him bear it."

"It would be ill-advised," said Beluk.

"But it would allay the doubts I know the other clans have. He came here, claiming descent from a lost clan on the grounds of a name and a blade. It does not sit well with me, and we are all aware of the duplicitous nature of the southernfolk."

"His features are clear enough to see that he bears the blood of our people," said Sejun. "He shares the same eyes as *Svewyll*. There are few that could make the same claim, and in their line, all shared those same pale orbs."

Karja grudgingly nodded. "I am not used to the idea of having an enemy so close to home."

"He has not proven to be any enemy," said Haljn. "I know that it is hard to consider having someone who shares their blood so close to our own."

"You are worried then."

"I always consider the threats to our people," replied Haljn. "I agreed with Nyeth because I believe in her. She is sound of mind and has already proven time and time again that she works for the betterment of us all. If she believes the southernblood to be a viable chieftain, then I will agree. Only time will be the judge of her decision."

All of them, barring Karja, nodded. He glanced over to the bonfire, noting that Sehren seemed to have moved on as well. After finishing his meal, he excused himself.

"I wish to speak with Nyeth. Perhaps then, I can ease my misgivings," he said to Haljn. With a nod, the chief gave him leave.

Karja walked along, weaving through the people and watching for the playing children. He saw Nyeth seated with Ghorun, both in deep discussion. They were deeply engrossed. Karja was not certain if it was his place to speak with her. His gaze trailed off before landing upon Sehren bowing to Korrenth as she took her leave. He met Karja's gaze and bowed his head respectfully as he made to leave.

Karja beckoned towards him, signaling with his head. Surprised, Sehren followed behind.

"You seem to be the only one armed," said Sehren after a moment. Karja looked over his shoulder to regard him.

"The job of a *krusho* never wanes. There are times I have to be ready even if all seems well."

"I am familiar with that mindset," said Sehren. "I just noticed that none of the others seemed similarly armed."

Karja rested his palm on the pommel of his blade, "I take my duty seriously."

"That is comforting," replied Sehren.

Karja gave cursory glances to Sehren as they walked, taking note of his smooth gait. It was a warrior's gait, one that Karja knew all his people shared, but to see it so effortless in Sehren was surprising.

"I admit, I am unsure of the reason for your interest," said Sehren.

"Have you spoken to other *krusho* before?"

"Only in passing. Most seem to share a detestment of me, and while I do not blame them, I find it wearing on my patience."

24

"Haljn mentioned that it would be good for our people to start fostering good will between our tribes. We were once close people, before…" he cleared his throat, trying to shield his burning cheeks.

"Days long past," said Sehren, seeming to miss Karja's pause, "and not ones many wish to dwell on."

"I knew your grandfather," said Karja suddenly.

"Many did."

"He was a stern and strong man, but it seemed even he could not escape grief's withering touch."

Sehren remained silent.

"Nyeth once mentioned you were a soldier of sorts, before you traveled here," remarked Karja as they continued walking. He led Sehren to a brook before kneeling down and washing his hands in it. When Sehren did not give him a response, he shook his hands of the stinging, clinging droplets before meeting his gaze.

Sehren's face had not changed much, barring a small spark of inquisitiveness. His eyes, his grey eyes, however, held hints of suspicion.

"At least, I think that is what she meant," continued Karja.

"I do not recall mentioning anything of the sort to her," replied Sehren.

"She mentioned that you seemed well armed coming into the lands," said Karja, standing up once more.

"If you mean to mention the blade I carried, then yes, perhaps," Sehren cocked his head, his grey eyes searching Karja's form. Karja was used to such scrutiny, however, and remained calm, his face betraying nothing.

"I think so. Long has it been since the Ombroj walked among us, and I am sure she was surprised to see you bearing their blade."

"Its notoriety still escapes me," replied Sehren. "Nyeth was cryptic about it and remains cryptic to this day, if I ever have the presence of mind to mention it."

"Is that so?" Karja placed his hand on his chin, taking a moment. "I would have thought Nyeth would have given you the details of your people's history."

"She did. Enough for me to understand where we once stood. She mentioned little outside of what she thought was needed."

"And you have no curiosity?"

"There is little need of the stories where I live," Sehren's pragmatic tone stole Karja's following question, the starkness stealing away his momentum.

"I thank you for the conversation," said Sehren. "While I understand your expressed interest in developing the bonds between our people once more, I do not believe that goodwill can be fostered."

Karja cocked his brow, "Why do you think that?"

"The girl lives and will continue to so long as I do," stated Sehren, his voice firm.

Karja's stomach bubbled with disdain at the mention of the southerner. Sehren was resolute, and Karja was certain that nothing would befall the girl so long as he still drew breath.

Which unnerved him.

With a stiff nod, he gave Sehren a bow, with Sehren returning the gesture before he walked off to continue speaking with the other members of the tribe. Once again, Karja watched as he seemed to glide with his movements, every step perfectly controlled and balanced.

His hand rolled across the pommel of his blade. Grinding his teeth as he thought, Karja wondered.

He knows not what he asks.

Karja rested his hand upon the hilt of his blade, continuing to watch as Sehren returned back to the bonfire. He was accosted by Aida once again, and Sehren followed the woman to sit beside the fire, intently listening to every word she said.

Karja knew he would have to keep watch. Although Sehren had mentioned that he would be doing little to foster relations between the clans, it seemed he was already on his way with the Kabrea.

Just what do you so possess, southerner?

It still escaped him that Nyeth would push so much for a member of the kingdom to share a bond with them all. He could still remember the anxiety he felt watching his father leaving for war. He still remembered the aches in his heart when his mother had fallen in their flight. He still held the grief as the cruel cold took other members of his tribe. He remembered Nyeth then, just a small girl with sparkling silver eyes filled with fire and determination.

And vengeance.

Yet Sehren had managed to assuage that anger, that grudge buried so deep within the survivors of their people. The woman that had once fiercely patrolled their lands had softened in regards to him. Nyeth had let him and his companion live once they had crossed into their lands, and none had questioned her decision. The first time Sehren met with the chiefs, he had faced a rush of hatred, but he stood firm, his face holding empathy and acceptance.

And Karja couldn't understand why.

He bit his thumb, the sharp pain as his teeth sheared off the tip quelling the conflux of questions within his mind. He tasted blood.

But for Karja, it was a familiar and comforting taste.

ROSLINE.

"We will need the medicinals restocked. The spring was unkind to us, and I don't wish to be unprepared for what the gales of the summer might bring."

"Yes, Lady Rosline."

"And have we properly sent out the couriers to the trademasters so that we can get the shipments arranged correctly? Lady Eleanor wishes to send out the first shipments once we can confirm that the last of the spring thaw has finished."

"The couriers were sent a tenday ago, but I shall get another sent for a continuation and update."

Rosline nodded, "Good. That's all then. Dinner will be ready once Lady Eleanor returns, yes?"

"It has been stewing all day, and I believe the kitchen accounted for her elongated meetings for it to be done by then."

"Perfect. Very well, you are dismissed then."

The servant bowed to Rosline, who returned it with a modest curtsy. As they left, Rosline took a deep breath before heading upstairs. She walked along the hallway, other servants bowing their heads as she passed by. She approached a door, turning the knob and stepping inside as she let out a long breath.

I will never get used to this.

Rosline glanced around the room. Her room. The notion still amazed her, even after all these long years. Eleanor had given it to her after her first year, not content to have Rosline staying among the guest rooms. At first, Rosline hadn't known what to say, but Jaks had taken her hand in his and, with his comforting smile that always hinted at amusement, told her she deserved it.

It contained more things that Rosline had ever owned. A tall bureau held several different dresses that had been tailored specifically for her. A dresser stood by the wall, next to a desk with several books upon it, all gifts from Eleanor to help foster her into the life as her handmaiden. She even had her own maid, Geneve, who tended to her room and chores when Rosline had to act in Eleanor's stead.

And still, even with five years passed, Rosline had moments where she believed this was all beyond her. She traced the sturdy post of her bed, it and its other companions holding long, gossamer sheets that Rosline could draw around her when she slumbered. The fine sheets and blankets that laid within the chest at the foot of the bed were not moth-worn or threadbare, but soft, sumptuous, and soothing.

She pulled the lace net from her head and uncoiled her cinnamon-hued hair from the intricate bun that Geneve had set hours earlier. She left the braid in though, draping her hair over her shoulder, knowing she should still try and keep proper in case Eleanor had decided to bring a guest home. It was becoming more and more of a common occurrence these days, and Rosline wanted to do the best not to embarrass her lady.

She stepped into the small washroom connected to her room, another luxury that Rosline was still unaccustomed to. A long tub sat by a curtained window, with a set of steps beside it to help Rosline climb into it. Geneve had left sweet potpourri out, imbuing the room with a delightful, cloying scent.

Rosline rinsed off her hands in the basin, before reaching up and untying the length of cloth that rested over her eyes. She blinked before doing so, slowly opening her eyes as she stared into the silver mirror over the basin.

Dark eyes stared back at her, almost inky black. Rosline could see the swirling within her irises, a phenomenon that led her to continue wearing the cloth over them all these years. As the world slipped into view beneath her umbral gaze, Rosline took a moment to focus and steady herself as she stared deep into her inky orbs. They had regained their luster over the years, the advice of Eleanor coupled with Rosline burgeoning talents slowly healing the trial she had endured. However, even with the shadowy black that once rimmed her eyes dispelled, Rosline's eyes had never regained their dark brown glow that had made Jaks smile.

Rosline traced her finger along the length of her cheek, her eyes following the movement carefully. The movement, so innocuous, threatened to pull her gaze into the world she had become familiar with over the years. She had learned focus, however, and tempered her curiosity with the discipline gained from her failures. She closed her eyes, steadying herself with a deep breath. The world around her melted away, only showing where she was looking and after a few more moments, it fell into its normal hue. Pleased with herself, Rosline tied the length of cloth around her wrist, not wishing to be without it should her focus break. She rinsed her hands in the basin beneath the mirror once more before a knock on the door drew her attention.

She ambled over to it, opening it and smiling when she saw the little girl eagerly waiting.

She had a thicket of brown-hair, streaked with light highlights. It was a tangled, curly nest, but it framed her kind face. Nestled within were excited eyes the color of dark honey, filled with inquisitiveness and curiosity. Her child-like grin warmed Rosline's heart, and her voice chirped, "Mama!" when she saw the door open.

"Come here, my little dove," said Rosline, kneeling down and holding her arms outstretched. The girl jumped into her grasp, nuzzling her cheek against Rosline's before pecking it lightly with a kiss. Rosline lifted her up, before she met the gaze of the servant waiting politely for her. "Hello Kurtis. Did she do well today?"

"Kyrah's lessons are going exemplary, Lady Rosline. She takes to most of them with ease but it is a trying matter to keep her focused." His voice was calm and even, and Rosline could see that he was incredibly pleased with her.

"And I take it she finished early," she looked down at the girl in her arms, and a proud smile stretched across the child's face as she nodded eagerly.

"I thought it unwise to push into new topics when she had already accomplished so much," said Kurtis. "I spoke with a few of the others, and they told me you had already returned to your room. I hope I was correct in assuming you were finished for the day."

"You were," replied Rosline. "I was merely preparing for any guests that might be coming with Eleanor this evening, but I can take Kyrah for the afternoon if you wish to rest yourself."

"Whatever you desire, milady," said Kurtis with a bow. "If needed, I can take her during dinner if there is a guest brought along. I have a few more stories that I believe she would like to hear."

Kyrah's face filled with delightful eagerness, "Yes. Please!" She added, almost as an afterthought.

Kurtis gave her an endearing smile before bowing to Rosline and ambling off.

"Mama, are you happy for me?"

"I am, my dear. You are so talented."

Kyrah beamed, her eyes sparkling as Rosline carried her back into the room and deposited her upon the bed. Kyrah immediately climbed down, watching her mother as Rosline took a seat at a desk.

"Do you have things to do?" asked Kyrah.

"Just a few," admitted Rosline. "But if you'd like, you can sit and watch."

Kyrah beamed, climbing into the other chair adjacent to the desk. Rosline slowly wrote in a ledger, with Kyrah watching for a moment before fiddling with the candle holder on the desk. Rosline watched her ball up some of the old wax and turn it into a small caricature of a mouse, using soot to color the wax to make its eyes.

She smiled. Kyrah asked questions all the while but continued molding, eventually finishing with small strands of her hair for whiskers.

"Mama, will papa come by later?" asked Kyrah.

Rosline gave her a kind gaze, choosing her words before answering, "Not tonight, I don't think. He is still out of the city, making sure that things for his job continue to go well."

Kyrah pouted, "But he will be back, right?"

"Of course, dear. Nothing would stop him from seeing you."

Kyrah beamed again. She hopped down from the chair and moved to the wide window to peer out it.

"Be careful," said Rosline. "Don't lean out."

"Yes, mama."

Rosline watched Kyrah's sparkling eyes dart around as she watched the people in the gardens and avenue beyond. Seeing her daughter preoccupied, Rosline took a steadying breath before letting her gaze slip into the umbral haze as she began searching.

Almost at once, as though it was waiting, her vision flickered to the myriads of blacks, greys, and whites that were so starkly disturbing. Rosline focused and the shifting shades took form, with several amorphous figures scattering at the edges of her sight.

She peered southward, trying to see if she could spot her love, but after sorting through the countless faces and feeling her temples start to ache, she shook her head and started making efforts to return her gaze to normal when a flickering to the north caught her attention. She latched onto it, feeling her sight pulled far from the city, far from the rolling farmlands, until it landed in a small village, with several people garbed in fur lined leathers. Pressure built in her temples, but grasping the pendant that hung at her neck with a steadying breath, she pushed forward.

The image shifted, the blackened ground giving way to the altering shades of people. One, a man with a calm face, stood before a bonfire, his eyes studying it. Even in the shrouding shade, she could clearly see their pale grey hue, as if illuminated in the gloom. He flickered his gaze towards her for but a moment, Rosline flinching as she saw his face shift into curiosity, but the pain grew to be too much behind her eyes, and she eased herself back into the lighted world, rubbing her temples soothingly as she regained focus.

"Mama?"

Rosline turned to Kyrah, who was watching her, her honey-hued eyes filled with curiosity and concern.

"I am fine," said Rosline with a smile. "I just got caught up in my thoughts for a moment."

"Can we go to the garden?"

Rosline cocked her head as she considered the ledger on the desk, before smiling and saying, "We should. It's a wonderful day outside."

She grasped Kyrah's hand and feeling her small fingers in her grasp melted away all the aches within her head.

Eleanor returned late that afternoon as the sun dipped below the horizon. Garbed in a fine dress suited for a woman of her station, she was escorted by Railand, her own personal guardsman. Everything about the man screamed knight, but he never took the vows of the illustrious Knights of Isle. Railand was not fond of the band of soldiers, a fact that he made abundantly clear. He considered them little more than upjumped sellswords, trading their lives for standing, and while that had ruffled the feathers of some aristocrats, Eleanor appreciated the man's forthcoming nature. From what Rosline had heard and seen, he was adept with his blade and incredibly perceptive.

His mixed heritage was evident as well, his face and skin holding his telltale lineage of Naciniman heritage. He had burgundy eyes, with shoulder-length black hair. Many believed that he was part Candraman, but Railand had never confirmed that with anyone. Even the blade at his side, a rather peculiar curved variation of the longsword, was imbued with the legacy of his heritage, and while most guards opted for mail and shield while on duty, Railand tended to wear a simple scaled cuirass with a thick cloak.

"Milady. Railand," said Rosline as she bowed her head. Kyrah at her side followed suit, drawing a kind smile from the man.

"Shall we go to do something fun while they talk?" asked Railand, crouching before Kyrah. She sought Rosline's permission, her eyes alight with excitement.

"You can."

"I know a fun spot in the garden!" said Kyrah excitedly, and she ran off with Railand following after her.

"She is spry," said Eleanor.

"She is. Takes after her father, I suppose."

Eleanor smirked before walking towards the dining room with Rosline following close behind. Servants bowed before both of them as they passed and, once they sat themselves down at the table, Eleanor let out a deep sigh.

"I'm guessing the meeting didn't go as well as planned," said Rosline as the servants brought in food.

"You would guess correctly," said Eleanor. "Many of the other merchants that I've come to do business with are finding themselves lax in the melt, with most of them not chartering caravans until the start of the next month."

"That is... ridiculous," replied Rosline at length.

"Indeed. It took a while to express my disdain without being, as they say, 'off-putting,' but I believe I was able to convey to them that this is unacceptable and cannot continue."

Rosline shook her head. While Eleanor had inherited her father's business, many of his contacts had not found the woman a suitable replacement for the man. That is, until Eleanor had turned their businesses on their heads. She was devilishly smart and intuitive, with Rosline learning that Eleanor had a knack for seizing many advantages from her station while doing her best to mitigate the disadvantages of her sex. Indeed, Rosline had taken note during her years as her apprentice, becoming startled to see that even the most mundane of Eleanor's techniques yielded grand results.

"With everything sorted, we should be able to ride through the spring and most of the summer without a hitch," said Eleanor as she navigated her plate one-handed. Quietly, she said, "Keep an eye on them, if you would. Especially Marquis."

"Yes, milady," said Rosline. She watched as Eleanor poked at her plate, and she could tell that even with her optimistic evaluation, she was bothered.

"I think I saw him today," said Rosline quietly.

Eleanor froze, her green eyes snapping to Rosline. They were filled with yearning. "You did?"

"He has pale grey eyes and black hair, yes?"

Eleanor nodded.

"Then I think so. He was in a village, watching a bonfire."

Eleanor sat back, her gaze fixed on Rosline. "Village? He wasn't alone?"

"No. It seems he found something in the north."

Eleanor broke her gaze for a moment as she thought, "He is still alive…"

"And faring well, it seems."

Eleanor gave an indulgent smile, before meeting Rosline's gaze, "Thank you."

"Of course."

They continued speaking in low tones about the merchants and their laxness in regards to Eleanor, but Rosline heard a spring in Eleanor's voice.

As Rosline finished her meal, she rose for a moment, before bowing to Eleanor.

"Don't forget that we have to investigate," said Eleanor as Rosline pushed in her chair.

"I haven't. I was going to wait until after Kyrah was asleep though. She caught me earlier."

"Do you think she shares your talent?" asked Eleanor, her voice innocuous.

I hope not.

"I don't know, but she seemed worried, and I don't think that's a good thing for a child to be fretting about."

Eleanor nodded, her eyes flickering with contemplation before saying, "I'll call for you if I need anything else. Thank you for sorting out things today."

"Of course milady," Rosline gave her one last bow before excusing herself to her room. She passed by the foyer, pausing a moment. She walked to the door, opening it and peeking out through the gardens. She could hear Kyrah's exuberant voice as she raced through the garden, and she saw Railand's amused face as he followed behind. They locked eyes for a moment, with Railand giving her an assuring nod before following along.

ARUHN CARVER.

Aruhn stepped down from his quarters, his brown eyes scanning the common room of the tavern. His tavern. It was filled this evening, with many guests packed into the tables and booths that lined the walls. His barmaids wove about the tumult, with glittering coins dashed upon their trays as they deposited drinks into the waiting patrons. Aruhn heard the barks of orders come from Celeste as she continued dealing with the guests, and the calm calls from another.

Aruhn looked upon Diyane, the woman calmly watching each guest, her hazel eyes taking stock of each person. They flashed at Aruhn, and she gave the shallowest of nods, before continuing her search.

The barkeep strode through the common room, occasionally stopping to talk with a familiar patron or friend, before reaching the woman.

"No one's here tonight," she said simply, her hand calmly resting on the hilt of her peculiarly curved blade.

"That's a relief," replied Aruhn as he walked past her and took his spot behind the bar. Diyane took the seat nearest the end of the bar, her back resting against it.

Aruhn set her a small glass of wine before turning to deal with the other patrons at the other end of the bar. Celeste made her way by, nodding curtly at Diyane before heading back towards the kitchen.

The clamor built throughout the evening, with Aruhn taking note of who was passing through. He stopped his bartending now and again to refer to a small ledger he held beneath the bar, jotting things down now and again. Diyane would give small reassuring nods whenever Aruhn beckoned towards her, his gaze focused on a particular patron.

"So many unexpected faces," muttered Aruhn to her as he grabbed her empty glass.

"Unexpected for you perhaps. Trade season is starting late, and many that are meeting here are trying to pilfer the best deals." She continued scanning the place, her gaze narrowing when she spotted a man approaching the bar.

Aruhn snapped to her gaze, letting out a scoffing laugh when he saw Jaks approaching. His golden hair hung loose this evening, with his trademark bandana tied around his neck. Nimble steps brought him to the bar, and he slid into the seat next to Diyane, his gold and yellow segmented eyes glittering with mirth. Aruhn noted that some of the female patrons, as well a few male ones, took a long gander at the Duhoviman before returning to their own conversations.

"Gracious days lead to wondrous nights, wouldn't you say, Aruhn?" spoke Jaks, a roguish grin spreading across his face.

"Wondrous nights with many sights," chimed Diyane, her gaze returned to the crowd. Jaks' eyebrow arched, his grin widening as he regarded the woman. He looked her up and down, an appraising look upon his face.

"Is that so?"

"And most noted," continued Diyane calmly. "Don't look so surprised. It's what you pay me for."

Jaks let out a bark of a laugh before turning back to Aruhn, "It is good to see that you work well with Aruhn."

"He's shown to not be as forgone as I thought he might be." Diyane rose from her chair, adjusting her belt before heading to the door to step outside.

"You've grown on her," commented Jaks.

"Aye and I admit, she's grown on me," said Aruhn, setting down a drink for the wily Duhoviman.

"None for me tonight. I have another appointment after this that is long overdue, and I'd rather have a sound mind for it."

Aruhn laughed, his eyes darting over the crowd. Few were paying attention to the pair of them, caught up in the wiles of the night with the slapping hands of barmaids snapping them into revelry.

"I know I asked yeh before…"

"And yet again you wish to know. But even my eyes have their limits Aruhn. By all accounts, she is safe and well."

Aruhn let out a sigh, grumbling a bit but knowing that little could be done. "It's been years."

"Yes. Did you expect otherwise? The fact that I can't find her means that no one can, my old friend."

Aruhn frowned at him but as he cleared his throat he couldn't argue with the man on either count. The years had startlingly caught up to Aruhn. After the attempt on his life, it had been months before he had been well enough to work. It had been rough, each day punctuated with aches and stiffness. Without Celeste and his maids, he believed his place, his tavern, would've gone under.

Even these days, he swore he still felt the ache of the biting steel on his ribs or the twisting of the puckered flesh beneath and some nights he wanted to beg off ill.

"I still worry that it wasn't the right thing to do…"

"That is because your daring fire has smoldered for far too long, my friend," replied Jaks. "It was a perfect match with a sound plan. Few in the kingdom were on par with our friend and as we both learned, even the Knights found they couldn't contend."

41

Aruhn repressed a shudder at that. The discovery of Sir Irving's death had raised an alarm in the city. It was like a distressed hive, each day the order evaluating what they could bring to bear.

"And we know they left north. Outside their reach. But from there," Jaks shrugged. "No one truly knows anymore."

Aruhn nodded, tending to a new patron as Jaks whistled merrily beside them. Diyane returned from outside, taking her spot at the door with her hand on her blade and her gaze upon the crowd.

"I reckon I owe you for her too," said Aruhn.

"It's not a situation I am unused to. I would find it odd if you didn't owe me in some way," Jaks grinned at him, his odd eyes sparkling with cunning as he did. He scooped up the glass that Aruhn had set before him, drawing a confused look from the barkeep.

"Thought you had an appointment?"

"I do. It's for them," he rose from his seat before giving a wink to Aruhn. "Don't worry, I'll return the glass as usual."

He whistled as he walked away, winking at Diyane before stepping outside the tavern. The woman watched him for a moment before continuing her watch.

The tavern emptied out over the hours, eventually leaving the common room empty save for those that had booked lodgings. Aruhn was helping the last of his maids pick up before sending them off, locking the door before returning to the bar to tally up the night's take.

Diyane slid into the seat before him, once again resting her back against the bar and she stifled a yawn with the back of her hand. Aruhn saw the sleeve of her shirt ride up a bit, revealing the lotus flower tattoo upon her shoulder.

"I'm surprised yeh ain't gotten rid of that yet."

"I still work, Aruhn. Most of them believe I'm sitting on you for information," she yawned again. "Which isn't entirely untrue."

He laughed, "For this long?"

"You were the last one with her. It's a simple link, even for the dullest members."

42

"I guess." Aruhn watched the woman, still wondering about her. He'd come to learn a bit about her over the years, but the most startling thing he found was that she was never far away. The years had done little to loosen her lips though, but there were rare moments when she would let some of herself slip out. Some nights, she had even told him about her home in Nacinima, and in those moments, he thought he saw a bit more of her.

But he still kept his distance. Unlike Jaks, Diyane made her intentions clear, and he knew she only stayed around because Jaks told her too. She was a cutthroat woman, with Jaks telling him that pragmatism was her defining quality. However, Aruhn saw a few times where the mask slipped, and she acted on her own accord with something of benevolence. Twice, she had dispatched follow up assailants on Aruhn, with the second incident giving her a grievous wound. Aruhn had given her a room at the tavern to recover, and deep down he knew she appreciated that.

"Yeh ever think about goin' home, lass?"

"All the time."

"Why not go? Yeh have the means to."

Diyane's sharp gaze turned to him, "Why did you never close shop and leave Isle?"

Aruhn gave a sheepish shrug; she knew the answer. And so did he.

"I guess we're both a buncha fools, eh?" He chuckled and she gave him a wry grin.

"You may be. I consider myself a professional."

Aruhn took the barb as a jest. With another chuckle, he eyed Diayne, the woman taking a measured sip from her glass.

"I wonder, still to this day, how'd you manage to get so far."

"By taking the paths I needed," she replied easily. "It is not so hard to get what you want."

"Even against those that fight for what they need?"

"Is that not what you once did?" she asked rhetorically.

43

Aruhn quieted at that. He'd been a broker for years, harboring the best kept secrets within the City of Isle to be sold not to the highest bidder, but to the right person at the right time. He'd been instrumental in keeping the chaos under control, all while living the life he'd wanted.

"Aye."

"Your age is showing, Aruhn."

"This game— It's not an old man's game."

"Aye, but those should beware old men in a job where they die young," said Diyane. When Aruhn wrinkled his brow, she said, "I heard it when I first got here."

"From Madrid?"

"From Madrid."

"Yeh knew him from the start, didn't yeh?"

"I wasn't content to deal with the rite of passage that they had set for me," said Diyane. "And I found my place, rightfully so."

"Do yeh think I did the right thing, all them years ago?"

Her eyes flashed at him, "Which thing? The wife or the daughter?"

Aruhn's throat tightened as he considered her answer. Her eyes were like a hawk, scanning him for the slightest movement. In the past, he had learned to control that impulse, that fear nestled within him that stemmed from his doubts. But in the years present, with the wake of his actions ever-present before him, the mask was slipping.

"Both, I reckon."

Diyane paused, scanning him a moment before setting down her glass. "You did what you needed to in order to survive. Right and wrong are a matter of perspective, and try as you might, you'll never match someone else's."

Diyane turned her head to the door, "You mean, however, that you wonder if I'd have done the same, if in your situation."

"Aye."

"I was there for the wife," said Diyane. "I stood alongside, there to assure Madrid that if she did anything strange, she would die. It was an easy job assigned to me, but not an easy task to watch."

"I thought yeh were hardened."

"As I thought of you," she retorted simply. "And yet you asked me. I am a survivor, Aruhn. To that end, what matters most to me is my survival. Not the weighings of someone else's conscience."

"And yehr conscience. Yehr thoughts?"

"Those can be quieted just as easily as anyone else's." She met his gaze once more, calm. "You are a survivor. Don't let your affinity towards the daughter impact your thoughts on what you did to the wife. In the end, both survived."

"Aye, both survived," he quieted, opting to take up Diyane's glass and head to refill it. He unstoppered the bottle, watching the dark red liquid fill the glass. He saw a swirling of a red mane in the pour, a flash of blue in his mind's eye. He saw a splatter of blood with a pit in his stomach.

He returned the glass to Diyane, who waved it away from him. Aruhn palmed it, before taking a swig himself, the wine feeling like a balm in his throat.

"Yeh never intended to kill the wife," he surmised calmly as he wiped the wine from the corner of his mouth.

"I had every intention of fulfilling my role," she replied simply. "I'd never risk my life for someone like her. And neither would you," she finished curtly.

Aruhn nodded slowly, taking another sip. She was right, as usual.

"We live for this life," she said suddenly.

"Ain't really much else like it."

"Yet you feel guilt for the daughter."

Aruhn shrugged. "I just want her well. Always, that's what I've always wanted."

"She has a chance as good as any. Moreso, with the knight."

"Aye, that's what Jaks feels too. Sometimes though, it feels like it wasn't enough."

Diyane took one last fleeting look at Aruhn, before rising from her seat and striding over to the staircase. "None were here this night. Sleep well."

"Aye. Thank yeh." Aruhn listened to her soft steps as she climbed up before digging through the bar and pulling his ledger out. He had made some more notes in it this evening, but nothing had particularly stood out to him. He tucked it away, locking up the tavern and closing the shutters before taking a glance at the rack near the kitchen, where an old apron had hung for years.

He climbed the stairs, eager to find sleep.

KARJA.

The next morning found Karja much too quickly for his liking. He roused himself from his tent, taking a moment to dress before looking to the slumbering form that had shared his tent. She snoozed beneath the fur covers, her steady breaths tousling the tangled hair that rested beside her cheek. Karja pulled his belt about his waist, securing his blade to his side before pulling his hood high and pushing forth from his tent.

Thin rays of light slipped into the village, with only a smattering of people out keeping watch for potential predators. Karja walked to the remnants of the bonfire, only a smoldering mass of ash and soot by this point, and held his hands over the embers. He scouted around, taking measure of which clan members were currently up, and keeping watch for the telltale glint of silver.

Sure enough, after a few minutes of warming himself, he spotted Nyeth walking into the village along a path, guiding the small Mikja by the hand as she did. The boy seemed to be listening intently to his mother, but Karja saw the energetic spring in his step and wondered how much of what he heard stuck. He waited a moment, watching as Nyeth ushered him into a cabin, before rising from the embers and approaching her. He cleared his throat before bowing low to her.

"*Cesogez.*"

"Karja," she replied. "You are up early."

"I was making sure that there were people out to keep watch for any beast that might try to break their way in."

Nyeth gave him an approving nod. "I see."

"And you?"

"Sehren was departing and Mikja wished to see him off. I had told him that he could if he woke early enough to do so. I found him awake before I was." Nyeth smiled before looking back towards the path she walked. As she looked back to Karja, her smile faltered and her eyes narrowed. "You look as though you ate something sour."

"My apologies, chief. I still find the idea of the southernblood distasteful."

"You and many others," she said. "Do you believe I made a mistake?"

Karja measured his words here, "I find that I lack the wisdom you have about him. I am unfamiliar with the southernblood, and although I tried to bridge that yesterday, I believe he was still wary of me."

"It was you that asked about his past, then," she surmised.

Karja was caught off-guard, "I am not sure what you mean."

"He spoke of a man who asked about his background before coming here. He was vague about it, but told me that he thought the conversation did not go as expected."

"I did ask him about it. I thought if I could learn something of him, I could allay my own concerns."

"And what concern is that?" asked Nyeth. She crossed her arms over her chest.

"I do not trust his reasons."

Nyeth watched him for a moment, but unlike Sehren's scrutiny, Karja found it hard to maintain his gaze with her.

"Reasons?"

"You said he came north and bears the blood of the Ombroj. From what I could tell from him, I see no reason to doubt his claim. Yet, he cares not for reclaiming his ancestral lands, as is his right, over—"

"His companion. Yes, that is correct." Her gaze softened on Karja. "In truth, I thought that he would reconsider."

"It is just— I know many people will wonder just why he came to the north, and why he brought her along. If he wished to be among people he thought would be closer to kin, then why keep the southerner?"

"Are you asking me, or musing out loud, Karja?"

"If I could, I would like to know what you feel," he replied firmly. "I just wish to understand this guest turned chief, for the future of our people."

Nyeth considered him for a moment, before saying, "Sehren never had intentions of being in our lands. That much was certain from the moment we met. When he asked for passage, he wished for a place that was desolate of other souls, of others that would be able to bother them."

Or track them.

"And you took him to *otedien?*"

"Upon hearing his desires, I thought it best. I did not believe that anyone, let alone who I perceived as weak southerners, would survive out there. If they did, they would be far from us. If they did not, then the problem would resolve itself."

"But why offer him it?"

"I did not wish to spill his blood. Even before, his heritage was evident to me," she replied.

"And the girl?"

"She was a child, and it seemed already on the mend from a grievous injury."

"Is she his daughter or…?"

"I know not. All I know is that he would not consider leaving her then, nor would he return back south."

"So you took him as far away as you could."

Nyeth nodded. "You seem very curious about this matter. Are the Chuyara that unnerved by the claim?"

"No one knows of the girl's past or her relation. When we heard that you offered him the lands of his people and he refused because of her, we grew concerned why."

Nyeth's mouth thinned to a line, but Karja sensed that it came from a similar opinion on the man. "I admit, I do not know of the girl's past or origin. All I know is that she is important to him."

"Is that wise, considering your desires to include him in our people?"

Nyeth narrowed her eyes once again, "What is this about, Karja?"

"I was there when they came, Nyeth. Same as you, and same as many of the people here," he said. He flared a bit with resentment, but never forgot his respect towards the woman. "I know you say he is of our blood, and I can see that, plain as any. How he lived through *Javeaf* is beyond us as well, but I sense a strong inner strength in him. However, to have one of those cursedbloods so close… to allow them through our lands… It turns my gut and brings a tightness in my chest. I do not trust her, nor do I think any other will, and for all we know, he whispers into her ears at night all that he has learned of us so that she can turn south and bring ruin to us once more."

Nyeth chuckled, confusing Karja, "Yes, men do tend to reveal more than they should when in the throes of their passions. You believe her some temptress, then, that brought him north as an instrument of ruin?"

Still shaken by her amusement, Karja clarified, "I worry for all that we have recovered and regained over the years, chief. I worry for the growth and security of our young and old. We have grown strong, but if they came back—"

"They will not," she cut him off. "None cross into our lands unfettered, and those that have cannot tell tales."

Karja nodded, believing her. "It is just my concern, chief. Forgive me."

"There is no forgiveness needed. So long as you remember your respect and speak openly, I shall not reprimand you for that," said Nyeth. "But while I too wished for the snows of the northlands to claim them, I found myself curious when time and time again they proved the better. Sehren tells me the girl is an adept huntress, and that she brings back many of the pelts and bones that they have traded to our people. He also says that she has never asked more than curious questions of our history, not of our present."

"And you believe him?"

"I do. Of all that I can say for certain of the man, is that he is not deceptive or duplicitous. He has proven to bear no ill will towards us and shown that all he desires for he and his companion is peace."

Karja bit the tip of his tongue, wondering once more.

"You are still not at ease."

"I likely will not be until more time passes, chief," admitted Karja. "Nor will many within the Chuyara. Our memories are long."

"As are the Katski's."

"But it seems our idea of danger has shifted over the years," replied Karja. "We will remain watchful, but we are concerned."

"And that concern is understood. Do not think I have so carelessly dismissed the threats of the southerners. But I am of the mind that no one is looking for them, Karja. Sehren has told me that his flight was one of self-decision, and the pain in his voice and eyes tell more than he believes. He has fled the south, both in mind and body."

Karja bit his tongue again.

"I know your hate, Karja," said Nyeth. "It runs deep in many of us. However, this time, this ceremony, is about letting the hate heal. We will remain cautious, but now we must plan ahead. Our numbers grow strong once again."

"I understand, chief. Still, I shall worry, and so too will the Chuyara."

Nyeth nodded.

Karja bowed low to her again, watching her step inside the small cabin. As the door shut, he chewed on the tip of his thumb again.

Nyeth had a high opinion of Sehren, and from the sound of it, she had a grudging respect for the girl. Even if it was true that they intended to stay in their own lands, Karja felt the looming threat of the south before them. Her estimation of Astoria's prowess only fuelled Karja's confirmation of her lineage.

It is as he said.

Karja walked off, letting his mind rifle through what he'd learned and what he thought he should do.

Karja waited beside an aging tree, pacing around the gnarled roots that wormed their way through the earth. The sun was quickly approaching the horizon, and he frowned as he considered its descent. His movements were marked with agitation with each step punctuated by a grumbling remark.

"I wish this would be finished already..."

He glanced southward down the path, away from the gnarled trees and darkened forestlands. The border between their lands was unclear, shifting as the years went by, but he knew that where the serene cover of the trees ended, so too did the comfort of their lands.

His pacing continued, his hand resting easily on the blade belted on his side. His dark eyes trailed once more down the rough path that spiraled into the lands of that blasted kingdom. Instinctively, he loosened the blade in his scabbard, readying it to draw. His hand clutched the pommel causing his pale skin to whiten even further. After taking a deep breath, he blew out his tension, relaxing for a bit before pacing around once more.

Hooves and clinking barding alerted him a few moments later. He paused as the hoofbeats drew closer, bringing forth a hooded man wearing silvered mail and plate. A hood covered his face, attached to a simple brown roughspun cloak that trailed down his back. As if practiced, the horse slowed to a stop before crossing into the forested lands, snorting as the rider climbed from atop of it. With slow, methodical steps, the rider approached.

"And here I thought I would be the early one," said the man in a cool, even tone. "Good to see that you are punctual, Karja."

With an annoyed grimace, Karja spat at the ground at the rider's feet, "Do not bother with flattery. What news do you have?"

The hooded man let out a sigh, "And yet, still lacking courtesy."

"I am still perplexed by your knowledge of my tongue."

"The kingdom has many resources available, especially to those willing to utilize them against its enemies. Do you think I am soft of mind, not able to learn your simple language? It fouls my mouth for certain, but it is no more complex than the ravings of the southernfolk."

Karja gnashed his teeth at the man.

"No matter. It seems my suspicions were correct."

Karja grimace turned to a frown, "You had many of them. Which ones were correct?"

"It appears that most of them were," replied the man idly.

Karja, already agitated about having to meet with the man, growled at him, "Quit your vague responses, Ricard. Which suspicions?"

Ricard pulled his hood down, revealing his blonde hair and blue eyes. His face was even as he said, "The king is beside himself with the abduction of his heir. The man that you know of, the one that came north so many years ago, stole her away to secure his passage to the north. We only found out about her lineage later on after he had departed our lands."

Karja muttered, "Deplorable honor. Typical southerners."

"What was that?" asked Ricard.

"I said, I know of the man you speak of," said Karja, drawing Ricard's gaze back. "He walks with a woman with red hair?"

"He does," confirmed Ricard. "It took us a while to confirm her identity, but after finally talking with the right people, we determined that she was indeed the king's heir."

"And what does that have to do with me or mine?"

Ricard raised his eyebrow, "King Mistletain—"

Karja spat on the ground.

"—has indicated that he has come to the point where if the people of the northlands will not aid in returning his heir, then he will march his armies through the forests and retrieve her himself." finished Ricard.

Karja froze. His voice took on a dangerous edge, "You would never cross into our lands."

"I know of your concern," said Ricard, his tone becoming soft and understanding. He got an empathetic gleam in his eye as he regarded Karja. "Neither of our people wish to go to war again. The Blight Winter, while so long ago, is still a fresh trauma on the minds of our people. Needless to say, another war would cause pointless suffering for your people and mine."

"Then convince your king otherwise," barked Karja.

"If only it were that simple. The man lost his presumptive heir years ago, and with the death of his wife and new heir as she labored with their child, he has become sullen and melancholic. He will not respond to reason or logic, and in his grief, his paranoia that his family's lineage is coming to an end guides his actions. The pain he's experienced over the years is staggering."

"I care not for the pain of the king that made our lands bleed."

"Truthfully, I did not expect you to. However, perhaps you care for the future of your people," answered Ricard, his tone becoming grim. "He will seek out his only remaining heir, and having found that she resides in the northlands, in your lands, he is willing to step into his armor once again to retrieve her."

Ricard let out another deep sigh, "Another war is something your people can ill-afford."

Karja clenched his hand on the pommel of his blade. He had survived the Blight Winter and remembered his people's retreat to the far north after many of their warriors fell. The following years had been rough, with them relying on the elders for guidance while children protected them. Those who had survived and were capable of fighting ran through the woods hunting and reclaiming small parts of their lands from the wilds that had reclaimed them. It was a long time before his people felt safe enough to return to the lands of their families.

"So you wish for me to convince this woman to return," said Karja.

"We need the heir back in the kingdom. There are rumblings of discord throughout the lands, and without an heir, the people are growing restless at the idea of a new family leading," explained Ricard.

"She does not seem of royal blood."

"She is. Based on what you've told me of her appearance, she is mix-blooded, but her father is the king."

Karja laughed derisively, "The kingdom rests on the shoulders of an unwanted maiden?"

Ricard's face grew shrewd, "She bears the blood of the king. That is enough for the people and for the king himself."

"She will not go willingly," warned Karja.

Ricard nodded, "And I imagine if her captor was to find out about this, he would protest as well."

A chill ran through him at that, and he instinctively loosened his blade once more. "They are close."

"He is an honorless traitor," spat Ricard. Calming, he said, "I would go retrieve her myself, but you and yours have made it apparent that we would not survive if we crossed into your lands."

"You are correct. The *cesogez* would not permit it."

"Be that as it may, we need her back unless the tragedy of another war arrives at the edge of your forests," said Ricard. He gave the man a curt bow before returning to his horse. He began climbing atop it when Karja spoke.

"And if he protests?"

Ricard met his gaze, "Kill him."

NYETH.

Nyeth followed Mikja into the cabin, watching as the young boy immediately crawled back into the bed and tucked himself beneath the blanket. Nyeth sat at the side of his bed, listening to him as he scrambled beneath the blanket and eventually settled himself to sleep. She listened to his soft breathing, each breath bringing a rush of warmth through her.

She pondered what Karja had said, comparing it to the other statements she had heard the night before. While the chiefs had followed her lead, Ghorun had told her that there was dissension within the other tribes, especially from the elders that had survived the *Javeaf*. Grumblings of the southern girl were commonplace, even within her own tribe, and with the pointed ponderings of Karja fresh on her mind, she fostered some doubt.

Astoria, as Sehren called her, was indeed of the south, but whenever Nyeth had asked him for more details about her, he had curtly rebuffed her. The third time they had met after he'd settled into *otedien*, Nyeth had made an offhand remark about the girl, stating it would've been wiser to leave her in the wilds, and Sehren had immediately gathered his things and left without a word. From that moment, Nyeth had always broached the subject cautiously, drawing more information about her, but Sehren was quick to defend the lass whenever Nyeth made a disparaging remark.

Nyeth felt the clinging hatred in her heart as she considered Astoria, even when the lass was lame and injured when they had escorted them all those years ago. Still, Nyeth could not deny the light that shone within her pristine blue eyes, and from the first moment they met, Nyeth knew that the girl held boundless potential. Sehren told her that she was not his daughter, nor any real relation, but that they needed one another. Over the years, whenever Sehren had a large pack of goods to trade, Nyeth had seen Astoria shadowing him, her eyes watching with a calm attentiveness that reminded the woman of Korrenth.

On several occasions, after Nyeth had stated it was okay for the girl to move closer to their meetings, Astoria had surprised the woman with knowledge of their tongue, speaking fluently, if simply, in the presence of the woman. Even when she lacked the knowledge to properly convey what she wished to say, Astoria never shied away from trying, pulling assistance from Sehren, and to her own surprise, Nyeth when Sehren was also lacking.

Nyeth, despite her prejudice, held a grudging respect for the woman, and she could even see parts of herself within her. She shuddered, heat rising in her face as she grew agitated by the comparison.

Even with Sehren's dedication to the woman, Nyeth knew none would ever allow Astoria to live in their lands. Nyeth could talk to them if she had the mind to do so, to try to allay their angst, but all knew the deep-seated grudge that had nestled within. And regardless of the woman's potential, she felt the same way. A kinship had built over the years between her and Sehren, his competence combined with his clear heritage soothing her initial disdain of the man. That kinship, however, would never extend to the girl.

Nyeth watched Mikja sleep, his soft breathing telling the woman he had drifted off once more. She rose from his bed, taking one more glance, before departing the cabin.

Nyeth checked with the patrols, pleased that nothing had occurred through the evening. The hunters had already gone out, early before the sunrise, and Nyeth knew they would be back to bring food for the people still there. One of the tribes, the Thunzi, had already departed alongside Sehren. While he traveled east, they turned west, marching off to return to their lands in the wake of the remembrance.

Their chief had been resistant to Nyeth's claim, and even though she had explained herself in length to them the previous night, she knew that it would be long before they would be content with her decision. They may grudgingly accept her decision, but Nyeth considered herself fortunate that none had tried to contest her.

The pyre was smoldering as it was the final day, and Nyeth knew that soon it would be out, heralding the ceremony's end. She was proud of her people's growth. The clans before had fostered resentment towards one another, the days long past having built strife between them. It was only in the wake of the war that they had set aside their differences to survive, and even in the years past, where Nyeth could see the old grudges rising up again, she saw them tempered by the communal need to survive. It would do poorly for them to turn against one another when they had made so much progress in reclaiming the northlands for themselves.

As she walked through the village, many gave her bows of deference, even if they had quickly quieted their discussions before she arrived. Their hushed tones and wary glances told her the nature of their conversations, but Nyeth never had a need to control what the people spoke: let them talk safely, comfortably, if not with her then with one another, so that should their concerns become palpable, they know they have someone to rely on.

She walked to the edge of the village, nodding at several more guards, before she took a steadying breath and shut her eyes. She reached within her, for the familiar feeling she had so honed over the years, one that would take her senses beyond what she could normally see.

Immediately, she felt the others around her. She felt the footsteps of the Thunzi people as they marched back towards their lands, each step rhythmic against the earth. She found the hunters, walking in tandem, and knew they had successfully brought down their game and were returning to the village. She sensed every individual within the village behind her, some slumbering while others walked about getting ready for the day.

Opening her eyes, she peered around. The world was dark and grey to her now, the once vibrant boughs of the trees shaded in ashen hues. She glanced around, spotting several animals within the reach of the village, some coming to check upon the place while others kept their distance warily. There were shadows flitting about, some stopping upon the pyre while others melted away into the world, their forms becoming indistinguishable from their surroundings. Nyeth never paid mind to the shades, except to note the ones that took notice of her. Tinged with mild animosity, a feeling of acceptance came over Nyeth, and she let herself slip from that lightless world, her vision returning to the hues she was accustomed to.

"Korrenth," she called, turning to the woman as she approached from behind. Her dark hair was tied in a loose tail, with her dark eyes looking concerned.

"They told me you had left early."

"I did. Mikja wished to bid Schren farewell, and afterwards Karja wished to express his concerns over my decision."

Korrenth frowned, "He is unhappy?"

"He is worried. He and his kin. Although, I expect I will hear more about it in the coming day, with the ceremony now coming to an end. Few wish to cause upheaval during such a tender time."

Korrenth nodded, "And do you find their concern valid?"

"Years ago, I would have been at the forefront if another chief had called for such a naming," admitted Nyeth. "Even knowing the Ombroj, I would have readily defied any attempt to integrate him into our own."

"But now it is you that wishes to have him join us."

"He has not been what I expected from a southerner. He and his companion. The surprises they have given over the years have become so common to me, I expect something new to arise whenever we meet."

"Surprises do not mean that they are fit for our people," said Korrenth.

"He is Ombroj, through and through. I can see it every time he meets my gaze," said Nyeth.

"I see it too. It is odd that he was never groomed by any member, and yet he holds their ideals and values so close to him."

60

"He must keep his lessons from his mother close to heart," agreed Nyeth.

Korrenth looked contemplative for a moment, "Do you expect rivalry?"

"No. I do not even expect that the concern will last through the summer. Those that have met with him know I was correct in my estimation, and those that have not will trust in my decision."

"You have guided us for so long," said Korrenth. "Your decisions have brought us to where we are today."

Nyeth met her gaze,seeing that her dark eyes were filled with admiration. "But still, I am worried."

"As expected. To lead is one thing, Nyeth, but you are also allowed your own doubts. However, remember: you have brought us here. I doubt anyone else, even another from our tribe, could have managed to bring us back so surely from those dark days." Her gaze trailed to the smoldering fire.

Nyeth agreed. She had inherited her father's mantle long ago, and while challengers had risen to claim rule, she had, as taught, put them in their place, all while nurturing the bonds that were so vital to their people. No, she had never doubted the path that she led her people.

"Thank you, Korrenth," said Nyeth. The woman bowed to her, before stepping to her side as Nyeth walked back into the village.

The hunters had finally returned, dividing up the game they had found and beginning to cook it. Several of them stood hastily as Nyeth passed, bowing in deference to her before returning to their work.

"Chief," called one, drawing her attention. He held several slabs of freshly trimmed meat, wrapped in a portion of the beast's hide.

Nyeth took it, "Thank you for your work."

He bowed, a smile on his face.

As Nyeth turned away, she spotted Aida similarly trimming some meat for her people.

"Korrenth, will you take this to the cabin?"

"Yes, chief," she said, taking the bundle from her. With a bow, she departed.

Nyeth approached Aida, who was enmeshed with her work. She cleared her throat, drawing the woman's attention.

"Oh, chief," she said, rubbing her palms on the sides of her pants, "what is it?"

"How are you and yours?"

"We are well," said Aida, giving a glance back to the gathering. "The remembrance has put a fire within them. They are desiring to return home so that we can grow more."

"And you?"

"I feel their excitement," said Aida, her eyes flashing. "Seeing the others again, it brings up a sense of competition. One that I think is good for us as a people."

Nyeth smiled. Aida was over a decade younger than her, but her spirit coupled with her prowess made her stand out compared to the other chieftains who were mostly older than the silver-haired woman.

"Have you heard any grumblings regarding my decision?"

"Only my own," replied Aida, giving an impish smile, "but I am used to such things. Let me learn more of the Ombroj and that too will settle."

Nyeth chuckled. "You approve, then."

"He is the blood, through and through, if my father's stories can be believed," said Aida. "It will be interesting to see him grow from here."

Aida heard a call from her people and bowed to Nyeth before heading to see what they needed. Nyeth watched as several children ran to Aida's side, their faces filled with glee at the woman as she spoke with them. One of them tried to get the woman to chase them, but Aida just laughed and waved them off as she continued getting her people ready for travel.

With the ceremony at its end, Nyeth was glad to see the mingling of the children from the different tribes. The bonds they would create would help keep her people alive, and eventually maybe

62

even the old grudges would fade away at the hands of the young. She thought of her own son, and thought of what she would want to leave behind for him when she stepped down in favor of a younger chieftain.

Years from now. Decades even…

Still, it was something she spent many nights considering. She cared not for legacy; that could help little in the cold winters with scarce food, or against roving men turned wild upon the lands. No, she wanted to leave stability and cooperation at the end of her reign, with the calm reminder that hers were a people that would fight for a tomorrow. Regardless of the obstacles.

She looked back towards the road, where Sehren had taken his leave earlier that morning. Many questions would arise in the coming weeks, but Nyeth was certain she was taking the right path needed to preserve her people.

ASTORIA.

Astoria finished packing the hides together, tying them into a large stack with a rough piece of cord. She dusted her hands as she finished before there was a tug at her senses. The small pendant that rested in the crook of her chest seemed to thrum, and Astoria turned her gaze to the outskirts of their camp. She grasped the blade that laid beside the entrance to the tent, belting it to her side as she left the encampment.

Her senses tingled, and a smile tugged at the corners of her mouth as she saw a lone figure walking towards their camp with a pack on its back. She raced out to meet them, and her smile went wide as she regarded Sehren marching towards her, a serene look on his face. She drew up right before him, pushing him to a stop.

"You're early," she said, looking up into his face.

"I am. Nyeth had little left to tell me after the ceremony, so I took an early night and thought it best to get here early in the day." He held a small smile on his face while admiration sparkled in his eyes.

Warmth rushed through Astoria's face as she took up stride beside him. She glanced over the contents of the pack, feeling elated to see more supplies and varied foodstuffs for them. "They were generous."

"They said it is an offering for the new chief."

Shock ran through Astoria, followed by delight, "They agreed to it?"

Sehren nodded, the tension leaving his form as he did. "Aye, they did."

Astoria turned to see his face and felt pride in her chest as she saw the satisfaction in his eyes. They continued walking in relative silence until they reached the encampment, with Sehren walking towards the center tent to place the pack within.

Astoria followed behind him, taking a moment to watch him. He moved with an excited energy, one that Astoria hadn't seen in a long while. As he revealed all the new gifts they had given to him, Astoria knelt beside him, leaning against him as he sorted through it all. He leaned against her in return.

"We have plenty for the summer and even perhaps autumn."

"And if not, I finished cleaning another *davoarth*."

Sehren gave her an appraising look, "Another one?"

"It ate my deer."

He chuckled. As he picked through the supplies and set them throughout the tent, Astoria left him a moment to go grab the bundle she was preparing earlier. She dragged the litter into the tent as Sehren finished unpacking, and he walked over to her.

"I never stop being amazed by your prowess, Astoria."

She flushed as she grinned, "Felled it in a single stroke too. Didn't even put up a fight."

He chuckled again, wincing slightly.

"The travel?"

"Aye. Nyeth gave me some advice about how to better mitigate the fatigue I feel from it, but I admit, it is still a trying endeavor."

66

Astoria was concerned. During one of his meetings with Nyeth, he had learned secrets of his people. When he had returned, he was out of sorts. Astoria had grown worried, but one evening, when they laid within the tent, with everything around them tended to, Sehren told her of something that the Senakamans called the *kymbra*. When he explained it to her, she couldn't believe him, and over time, he came to demonstrate for her. Astoria had been unnerved by the sight. He had been shrouded within a gloom and from that, vanished, only to return at the other side of their encampment, lathered with sweat and heaving for air.

Astoria couldn't comprehend what had occurred, but as the years passed and Sehren's familiarity with it grew, he utilized it more and more. She found that as she grew accustomed to his practice, if she focused hard enough, she could feel something tugging within her mind, telling her that something was there. Eventually, she came to trust this sense, and from it, could guess when Sehren would be returning whenever he traveled.

"There is so much to learn," she commented, "maybe you shouldn't be so earnest with it."

"She mentioned as much when I told her about it," conceded Sehren. "I believed that I have practiced much but to travel that far with it… It takes its toll."

"Hopefully not too much though," said Astoria.

Sehren smirked, "Worry not. You are stuck with me for a while, Astoria."

She gave him a soft laugh, taking a seat beside the fire pit. It was already burning bright, with tendrils of smoke carried through the small hatch over the top of the tent. Sehren joined her, settling beside her and leaning against her.

"I admit, in the excitement of the news and all of the supplies they offered me, I did not think to bring you a memento of the ceremony."

"A memento?"

"Spring has ended," said Sehren simply. "I know it is hard to keep track of which day exactly it is, but your birthday recently passed, no?"

Astoria smiled, "Yes."

He reached down to the thin chain that held the pendant that rested against her chest, tugging the stone up, "I admit, I doubt I could have found something as grand as Jaks' gift to you, but still, I should have remembered to bring something."

"That's okay. I already know what I would like," she said as he let the stone slip back beneath the collar of her shirt.

Sehren's eyes crinkled with amusement, "Is that so?"

"It's what I've wanted for years," she said simply. She gave him a smoldering look, to which Sehren let out a jovial laugh.

"Ah yes, your request. You know the deal, however," he replied.

"I can beat you," she said earnestly.

"Oh, do you mean to try today?"

"It's as you said: you don't know which day it was, so why not celebrate now, in the wake of such good news."

Sehren laughed, "Of course. I see now."

Astoria rose, grabbing the scabbard by the furs and sliding the alabaster blade from it. She looked to Sehren, who was still seated by the fire.

"Now?"

Astoria nodded before silently walking through the entrance of the tent. She strode from the entrance, turning back and waiting. Her heart raced as she heard the flaps open, with Sehren gripping the sheath of Samuel's sword. He pushed himself free, an amused look still on his face.

"You are ready?"

"I always have been," she whispered quietly. Sehren slid the blade free from its sheath, and took his stance, his right hand leading.

Astoria mirrored him, watching for the smallest hint of movement. The hairs on her arms rose in anticipation, and the smallest rush of air over them sent chills down her spine.

"On guard," he said, stepping to a swift sword rush.

Astoria turned the blade expertly, letting the steel ride alongside one another before pushing off and taking a short swipe across his chest. As expected, his parry was aligned in time, driving her blade downwards before he stepped into it, trying to use his weight to destabilize her.

She was already dancing back on the balls of her feet, keeping him at length before rapping against the handguard of his blade, "I could've stung you then."

"No, else you would have," he replied. He had not broken his gaze with hers, and she could see the intensity within them. But she also saw the fatigue marring his face, and her heartbeat quickened.

She pressed the advantage, taking measured thrusts at him, which were battered aside with swift cuts of the tip of his blade. He swiped at her, stepping into the cut as both hands grasped the hilt. Astoria tucked her blade against her shoulder, using the steel to let his swipe push her away, the tip of his blade coming a finger's breadth from her cheek.

Still, she didn't break her gaze with him.

Their steel clashed, each movement they made almost harmonious as they danced through their combat. Astoria would find an opening and strike, only to find his guard aligned and riposte sent her way, only to be dissuaded by her own parry with her own counterattack already responding. They came within inches of their edges kissing the flesh of one another, but Astoria and Sehren knew each other's expertise well, knew the limitations of their reach, and knew exactly how much force to use.

High.

Their blades locked overhead, sliding along one another as they disengaged.

Low.

Two low sweeps, aimed for the thighs, clashed against one another before they pushed away from each other. Astoria saw Sehren's delight, knowing that there were few in the world that could keep such a pace with him

She repressed her smile, wanting, yearning so much to beat him that day. Sweat beaded her brow, as it did Sehren's, and their dance became more frenzied, each strike measured with tempered fury. She knew what it would mean if her guard slipped, but she also knew he recognized the same risk. They continued to up the pace, as if they were fighting to the death, but Astoria met his fervor with her own. She saw it then, his stamina failing, as she had hoped it would because of his travel. She worked his guard high, trying to avoid springing an overhead swipe, while stepping into his reach, seeing the perfect strike.

The middle of his left side.

White steel sung through the air as she turned the blade to strike on its flat, and she felt jubilation as she saw he would not, could not, align his guard in time.

She growled in frustration as her blade caught nothing, his form melting away before the steel.

There was a slap against the lower portion of her thighs, beneath her buttocks, and she almost screamed in frustration.

"You cheated!" she said, rounding on him.

Sehren was laughing, his smile wide. "You picked this day to fight, with her advice still clear in my mind."

Astoria growled at him, clenching her fists until her knuckles turned white. Sehren grinned at her, placing his blade point down into the earth before approaching her confidently.

"I believe I won."

"You cheated," she said, her bluster playing out as he drew close. She planted the tip of her blade into the earth as well, untensing as he approached.

Sehren traced his hand across her cheek, the callouses catching on the whispy hairs. "Still, I won. You can win as many fights as you wish, Astoria, but you can only lose one."

Her heart hammered in her chest as his grey eyes softened. She leaned into his grasp.

"Best two out of three?"

He laughed, "Not this day. However, that is further than you have ever pushed me before, and that is astounding."

She peered into his gaze, his eyes filled with wonder. She saw a flicker of reluctance, but her heart beat away as he drew close.

His lips locked against hers, and she felt that losing this day perhaps was better than she could've expected.

AMOS GREYFIELD.

Amos gazed out over the city, his mind teeming as he considered the darkened lanes of the capital. He saw a few of his men out in the city, their languid paces telling him that the patrols of the night were soon to be replaced by the morning shift. The sky lightened, with each moment dimming the stars as the horizon turned flusher with light.

It was not the first time in the passing months that the commander had watched the encroaching dawn, his mind filled with errant thoughts and stratagems. Even now, with the prospect of a new day, a new beginning put before him, he found his mind lingering on the past mistakes.

The City of Isle was once again at peace, with the garrison of the illustrious Knights of Isle at an all time low within the city. The people had survived the winter in spectacular form, and already plans for the festivals and ceremonies to usher in a bountiful summer were already put forth to the Lord Commander, in hopes that they could secure enough manpower to bring security to the merchant lords when they gathered once more. They wanted more members of the order present after the thaw so that the ceremonies could be handled efficiently and quickly.

It turned bile in his stomach to think of the brotherhood, the men he had fostered and nurtured over the years, regulated to such menial and mundane tasks. Amos had repelled two attempts during the past years to push him from his station, holding true to the bonds he had built over the years of his tenure. However, it was abundantly clear to the elder knight that something had grown rotten despite his guiding hand within the order. The knights of the new held little stock in the wisdom and accomplishments of the knights of old. It was not uncommon for him to hear of dissension in the ranks through the channels of society that were supposed to have little influence over the movements of the knights.

And yet, only two nights ago, he'd learned of several upjumped recruits using their newfound prestige to maneuver around tradition within the city. There were mutterings of subjugating those that had little or no connections within the brotherhood as well.

It has become a nest of braggarts and ruffians.

Amos had done all he could in the years to mitigate the growing influence of the merchant lords within the order, but even with his decision to spread the men around to the other forts of the kingdom, their influence grew.

And still, the prison remains full to this day.

His gaze traced to the docks of the city, far from where he could see. While out of sight, he knew off on the island nestled within the cold waters of the bay were many men in chains, their sentences unfit for their crimes.

The folly of the witch hunt, he knew. Influencers within the city had driven the officers of the brotherhood to push forward with trials against their brothers, with many facing sentencing to the prison in order to quell potential corruption.

He heard the whispers as well, the uttered voices from within about the changing of the times. His Majesty Mistletain, now widowed and seemingly going mad, saw few visitors these days save for the men sworn to protect him. He rarely graced the people with his presence, and even only attended the most sacred of ceremonies, for his absence would be a slight against the Lady herself. Yet even then, King Mistletain was sullen and forlorn, taking stock only of what was needed of him before retiring from the ceremony to leave his advisors in charge in his stead.

The whispers grew that the end of the Mistletain era was approaching, and it would only be a moment's time before the Council of the Four Kings convened to determine who would rule the people of Candrama. Amos had attended many formal meetings with the other noble families, but rumor had it that Xander Estocri was favored for the position, using the catalyst of his fallen daughter as fuel for support. Some spoke that he would take the seat within Isle, and that his son would remain the regent in the east until he claimed the throne. Others, however, thought that Xander would oust Saiho before then, and let his son rule as he advised from their home.

If only they knew the truth.

A wrenching pain in Amos' arm pulled him from his thoughts, the shock causing his fist to become gnarled and pained as it became a claw-like vice. He focused on his pulse, using each heartbeat to dull the pain until the ache was stymied. After a few minutes, the shock ran up his arm, dissipating once it reached his elbow as it always had. He flared his fingers, finding reprieve as the muscles in his forearm stretched and relaxed. Clenching his fist, he felt grim.

He was growing old, and the mornings he actually slept he felt it keenly when he rose from his bed. While he maintained his limberness with training, his joints would ache if he worked himself too hard, and there was a heaviness in his movements that grew with each passing season. Amos worried that soon there would come a time where he could not act in the manner he was used to, and he hoped he could right what needed to be done before that time came.

The sounds emanating from the floor below told him his servants were up and about, getting ready for the new day. Amos had retreated from his bedroom earlier that morning, stating to his wife that he didn't wish for his restless sleep to disturb her sleep. She had merely groaned her compliance, but Amos knew that once she realized he hadn't slept at all that night, she would be cross with him. Still, it spared him guilt of disturbing Elaine, and Amos hoped that his mounting exhaustion would eventually grant him the peace of mind to sleep fully the coming night.

That would have to wait for later however. He had things that needed to be sorted that day, and with his mind still filled with errant thoughts, Amos made his way down to the foyer.

Several of his servants bowed their heads as he passed, one only pausing a moment to ask if they should inform the cooks to start working on breakfast. Amos merely nodded before turning down the hall and finding his way to his study. He shut the door behind him after entering, and took a heavy seat at his desk. Coiled scrolls sat waiting for him while others lay half open upon the tabletop. He leafed through them, dismissing some almost immediately as they were requests to transfer men from one fort to another. Amos knew the aristocracy grew nervous with their sons separated so far, but he also knew that to let them sit together at meal times and to share watches would only spur the growing dissonance within the order.

He found the letter he was looking for, checking the semi-tidy scrawl to make sure he hadn't forgotten the date of appointment. He looked at the signer's signature, a small smile gracing his face as he read it.

Gavin.

Amos had assigned him to watch over Eleanor in her time of need, and knew that the man had become a close friend to the woman in the following years. He knew that the priest abhorred the wanton imprisoning of other men within the order of the Knights, and like Amos, believed something was quickly growing foul within the order. He had requested the Lord Commander's presence before the season's change, with the clergy requesting more funds and manpower to help better plan and oversee the coming festivals.

Amos gathered his thoughts before retrieving a brigandine and fastening about his torso. He covered it with a light coat, wanting to look formal as he went to the Cathedral. As he belted his blade to his side, a knock sounded on the study, soft but insistent.

He approached the door, opening it to see Elaine seated there, a frown on her face. "You didn't mention you were going to be going out today."

"I've been a bit remiss in more than just my sleep, my love," said Amos placatingly. "It's time I remedied that."

76

"Are you planning a visit to the Cathedral?"

Puzzled, Amos nodded, "Yes, that is my intended destination. How did you know?"

She smiled at him as she smoothed out the wrinkles in his coat and straightened the collar, "You always wear that same coat when you go to the Cathedral, Amos. It would be odd if you weren't intending to go there."

Amos let out a short laugh, his appreciation bubbling for his wife.

"Is there something amiss?" she asked quietly.

"I'm meeting with an old friend," said Amos. "And it is much better to be seen meeting someone at the Cathedral than out and about in the city."

"With the rumors abounding, I'm sure that's true. Will you be taking anyone with you?"

"Not today, no."

Her eyes flashed with concern, but Amos set a steady hand upon her shoulder, "I will be careful. I'll need you to manage the household affairs today. If someone asks, I merely have an appointment."

Elaine nodded after a moment before she headed off to the foyer. Amos watched her go, grateful for the woman that had shared the past three decades of his life. He followed in her wake, but merely nodded to the servants as he departed his home.

His hurried gait brought him to the wondrous Cathedral of the Lady, its white marble walls suffused with the orange of the morning glow. Several young acolytes were tending to the outside wielding stiff brooms and brushes, but all of them rose and bowed deeply when Amos walked up the steps of the temple. With a wave of his hand, they returned to their work, their movements infused with a vigor that hadn't been there beforehand.

Chuckling, Amos pushed open the wooden doors, hearing greetings from passing priests as he shut them behind them. He simply nodded their direction before heading to one of the small chambers, comfortable private places for meeting with a member of the clergy without the pressure of the rest. He called for an acolyte before setting himself up, asking him to retrieve Gavin for him.

"Yes, Lord Commander," said the acolyte with a deep bow, before hurrying off. Amos entered the room, sitting at a small, round table while he waited. The door opened behind him and several calm footsteps revealed Gavin.

His hair had grown to his shoulders, neatly trimmed, with a thick braid woven in the left. He had a well-groomed beard and moustache and wore a long-sleeved robe of the clergy that did little to hide his musculature.

"It's a good day to sit before the Lord Commander," said Gavin, his dulcet voice filled with shared appreciation.

"That it is, Gavin. How is the life of a high priest treating you?"

"Same as before, except now I have more to look after and more headaches to manage," he replied with a laugh. "I admit though, my new quarters are more comfortable if I actually had the time to enjoy them."

"The burden of power," chuckled Amos. "I recall before I was commander, as a marshall, that I believed having such a large home for me to simply sleep in was folly. It's only in recent years that I have actually had the time to appreciate such a sprawling place, and now my bones and joints creak too much to enjoy it."

"The inevitability of age," said Gavin sagely. "With wisdom of the mind comes the frailty of the body."

"Something you won't have to deal with for years to come," said Amos. The priest was barely older than Sehren, and while wrinkles had begun to show on his brow and at the corners of his eyes, he was still vital and strong.

"Aye," nodded Gavin. "As much as I would love to share sentiments with you, Lord Greyfield, I do have limited time this day."

"Of course. You requested funds for the ceremonies and the manpower to help with the change of the season, and the treasurer has approved the wages for the Knights you need. I simply have to send out the letters, and they'll be here within a fortnight."

Amos saw a flicker of concern within Gavin's face before the man cleared his throat and said, "Would it be possible to allocate the funds to volunteers that have shown interest in helping with the ceremonies? I doubt we need such martially trained men to simply get the chores done and that would free you to keep your men at their posts."

Amos furrowed his brow.

Gavin continued, "I just believe that the volunteering men would be more suited to the jobs, Lord Greyfield. I feel it would be better to spread the Lady's wealth around to those more deserving."

Amos gave him a knowing smile, "You can speak plainly with me Gavin. There's no one listening, I take it?"

"Of course not, Amos," said Gavin, tension releasing from him. "I find the younger men of the Knights lacking, and there are many less fortunate within the city's walls that would find the boon of extra coin in their pocket a blessing."

"A sentiment we share," replied Amos. "There's been too much upheaval within the order. Go ahead and tell those that wish to help to do it. I'll sort out the wages and get you the coin."

Gavin bowed his head, a kind smile stretching across his face. "Have you met with Eleanor lately?"

"I haven't, though we hosted her for dinner but a few months ago. How is she?" Amos knew that the priest met with her regularly, mainly for someone for Eleanor to confide in with utmost confidence.

"She fares well. I spoke with her a little over a week ago, and she seems to be in finer spirits than I've known her to be in for a while. I'm certain that with the season's change coming and the city reaching the height of trade, she's eager for the new season."

Amos nodded, knowing that Eleanor had spent much of her time growing her late father's business over the years. "Does she still have her moments?"

"I find that I'm uncomfortable discussing that with you, Amos," replied Gavin. "Eleanor has my confidence, just as you do, and I wouldn't wish to mar either of them. Even for the concern of her old husband's mentor."

Amos gave him a smile, "My apologies, I got ahead of myself there."

"No need for apology. I know your concern comes from the heart. I merely wish not to make a habit of it, even for such an old friend."

Amos met Gavin's gaze, the kindness in his eyes allaying the elder man's concerns for the woman. "You have given her much strength."

"I do as the Lady wills to help all that I can," said Gavin. "But I do find myself glad that she has found happiness these days."

Amos rose from his seat at the table, before extending his hand to Gavin. The priest took it, giving a hearty shake before saying, "In time, this madness will stop, Amos."

"I hope so. I have done what I can to remedy the follies of many, but it is trying upon the soul."

"If you find you need an ear, simply call for me. I can always make time for the Lord Commander and an old friend."

Amos gave him a nod before heading from the room, his spirits lifted. He saw Gavin instruct one of the acolytes before leaving the temple, taking the steps as he mused about his other appointments he'd been avoiding.

Perhaps it is time I did what needs to be done before stepping down.

He walked back home, pondering.

ELEANOR DEVILLE.

Eleanor knocked on the door to her study, calming waiting for the expectant reply. The door swung open, with Rosline looking curious before saying, "Lady Eleanor!"

"I know it is early, but I was wondering if you had taken a chance to look into Marquis for me. I have a meeting with him this afternoon and I wish to be prepared."

"Of course!" Rosline stood aside as she let Eleanor in. She stepped into the study, pleased to see not a hint of cobweb or dust. Knowing that her mother's sanctuary was once again being used to its potential sent a surge of pride through Eleanor.

Rosline beckoned her to a table, where several different stacks of parchment were sorted into neat piles. "That one is for Marquis," said Rosline as she took a seat at the table.

Eleanor considered the stack, reaching down and picking up the first sheet. With a raised eyebrow, she looked at Rosline. "Really?"

"I was surprised too, but I continued watching and searching, and it all points to the same conclusion."

"To think he has such a fair wife too," said Eleanor as she sat beside Rosline. "And this is his business partner?"

"I believe them to be the reason he is so capable of avoiding the tariffs. He owns several boats, most that make deliveries to his warehouses."

Eleanor smirked, pleased with Rosline's ability. "You've gotten so good at this"

"Thank you," said Rosline, beaming. "It's kind of like what I used to do when I was a barmaid. Aruhn always gave us a nice bonus if we found a particularly interesting tidbit."

Eleanor felt a cold sliver go through her at the mention of Aruhn, but she reserved herself. Rosline had given her more and more tidbits about the man over the years, but she could still sense a loyalty to him. She never pressed Rosline, instead slowly drawing out more and more about the man. She'd known him to be a broker, but between her and her other source of information, he was much more than that. He'd been the leader in disseminating information to Eleanor and her competitors before.

And she had determined that he was the one who figured out her identity and sold her out.

Her wrist twitched as she thought about that dark day over five years ago, repressing a shudder as she painted a kind smile on her face.

Everyone gets theirs, she thought idly as she set the parchment back down.

"Everything okay, Lady Eleanor?"

"You know you can call me Eleanor in private, Rosline," replied Eleanor with a soft smile. "And yes, I was just contemplating how best to use this information."

"Oh, right." Rosline's face flickered a moment before she continued penning down something upon another piece of parchment, her hand gliding slowly so she wouldn't make a mistake.

"It'll do us good when I go to the meeting tonight. Is Kyrah taking her lessons today?"

"Oh, yes! She is taking to them very quickly so Kurtis is finding other ways to keep her involved during the day while I work." She gave

Eleanor an appreciative smile, "Thank you for taking him in your service. He has been so helpful."

"Of course, Rosline. You've been such a hard worker over the years I thought it only fitting to find someone that can help nurture your daughter while you work. She's so bright, it would be a shame to have her potential go to waste."

"And I know she'd get up to mischief if she was left to her own," laughed Rosline, "She takes too much after her father sometimes."

Eleanor shared the laugh with her, "Speaking of, when are you expecting him to come by?"

"I think he got back into the city today, so hopefully this evening. I was going to ask if it would be okay to finish my duties earlier, but I know you have the meeting with Marquis."

Eleanor shook her head, "Take the night for you and your daughter. With your information, I should wrap that up relatively quickly and if anything, it will give me a reason to keep it prompt."

Rosline nodded before returning to penning down the information she had found. Eleanor sat with her a moment, her hand trailing down to the cloth wrapped around her left wrist. "Don't tense your wrist so much and the ink will be less shaky."

"Okay, I'll try."

Eleanor scratched at her wrist, frowning when she looked down at it. Over the years, it had pained her less and less, especially with the tender care that Gavin had given her in regards to it. Occasionally, it would twitch or itch, but she found herself squeezing it like she used to when the sharp pains used to rush through it.

"Are you certain you're okay?" asked Rosline as she set the quill into the inkwell. She looked down to Eleanor's clenching hand, her eyes filled with a solicitous gleam.

"I will be," said Eleanor with a disarming smile. She rose from her seat, "I'll be leaving in a bit to make my way to Marquis' home. With the new information, it would be best to negotiate in an area that he is comfortable in, as not to scare him off completely."

Rosline laughed, "Of course. Will you be taking Railand with you?"

Eleanor nodded, "I'll need you to look in on the wagons to make sure everything is getting packed accordingly. I can't fluster the merchants if I'm not ready to have the stuff ship at a moment's notice."

"I'll take care of it," said Rosline confidently. "You won't have to worry about a thing."

"As always. You've learned well, Rosline. Truly, my life is better with you in it."

Rosline's tan cheeks flushed as her gaze trailed to the floor, "Thank you, Eleanor."

"And as I said, once Jaks comes to call, you're welcome to take the evening off. I know you must have much to discuss."

Her face flushing deeper, Rosline simply bowed her head before returning to her work with vigor, her eyes filled with determination.

Eleanor took her leave from the study, a contented smile on her face. As she walked down the hall towards the staircase, she felt a tinge of annoyance that she couldn't place. She thought of how she was going to wrangle Marquis and how this trade season would bring her much more profit than the last two combined, but it seemed hollow. Familiar footsteps stirred her from her thoughts, however, as she heard the subtle shifting of scale.

"Railand, good day to you," she said as the man drew up to her.

"Good day to you as well, Lady Eleanor," said Railand, giving a bow of his head. He was garbed for travel, his curved blade hanging from his back, his cloak caught upon the pommel.

"It seems you're ready to go," said Eleanor as she eyed him.

"You pay me well for my services. It is only fair that I am always ready at a moment's notice," he replied easily. A maid passed by the two of them, and Eleanor watched as her face pinkened as she looked over the man before looking at Eleanor and rushing off.

"Where are we headed today?" asked Railand, his hands resting upon his belt.

84

"To Marquis," said Eleanor, still watching the wake of the maid before turning her attention back to the man. "I've come into some information that will rebalance the deal we had made."

"Fair. And after that?"

"I have little today for appointments, and I promised Rosline once I was finished I would hurry back to give her time with Jaks."

Railand's face soured at the mention of the Duhoviman, "That's charitable of you."

"You don't like him."

"I'm rather familiar with Duhovimans, my lady. None that I have met have ever merited the privilege of my courtesy, and him even less so."

Eleanor smirked. Railand had been in her employ for almost three years, but he had never bothered to speak with Jaks when the wily man arrived to visit Rosline and eventually their daughter. Jaks opted to keep his distance, sensing the man's obvious dislike, but the gleam in his eye told Eleanor that he knew much more about Railand than the man would ever realize.

"Even still, Rosline is sweet on him, and they have a child together. He will be a fixture in my life, and as long as you are in my employ, yours as well."

"I merely am pointing out my distaste for him," replied Railand. "It isn't my place to tell you what company to keep, only that I keep you safe from them."

Eleanor smirked at him. "You have met Marquis before, yes?" She started walking off, and dutifully, Railand followed behind, to her left.

"Only on outings with you. The man is plump, flippant, and otherwise unappealing."

"He has much money and influence."

"A poor fit for you if that is what you are implying," said Railand.

Eleanor laughed, looking at him incredulous, "Yes, he would indeed be a poor fit. He is wed, after all."

"Marriages can be broken," he replied simply.

"Even still, in your limited visits with him would you find him duplicitous?"

"Aren't all you aristocrats in some manner duplicitous?" asked Railand in a serious tone. Eleanor set a look upon him before smirking once again. "No offense to you my lady, but I have gone on many an outing with you to know better."

"I shudder to think what you would tell one of my competitors," chided Eleanor.

"Nothing, for that's what you pay me for."

"And after?"

"New contract, new rules, but don't think me so petty to turn informant," he responded. "Else what would be the point of having a guardsman to yourself?"

"Fair enough," conceded Eleanor. She had played this game with him before, constantly poking to see where his loyalty truly lay. Eleanor knew that gold kept him in employ, but he had a warped sense of honor that extended past that. She attributed it to his heritage, but still had her doubts that a bag of gold wouldn't loosen his lips.

Rosline keeps a good enough eye on him.

Eleanor smirked as she walked down the cobbled path towards the gate of her grounds, Railand's easy stride bringing comfort she hadn't known in years.

ROSLINE.

Rosline rested easily beside Jaks as he traced circles on her back. He planted a kiss on her shoulder, sending warmth through her as she turned to face him.

He was watching her with his customary smirk on his face, his odd eyes sparkling with mirth.

"It's good that you're back," said Rosline quietly.

"It is indeed. I missed spending my nights with you. I was surprised that Eleanor allowed you to take a whole evening off just for us."

Rosline felt heat rise in her face as a fluttering ran through her stomach, "She's been very pleased with my work for her, so she thought it only fair to have some time to myself."

"Of course. You've been quite busy for her," said Jaks. He pulled himself from the blankets and pulled on his trousers as he reached for a small bundle that laid upon the night stand. With a practiced hand, he procured a pipe and packed it full of a mix before heading to the balcony. An orange glow filled his features as he took a long draw, and Rosline caught a waft of the sour smell of his usual blend. However, the smell wasn't as repugnant as once before, and she got a nostalgic feeling of when Jaks used to take her to a fancy tavern room for the evening many years ago. She pulled the blanket around her tightly as she thought, stirring only once Jaks returned to the bed, the scent of his pipe clinging to him like an acrid perfume.

"Sorry for not letting it drift away," he said as he climbed back into the bed beside her.

"It's fine. I'm finding, oddly, that I missed it."

"Are you well?" he said in a facetious tone, raising his hand to her head.

Rosline laughed as he grabbed his wrist, "I am fine."

"I remember you made me leave my clothes outside the first time I smoked around you," he said seriously. "I was so affronted; no one had ever told me that the smell was foul."

"I'm sure they had, but you actually cared about what I said," retorted Rosline.

"Perhaps just a bit," his face spread in a grin, "but not said. Say. As in present tense."

"I know." She smiled as he crawled behind her, wrapping his arms around her and pulling her close. The warmth of his skin pressed against her back, the steady beat of his heart comforting her.

"How is Eleanor these days?" asked Jaks.

"Much better now that she's getting the respect she deserves," said Rosline.

"With much thanks to you, I'm certain," said Jaks. "Being able to needle the soft points of soft folk must give her a dangerous air."

Rosline blushed, "Jaks…"

"Oh, right, I'm not supposed to know that," he said in a faux-defeated tone. "But how can I not exult when I have such a talented woman at my beck and call."

"The only one I hope," said Rosline quietly. She could hear him grin.

"Of course Rosline. I would never imagine finding another woman like yourself."

There was a tinge of unease as she thought about his comment, but a kiss on her neck blew that away.

"And Kyrah?"

"She is doing well in her studies," said Rosline in a proud tone. "I'm sorry you couldn't see her before her afternoon lessons."

"It is fine, she knows I'll have her to myself all of the morrow," he said. "As for her talent, why, I would expect no less from a child of my loins."

Rosline bit her lip, once again wondering at the tone in which he said it. She had never asked about his previous dabblings with women, and the few times she had sought him out in her vision, she found nothing to indicate he bore other children. And yet, she knew him before as a womanizer, a scoundrel, and most importantly, Jaks.

"You are much in your thoughts this evening," said Jaks.

"There's been a lot to consider," said Rosline.

"I imagine so. We both work in worlds where the other is not familiar with what their partner does," Jaks observed, resting his head in the crook of her neck. "And yet, we have a child and a growing life."

"We do."

"Does that make you uneasy, Rosline?"

She knew the answer she wanted to say, but she also knew that there was nothing, including a child, that would take Jaks from his path.

"It makes me wonder what Kyrah will think when she's older."

"Whatever she wants. She is a gifted child, Rosline, more so than any of the pumped up children she will come to know in the coming years. She will grow restless with the blood of Duhovima in her veins, and eventually she will forge her own path."

Rosline didn't know how she felt about that. Her gaze trailed around her room, to all the comforts she had come to know from her work. "I just worry for her, Jaks."

"Indeed, as is normal for a mother for her daughter."

"And you don't?"

"Only if she would end up meeting a man like me," he said sagely. "There would be chaos that not even you could peer through."

Rosline gave him a smirk, seeing his glittering eyes smiling down at her as he held her.

"Are you still uneasy?"

"Always, but that is from uncertainty. Not from you."

"I would consider both normal, but the former much more so," he said, drawing a laugh from her. "Are you certain about Eleanor?"

Rosline shifted, nestling in his gasp as she answered, "She is kind, smart, possessing both wit and cunning that I envy. And she works hard."

"Perhaps not hard enough," he said in a sharp voice.

Rosline knew he was referring to her eyes, the promise that Eleanor had given that she could not fully deliver.

"She didn't know, Jaks."

"It doesn't change the result any more or less," he replied. "And yet, I admit she did more than I expected from her."

"You thought she wouldn't want to help me?"

"Not solely for you, no."

Discord ran through her, but she knew that Jaks had an odd intuition about people that she would never match. He made a living reading people. However, despite his gripings, she knew that he was fond of Eleanor.

"Do you regret our meeting, all those years ago?" asked Rosline.

"No. Do you?"

Rosline shook her head emphatically. "She has given me more than I would have dreamed of."

She heard him smile again, "Good. But don't let your dreams end there. Continue dreaming and perhaps those will come true too."

Rosline shifted uneasily, having had an old dream only a few nights prior. "Is she… okay, Jaks?"

"You're just like that old barkeep," he said with a sigh. "I know many a thing, Rosline, but even I can't tell you for certain that she is well. She is free though, just as you are."

Rosline nodded, having to believe that Astoria was okay. Every few months, she would have that same dream where she watched her lying cold and scared on the ground. But, when she woke, she realized she saw less and less, and last time she realized she couldn't remember if she had freckles or not.

Everything fades, I guess.

Jaks cradled Rosline in her grasp, bringing back the sensation of comfort and security.

"Would you ever go north like they did?" she asked.

"I find that the snows of the north do little to alleviate my derision of the kingdom," he replied simply. "Let the burly northmen and the beasts of the forests lay claim to the frigid lands. I am quite content to rest in the warmth within this city."

Rosline laughed as he had punctuated his sentence with a grope. She tilted her head up and he kissed her, warmth flowing through her. "Did you think you'd miss us, Jaks?"

"Surprisingly, yes," he said with a grin. "But don't let that go to your head. It's much simpler to worm my way into a bed I'm already familiar with."

Rosline swatted him, frowning as he chuckled. "Sometimes, I wonder."

"Good, that means you are thinking, and that's what will keep you free."

Rosline laughed again, before she quieted. "Have you heard the rumors?"

"I've heard many," he replied, his voice losing its charming tone. "The king is ailing. His mind is going and people whisper that the end is near for the family's rule."

"It's just a whisper though," she said, pondering. "Do you think things will be okay?"

"Do you wonder if a scion of the Zweihanz family takes the throne whether those of southern descent will still be welcome?" he asked her, his eyes meeting hers.

She gave a small nod, worry bubbling in her chest.

Jaks grinned, "Fear not, Rosline. Not all rumors are true, and even the ones that are can be contested."

Rosline smiled weakly, remembering again that while she had spent much of the past five years with Jaks, he still was Jaks.

KARJA.

Each step took him further into the untamed land, his breath coming in puffs. The melt was already long underway and yet the ground was still hard with packed ice, the thickets of grass shone by sparkling frost early in the morning. Karja hadn't realized how long of a trek it would be and lamented the fact that he couldn't muster the *kymbrah* as his chieftain could.

Blasted otedien.

His steps were punctuated by the crunching of the grass beneath his boots. His breath hovered before his face, caught by the fur lining his cloak, but that did little to lessen the bite of the chill in the air. It was a harsh land, and yet somehow they had survived.

As the sun hung high in the sky, Karja broke for a meal, starting a small fire to heat some of the rations he had brought with him. Even with the directions he'd learned from Nyeth through careful conversation, he still hadn't the faintest idea when he was supposed to arrive at the encampment of Sehren and his southern ward. He ripped a piece of jerky as he heated up the rest of his meal, his eyes scanning the horizon. There were several copses that could potentially hold the camp, but between the taller thick grasses within the vast expanse, judging distance was proving to be a laborious chore.

Karja ate, musing. He believed they could force the pair of them from the north if need be, but he wanted to gauge just how invested they were. If they had built solid structures, or had made land arable, it would indicate to Karja that they were ready to stand and fight. But something that could easily be moved would be telling, as if they hadn't known whether they planned to stay or not.

And Karja thought that if the latter was true, it wouldn't be hard to push them away.

As he ate, a shudder ran up his spine. Peering around, Karja felt the sensation that he was being watched. One hand dropped to the blade at his side, loosening it in its sheath as he slowly rose. He stopped chewing, letting his trained senses search for any sort of unfamiliar sound.

A soft footpad crunched on the frost, and Karja wheeled about, facing it.

Crouched in the tall grass was a wolf-like creature, but its dark fur and dangerously intelligent eyes told Karja he was in danger.

Eiravuk.

The beast, having been seen, tensed itself, pulling back its lips to reveal thick, sharp teeth. It let out a low, rumbling growl, a clear threat as its fur stood on end.

Karja clutched the hilt tightly in his hand, slowly moving to take stock of his surroundings. He ignored the racing heartbeat in his ears, trying to hear accompanying growls, and before long he heard a chorus of them.

Four or five of the beasts. Far too many.

He felt stupid. While they were rare in the traveled lands of his people, *eiravuks* were known to run rampant in the wilds that their people hadn't the time nor resources to reclaim. While normal wolves would hardly be a problem, these beasts were dangerously cunning and their dark fur lent them much better odds at ambushing their prey than their smaller kin. Furthermore, they were unafraid of most things, as their sharp fangs could pierce even the hardiest creature's hide with little effort.

Karja slid the blade from its sheath, the action drawing a louder growl from the beast before him which was mimicked by the others around him.

"Well then, come!" he shouted, rushing forward at the beast. Loud barks erupted. He could feel them closing the circle around him.

If I slay this beast, I can try and break away from their circling, and try to goad them one at a time.

He cut forward, but the beast jerked to the side, avoiding the reach of his blade before coiling its feet beneath it. It lashed out with a savage bite. Karja similarly jerked away from it, feeling grim as he watched the fangs effortlessly shred the outer layer of his armor. He spun, quickly kicking forward as one of the beasts from behind lunged at him, catching it on the snout and pushing it away. It recoiled with a yelp as Karja settled back into his stance, taking an even, side-stepping gait to try and prevent the beasts from circling around him again. He'd been right in his estimation: five of the beasts had come to hunt. He saw their ribs beneath their skin, and their slightly hollowed faces told him that their winter had not been a good one, most likely stirring them to stalk him. They approached, staying low as they did. Karja knew that he could not outrun them, and that the beasts would most likely try to corral him with lunges to preserve as much energy as they could.

Karja tried to prevent them from gaining an advantage against him, but they were quickly moving from his line of sight. He had to take the offensive now. With a steadying breath, he lunged forth towards the nearest of the beasts, his blade leading. The beast jumped from his reach as he heard a rush from behind, and he quickly spun, placing his blade between him and the *eiravuk*. He caught it by surprise and felt satisfaction as the edge cut through its fur and into flesh beneath. Before he could deepen the blow, however, the beast shook away from him, and there was a tear in his back as another beast took a lunge at him. He spun again, trying to catch it, but the beast was already retreating to a safe position before taking that loping gait again, its eyes watching.

Blood ran from his back, the armor he wore dissuading the fangs from piercing deep into his flesh but not preventing them from tearing into his skin.

Am I really going to die here?

Karja shook his head, gritting his teeth as he watched the beasts that circled around him. He didn't survive the *Javeaf* to get eaten by some damned beasts far from home. Steeling his nerves and steadying his breath, he waited for one of the beasts to take a lunge at him. It wasn't long before one of them acquiesced, trying to push him towards another with it. Instead he rushed the beast, placing the tip of his blade in line with it to attempt to skewer it. It tried to turn, but had no mobility mid-lunge, and Karja caught it in the shoulder before viciously tearing his blade free.

He turned around, expecting the follow up lunge, his foot arching through the air and kicking another beast across the snout. However, his victory was short-lived when another one tore at his side, this one pulling away a sizable chunk of his flesh with it. His blood flowing free, Karja grit his teeth against the pain, trying to find a way to win.

The beasts bayed and growled at him, but suddenly they raised their heads and sniffed, as if something was on the air. Two of them turned, their growls rumbling deep as Karja watched a swirling gathering of mist coalesce behind them.

The kymbra... but... who?

The mist thickened and from it stepped Sehren, his grey eyes widening slightly in surprise as he stepped forward. Sweat beaded his brow, and Karja saw his breath coming short, but he confidently walked before the beasts as he drew the steel from his side. Silver metal shone in the sun and the *eiravuks* growling increased, the beasts incensed by his appearance.

"Not what I expected to find," said Sehren as he looked over the scene, "but I admit, the beasts were making it hard to find game."

Karja, gripping his side, watched as the beasts seemed to fear Sehren. One lunged at Sehren, drawing its kin, but with a careful thrust, he pushed the first beast away, only to shear through the second beast's side as he sidestepped the creature's lunge. The beast tumbled to the ground, weakly attempting to rise and limp away as Sehren pursued it and thrust through its side. Swiftly pulling his blade free, Karja watched him square off against the first one, his blade catching its maw before it sunk into him.

It's effortless. He's not thinking.

Karja rose his feet as the other beasts started moving away from him to deal with Sehren. He felt that the wound in his side was dangerous, but not lethal, as he moved to help Sehren. As he approached, Sehren took stock of him, his face growing grim.

"You were ill prepared for them," he said, his eyes focusing back on the circling beasts.

"They caught me at meal."

"I see."

Sehren placed his back to Karja, watching as two stalked him. Karja, still gripping his side, considered him for a moment before looking to the other two that circled before him.

"Focus on them not getting to my back," said Sehren calmly. Karja thought he sounded calm, too calm. "Do that, and you shall live this day, son of Chuyara."

"You would strike me otherwise?" asked Karja, suspicious.

"No," said Sehren, looking at him incredulously, "but if you take the offensive in your current state, they will hamstring you before taking your throat. You are weaker than you believe."

He faced the beasts before him, waiting. Karja breathed through the pain, focusing on preventing the other two from getting to his back. Once more, one of them came lunging forward, but Karja swatted it away, shifting back into position as the other beast came behind. There was a thud against his back, almost toppling him, as Sehren moved against him, and a shadow darkened overhead as he watched one of the beasts, its entrails spilling from its body, thrown over them.

Sehren then rushed forward, startling the beast, and swung. The beast leapt from his reach, and Karja intercepted the lunge from one of his beasts at Sehren's side, swatting it away as he cut across its snout. He could feel the last of the beasts coming for his side, and while he knew to turn, his movements were sluggish, the loss of blood catching up with him.

He was thrown to the ground as Sehren pulled him down, his blade singing as it swung through the air, the silver steel cracking against its skull. It yelped, recoiling in pain as it shook its head, but Sehren cooly stepped over Karja as it retreated, and with two careful strokes, felled it.

Karja rose, his side smarting, but the other two *eiravuks* were no longer circling, as if reconsidering. They saw Karja though, wounded, and again stalked towards him before Sehren interposed himself between them.

The silver steel in his hand was stained red, but Sehren breathed easily. His gaze told them in no uncertain terms that they were going to die this day. Karja repressed a shudder. Hungry, they continued baying and growling. Sehren goaded them forward, moving from Karja, and he knew that it was to draw their attention away from the injured man. Once again, they tried to lunge at him with alternative timings, but Sehren sidestepped and swatted them away, taking his own measured strikes. It was almost comical to watch, Sehren tracking their movements effortlessly. Even when one was in his blindspot, the man seemed to know exactly how to move in order to avoid taking a bite, and before long, both beasts, bloodied and limping, looked haggard and cowed before him.

"I am sorry," he said to them, his voice filled with genuine apology. "You should not suffer this way." He followed along as they tried to muster enough strength to flee, but Sehren quickly put them down with little effort.

Five of the beasts lay around them in cooling pools of their own blood, and Sehren wiped his blade on the grass Karja's heart was racing.

He's beyond me.

He didn't believe it. Karja had trained at Haljn's side for years and was widely regarded as one of the finest warriors of their people. Even Nyeth had spoken with favor towards him in regards to his skill. Sehren, however, was beyond him. Perhaps even beyond any chieftain of their people.

Maybe even... Nyeth.

He saw it then. The reason she had an unfaltering respect for the man. Sehren's movements were fluid, each strike planned three to four steps ahead. He had known what the beasts were going to do before they did it and had already mapped out how to kill them. It was simple to him.

Sehren set his grey eyes upon Karja, concern filling his face as he peered at the darkened stain of his side.

"Can you walk?" he asked, looking into Karja's face.

Karja nodded, "I have supplies I can use to staunch the wound."

"I doubt they will suffice. Something about these beasts' bites makes most poultices that your people use melt away. Tend it with what you can; we will walk to my camp from here." He moved to one of the fallen *eiravuks,* placing his blade within its scabbard while pulling a broad, short carving knife from his other side. Karja returned to his belongings, reaching for a poultice and placing it upon the wound. He hissed, the stinging mixture of herbs and oils flaring pain in his side, but as he began to wrap it, he watched as it became loose and as Sehren said, melted. Grimly, he wrapped his side with cloth, hoping that would stem the bleeding. Sehren continued cleaning the beasts, eventually removing their five pelts the best that he could. Wrapping them into a bundle and tying them with a belt, he carried them upon his shoulder before looking at Karja.

Karja gave him a nod, grabbing his things before following him across the tundra. He could still feel himself bleeding, and the cloth he had used to wrap himself was deeply stained by the time they arrived at the encampment.

"Astoria!" called out Sehren in Candraman, drawing confusion from Karja. A woman, a beautiful woman, with thick red hair and eyes the color of the sky, pushed her way from a large center tent, her face filled with curiosity. Her smile went wide as she looked upon Sehren, enhancing her beautiful face, before concern and confusion filled her face as she regarded Karja. They traded words in that strange language while Karja labored in pain, before the woman approached him as Sehren walked to another tent with the bundle on his shoulders.

"Can I see?" she said in Senkaman, drawing more surprise from Karja. She made tentative movements towards his side, and with reluctance, loosened his grip with a gasp. She palpated it as she spoke under her breath. "That needs tending," she said after a moment. She straightened, "Come then, I have the things."

"How do you know our tongue?" asked Karja, his voice filled with surprise and pain.

"Sehren taught me," she replied kindly. "Him and Nyeth. Now come. You will bleed through your leathers if that is not tended." She walked off towards the center tent, and Karja followed behind. He couldn't help but appreciate her gliding movements, the sway of her hips pinking his cheeks.

She spoke slower than he was used to, but her proficiency with their language, coupled by her beauty, had offset Karja's prejudice.

She's of the south.

He knew she was. He knew she was an enemy, but her bright eyes and kind smile as she pulled out a small kit filled with strange bone needles and myriads of thread disarmed him.

"Can you sit there," she asked, pointing at the log by the fire pit, "and remove your clothes? It will be easier this way."

Karja watched her for a moment as she took stock of one of the needles, before drawing it and holding it to the flame of the pit. "Now, if you want to live." There was no hint of threat, nothing in her kind voice that regarded him as an enemy.

Karja removed his shirt, his back stinging. He hissed as she said something else in that same language, examining his back as well. "*Eiravuks?*" she asked as she looked.

Nodding, Karja asked, "You know of them?"

"Who do you think kills them most of the time?" she said with a laugh as the tent flaps opened. Sehren walked in, setting his blade beside the entrance. "Certainly not him, as he is too busy seeing things."

"If I had not been busy, he would be dead," countered Sehren with a kind smile and laugh. His eyes narrowed with concern, "Is it deep?"

"His back is not. But his side is dangerous. I am not confident that I can tend to that one."

Sehren nodded before removing his leather coat and rinsing his hands in a pail. "Tend to his back then so you can get practice, and I shall do his side."

Sehren brought a waterskin to Karja, who thanked him and took a deep draft before hissing as he felt pinpricks in his back. "What are you doing?"

"Closing the wound," said Astoria, her voice steady as she worked. Karja tried to turn but she placed a hand on his back. "Please do not move. This is hard enough as it is."

"With the wound closed, whatever is in their saliva will fade away, and you will heal normally," said Sehren as he sat beside Karja, examining his wound. "Something in there eats through cloth. This is the way we know how to treat it."

"And you have treated them before?"

"Many times," said Sehren, his eyes filled with certainty. "Once she is done, I will tend to your side, and you can rest here."

Karja gave another nod as he felt more pinpricks in his back as well as a slithering feeling. Astoria and Sehren spoke to one another in their strange tongue, sending suspicion and shivers through Karja.

"I admit, I was not expecting a son of Chuyara this far from home," said Sehren.

"My curiosity of you had grown after our talk all those weeks ago. I wanted to meet with you."

"Alone?"

"Most of my closest companions are *krusho*. We could not all come."

"Still, one extra could have saved you trouble and pain," said Astoria as she worked. "That should do it," she said afterward.

Sehren nodded, "I need you to sit as still as you can. Once the flesh is closed, you will have to resist stretching else you will reopen the wound."

Karja looked puzzled as he watched Astoria thread one of the small bone needles and pass it to Sehren. "What is that?"

"Sinew. The saliva that remains in the wound will melt it as it heals but your flesh should be healed by then."

Karja looked suspicious and clenched in pain as Sehren began. Sehren stopped before calling to Astoria. She left the tent and returned with a small bit of wood. She cleaned it off with some water before offering it to Karja.

"Bite on this," she said.

"To ease the pain?"

"To withstand it," she corrected. "It will hurt, and this will help you not squirm."

Karja eyed the wood for a moment before placing it in his mouth. As Sehren worked, he clenched as hard as he could, his teeth feeling as though they would break.

"That should do it," said Sehren after what seemed ages. He clipped the thread and tied it.

Karja glanced at it. The once wide tear in his side was closed with a series of looping stitches. He tentatively palpated the sewn flesh. "That is new."

"It is something I learned long ago," said Sehren as he returned the supplies to their place. He brought another waterskin to Karja, "As I said, try to stretch as little as possible until the thread melts."

Karja nodded, his mind racing. Astoria gave Sehren a glance that sent a surge of jealousy through the man before heading from the tent.

"Your curiosity could have cost you your life," said Sehren.

"I see that now. Your lands are much more wild than I anticipated."

Sehren let out a short laugh as he rose and departed from the tent.

He'd come to save Karja. They tended his wounds and left them in their home unattended.

He heard them talking again in that strange tongue, the woman's laugh broken only by the sounds of a swift kiss.

Karja was at a loss.

ASTORIA.

Astoria woke up before Sehren. She pulled herself from their bed of furs, moving as quietly as possible to let him rest. She knew he was still recovering from his watch yesterday but knowing Sehren, he would rouse a few moments after she left the tent. She smirked.

Karja had stayed only long enough for him to rest and feel confident enough to make the trek back to the Senkaman lands on his own. Sehren had offered to guide him just in case another wayward pack of beasts came upon him. Karja, however, had refused. Still, that hadn't prevented Sehren from sparing concern for the man. Sehren had spent his time keeping watch out, exhausting himself the day before. Astoria still didn't understand how something so simple could be so taxing for him but when he told her that he had made it safely from their territory, his face had been covered in sweat and his breathing had been harsh.

Today though, she knew he would be tired, and while she had lost their sparring bout before, she felt a bit vengeful today. Before that though, she grabbed his blade, pulling the white steel from its scabbard and turning it sideways and eyeing the edge. She dared to not test the edge as she would their other blade, and her practiced eye saw no burr or nick in the metal. Sheathing it, she belted it on her side before pushing her way from their tent.

It was quiet outside, the steady rushing of the stream the only thing standing out to her. It was bracing but the sky was clear. She took a deep breath, the cold air surging through her lungs and invigorating her. With a deep exhale, she walked around the perimeter of their camp, checking the fencing for any breaks. While she knew it wouldn't hold up against anything serious, the mere presence of it had deterred many of the wild beasts that wandered through the tundra. She saw a loose portion of it, seeing the rope they had tied the beams with slacken and frayed. Astoria fixed it, her movements automatic as she continued peering around. Satisfied with the repair, she made her way around, eventually taking a moment to approach a small cairn that sat beside their crop field. Astoria was somber as she approached and knelt before the rough stone that marked the grave.

Termesa.

She sniffed as she remembered the horse. She had been a valiant steed, carrying her and Sehren from the City of Isle steadily and without complaint. Even when they had to push further north, the warhorse hadn't faltered, almost as immovable in her resolve as Sehren had been. Her last act had been to protect Sehren from a *davoarth,* the savage ursine creature having battered Sehren and stolen their food. She had intervened on his behalf and even cracked the beast's skull with her powerful hooves. But, weakened and tired from hunger, her luck had run out.

Astoria bowed her head, clutching the small pendant around her neck as she said a prayer for her. She didn't know if the Lady of Isle cared about her anymore, or even heard her prayers so far away from her lands, but Astoria felt better trying to commune with her.

"She was a great friend," said Sehren's voice quietly. Astoria smirked, knowing Sehren hadn't meant to sneak up on her but still managed it even to these days. Astoria took stock of him as he knelt beside her, his hand running over the stone as he gave a solemn smile. His eyes were dark, but Astoria knew that he was focused on all the good times that he had shared with the warhorse. She'd heard plenty of the stories and while some of them seemed embellished, it only took

Astoria remembering that night against the *davoarth* to dispel her disbelief.

"She was," Astoria reached for his free hand, lacing her fingers through his and clutching tightly. Sehren took a moment, bowing his head before nodding to the stone and rising up.

"I hope you are ready for practice this morning," said Sehren. Astoria smirked again, noting that he bore Samuel's blade on his side.

"First to three?" She asked as she rose, stretching her arms up as she asked.

"I was thinking five."

Astoria laughed, "A long one then. Do you think you can manage after yesterday? You seemed rather exhausted."

"Is that fear I hear, Astoria? I thought you would be more eager considering our last match. Or have you already put it behind you?"

Astoria gave him a dangerous smile, "The one you cheated in? Oh no, I haven't forgotten that one."

Sehren laughed, "I would hope not. Needless to say though, I do not believe that I could manage that trick again."

They had made their way towards a cleared area where the grass had been worn away from their constant fervent dances. The sky was still dark blue, the sun barely touching the edge of the horizon as they strode before one another. With a slither, Astoria drew the alabaster steel from her side, Sehren mirroring her movement with the dark steel of Samuel's blade. They circled, their movements in time with one another. Her heart quickened in anticipation, but she quelled the distracting beat and solely focused on Sehren. The tip of his blade twitched, and in a rush, he was before her.

Reflexively, she caught the steel with her own, their blades kissing one another before she responded with a riposte. Sehren swept that aside with an elegant parry, already moving into his own response, to which Astoria had her own guard in line to deny the edge of his blade. It was second nature, her eyes watching his pose and stance more than the singing steel.

A foe will tell more with their eyes and body and the position of their blade. Once you know where the steel is, watch their body for the followthrough.

Astoria had studied Sehren for years, her waking hours training to try match the grace that he had honed over decades. She knew that her prowess had grown exponentially, Sehren's careful and impassioned training shaping her into a fine duelist, and by Sehren's account, one of the finest fighters he'd had the pleasure to train.

But her own practice pushed her further, her desire not to impress Sehren, but to defeat him driving her more than anything else. She was taken from her thoughts as a whizz passed by the side of her temple, the sound reminding her that even if she could walk through his routine, could memorize the dance of his mother, she still lacked the experience to push past that.

As the steel clanged and their shirts clung to them with sweat as the sun rose over the horizon, Astoria contemplated his last victory.

Left.

Her once weak side, one that Sehren had shaped over the years with stinging welts, was her strongest asset now as she caught and turned his blade high. She saw him unsteady for a moment, saw the moment to strike his thigh, but her experience with him told her the truth. She aimed higher, for his shoulder, and managed to sting the side of his arm with the side of her steel. Her elation was short-lived though, as she felt a retaliatory sting on the inside of her arm.

"One," she growled in between breaths. He grinned, his eyes flickering with applause. She repressed her own smile, knowing that it would steal a moment's thought from her, and that would be a moment too long.

"No smiling," she said shortly as she repelled a thrust with a downward sweep, resetting their stances as they both went wide. They circled one another, taking a moment to collect themselves and gather their breath.

Endurance is the most important thing for a fighter, Astoria. If you rely too much on closing the fight within moments of crossing blades, and find that you cannot, you will lose.

Steadying herself, she raised her blade once more. Her muscles were growing tense, but Astoria knew that she had much more left in her. Dashing forward, she grasped the blade with both hands, driving a swift cross cut across his body.

Sehren reacted as expected, his own blade before him. However, instead of trying to catch the steel on his once, he deflected her swing high before trying to quickly thrust.

Astoria followed the momentum as she sidestepped and almost slid along his thrust. Were her blade not so high, she would have given him a whack on his head. Instead, with a quick backstep, she lowered her blade and attempted a thrust of her own, hoping Sehren would be too immobile to shift in time.

He wasn't though. He never was. Her thrust caught nothing, Sehren already several paces away from her aim. She could feel the blade cutting through the air to her back and quickly turned, trying to catch it on the side of her own. The steel in her hands jarred against his, causing her teeth to rattle as she parried. However, she didn't let that addle her thoughts, already backstepping to create distance as her blade tangled with Sehren's.

"I doubt you would've been able to stop with such a vicious thrust," said Sehren as he watched her, his eyes filled with mirth.

"Or you, with that savage swipe," she retorted, smirking.

"I knew you could catch it."

"I know."

Astoria had to repress the surge of pride coursing through her. Sehren had never pushed her farther than she was able to manage. He said it was from experience of training so many, but she believed it was from an intimate understanding of one another. They had used leather covers when she had first picked up the art again, but Astoria had requested that they remove them and be careful, the leather feeling odd on the normally light blades. They had few scars from their sparring, mainly Sehren more than Astoria, as when she was less experienced she couldn't always turn the blade on its side in time to sting rather than cut. There were no complaints between them though, and even now if one of them drew blood on accident, they continued on until the number of strikes was met.

Sehren took the offensive again, working her through a swift flurry of cuts and thrusts that Astoria deflected with hardly a second thought. He forced her to backpedal though, and she worked on keeping her feet underneath her while driving away his steel. Sehren was trying to corral her she knew, but she understood that the most dangerous thing she could do would be to try and force her way through. Each flurry was timed with one another, and Sehren would have already predicted her response to try and break through as he guided her. Once it ended, however, Astoria retaliated, the white steel in her hand almost becoming a blur as she went through her own flurry of her own. She knew where each strike was going to land, and knew how she wanted Sehren to parry, but he had put distance between them almost immediately, causing her to overstep.

She was already wincing when she felt the two welts on her side as she tried to compose herself, growling as she tried aligned her guard in time.

"Patience, Astoria," he said calmly.

They paused for a moment, and just as Astoria was getting ready to strike again, Sehren rested the tip of his blade into the ground, wiping the sweat from his brow.

"Should we break here?"

"You were the one that said five," she countered, her tone challenging.

He laughed, smiling, "Yes, I did. And you will not reconsider, will you?"

She shook her head, sensing his fatigue.

With another laugh, he pulled the blade from the earth, "Very well."

He swapped his blade to left hand, and Astoria frowned, thinking he wasn't taking her seriously.

"If you can sting me twice while I use my left," he said, twirling the blade, "then I will consider you having won this one."

"You think that's wise?" she asked.

"I need the practice."

110

Astoria shook her head as she smirked, "You're bored."

"On the contrary, Astoria," he replied. "I am having the time of my life."

She saw the sincerity in his eyes as he said that, and with another shake of her head, took the initiative, closing with an overhead chop. Sehren sidestepped it, and as she followed, he took more and more evasive maneuvers, studying her. His eyes flickered, and Astoria knew what he was going to do, already launching her riposte as she knew his feint would land short. She felt another sting though, her surprise full as her own strike fell short and his blade slapped the inside of her forearm. Drawing back, she tried to steady herself, but let out a sigh as she knew, resigned, that he had won. She lowered her blade, sitting upon the ground.

"You tricked me."

"Of course. You are far superior than I am with my left," said Sehren.

"You were going feint for my left shoulder, then duck beneath my guard and strike my torso. I would've shored up my guard to prevent the hit, but you would've struck my left shoulder blade, using the feint and shortened reach to step past me."

"You are learning," said Sehren with a nod, "but that is hindsight. You fell prey to it again."

"I know, I know. Arrogance."

He sat beside her, "Even still, that is why we practice, Astoria. You have become one of the finest swordsmen I have ever trained, and one day I believe you will match me."

She raised an eyebrow, "Really?"

"Aye. It is only a matter of time. Mastery comes in terms of years, but with your drive and our constant training, that can be shortened."

Then maybe, I'll finally get the win I want.

Astoria rested her head against his shoulder, "And then what…?"

Sehren fell silent. The last five years had passed in almost a blink as there had been so much to do. The first year, Astoria had been filled with a vitriolic angst towards Sehren. She thought she would go mad as she wiled away the days within the tent as Sehren hunted and provided for them. Her curiosity had been her saving grace, her inquisitiveness pulling her from the confines of their shelter and helping Sehren with the chores they needed to survive.

Now, they thrived in the tundra. The encampment spanned the entirety of the grove that they had first arrived at, and between both of their efforts, they had stored meat, grown plentiful crops, and widened a spring of freshwater. Their tents had become thick and resilient, holding off the bitter chill of the autumn and winter months. They had even managed to cobble together crude furniture from the remnants of the wagon after it had broken down from disrepair. After Sehren had fostered relations with Nyeth, they were able to trade the things they held in excess, grabbing clothes and comforts that had been foreign to them for the first few years.

"Do you wish to prepare the meal today, or shall I?" asked Sehren as he rested his head against hers.

"I think you should. You still need a bit more practice for not undercooking things," she teased, smiling. Sehren laughed. He did that often these days, a carefree bark of laughter that dispelled her misgivings for the future.

"Very well. Make sure you check the meat for spoilage and water the crops. If we plan right, we should have a great store for the winter."

Astoria nodded, feeling him stand up. He held out his hand for her, and she took it, his sharp tug effortlessly pulling her to her feet.

As he walked off, Astoria adjusted the sword on her side before walking around the camp. In truth, she much preferred doing the other chores around the camp rather than cooking, and Sehren was inclined to allow her the freedom of her choice. She also much preferred hunting, but as she went to the tent that sat atop the widened stream and checked the nets, she saw that they would be fine on meat for the coming weeks. Astoria carefully set the netted venison back into the rushing water, scouring with a small, wooden spade to make sure that the stream didn't settle and become slow again.

112

As she exited the tent, she smelled Sehren cooking and took a moment to water the crops before returning to the tent. He had set the skillet with the still sizzling meal beside the pit, dishing its contents onto a plate before turning his head towards her and offering it.

"Smells good," she said as she picked up a small piece of the roasted meat with her fingers and popped it into her mouth. With a satisfied smile she said, "You actually cooked it all the way through this time."

"If you can learn my mother's dance, then I can learn the lessons you have taught me as well," said Sehren. "I often misjudge based upon the outer layer. The charring is still something I will never be able to make consistent."

They ate together, Astoria leaving small bits of the tougher parts within her plate as she ate. "Sehren?" she asked between bites.

"Aye?"

"How's it feel, being a chieftain?"

He chuckled, "The same as being an outcast, renegade knight."

She grinned, "On top of being the Steadfast?"

"That too. It is all the same to me, but I admit, being recognized for accomplishing what no one else from my kin have been able to do is satisfying."

"And eventually, you can claim your lands back!"

"If I ever desired to, yes."

Astoria pursed her lips, "But that'll happen when I'm queen, huh?"

Sehren met her gaze, mirth in his eyes, "Precisely. Once you become queen, Astoria, I shall go to Senkama to claim the lands of my heritage."

She laughed as he rose from the fire pit.

They continued tending to their home with Sehren once again falling into a deep, meditative state as he seemed to keep a watch over their lands. Astoria didn't fully understand what he did exactly, but recalled him stating that he could feel the presence of others when he set aside everything else. He said it was like seeing the world through a fogged window, with beacons and pinpricks all around. Nyeth had taught him about it, but it was something that no matter how much he did it, it wouldn't make sense to her.

Still, being able to find Karja proves that he is doing something. Even if I can't see it.

Astoria took some time to patrol around close to their camp, not expecting to find much but still hopeful of being able to snag something for them for the evening. Eventually, night overcame their encampment, and she found Sehren staring up at the sky. Astoria joined him, her gaze going skyward to the bed of stars above.

"I'll never get over how beautiful it is," she said as she gazed. The conflux of stars sparkled overhead, lifting her spirits as she beheld them.

"Aye." Sehren broke his gaze for a moment before beckoning Astoria to sit with him. She joined him, considering him for a moment before turning her gaze upward once more.

"Sehren?"

"Yes, Astoria?"

"Do you think we will ever return to the kingdom?"

Sehren turned his attention towards her, his face becoming pensive. She felt foolish asking and knew that it pained him to think about it.

He gave her a solemn smile before saying, "If you wish to return back, we can go, Astoria. I think I am ready."

Astoria watched his eyes flicker back up to the sky, her heart aching slightly. She shook her head, fighting back tears as she said, "Perhaps next spring."

AMOS.

A desk of cherry, polished to a high sheen, laid along the center of the room, a high backed chair behind it. Piles upon piles of scrolls and parchment rested upon its glossy surface with pen and ink seated beside them, waiting to place their marks upon the missives and issues that waited for them. Books lay nestled in tall oaken shelves, their spines etched with myriads of colors and titles.

The King's Study.

Amos once was a frequent visitor to the king while he sat in this very room, working with the man to discern the largest threats to the kingdom and working together to remove them. Now though, he was a seldom visitor, the king refusing to see most of his advisors outside of the captain of his guard.

Amos walked around the room, eyeing the different volumes of knowledge that lay within. While nowhere near as grand as the archives of the brotherhood, it still stunned Amos just how much knowledge was packed inside the lavish room. Decades of information lay within, their leathery covers the only gatekeepers of the knowledge held therein.

That, the Aegis, and several more guards of the city.

Amos turned his gaze to the door, where one member of the prolific order stood, his hand at his side upon the hilt of his blade. He gave Amos a steady nod, his eyes taking note of every action, every movement made within the room. Diligent and unwavering.

Footsteps upon the stairs turned Amos' gaze towards the king's quarters. He bowed his head as the king made his way down the steps. Garbed in finery few peasants could even dream of, Saiho's regal gait brought him to the desk where he sat heavily into the seat, his dark eyes rimmed with dark circles and a somber look upon his face.

"My liege," said Amos with a respectful bow. Saiho waved at him, letting him know that the courtesy was unnecessary.

"What brings the Lord Commander to my study?" said Saiho. Amos resisted frowning. His voice, once vital and filled with stern authority, was gruff and tired. "Are you still dissatisfied with my decisions regarding the festivals?"

"No, I settled that matter already with the treasurer," replied Amos. "This call comes from more of a place of concern. Ricard tells me you are continuing the search through the order to find more men of deceitful nature that could threaten the kingdom."

"Aye, I am. What of it?" Saiho's tone was already petulant, resting his head upon his arm at the desk.

Resisting offense, Amos stated, "The matter regards men within the Knights of Isle, my liege. My men. My order."

"Ricard mentioned you had grown provincial in the past few years," said Saiho, sitting back up. His eyes scanned Amos a moment before letting out a sigh, "I see he was correct."

"Provincial?" said Amos, his tone growing agitated. "These men are under my purview and command. I should have been informed that you were planning on continuing to investigate them. I shouldn't have had to hear it from Ricard that you weren't planning on stopping."

"Aye, these are indeed the men that you command. But you forget yourself, Amos," said Saiho. "You are under my command, and therefore, these men are as well. As for Ricard informing you of my decision, I thought it foolish to have you make your way all the way to my quarters to simply inform you of my actions."

"A habit you seem to be making of all affairs regarding the city," responded Amos.

Saiho raised his eyebrow, "Am I to personally get myself involved in every matter within the city and kingdom, Amos? Is that not what I have you and my council for?"

"You do, but more and more it seems that you resort to using Ricard as your courier rather than for his intended station of protecting you. To many, it seems that the words come from his mouth rather than from your own."

"What did you just say?" said Saiho, a dangerous edge in his voice.

"I speak the truth, my king," said Amos, not crumbling at the man's glare. "Many grow concerned throughout the city that you've become disinterested in resolving matters and instead are allowing Ricard to act with the permission of the king. If that is the case and your intent, then I merely wished to have been informed by you that he was speaking with the king's voice."

"Ricard serves me in the best way he can," replied Saiho, "but know that the words he utters are directly from me. You think I would be so incompetent to let him foster decisions about the welfare of the people?"

"Not at all. I came here today because I am concerned about what may come from the appearance." Amos had stung the king's pride, and he knew there was no better way of getting a direct answer from the man.

The king let out a deep breath, before saying, "Your concern is noted, Amos. Misplaced, but noted. The decisions regarding your men are mine, among the other decisions I have come to ask of late. Do you find that an apt answer to your concerns?"

"Aye. Still, I wish you had consulted me about the order before relaunching another investigation."

"After those knights defected two years ago, Amos, it came to my attention that letting the order know of what may transpire could cause more uproar than needed."

Amos winced, remembering the incident. Almost fifty men had fled the city rather than face the investigation that was being conducted. No charges had been levied against them and yet instead of

117

cooperating, they had stolen supplies and rations, before fleeing. They were still somewhere within the kingdom, but whenever sorties had been made to apprehend them, they either turned up too late and the defected knights had moved on, or found no evidence of their passage. To this day, Amos had only heard of the band of knights from disgruntled land owners that said poachers were running through the land. Unlike other bands of brigands or lawless men, the defected knights had done little to stir chaos in the kingdom.

"I understand, my liege," conceded Amos. "Will you be conducting the investigation as before, with convening of officers within the order to review those that you believe are a threat?"

"Something to that effect," answered Saiho. "These are times of revelations, Amos. Men that once were stalwart and the backbone of the kingdom are proving to be instead petty glory seekers looking to fill the coffers of their forebears while lining their own pedigrees with silver threads of knighthood. It is despicable."

Of that, we agree.

"I remember learning of the formation of the Knights of Isle, Amos. I was barely more than a lad as my father first spoke of them. They were first and foremost men of the Lady, knights said to be exemplars because of their devotion to kingdom and faith."

Amos nodded, also knowing of the almost legendary stature of the knights of old.

"At first, they were simply the knights of this city, the stronghold a key within uniting the different dominions of the kings. So close to the north and yet well within the grasp of the south, they were regarded as some of the finest men to ever bear arms with the Lady's sigil upon them. Few threats could stand against the brotherhood in their founding days, and eventually they expanded their order, each fort they erected a sign of peace and order within the lands they laid the stone. They, alongside my ancestors and the other forebears of the royal families, tamed and shaped Candrama into the nation that it is today."

Saiho let out a deep sigh as his eyes trailed over to the window to peer outside, "The order has become a ghost of itself, a shell of its former glory. The men, boys really, are unfocused and the new stock is

118

of almost unrecognizable ilk. But worse are the whispers of dissent, Amos, ones that I cannot overlook simply because I prefer the values of the old over the ignorant exuberance of youth."

"You plan on rooting out the corruption that has nestled within. I can understand that, your highness, but why not include me in that so that together we can solve the issues that so plague the order?"

"I admit that I have been a bit remiss in considering you in my decisions, Amos. Over the years, I can see the folly in not truly consulting you in regards to the order."

"Among your decision to replace me," added Amos in a biting tone.

Saiho winced, "It was not a decision I made lightly, nor do I think it was a poor decision overall. Your continued determination to try to solve for truth within the order as well as your dedication to the men regardless of mixed opinions upon you have shown me that the order was of sound and disciplined mind. And even now, with my grievances of the new recruits laid upon you, you stoically listen but I know you would defend the men under your command with biting words and necessary retorts if needed."

"Thank you," said Amos, bowing his head.

Saiho sat back in his chair. "I will leave it to you to best determine how to go about this investigation, Amos. I understand your protests before, but you also understand my concern. I hope that we can figure this out together to create both a better brotherhood, and a brighter outlook for the kingdom."

Amos bowed once again before saying, "I shall take that to heart, my liege. Allow me a moment to discern where the threat may lie first before we act this time. I agree that it would be folly to bandy about with your intent, but the men deserve a modicum of respect and transparency else distrust will grow like a weed within the order."

Saiho took a moment to consider before nodding and saying, "Very well. But do not let this fester, Amos. I take this matter very seriously."

"As you will," Amos approached the king, extending his hand to him. Saiho rose from his seat and clasped wrists with him, his grip still strong. Amos gave him one final bow before leaving the room, giving a cursory glance to the member of the Aegis that was by the door to the study.

Let Ricard hear of this to be reminded where I stand with the king. That will help with my decisions and from there, hopefully we can put an end to this madness.

Amos left the palace, his appointment taking a bit longer than expected. He knew that the older generals of the order would heed his call, as they were staunch supporters of Amos and his decisions. The younger officers would be the point of contention, seeing his actions as intrusive to their given superiority. It wouldn't be the first time that one of the newer men had become an upstart, and Amos knew for every sincere man who wielded power solely because he was told to, there would be three that would covet it and abuse it once they obtained it.

Amos also knew that some of the younger men were growing anxious about the potential power shift. Rumors were growing about Saiho abdicating the throne for another one of the royal families to take the seat of power over Candrama, and as such, some of the men grew worried about the order. The Knights of Isle had been given the resources that had fostered their growth initially from the Mistletain family, and if Saiho returned to his ancestral keep in the west, many were concerned how another family with little investment into the brotherhood would maintain them as the Mistletains had for decades.

It was a growing concern for Amos, but even if Saiho did find the burden of the crown too much for him to bear alone, he would maintain the order so long as he was Lord Commander. He would advise the new king on the importance of the order, and assure whoever it was that the continued support for the Knights of Isle would be beneficial to the sovereignty and security of Candrama.

So long as they can set aside their own grudges for one another, it won't matter who leads.

ARUHN.

Aruhn swept the common room of his tavern, the night's wiles coming to an end. Stifling a yawn, he took comfort in the soft scratching noise of the bristles against the hardwood floor. His maids were chattering in the back of the tavern, cleaning the remaining dishes before they themselves headed out. Aruhn listened to their energetic conversations, smiling as he thought of the haul they were bringing in for the tavern.

Maybe another year or so, and I'll be able to call it quits.

The thought came to him more and more as the years had gone by, exacerbated by the cough he continued to carry since the failed attempt on his life all those years ago. He thought of the days where he could take his earnings and pass the torch to someone else, but sadly, his pride in his tavern and its legacy always made him reconsider. There simply wasn't anyone that was good enough to continue the Friar's good name. He'd spent decades of his life in the tavern, building its repute and fame all while dealing under the table to supplement his income. While the thoughts of turning to a simple brewer were tantalizing, he knew that he would most likely work in the tavern until his age caught up with him and he could no longer run it well.

Another sweep along the floor cleared his mind as well as it cleaned the dirt and dust from the night. It had been another full night, with clinking glasses, jovial voices, and much wealth spent on his food and drink. His maids were going to have a good season, and feeling generous, Aruhn had already started setting aside small bonuses for all their hard work.

With a rub of his nose, his eyes made their way to the door, the latch shut and locked. He was waiting for one last appointment before he could truly shut down the shop, and he heard the faint knocks that drew him to the door. As he unlatched the locks, he creaked the door open, letting out a sign when he saw the telltale smirk.

"Forgive my tardiness, Aruhn. I found myself wrapped up in the embrace of a beautiful woman, and thought not to waste the moment."

Aruhn just gave him a gruff, "Uh huh," before letting him in and shutting the door behind him, resetting the latches.

Jaks took a seat at the bar, sending a wink to one of the younger barmaids which sent her off to the kitchen, flame-faced and embarrassed. Aruhn took a seat across from him, wrinkling his brow with expectation.

"Are you somber this evening, Aruhn? No witty remark or other comment?"

"I know yeh like to hear yehrself talk, so I was just waiting for a lull in the conversation."

"I do indeed enjoy the cadence of my own voice, this is true," said Jaks with a mirthful smirk, "but why would I ask to meet with you if I merely wished to hear myself talk?"

Aruhn just shrugged as Jaks shifted in the seat, his eyes darting now and again towards his maids with an appreciative look, "You're going to miss the sights, Aruhn. How can someone so willingly give up such a bevy of young wenches?"

"I'm findin' that there's more than just linin' my pockets and eyeful sights, Jaks."

"Your guilty conscience must be weighing on you then, Aruhn," said Jaks wryly.

Aruhn frowned at him. "And if it is?"

"Then it's a little late to the situation," replied Jaks. "but I understand. You've spent the last few years wary of someone ending what you have left, and that, alongside your tavern's prosperous growth in the face of lacking competition, you've become comfortable. I too find that things have been lacking their usual subtlety. While the Lotus has still been active, they haven't mustered the gumption to move against me as they once had before."

"I'm sure yehr contacts within prevent that."

"I had contacts before, Aruhn," countered Jaks. "It's my job. But there isn't even a sect within the clandestine group that has tried vying for power or tackling the status quo. It's all so boring."

Jaks let out a dramatic sigh as Aruhn shook his head. He bit his tongue, but Jaks gave him a withering look as he said, "If you have a question, ask it, Aruhn."

"Is this all just a game to yeh? Are these people's lives that meaningless?"

"All lives are meaningless, Aruhn," replied Jaks seriously, raising an eyebrow at the man. "From the king himself who is in the clutches of despair because his lineage comes to an end, to the newly wailing babe that seeks comfort at his mother's teat. Because they are meaningless, they get to decide what they want them to mean. Should I choose the security of the kingdom while I wallow away as a peasant, barmaid, or some other menial member of society? You can, if that's what brings you comfort and safety. There's nothing wrong with that, but to resign yourself to the idea, the notion, that you were fated to be nothing more than you find yourself as is why people find themselves trapped in despair."

Jaks rested his head on his hand, before continuing, "Why engage in something so pointless? Most who claim that only the talented and fortunate can climb the rungs to escape the dirt have rarely taken the first step needed to bring their own meaning. If I can take such an existence and give it meaning, then my game is worth more than the wallowing they would have spent decades doing, even if it's cut short, is it not?"

Aruhn's frown deepened.

"You think me crass and uncaring, and you'd be right on one count. But I very much care in the way my own goals are resolved, and through that, the people I watch to that end. Should I lament for those that chose to play the game without fully understanding the rules? Or should I take sympathy upon those who tried to dip into my world only to find themselves far outmatched?"

"Yeh could show some kind of remorse for the people's lives."

"Like you did all those years ago?" accused Jaks, smirking with his eyes glittering. "When it suited to serve you, you threw away a name without nary a thought."

"Never without a thought," said Aruhn, his admittance flushing his face. "I knew most of the people that got tangled into things they shouldn't have. That didn't make their lives worthless."

"And when it came down to it, Aruhn, you chose yourself over them. You chose that your life would have meaning even if their actions didn't give theirs meaning."

"But not without guilt," countered Aruhn, slamming his hand upon the counter, drawing the attention of the maids. He waved them away before continuing. "Even as a youngin, I always took it hard when I saw what my actions could and would bring."

"Just not enough to stop," said Jaks.

"Yeh always have an answer," said Aruhn.

"Because I have meaning. A purpose. And you did too, for years. It was your tavern, your name, your reputation. You used to relish the respect you garnered from people like Marson and Gaius. A barkeep that could dance the same dance as us? A coveted position, for certain. You touched elbows with prosperous members of society, and even met Madrid in person and lived to tell the tale."

Jaks leaned towards hims, his voice dropping, "You held the future of the kingdom within the fours walls of your establishment and reared her, treating her as your own, before relinquishing her to the company of a renegade knight with a malicious, conniving wife."

Aruhn was taken aback at the amusement and excitement in his voice, his odd eyes glittering with glee as he continued. "How can you possibly say you didn't enjoy that?"

124

Aruhn shook his head. "It was for survival."

"Then why not leave, when you made your first score? Take the gold, get a wagon, and flee. Even I don't have arms and eyes everywhere, Aruhn. You could have settled somewhere and been free from all this that you seem to find distasteful. Look at our mutual friend: He gathered his things, fled to the north, and no one knows what became of his fate. Maybe he perished fighting the perils of the north. Maybe he found a place to hide away. But he found something else, away from what he found so distasteful."

Jaks turned a knowing eye onto him, "But you didn't. You threw your lot in with the rest of us, and you chose to cut your teeth in our world."

Aruhn let out a sigh, "I'm old Jaks. I want peace, and all this is comin' to show that you hate peace over all."

"I am flattered for you to think that my actions alone will steal the peace from the kingdom. Even now, there are machinations and rumors abound that I have nothing to do with. Era's end after all Aruhn, no matter how withered hands futilely grasp onto them."

Aruhn was shocked, "The king's dying?"

"No not that rumor," said Jaks, bringing confusion to Aruhn. With a malicious grin he said, "It seems the Klins province is growing tired of the idea of being in service to the king. There are talks of them declaring independence from the kingdom, especially if Saiho shirks his responsibility before his time."

Aruhn was stunned, "They've always been the most earnest supporters of the crown."

"And it seems that era is coming to an end," said Jaks, his grin wide and devilish. A chill ran through him, prickling his skin. He could hear Jaks' mind working as he thought of the chaos that would ensue from the splintering of the kingdom.

"A kingdom in chaos, Aruhn. Can you imagine? Who knows if the Desmond or Cerus provinces will follow suit? A once united nation, fractured due to greed and doubts."

Jaks closed his eyes a moment before saying, "And to have agents in all four nations, working together against the Candraman greed. It stirs the mind."

Aruhn said, "But that's not yet, right? It can't be on the Kris family mind so readily."

"Aye, not yet, but once one family goes, then soon the next comes quicker and the next quicker after that."

Aruhn frowned. He'd heard some of the aristocrats were concerned about what the king had been doing lately but nothing to indicate the kind of dissent that Jaks hinted at. However, even though he wouldn't admit it, Aruhn's information network had declined in the past years, with some of his patronage taking their business elsewhere when Aruhn needed his time to recover.

Jaks, however, had his people wherever they needed to be. It was uncanny these days to not find the rogue at the heart of all the rumors abounding, but he'd taken a spectator's role in watching the city. There were threads unraveling between the families, but Aruhn had to admit they were not by his hands.

"How's Rosline?" asked Aruhn, clearing his throat.

"Fair as ever, with an embrace to die for," he says with a roguish grin. "She finds that the high life suits her, and although she was once a slow reader, is much more capable now."

"I'm glad to hear that... I hadn't seen her in a while, and I hoped she'd been well."

"Aye, and sometimes I feel bad for picking her from your lovely stock," said Jaks with a mocking lament in his voice, "but I think she's far better off with her job that she has now."

"What is it she does these days?"

"She's a handmaiden for a rich household and an impressive noblewoman."

"Ah, that's right." Aruhn drummed his fingers on the bar top as he took a deep breath, "About Diyane?"

"What about her?"

"Will she be stickin' around?"

"Most likely. I haven't found another place where she would be better served," Jaks looked at Aruhn. "You've grown fond of her."

"She's good at what she does."

"It would be wise not to forget that," said Jaks, rising up from his seat. "Clearwind at the end of the day is solely loyal to herself."

"She wouldn't move against yeh though," said Aruhn.

"Not if she knew she could fail," corrected Jaks. "But I make it a point to trust few people Aruhn, and she doesn't warrant that list."

Aruhn frowned, "And yeh leave her here?"

"Of course. I trust you."

Aruhn watched the wily Duhoviman smirk before walking to the door and unlatching the locks. He gave a tilt of his head before shutting it behind him as he took his leave. Aruhn took a moment to mull over his words, concerned about what would happen if the kingdom splintered. His thoughts swam to Astoria and relief worked its way through him.

I'm glad yeh're gone from here, lass. Too many secrets and too much to hear. Yeh're better off, wherever you are.

He went to the door, latching it and bolting it shut before calling to his maids that he was heading in for the night.

ROSLINE.

Rosline woke early, the soft breathing of her daughter beside her as slept on. The sky was still dark past the gossamer curtain, but Rosline knew that it was better for her to stir now than to take a lie in and risk waking up late. She noticed that Jaks hadn't returned that evening, but honestly hadn't expected it; the man had his own agenda to tend to now that he was back in the city. Still, she found that much preferred waking with him at her side.

Clearing her thoughts, Rosline began to ready herself for the day. As the sky began to lighten, she heard a soft knock, followed by the careful opening and closing of her chamber door, turning her gaze. Geneve was walking in with a bundle of Rosline's dresses and clothing in her arms. She smiled at Rosline and began to speak until Rosline pressed a finger to her lips and indicated at her bed, where Kyrah had bundled herself within the blankets. Beckoning Geneve to the washroom, the maid tiptoed carefully to her before she shut the door behind her.

"Morning, madam Rosline," said Geneve, her face lighting up with a smile. "Just got these off the line and thought it best to bring them up to you."

"Thank you," said Rosline. She reached for the cloth that laid folded by the basin, unwrapping it before placing it over her eyes.

Geneve immediately set the clothes down upon a small chest within the room and moved behind her, tying the cloth expertly as she had for years.

"There we go, nice and proper. Is it too tight?"

"Not at all. It won't come off if I turn my head too suddenly, but it is loose enough not to pinch."

"Great!" Geneve picked up a brush from the basin, and working her way from the bottom of Rosline's hair, she softly brushed the tangles and combed out Rosline's natural curls before braiding it into a long plait that she hung over her left shoulder. "Just like Lady Eleanor!" she said with a proud smile.

Rosline's face spread in a wide smile, her thoughts going back to her days at Aruhn's tavern when she used to get all fussed up with the other maids before shift. Astoria would watch them, helping where she could as she listened to the rambunctious maids and their sometimes exaggerated tales of the suitors they had been with. Before, Rosline had been particular about her appearance because she got more tips the better she looked, but for days like today, she knew that she would be representing Lady Eleanor. Her appearance, demeanor, everything she did had to be impeccable.

Geneve picked out one of the dresses, an elegant maroon number that tapered well at the waist and had a modest neckline. She helped Rosline step into it and tied it up the back for her, smoothing out the small creases in it. Rosline took the small stone pendant and tied it about her neck, letting the onyx jewel sit in the crest of her bosom before tugging at the sleeves of her dress and smoothing the creases there.

"You look marvelous, madam," said Geneve as she smiled brightly.

"Hopefully it will be enough. I am meeting with a few familiar faces and several new ones today."

"Lady Eleanor is out?"

"She will be for most of the day. She has a meeting with Gavin."

"And that means Railand will be gone as well…" Geneve got a saddened tone in her voice as she gathered the rest of the clothes for Rosline and moved to the door.

Rosline smirked, "Yes, he will be with her, although I don't believe he goes inside the Cathedral with her. I've heard he's not fond of the faith."

Geneve's face pinked under Rosline's knowing gaze before she quietly opened the door and made her way to the wardrobe. Rosline followed behind her, before sitting on the edge of the bed and watching Kyrah sleep.

Each breath she took tousled the curled hair that laid in front of her face, and Rosline pulled a few strands away from her before kissing her on the forehead. Kyrah stirred then, her face spreading in a smile as she rubbed the sleep from her eyes.

"Mama," she said, yawning widely as she did. "Is it time to get up already?"

"It will be soon. I'll send Kurtis up to help you get ready for lessons."

She frowned, "I thought I was gonna be with Papa today?"

"You were with him yesterday and the day before," said Rosline with a smirk. "He also has work to do today so you will have to be with Kurtis."

With a pout, she coiled herself in the blanket and laid back down, her eyes shutting as she said, "Okay, mama. Can I sleep 'til Kurtis gets here?"

"Of course, my dove," Rosline kissed her forehead again before rising from the bed. She followed Geneve out of her chambers, shutting the door softly as they walked together.

"I have a meeting soon this morning, so I'll be taking my meal in the conference room. Once Lord Wycht or his courier arrives, have them sent in will you?"

"Of course madam. I'll get breakfast sent to you as well." Geneve bowed deeply before heading off, leaving Rosline to consider the meetings.

First Wycht and his talk of tariffs and taxes that should be accommodated for, then Duwain and his gripes over the costs of the wagons we need, and if I'm lucky Arnstein will only have a short meeting about why his hunters have been lacking as of late. Eleanor took care of Marquis so it should be a fairly brisk morning.

Still, Rosline felt her nerves creeping up on her. It was only in the past year that Eleanor had elevated her to sitting in her stead while the lady was out with her own affairs. Before, Rosline had simply stood quietly at her left, listening to the lords and ladies that came to call, and most importantly, taking stock of who they were. With Eleanor's faith in her, Rosline knew that she had to be careful with her dealings else she could cause a rift between her peers.

As Rosline finished her plate of food and took a sip of wine to wash it down, she saw Geneve step into the doorway of the conference room, a look of seriousness on her face.

"They're here."

Rosline nodded, sitting up in her seat and trying to make herself as poised as she could be.

After a long morning with dry, stale conversation, Rosline was finally free as Arnstein's courier departed with a deep bow. Letting out a satisfied sigh, she leaned back in the chair to reflect for a moment. It went well. Rosline had managed to navigate the condescension of the lords with proper courtesy and maintain the relationships with them. As she rose from the seat though, she let out a deep breath, knowing that there was still more work to do. She walked past the guards at the door, thanking them for keeping her safe, and she smiled at Geneve as she cleaned up the conference room afterwards. Rosline made her way back upstairs, nodding and greeting the servants she passed. She arrived at the study and let herself in, locking the door behind her after she entered.

With a deep breath, she removed the cloth from her eyes, taking a moment to let her eyes readjust to her umbral vision. She set the cloth atop a desk laden with scrolls and parchment before moving to the array that was painted in the center of the room. Standing in the center, she removed the pendant from her neck, wrapping the chain around her right hand as she clutched the stone within her grasp. Her eyes shut as

132

she took another breath. Rosline beckoned to the pendant and opened her eyes once more.

She saw beyond the room, the grand city of Isle and the lands beyond masked in a myriad of greys. With each turn of her head, she saw several figures wandering about, scurrying like ants alongside a flowing river. She took a moment to focus on several of them, the faces of old friends and acquaintances flowing before her vision as she watched. Steadying herself, she recalled the faces of the men she spoke with earlier.

Wycht.

Her vision flickered as her gaze pulled into another manor, one smaller than Eleanor's. He sat with another lord, talking eagerly with a smile on his face. It was almost an entirely different person than the shrewd, depreciative man she had hosted only hours before. As she watched, the pair of them swapped notes and purses of coins. She came to the determination that he was mustering a new deal, perhaps in relation to the deal they had just made, but most likely to offset the losses he would face from the tariffs while doing business with Eleanor. Rosline watched them for a moment, taking care to try and memorize the other man's features as well as she could. If Eleanor could garner a meeting with him, perhaps they could cut Wycht out entirely for their own dealings while offering a more companionable business partner.

Duwain.

Her gaze lurched once more as she felt a tug to the southern side of the city. The man rode in a carriage with a woman, one that Rosline was certain wasn't his wife. He sported a hungry grin as his hand clenched her thigh, and she gave him a tinkering laugh, swatting at him playfully. Rosline knew this one could be precarious to deal with, so she simply memorized the route they took and the abode they stopped at, a much more lavish estate than usual in the destitute portion of the town.

Arnstein.

Rosline saw naught but grey and black for a moment before she realized the man was seated in his home, expecting something. A door opened beside him, and Rosline recognized the courier she had spoken to, his head shaking as he spoke. Arnstein shouted at the man, which brought a satisfied smile to her face knowing that she had been able to broker the deal for Eleanor at his cost. They traded words for a while, with Arnstein angrily waving off the courier before penning something along a scroll. He rolled it up and sealed it with wax before handing it to what looked like a member of his guard and barking at him. The man nodded timidly before setting out. Rosline kept an eye on the guard, watching as he navigated through the city before arriving at the docks. He glanced around, meeting with the dockmaster and handing him the scroll. As the dockmaster read it, he gave him a stern nod before heading off.

It seems he's already trying to circumvent the deal.

Rosline released her vision for a moment as pressure built behind her eyes. Slowly, her sight gazed only at the room around her. She wiped the sweat from her brow before heading to the desk. With a steady hand, she began penning down what she had seen, as well as features of the others that the lords had met with. Her penmanship wasn't the best so she took her time, making sure that Eleanor could read her script. She would be pleased this day, knowing that the best way to handle the other aristocrats was to see through their duplicity. Rosline was her key to that, and Eleanor rewarded her greatly for her talents.

After finishing her summary of Arnstein, she leaned back and massaged the cramp that had built in her wrist. As she rose from the chair, she took a passing glance at the array, pensive. With a nod, she stood in the center and once more slid into the shadowy vision, before peering off northward. Past the city of Isle, past the North Road, and past the lands of the Kris family. She searched, hoping to find her, to see her, believing her to be well but yearning to know. The pressure built quickly as she searched and Rosline released her vision, feeling a splitting headache coming on.

I wouldn't even know where to look. Or even what she looks like anymore.

Rosline sighed as she rubbed her temples, pondering. She was pulled from her musing by a soft knock at the door, followed by a rousing one that Rosline recognized all too well. Smiling, she clasped the necklace around her neck before flipping over the topmost of the

134

notes she had written. She moved to the door, sliding the bolt and creaking it open slightly.

Two pairs of honey-colored eyes watched expectantly, with Jaks holding an excited Kyrah in his arms.

"Mama! Papa says he's finished for the day. He wants to play in the garden."

"Would you like to join us, Rosline?"

Rosline glanced over at the stack, feeling that she had accomplished all she could today. With a nod she stepped from the study, locking it with a key before grasping Jaks' hand and walking with him to the meadow.

KARJA.

It had been weeks since Karja had found himself at Sehren's camp within the vast untamed lands. He hadn't told anyone of his trek, saying that he had been ambushed by the *eiravuks* when he was out hunting. Concern had risen from his spotting of the dangerous beasts, but he assured the members of his tribe that they were far from there, and they had run away haggard from their battle. He'd refused care for his wounds from his people, not wanting them to see the strange stitching on his side and back.

Karja felt ashamed of his duplicity, but his pride stung from the fact that he had needed to be rescued from the wretched beasts by Sehren. The man had struck so effortlessly, so easily that it hadn't seemed to even be a true danger to him that they had been surrounded. He could still see Sehren's flowing movements, his dance of battle more refined than he could have anticipated. None of the beasts had touched him, and before Karja had known it, it had all been over. Even still, Sehren had watched him to make sure he was okay before leading him to their camp to tend him

He was also confused that Astoria had tended his wounds so readily, her smile still on his thoughts, but deep down he still nursed resentment towards her simply for who she was. She was beautiful, it

137

was true, and there was a spark in her eyes that hinted at greatness, but all Karja saw was the threat ever present to his people.

She's the true danger. She could bring ruin to us all.

Karja shook his head, trying to dispel the encroaching thoughts before he entered the cabin before him. He was glad to see Sejun and Beluk already waiting for him. Both of them stood quickly and bowed their heads in respect to him as he entered. He unbelted the blade at his side, setting it against the door before he took a seat with the two other men.

"How are you faring?" asked Sejun.

"My wounds are on the mend. The skin already has closed and while I still feel sore, I am more than confident that I will be well with another week or two of healing."

They grinned, sharing a look with one another. Beluk said, "As expected. I had never known anything that could slow you down too much, Karja."

"Aye," said Karja. "I have things that I need to discuss with you both. What I say though must stay between us unless we all agree that we should inform Haljn."

They traded serious glances, nodding firmly. Karja knew they trusted him implicitly, as he trusted them, but his tone had told them that it was a grave matter.

"You know of the woman that walks alongside the Ombroj chief, yes?"

"The southerner? Aye," said Sejun, frowning.

"Many months ago, a man approached the south. A knight. He stayed along the edge of our lands, and I went out to meet him when I had been informed."

"Aye, you mentioned him to Haljn. You said that he had been taken care of."

"He wanted to speak with one of us, someone from our people to voice a concern of his."

Beluk shook his head, "Pah, a southerner's concern. You should have just taken his tongue."

138

"Acting against a knight of the kingdom is not in the best interest of our people," warned Karja. "While they don't readily march against us, the threat of them coming into our lands cannot be underestimated."

Both Sejun and Beluk agreed with disgruntled nods. "What did he want?"

"It seems the king was searching for his heir, a woman with red hair that may have fled into our lands. He sought her fervently, the knight said, and would do anything to find her in the north lands. The knight told me she would likely be with a man, who had used her to secure passage north without danger, and that he would be a formidable foe if crossed."

"That sounds exactly like Sehren and his companion," observed Sejun. "He used her as a hostage?"

"That is what I was told. I had no idea when the knight told me if he was speaking the truth, as I had never seen the woman, but in addition to this that I hid from you all, there is something else I need to tell you in confidence."

They nodded, and Karja smiled, knowing his brothers in blood would always stand beside him.

"The *eiruvaks* that I came across were not in our lands. I had gone into the *otedien* to meet with Sehren, to speak with him about the matter. I was ambushed there, and he came."

"He passed by you during the ambush?" asked Sejun, incredulous. "That is a coincidence."

Karja shook his head, "He stepped from the *kymbra,* as if he had been watching before and came to intervene. He was surprised to see me, but it was with his intervention that I lived that day. I followed him afterwards to his camp where he tended the wounds I suffered. That is when I met the woman, and she was exactly as the knight had described her: Red of hair, fair of skin, with blue eyes. It was apparent to me that she was not Sehren's kin, but if she was his hostage then she is no longer."

"Why would she stay then if he was her captor?"

"I know not. Perhaps she fears what awaits her in the kingdom. Perhaps she feared her death before. They seem close, however, and she looks upon him with much affection."

Karja saw the disbelief in their faces as he continued, "But the knight told me that the king was adamant that he would march north for her. He said that anything in the way would be scoured in his search."

"And you believe him?"

Karja nodded, "I still remember the *Javeaf.* That king and his men. They left nothing but ruin when they marched. If they were to march in force again, we would be unable to stop them. I also feel we would not recover from it."

Beluk sat back, "This seems like much for a single woman. I thought they only followed kings in the south."

"I am unsure. I am not familiar with their ways, but the knight seemed grim indeed when he told me. However…"

Karja had to tread carefully here, he knew. "He told me that Sehren would not be willing to part with the woman, even if we came to him with our concerns."

"The man refused to settle in closer lands and reclaim his people's home solely because she was not welcome in our lands," said Sejun. "I do not doubt he would be incensed at her mention."

"But if the risk is there, even if it is miniscule, it has to be addressed," said Beluk. "That is our task, after all. Our job to our people."

Karja continued, "I sought to converse with Sehren the day I went alone, but injured and uncertain, I did not wish to mention it in case he became incensed and thought the best solution was to kill me."

"You think he would?" asked Beluk. "He treated your wounds."

"I am not certain. I told him I merely wished to learn more of him. Chuyara and Ombroj had once been close with one another, and I brought that up to him during the remembrance. He seemed reluctant, but during my stay with them, he was more relaxed."

"What do you think we should do then, Karja?" asked Sejun.

"I wish to bring the matter to him, to tell him what happened. If the knight is to be believed though, Sehren will not relinquish her lightly. It could turn violent, and I would want you there in case it does."

"To help your case," nodded Beluk.

"And to fight alongside you, if needed," added Sejun.

Karja nodded, feeling confident. They had trained together for years, and while Sejun was young in comparison, he believed that there was little in the lands that could stand in their way.

"I shall also be asking Haljn if I can borrow his blade," he said, the statement making the other's faces grim.

"Worried?"

"He can use the *kymrba*. While I am usure to what extent he has trained with it, it seems prudent to bear the blade just in case."

A tenseness passed between them before Beluk asked, "When do you plan on going to speak with him?"

"After a few more days. I still feel sore and I wish to be in the best health possible if it comes down to trading blows. Rest well, I will let Haljn know we will be attempting to hunt down the missing beasts that attacked me."

They looked uneasy at the lie, but Karja knew it was a necessary evil if they were going to act so boldly against Sehren. Regardless of how he felt about the man, Sehren had been accepted as a chieftain within their people, and if they came to him with danger and threats, he would be more than justified in striking against them. However, if the others knew that Haljn had consented to the actions of his *krusho,* the backlash against his people could be staggering. They had to tread carefully, and for that, Karja would stain his honor with the lie.

He had to believe that, had to believe that the threat was real else he wouldn't know what else to do.

SEHREN.

Sehren walked through his camp, taking a deep breath as the summer air filled his lungs. The grasses were verdant, the late spring showers blossoming the tundra around them from their bleak greys and browns to vibrant greens and yellows. Sehren could hear chirping of the birds that had grown accustomed to their presence, nestled high in branches of the white-barked trees. He took another deep breath, tasting the crisp air upon his tongue. He smiled.

This was their land.

He knew it. It had been a struggle, with many days slipping by as he and Astoria had fought to make a place for themselves in the wild land. He thought it would break him, as the loss of Termesa once did, but he found within himself the same vigor, the determination that had so driven him during the Blightwinter, and with that, he had pushed through. Eventually, each day had become not a fight for survival, but rather a challenge to thrive, an obstacle to be removed, and an endeavor to survive. He had learned from the beasts of the lands, finding that which could be consumed readily and storing away that which could not. He followed and stalked, each failed hunt and aching stomach a reminder of patience and foresight.

But he had not been alone. Each outing that ended with empty hands had brought not just discomfort and hunger to him, but to

Astoria. Her eyes used to watch him accusingly at first, which was something he could bear. Each moment she would look upon him, he saw resentment and anger simmering within her, her disappointment for the life they led obvious upon her face. She had hated him, but he could handle that, and he had eventually grown used to her pointed glances and depressed sighs as he returned with what he could find.

Eventually though, her eyes had lost their luster, the vibrant blue constantly clouded by the specters of melancholy and despair. Hope had left the spring in her step, and a steady resignation for a life only lived rather than experienced had filled her gait. It had crushed him, his sleepless nights spent formulating, contemplating, and even suggesting that they return to the kingdom. But never together. He planned only for her to return to the City of Isle so that she could be reunited with those that Sehren knew she held closest to her heart. Whenever he brought it up, however, Astoria refused, and her accusing gaze would be set upon him, a reminder that he had chosen this life for them. He fought, scouring his mind for the lessons from his mother and the lessons as a knight, desperately searching for something, anything, that could instill the lust for life she had lost.

Sehren pressed through, never relenting, never wavering, for even the crushing realization that he had destroyed that light in her eyes with his stubbornness, his need to flee from everything around him, had not broken his spirit. Her despair became his cause, her melancholy his reason, and he fought against those tides as heatedly as he had fought against the crushing presence of the Duhovimans in the south. He could bear her sadness, and every success he achieved rang out for him as a conquest against the baleful grip that so desperately tried to waylay them.

The years had trickled by, but Sehren had grown wiser and Astoria ever stronger. She saw his determination and eventually was moved by it, his need to fight never quenched by any stinging barb or insult she sent his way. Eventually, he parleyed with Nyeth. At first, the woman had threatened to kill him should he ever cross back into her lands. Their contact had been tense, but still Sehren had refused to relent. He had stood before her, bearing what he could salvage, dragging the wagon needed to carry the bones and hides of the creatures he felled with no complaint. Nyeth had not been receptive at first, showing only when Sehren would make his camp upon the edge of their lands, believing he would stir someone, anyone, that could help him survive. Time after time, she appeared, usually escorted by Korrenth or Ghorun, always with disdain, but eventually with goods of their own.

Even that took a turn for the better, Sehren's consistency bringing curiosity from the chieftain. Nyeth soon began sharing meals with him, and her initial disdain melted away into her own inquisitiveness on how soft southerners could survive in such a bleak land. Sehren just continued their trade, each time bringing more and more along until the moment that Astoria had come with him, stating she was tired of being left alone. Sehren had seen the gleam in her eye though, the spark of inquisitiveness that had driven her questions before, the same spark that had fostered her desire to learn the blade and that had driven her to learn Senkaman. Nyeth had been cross with Sehren when he had brought her along, her attitude towards the girl in her absence all the more hostile. Astoria had taken it all in stride though, understanding that the Senkamans held a deep-seated resentment that Sehren could do little to mend. When it came time to leave and Nyeth spoke of Astoria in Senkaman, she had truly become incredulous when the girl had replied to her in simple, but fluid Senkaman.

Sehren remembered his amusement when he saw the confused look on Nyeth's face, and his determination had been restored when he subsequently saw Astoria smile, the same smile she used to wear when she knew she had impressed Sehren or Aruhn.

She wore that smile easily now. Astoria had taken to the concept of their land and their home, her excursions with Sehren bringing more and more of the vital spark from her, breathing life back into her smile. Every lesson Sehren taught her, be it hunting, gathering, farming, medicine, or even just leisure, Astoria took to with rapt attention. He knew that she was trying to seek forgiveness from him, to apologize for the months and months of strained silence and angry outbursts, but Sehren needed no apology. He felt the fault landed on his shoulders and knew that her earnest desire to help shape a better life for the both of them was her attempt to lift that from him.

Sehren tended to the crops that had sprung forth with pail in hand. As he predicted, their plot was overflowing with crops, leading him to transfer some of them to another patch of earth that he had subsequently dug out. Judging by the number, they would be well off in the fall, perhaps even enough to store away through the winter and into the following spring. Astoria was gone hunting as the last of their nets hung empty. While they normally tried to prevent their nets from being empty, Astoria had taken to long sparring bouts, her zeal driving her to try and defeat Sehren. She grew closer with every attempt, the angry welts and small nicks in his skin a testament to her astounding growth.

One day, she'll come to rival me.

Sehren was confident in that fact. The stings she received stuck heavy in her mind, and Sehren found that his usual techniques that would trip her up were fading away, his hits coming more and more as opportune strikes rather than fully planned series he had grown so accustomed to. Astoria's defense had tightened significantly, and her offense was growing to the point that she could become one of the finest duelists in the lands.

Sehren returned to the tent after finishing tending the crops, and he settled beside the fire pit. It was out at the moment, the cool stone within it black. He stared at it before taking a deep breath and considering the lessons that Nyeth had taught him.

Sitting on his knees, he steadied himself, taking a moment to blot out the world around him as he shut his eyes. He focused on the beat of his heart, willing it away until it melted into the world around him. There was a lull within him before he felt a tug, a beckoning, and at that moment he opened his eyes, taking care to not break the meditative state he had achieved.

A darkened world swirled around him, filled with shifting shades and a morass of shadows. He could peer through the patches of grey, watch as the woody monoliths around him swirl around his sight, and could feel the patter of the creatures that moved around nearby. He let himself fall deeper into it, feeling himself peer further out, reaching out and expanding his sight more. As he did, the once defined features started to melt together, and his senses turned more to a feeling of presence rather than a sensation of sight. He could feel his heart racing but willed away the beat within, focusing on watching and pushing past the obscuring shades that stood in his sight.

They stayed however, moving ever closer. His curiosity piqued, he willed himself to rise, one part of him focused on the shifting shades while the other called to his body to stand. He sought a moment of clarity, seeing a glimpse of the land around the shades and stepped towards it, pushing himself through the gloom. His sense of self melted away for a moment as a sensation of being drawn forth overcame him. He steeled his mind, pushing past the feelings of exhaustion, before he tasted the air around him and stood once more along the tundras of his land.

He steadied his breath, turning to find Karja and two others, their weapons drawn as if scared. They immediately lowered them upon seeing Sehren, their faces becoming worried and suspicious.

"We meet again, son of Chuyara," said Sehren as his heart steadied. He idly considered the other two, recognizing them from the remembrance ceremony but unfamiliar with their names.

"Sehren," said Karja, his voice clipped. "It has been a while."

"Have you healed well?" asked Sehren, cocking his head to the side. Karja raised his hand to his side where the beast had torn his flesh and nodded.

"As well as expected. I did not believe that it would mend so readily."

"Much trial and error led us to that solution, and as such we are quick to utilize it whenever necessary." He glanced at the other two men, his curiosity piqued. "I do not recall having met you before."

"This is Sejun," said Karja, indicating the man to his left, "And Beluk. They are friends of mine, interested in speaking with you."

"I did not think that becoming a chieftain would warrant so many visits. Perhaps I should have had Nyeth been more clear about that," said Sehren with amusement. Sejun gave a glance to Karja, and Sehren cocked his eyebrow, thinking the action odd. "What is it you wish to discuss?"

Sehren saw them shift nervously as Karja weighed his response. "The woman. Astoria was her name, yes?"

Sehren immediately narrowed his eyes, "What of her?"

"A man came to me, asking if I had seen a woman that matched her. He spoke softly and quietly but urged that she needed to be returned to her people."

"Who is this man?"

"He is a southern knight—"

"I thought Nyeth did not allow southerners to cross into your lands, and you mean to tell me that you conversed with a knight?"

Karja frowned, "He stayed outside our borders. The first moment he met me, he spent many nights alongside the edge of our lands as if beckoning. Eventually, I met with him. He merely asked about a southerner that may have crossed into the north. I interrogated him, but he took my aggression to mean that he was correct in his estimation. He told me that he was seeking a lass, who would be a woman now, that bore royal blood. The king was looking for his lost heir it seemed."

The hair on Sehren's arms bristled as his skin tingled.

Karja continued, "He said that the king is bereaved by the loss of his queen in childbirth, and that all he desires is to find and seat his heir upon the throne. Upon learning of her potential flight into our lands, the man told me that the king would march forth with his men to find her, no matter the cost to his people or ours.

"Preposterous," said Sehren, interrupting Karja.

"You do not believe that he would march north?"

"I know he would not."

The three of them looked confused at Sehren. He continued, "The kingdom of Candrama, while having no love for the north, is superstitious and close-minded. They fear the north and the beasts and people that inhabit it. It is said that the Lady of their faith cannot reach them in the frigid north, and without her watchful presence, they are scared to step into the forests. None of the common soldiers would dare march into Senkama without a regiment of the Knights of Isle at their head, and the Knights would never march without risking the raids of the south overtaking the kingdom there."

Their scrutiny was heavy upon him, but he knew this to be true. "Without the support of Knights of Isle, the king would not be able to muster enough support from the people to attempt such a campaign. What you were told is a falsehood. Whoever told you that tale was trying to prey upon your fear and paranoia. It seems they succeeded."

"You know much of the Knights," said Beluk, his voice fraught with suspicion.

"I was a Knight of Isle for many years," said Sehren calmly. He saw their eyes narrow more as distaste filled their pale features.

"Nyeth mentioned you were a soldier," recalled Karja.

"She never knew. She never asked. The only thing that would have tipped her to my past would have been the skill I possessed to defeat her in *kruparu*."

"Impossible," said Sejun.

"Ask her yourself," said Sehren.

Sounds of disbelief passed between the two others but to Sehren, it looked as though several things had been confirmed for Karja. He cleared his throat, his hand resting on his blade casually, but Sehren took it as a threat.

"Even if you believe that the threat is not real, Sehren, we cannot sit on our hands and do nothing for someone like her."

"How familiar. That is chief to you," replied Sehren, crossing his arms over his chest, "And that someone tended the wounds you sported from your folly of crossing into my lands without invitation. That someone fed you and watched over you as you recovered. Hospitality that took years for me to cultivate with yours was given to you without hesitation and now you stand here to threaten me?"

"It is not a threat. We came to speak with you about the matter because we desired to come to a solution about it."

"If that were the case, you would have asked about it when you first visited, not months later with duplicitous intent."

Karja looked stricken. Sehren knew he had struck a nerve with the man. He was honorable, dedicated to his people, and he followed their traditions and ways as diligently as Sehren had protected and fought for Astoria's survival.

"Who told you this rot?" asked Sehren.

"I told you: a southern knight, much like you had been."

"His name, Karja."

"I believe he calls himself Ricard."

Sehren felt a sliver of ice pierce him, the cold filling him as he considered it.

Ricard. He knows who Astoria is.

Karja narrowed his eyes, "You know him."

"Aye," said Sehren. "It was him that pushed me to flee the kingdom. He planned my death, and it is my belief that he plotted the crown prince's murder."

Karja shrank back, his face crinkling with confusion. "Why did you flee your home?"

Sehren repressed the memories. He had spent too many nights on them already, the flickering image of Eleanor's pained face as he spoke his refusal to stay. "Astoria will not be returning to the kingdom."

"And if they march through our lands? Will you be responsible for the death of our people?"

"Your people," corrected Sehren, "and that guilt will fall upon your shoulders. You could have simply told him that she had been killed already. You could have said that you knew nothing of the sort. But, based upon your requests here today, you already told him of our presence. It is not our people that you cared about Karja, but yours. I understand: I never expected to truly be welcome among the ranks of your people, but I hoped that perhaps the grudge could be buried."

Sehren drew the blade from his side, his action startling the three men.

"She will not be returning to the kingdom."

"You bare your steel against us?" spat Beluk.

150

"Aye. This is my land. My territory. You," he pointed the blade at Karja, "know how to find our encampment. I am sorry, son of Chuyara, but you cannot return back to your people."

Karja drew his blade, the action mirrored by the men at his side, "You throw away your honor."

"Honor? What little that means in a savage, wild land. You would sacrifice a woman that showed you naught but kindness for the lies of a man that cares for neither you or your own. I already know what he intends, and while I wish I could tell you to turn and leave and never return, you know how to find her."

Sehren felt true sorrow as he considered Karja. "Her safety is paramount to me."

"You make a mistake, southblood," said Beluk.

"You need not suffer for his mistake, son of Chuyara," said Sehren calmly. "Stand aside and let him face the consequences of his actions."

"And what if I told you all of us, including Haljn, know how to find your home?" asked Sejun.

Sehren merely set a resigned gaze upon him before saying, "The lands are vast. It would not be hard to place another body within it."

Sejun and Beluk traded looks of worry, but Karja stood defiantly before Sehren, raising his blade. "Reconsider, Sehren. Else, you die here today."

Sehren turned to the side, his stance growing tense as his heartbeat quickened, "Very well."

Beluk and Sejun quickly shifted into their stances as Karja rushed forth. Sehren rushed to meet him, but he stopped short, his hand reaching at a small pouch on his belt. He pulled two small pellets made of taut dried grass, slamming them at the ground as he turned his face away. An acrid cloud of powder erupted from them when they broke upon the ground, and Sehren heard them coughing as he turned away from the cloud before thrusting his blade through, holding his breath and keeping his eyes shut. He felt the tip sink into flesh before a clang of steel pushed him wide. Backstepping, Sehren swayed back. The air cut before his face, and he knew the wild strikes would come soon.

151

As he dashed back, he opened his eyes, taking a tentative breath to make sure he didn't get any of the stinging powder in his nose. He watched as Sejun was rubbing his eyes, trying to clear them as Beluk and Karja cleared themselves of the cloud, Karja nursing the side of his arm. Testing it, he nodded at Beluk, and they stalked towards him, their movements fluid.

Sehren knew they were familiar with one another, but he watched Karja carefully, knowing that Beluk would try to shore up his defense now that he was wounded. They would not speak, he believed, most likely familiar with their fighting styles to know how to compliment one another.

Karja led, as expected, but Sehren saw the feint as he made it, not bothering to put his guard up as Karja drew away at the last second. Instead, he interposed his steel between him and Beluk, the expected response to move away to prevent surrounding him. A poignant thrust was already aimed at his side, and Sehren turned it aside as he ran the edge of his blade against Beluk's arm, drawing a long line of blood. Beluk let out a hiss before attempting a backhanded swing to drive distance, but Sehren had already stepped into his side, the tip of his sword thrusting into his side several inches before he swiftly withdrew and pushed Beluk away. Karja was upon Sehren's back, but he already turned, expecting the assistance. The sight of his bloodied blade however enraged Karja, his dark blade cutting at Sehren's right shoulder viciously, a shrill whistle in the air from the speed.

Sehren threw up his blade, grasping the pommel with both hands. The screeching of metal filled the air as he guided the vicious strike upwards. There was movement beside him as he used the rest of Karja's blow to push him away, a whoosh beside him telling him that Beluk had tried to cut at his exposed back. Sehren broke away from the both of them, before seeing that Beluk had unsteadied himself with his attack. Sehren rushed him, using the injured man's left to shield him from Karja.

The man staggered from him, grasping his side as his breathing became haggard. Sehren saw the moment lost, instead preparing a parry for Karja. The man didn't follow through though, waiting for Sejun as the man had finally stopped coughing enough to join the fight. Beluk, however, swayed, his stance uneasy as he cupped his side.

"What?"

"Your kidney," said Sehren simply. Beluk tried to join Karja and Sejun as they approached Sehren, but his steps were hesitant and unsteady.

"Stay back," said Karja, his voice filled with concern. Beluk shook his head.

"Together. As it should be," replied Beluk, clenching his teeth as his gaze focused on Sehren.

He saw their resolve to one another was as deep as his for Astoria.

Sehren turned sideways, emulating the stance his mother had taught him all those years ago. They drew closer but Sehren waited, his eyes tracking their movements smoothly.

Karja first, then the injured one to surprise me and the last to close it off. Karja will strike in tandem with the third.

Sehren knew it true within him and judged how close they could get to him before they would surround him.

Break the third, his senses will still be dull. Karja is still recovering and the other's wound will slow him.

Sehren lunged, his blade drawing back in a swift thrust. Sejun planted, intending to parry him to make him unsteady so Karja could strike. Sehren saw him wrinkle his nose, the insidious powder watering his eyes. His parry was low.

A trap.

Sehren thrusted at his lowered guard, drawing surprise from Sejun. His reactive parry pushed Sehren to his right, in line with Karja who was already swinging his blade down at him thinking he would be staggered by the parry. Sehren stepped into his reach, tucked his shoulder, and thudded against Karja's chest, slamming against his sternum. A puff of air stole the speed from his swing, and Sehren slipped past him, turning on the vulnerable side of Beluk. He threw up his blade to intercept Sehren's swift swipe, however his grip was weak on his parry, and he stumbled back at the metal clanged together.

Sehren felt a cut at his back, and knowing that he wouldn't be able to evade in time, willed himself away. The blade passed harmlessly through him as he shifted, and he felt himself grow tired instead. He heard a sound of surprise from the man behind him. Sehren pushed forward, running his blade across Beluk's stomach as he swiftly drew it back and spun around to find Sejun behind him. He was set for a backhanded cut but Sehren ducked low as the steel sung over him.

He thrusted upwards from his stance, springing up and forcing Sejun back. He saw in the corner of his eye the dark steel of Karja's blade and reflexively, willed himself away again. He felt himself shift for a moment before the edge cut into his side. The edge passed through him, but something different this time, his side stinging as he shifted back. Sehren slid to his left as Beluk was quickly turning to him before swiftly thrusting into his back again. He seized up as he let out a cry of pain and stumbled forward, his legs crumbling as he did.

Sehren panted, taking several staggering steps back as his left hand went to his side. He felt the warmth of his blood. He spied blood on the edge of Karja's blade and saw the man's scrutinizing gaze.

"It is done, southblood," said Karja confidently as he observed the blood on his blade.

Sehren breathed, feeling a keen sting on his side beneath his leathers.

"You can use the *kymbra,* it is true, but you cannot run from this edge," said Karja, regaining confidence.

Sehren raised an eyebrow at the fallen form of Beluk, the man's meager attempts to rise becoming weaker and weaker.

"Good to know," replied Sehren, straightening himself. He could feel blood trickling down his side, but it was merely one of many wounds he'd suffered before.

Karja underestimated his endurance.

Sejun went to Beluk's side as he groaned in pain, "Karja, he is in danger."

"Quickly then," he said, glancing at Beluk before his face became grim as he considered Sehren.

154

His fatigue mounting but with a steady breath Sehren willed away the pain.

"Quickly, then," he echoed.

ASTORIA.

Astoria pulled the litter behind her, proud of the two deer she had taken on her hunt. She glanced at the sky, the sun partly passed its zenith and reckoned she would arrive back at the camp before it crossed the sky.

She looked over her shoulder, the cleaned kills bringing a smile to her face. They would give them enough for the next two, maybe three weeks. It would alleviate their worries for a while, and the abundant deer she had seen prance away filled her with hope for the coming seasons.

She steadily marched, wondering if Sehren was watching her. She knew he could reach rather far with his awareness, but she tended to push farther out from their camp as she wanted to be familiar with more of this land. Their land. The thought made her proud. Together, they had conquered the obstacles they had come across. It was as Sehren said it would be.

Their land to tame.

She smiled, redoubling her pace as she pulled the straps of the litter tighter on her shoulders. She pulled for a moment before she heard something very unfamiliar this far out from their encampment.

The clashing of steel.

She stopped a moment, listening carefully so the wind wouldn't deceive her. It was clear though, steel clashing against one another as though she were sparring with Sehren.

Sehren.

She dropped the litter, following the sound as best she could as she sprinted off. She stopped a few moments to make sure she was going the right way before continuing. Eventually, she came upon a startling scene.

Sehren faced off with a man, with one laying upon the ground while another was tending to him. The one facing Sehren seemed to be trading words with him as they squared off against one another. Sehren seemed injured as he palpated his side, and Astoria watched as the man tending his friend rose as well, grabbing his blade and rushing alongside the first.

Clearing her lungs, she pulled the bow from her shoulder and drew an arrow, but as she watched them dance and fight, she realized they were moving too much for her to get a sure shot without the risk of hitting Sehren. She almost released the arrow until she saw the third man staggering to his feet, grabbing his sword and turning to join the fray. Astoria drew the bow, but hesitated, her hand shaking.

He's attacking Sehren. Shoot already.

She hesitated, an ache growing in her arm as she held the arrow. His back was turned to her and the shot was clear but she couldn't do it. She glanced at Sehren again, and watched him repel a savage strike only to get struck across the outside of his thigh by the other man.

This is why you trained. Help him.

Astoria loosed the arrow before dropping the bow and unbuckling the quiver from her side as she ran to Sehren. She saw the arrow catch in the man's back and swore she heard the crack of his spine when it hit. Sickened, she drew the sword from her side, the alabaster steel sliding forth with barely a whisper. Sehren was struck again before she managed to get closer and she saw his blood dripping from his hand as it hung limply at his left.

Without hesitation, she cut at one of the men's back only to feel her strike caught by the other. She recognized him.

158

"Karja?!" She shouted at him, drawing a severe look from him. He sported several injuries, blood on his face but after his parry he responded with a brutal riposte, the tip of his blade spiraling towards her abdomen.

Sehren's blade caught the steel, pushing it away but his interception left him open for the other man, and Astoria watched as the other man's blade plunged into his side and drove into him. Sehren staggered as he withdrew the steel, blood seeping from multiple wounds, his breathing rough.

I slipped. He trained me for this, but I slipped.

Her heart almost stopped when Sehren dropped his sword to the ground as he stumbled from his feet.

"I warned you, southblood," said Karja through painful breaths. He rounded on Astoria, his eyes vicious as the man drew beside him.

Astoria felt anger, true rage. Sehren's voice, his advice, sounded in her ears but she couldn't hear it. She could see that Sehren had wounded both of them several times and that the other man was in no shape to fight. Karja stalked toward her though, his stride telling her in no uncertain terms his intentions. She saw the blood staining his and the other man's sword.

"You are dead," she said calmly in Senkaman, her statement bringing a look of surprise from Sejun. She dashed at him, the white steel leading, and as Sejun prepared to counter, she slid low along the ground, the edge of her blade cutting through his knee as she rounded behind him. He had tried to cut low at her unorthodox attack but had missed, catching the earth and howled as he stumbled to the ground. Leaping to her feet, she charged Karja who had taken a lethal rush towards Sehren. Hearing her steps, he turned, swinging wildly. Astoria sidestepped his swing, her own thrust already moving toward his chest. He lurched to the side, narrowly avoiding her deadly strike and was already aiming a cut at her shoulder.

Astoria gripped the blade with both hands, swinging with all her might at the oncoming strike. With a shout, they collided. The jarring impact ran through her arms, but she threw him off balance. She viciously thrust forth, the steel plunging into his lower gut. Karja lurched again, clutching, but she followed him. He swayed and Astoria saw the front: he was trying to appear more vulnerable than he actually was so she darted past him, his surprise strike catching only the back of her hair. She ran the edge of her blade against the back of his thigh, hamstringing him. He turned futilely, trying to catch her with another strike but she continued to move behind him, cutting his other thigh as well. He stumbled to he ground as she saw the other man regain his footing, his face filled with murder.

She dashed to meet him after kicking away Karja's blade. He locked against her for a moment before she slid off his blade while retracting her own and thrusting into his side. She ran the sword up until she caught bone and cut outwards, severing his backbone as she cut through his back. He lurched forward, blood seeping from his mouth as a weak strike came at her back. She parried it easily, kicking him to the ground and plunging her sword into his back and drawing it again.

Karja crawled towards his own blade, blood flowing free from his many wounds. Astoria walked beside him and as he reached for his blade and stabbed the tip of hers into his hand.

"Why?" she asked, her rage subsiding for but a moment.

Karja glared at her, "Because you threaten our people. You blight us all."

Astoria recoiled at the hatred in his voice. She wanted to hurt him, to make him suffer for what he did, but she instead withdrew her blade and ran the edge against the crook of his elbow, severing the tendons. He screamed in pain, the sound grating on Astoria's soul, but she blinked back the tears as she repeated the action on his other elbow. "Stay here."

She looked to the one she had shot, his body not having moved from where he had landed. The other hadn't stirred either, so she sheathed her sword and ran to Sehren's side.

"Sehren!" she cried, unable to stop the tears that welled in her eyes. There was a dark stain on the ground and blood stained both his left and right side with several other wounds over his body. He stirred at the call of his name, his grey eyes filled with pain but quickly filling with pride.

"Astoria," he said weakly.

160

She cradled him in her arms, trying to press pressure on his wounds. "Why? What happened?"

"Ricard knows," said Sehren, his breathing harsh. "They said... the king is looking for you."

Astoria was bewildered: no one had known her identity. "That can't be true."

"Ricard is. The king," he coughed "probably not. Even still, I could not let them leave. Karja knew where we lived."

Astoria felt shocked. Sehren was trying to protect her. She looked over at Karja, who was vainly trying to pick himself up but his ruined body wouldn't answer his call.

"Sehren..." she stroked his hair, her tears falling as she did. "You can't. You promised."

"Aye. I promised to stay with you..." he coughed again, his eyes filling with tears as he stared up into her face.

"That's right. You promised. That's why we stayed in our land, Sehren. *Our land.* That means me and you." Her tears fell freely now, running down her cheeks as she clutched onto him. She saw them splash onto his cheeks before she wiped them away. She kissed him, "so stay with me. Please. You can do it. I know you can."

Sehren reached his hand up, trembling with the effort. He wiped away the tears that fell from her cheeks as his grey eyes filled with their own. They streamed down his cheeks as he coughed, "I love you, Astoria."

Astoria shook her head, "Then stay. If you love me, stay with me." She dipped her head to his, sobbing "I can't do this alone..."

Sehren, with his last effort, placed a kiss on her cheek before whispering, "It's time to go home..."

He went limp in her grasp and Astoria screamed, her wails echoing through the lands.

She screamed until her voice became hoarse and her throat ached. Tears fell as she felt like she held him for ages, unwilling to let him go. With shaking shoulders, she tucked her head into the crook of his neck, sobbing into his shoulder. It didn't feel real. But no matter how she cried or sobbed, Sehren didn't stir, and with every passing moment the realization cut through her defiant denial.

He's gone.

No, he's not.

You need to get to the camp before night.

Not without him.

He's gone.

Astoria was dazed as she battled with her thoughts. A groan and shuffling sound wrenched her from her sorrow, and suddenly, she remembered why this happened. She hugged Sehren one last time before tearing her arms from him and, with simmering rage, rose from the ground. Karja had been slowly crawling away, blood seeping from his wounds. Hatred in her heart, she walked over to him and kicked him, rolling him over as he coughed.

Blood and dirt covered his face, with grass clinging to his hair and clothes. He grimaced in pain, but when he met her eyes, she saw hatred of his own within them.

"Why did you do this?"

He just glared at her, his face set in refusal.

Astoria drew her blade, setting it on his neck as she slowly said in Senkaman, "Why did you betray us?"

"There is nothing you can do," he spat, his eyes burning. He coughed, and Astoria looked to his elbows. His blood was running thin, and she contemplated a moment.

"You think you will bleed out before I get my answers," she said coolly.

Karja simply continued to glare at her, coughing now and again.

Detached, Astoria rose from him, looking around. There was an abundance of grass, some of it dry, and she started contemplating. Karja tried to roll onto this stomach but as he pressed his arms against the ground, a spurt of blood came from the injuries to his elbows.

"Your tendons are cut," she said as she gathered grass. She pulled a broad, skinning knife from her back, gouging a hole in the

162

earth as she set grass in it. "Even if you had the strength to move, you would not be able to do much." She finished before reaching into a small pack on her belt and pulling a wrapped bundle. She struck a rock against the knife, flicking sparks onto the tinder absentmindedly. Eventually, it began to smolder, and she blew on it, the smoke curling from the small pit. As the fire caught, she added more and more grass, looking around before setting the bundle within it. The fire caught it hungrily, and Astoria fed the flames with more grass, letting it burn hot.

Once the flames were burning bright, Astoria held the skinning knife in the flames until the steel turned black. She stood up, walked over to Karja, and rolled him onto his stomach. Seeing the blood seeping from his thighs, she knelt down and placed the blade in the cut, Karja howling as the skin seared black. Astoria held onto him strongly, her revulsion of the stench of burning flesh held away by her sheer anger. She returned to the pit, stoking it to bright flames again before repeating the process on his other thigh. After she finished his thighs, Karja stopped squirming. Astoria looked curiously at his face and assumed he had passed out from the pain.

She seared both wounds in his elbows before tending to the larger wounds that Sehrehn had inflicted upon him. Her steps were steady, her breathing even as she tried to fight the compulsion to plunge the white steel through his heart.

After she was finished with Karja, she left to return to the litter she had dropped. Clearing the fallen deer off of it, she dragged it back to the scene of the fight, glad to see that Karja was still passed out.

He may die yet.

Astoria pulled the litter beside Sehren, before kneeling down and looking into his face. She brushed hair from his cheeks before pulling him into a hug again as the tears fell. After taking a moment, Astoria pulled him onto the litter, adjusting him so that he wouldn't slide off as she dragged it. Looking at the unconscious Karja, she fought against the corrosiveness in her heart as she pulled his visible gear from him, before patting him down for other weapons. Content that he was not armed, she dragged him to the litter, hoping to find a way to set him up with it. When she started to pull him beside Sehren though, she shook violently and dropped him, her breathing coming harsh as she cried.

Wiping her eyes, she searched the other two Senkamans and took the few supplies they did have before she grabbed their weapons. As she grabbed Karja's blade, she noticed that the steel was dark black, almost as if it was held within a flame. However, no hint of soot or ash was upon it and when she ran her thumb along the steel, nothing rubbed off. It was a pristine black, but Astoria's curiosity of it waned when she realized it was that very same blade that had wounded Sehren.

Seeing the sheath of one of the blades was ruined, she cut the strap from it with her knife, using it to tie Karja's hands tightly before she stopped for a moment. Hooking his hands to the top of the litter, Astoria fought off her revulsion before setting it on her shoulders and marching off.

She arrived at their camp with the sun almost at the horizon. Karja still hadn't stirred, but Astoria cared little for that. As she passed through the gate and saw the expanse of the camp, she felt a hammering her chest and her breathing became short and hitched. She cried, thinking of being in the camp on her own. She thought of the crops they had cultivated, the river tent where they would hang their meat. She thought of all the medical implements Sehren had made from the various bones they had collected, and how none of them could help him now.

Astoria set the litter down, pulling Karja unceremoniously from it while gently setting Sehren within the litter to the ground. His skin was cool, and more tears welled in her eyes as she thought about burying him.

I can't do this alone.

She looked at Karja, the man still unconscious. She believed that he would die from blood loss despite her efforts but couldn't be bothered with tending to him. She went to the center tent, their tent, and froze after passing through the flaps. Their bed of furs lay at the side, the fire pit meticulously constructed by Sehren in the center. She felt light-headed, but steadied herself after a moment before grabbing a small length of rope. Returning to Karja, she removed the strap from his hands and tied his wrists to his ankles, as though he was a deer she had hunted. Confident he was secure, she returned to the litter, bringing Sehren towards the small headstone they had set for Termesa.

164

Astoria stared at it, understanding fully now what Sehren had felt before. Termesa had been his oldest companion, surviving everything through his knighthood with him. She remembered the stories of her endurance and speed, her tenacity, and her power. Sehren always spoke fondly when he spoke of the horse, even when he was down or ill. He would get a spark in his eye, a luster that told her that he had appreciated the warhorse more than he could possibly say.

There was an emptiness inside Astoria that she knew Sehren had once filled. She knew now that Sehren had held that emptiness from Termesa, from his old wife, and probably from everything he had known in the kingdom. And despite that, he had still been able to push forward everyday when she had been an insolent wretch, when she had screamed at him, and when she had told him she hated him.

She wished she could take it all back.

Tears fell from her cheeks as she crouched, hugging her legs to her chest as the night fell. With the summer on the rise, the nights had grown comfortable, but there was a coldness within her that she didn't know if anything would warm again. She looked at Sehren, his body on the litter, almost capable of being confused for being asleep without the blood and wounds. Astoria rose, cradling his head once more before kissing his forehead.

I don't know what to do, Sehren.

'It's time to go home.'

His voice echoed in her head, threatening to overwhelm her. She was home, but it felt nothing like it once did. She thought of laying upon the furs alone, without his steady breathing or heartbeat to tell her he was there. The thought sickened her, and she found it hard to catch her breath.

I can't do this.

Astoria's eyes traced the familiar campsite but nothing brought her comfort. Nothing could not steady the racing of her heart. She rose from Sehren, slowly and steadily gathering branches and twigs. Mindlessly, she piled them within the center of their camp, beside their tent, slowly and steadily building a pile. The summer night came upon them, the sun kissing the horizon and bathing her in a dim blue glow. She steadily continued gathering, until she managed a pile that came

165

up past her waist. She went to Sehren, dragging his litter over beside the pile before beginning to arrange the branches around him, slowly piling them up and creating a tapered pile. His head was left exposed at one end of it, and after she was finished, she started gathering everything she could, combining what she would need for her path ahead.

'It's time to go home.'

Astoria packed everything into two large bulging packs, which she strapped to the litter. She tied Karja to it as well after forcing water down the man's throat and coaxing it down, the action inflaming her disgust. Slowly, the path forward had burned its way into her mind. She knew she would get the answers she needed. Once packed, she returned to the pyre she had built, her breathing coming short once more. Kneeling down, she placed a shaking kiss on Sehren's head before stroking his hair and running her hand along his cheek.

"I love you…" she whispered into the night, placing one last kiss upon him before going to their tent. Picking up the tinderbox, she crudely wrapped a branch in old cloth and set it aflame before leaving the tent. Solemnly, she slowly lit the ends of the pile, setting flame to it in multiple places before throwing atop the bundle. It crackled and burned, the flames eagerly licking around and burning high. Astoria sat down and watched for a while, her grief filling her heart as she listened to the fire burn.

It's time to go home.

Astoria blinked back the tears before she looked to the packed supplies, everything she believed she would need to get to Senkama.

She wanted answers. She would decide everything else after that.

ROSLINE.

Rosline lurched awake, her skin covered in a prickling sensation. Kyrah snuggled into her, seeking her warmth as she had moved away. Jaks had retreated for the night it seemed, taking to his own errands as they had slept, but Rosline wished he had been around to talk.

It had been so clear, so vivid, just as it had been all those years ago. She had seen a woman with a thick mane of red hair and eyes the color of the sky. She had thwarted what looked like an ambush, her movements strong and precise with a blade of white steel in her hands. But that hadn't been what had stirred her awake.

She watched Astoria, for it had to be her, kneel beside Eleanor's old husband, his life pouring onto the ground beside him as she cradled him. Those small sprites, the small creatures that Rosline had almost completely forgotten about in her years, were dancing around him. She'd seen this scene before, over five years ago, when she thought Astoria had been slain. When Sehren had been cradling her, screaming at the sky.

Rosline saw Astoria cradle him and sob as he reached up for her, and for the first time in her visions had heard her pained cry, a wail that threatened to tear apart the world. The sprites had gathered around

Sehren, but at her cry, they had scattered before tentatively scurrying back to him before Rosline had been wrenched awake.

It's a dream. It has to be.

Rosline pulled herself from the warm comfort of her bed, reaching for a pitcher that was set upon the small stand beside it. She poured herself a drink and let the water wash down her throat and steady her nerves.

It has to be a dream.

Astoria had looked so clear though, tears streaming down her freckled cheeks as she cried with him in his arms. She could feel her lamentation, her sorrow and grief still pumping through her heart even as she stood tucked away in Eleanor's home. Rosline glanced at Kyrah. The small girl was curled beneath the blanket. Grabbing a robe to cover herself, she went to her washroom and grabbed the pendant that laid by the basin. Rosline carefully creaked her chamber door open and shut it just as lightly before making her way from her room to the study.

She passed no one in the hall and was comforted knowing that the guards would be set around the entrances of the manor at this hour. As she reached the room, she pulled a small key from her neck and slid it in the keyhole, the shifting tumblers rumbling on her spine in the quiet night. After shutting the door behind her, she made her way to the array in the center of the room, slipping the necklace over her head and resting it on her chest. She stepped into the center of the array before she drew her focus within herself. Grasping the pendant in her right hand, she tried to recall the image of her dream and tried to see Astoria as she had within her mind.

She felt a tug, her eyes immediately feeling tense and sore, but she tried to push past that. The haze grew thicker though as the pressure built behind her eyes. An outline of a grove came into her view, but as she tried to peer deeper, the pressure turned to pain and Rosline released the image, her eyes burning and her mind searing as her vision slid back into the lighted world. Tears ran from her eyes, and surprised, Rosline wiped at them, seizing when she saw they were dark. She rose hastily, opening the door to the study to see in the lighted hallway.

168

Blood stained her hand, and as she wiped her other eye, more blood joined it. Scared, she locked the study before heading back to her room as quickly as possible, a shiver of fear in her spine.

As she closed the door to her chamber, she was happy to see that Kyrah still laid sleeping, bundled beneath the blanket. Rosline went to her washroom chamber, lighting a small lamp that laid inside and looking into the mirror.

There was dried blood around her eyes. She pulled at the side of her eyes, scared of what she might find. She was relieved to see the white of her eye only slightly pinkened. She checked the other eye and again saw only a slight pinkness. Her irises looked worrying to her though, but no more blood leaked from her eyes, and she rinsed away the dried blood. After cleaning up, she took another look at herself in the mirror, concerned. She'd never experienced that kind of reaction before, even in her first days of training.

Even after my trial, I never had that happen.

Rosline ran her fingers around her eyes, relieved that the pressure she had been building had gone away so quickly. She still had complications trying to see past her normal vision. The times that Eleanor had asked for her to see a merchant or trader that had gone beyond her normal sight had left her bedridden with a splitting headache afterwards. As such, Eleanor rarely asked for Rosline to strain herself unless the need was dire and always gave her a day to recuperate afterwards.

Her worry abating, she left the washroom, leaving the pendant by the basin. Rosline crawled back into her bed, cradling Kyrah's head before shutting her eyes and trying to clear her head. She saw the images of Astoria return though, the tear streaks cutting through the grime on her face. The small little sprites followed her around with some of them bouncing around Sehren, as if they were dancing. Rosline opened her eyes, peering around the room, but didn't see anything else shifting around in the gloom. Worried, she tried settling herself again before shutting her eyes, grateful that all she saw was darkness.

As the dawn encroached over the horizon, Rosline was woken by Kyrah's soft voice, her excitement drawing her from her grogginess.

"You woke her, Kyrah."

"I'm sorry, papa. I was just so excited to see you."

Rosline rubbed her eyes, smiling genially when she saw Kyrah on Jaks' shoulders, his bandana wrapped around her head, holding up her hair.

"Good morning," said Jaks, grinning at her.

"Good morning," replied Rosline. She stretched, "I didn't know you were gonna be here so early."

"Eleanor said that it would be fine if you wished to do things today. She seems very impressed with your work."

Rosline felt her face warm before the memory of her dream came back to her. "I need to speak with her first, before we go anywhere. Is that okay Jaks?"

"I figured you would," he said with a laugh. "Sometimes, I think you're more dedicated to her than me."

Rosline laughed. "That's because she lets me in on her work."

Jaks grinned with a mischievous glint in his eye, "Come, let's leave mama to her wife."

Kyrah looked confused as he ducked her head under the door, speaking in Duhoviman with her while she chattered back to him. There was a soft knock on her door frame as Geneve stepped into the doorway, a smile on her face as she bowed.

Rosline, with her help, got dressed after a few moments before she dismissed her for the day. Excited, Geneve bowed once more before heading off. Rosline walked down the halls towards the conference room, knowing Eleanor would likely be there waiting for her first meetings for the day. She passed by Railand, who was headed outside. She bowed her head to the man, who gave a nod in return before going on his way.

Rosline walked past the guards flanking the doorway to the conference room, seeing Eleanor speaking with her steward before dismissing him as Rosline sat to her right.

"Good morning, Lady Eleanor."

"And to you, Rosline. I admit, I thought you would be out already with Jaks," said Eleanor.

170

"I wanted to make sure he wasn't mistaken in your intent," replied Rosline. "It wouldn't be good if I left when you were joking with him."

Eleanor smirked, "I applaud your prudence, but what I said to him was true. You can take today for yourself."

"Right," said Rosline, brightening, "thank you!"

Eleanor nodded as Rosline started to push herself from the table, but she paused, "I had a dream last night…"

Eleanor looked intrigued, "Oh?"

Rosline nodded, "It was similar to the one I had before…"

"Was Sehren in it?"

Slowly, Rosline nodded, "He was."

"Was he doing well?"

Rosline was conflicted. She didn't know if her dream was true, but its nature and the sprites tugged at her sensibilities, giving it a surreal quality. Even mentioning threatened to have it fill her mind's eye.

"Rosline?" asked Eleanor, concerned.

"No, my lady. He was not," said Rosline somberly.

Eleanor stiffened. "How was he, Rosline?"

Rosline swallowed hard, "He seemed in pain. He was being tended to by another, but from what I could see, it was grim."

"I see," Eleanor's face had grown serious. "And you mentioned it was like the one you saw before, when he looked well?"

"Yes" She took a breath, "Another thing…"

Eleanor cocked her head.

"With the image in my mind, I went to the study," she said, lowering her voice as she glanced at the doorway, "to try and see if I could see him. I was taken far north, to a small forest, but there was much pain so I released the vision."

Eleanor looked solicitous, "You must be careful not to strain yourself, Rosline. You could do more harm than good."

"I think I did…" continued Rosline, "when I released the vision, I felt tears on my cheeks. Thinking they were from the pain, I wiped them away before I saw they were bloodied tears."

Eleanor's mouth thinned to a line, "Are you okay?"

"I believe so. I didn't feel anything aside from throbbing after I stopped, and once I cleared them away, I didn't see anything wrong with my eyes."

"You have to be careful, Rosline," said Eleanor. "You have learned well and developed your vision much faster than I could have anticipated. But, our power has its limits, and if you push too much, you will bring hardship to yourself."

Rosline nodded, having heard this chastisement before. "I just wanted to get you a better answer, my lady."

"I know and I understand," said Eleanor as she took a steadying breath. "Thank you for telling me this. Let us hope that this dream you had was indeed a dream."

Rosline bit her lip: she hadn't told her about the shadow sprites, but seeing her already trying to move past it, decided against it. She rose from her seat, bowing to Eleanor before leaving the conference room and heading to the front door. Kyrah's laugh was sounding from the front garden, and Rosline smiled when she saw Jaks hiding from her as she ran around calling for him.

"Come here," said Jaks in a loud whisper, beckoning Rosline to his hiding spot. She tiptoed over, keeping her eyes out for her daughter, before tucking beside him as she suppressed a laugh.

"Did you confirm with your wife that you can accompany us today?" asked Jaks in a low voice, pushing back as Kyrah came running around some bushes before scampering off.

"I wanted to make sure she knew I would be out," replied Rosline.

Jaks searched her for a moment, a line of worry etching his brow as he said, "What's wrong?"

Rosline huffed playfully: There was little she could hide from his gaze. "I had a dream."

"Was she beautiful? Or perhaps, was it Eleanor?" asked Jaks coyly, earning him a swat from Rosline.

"Stop it," she grew serious, "it was like the one I had about Astoria all those years ago."

Jaks sobered up, his eyes rimmed with concern. He beckoned for her to continue.

"Except it wasn't her. I mean— she was there, but she wasn't the one hurt this time. It was Sehren."

Surprise crossed his face, "You're sure?"

With a nod, she said, "I had a dream about him before and Eleanor told me it was him. He was dying, Jaks. I could see it. Astoria was holding him, and she was in pain. So much pain. I could *hear* her, Jaks. Her anguish. And... there were shadow sprites. All dancing around him, like before."

Jaks looked pensive a moment, before hugging Rosline and saying, "I'm sorry, my love."

"Do you think... he's gone?"

Jaks shrugged as he held her, "I know you can see a lot, Rosline, but when it comes to your dreams, I don't know. You said you saw Astoria before, but by your own admission, she stood today. Older?"

Rosline nodded.

"Then I cannot say for sure. What I do know is that whether he is or not, we shouldn't let it mar this day too much. I presume you told Eleanor?"

"She seemed sad but didn't put too much stock in it."

"Because she knows your visions have their limits. Dreams are sometimes just that, Rosline. Dreams."

She sighed, "You're right. I just thought it was odd. I hadn't seen her in so long, to have that dream was just..."

"I know. I know," Jaks ran his hand through her hair, only stopping when Kyrah's playful cry pulled them from their musings.

"I found you, papa!"

"You did!" He said, picking her up and placing a kiss on her head. He helped her onto his shoulders, causing her to let out an excited shout.

Rosline chuckled as Kyrah chattered on about wanting to go to the park, before Jaks started talking with her in Duhoviman. She followed them out of the garden.

ELEANOR.

Eleanor listened as the man before her droned on, only half paying attention as her mind was racing.

He can't be dead.

She gave a cursory nod of her head, hearing the man speak of their terms and making sure that things were set for their deal.

"Yes. Of course."

"Excellent! I shall depart with haste then. It's been a pleasure."

The man looked expectantly to Eleanor, and she held out her hand, feeling disgust as the man lavished her with a kiss upon it. He stood up and left as Eleanor wiped her hand on her handkerchief. Her mind was fuzzy. She rose from the table in the conference room, walking steadily over as she called for her steward.

"Yes, milady?"

"No more calls today, please. I find myself addled," said Eleanor. "Explain to them that I wish to reconvene on a later day when I feel more apt for the conversation."

"Of course." He bowed as she made for the stairs, taking them swiftly. After reaching the landing, Eleanor took a brisk pace towards her study, before pausing and detouring towards Rosline's chambers.

She wasn't wearing it today.

Eleanor stepped into Rosline's room, seeing it was already straightened up. She made her way to the washroom and spotted the pendant resting beside the basin. Eleanor picked it up and hesitated, spying blood on the stone. Dipping it in the basin, she wiped it away, frowning as she thought of Rosline's bleeding tears before shaking her head.

I have to know.

Eleanor departed Rosline's chambers before making her way to the study, pulling a small key from her neck and unlocking it. As she crossed into the room, she shut the door behind her before she glanced around the room. It was well-kept, with several journals stacked upon the desk. An unlit candle rested in a holder on the desk, and Eleanor went to light it before opening the curtains. She stepped around the array on the floor and spied several dried drops of blood within it. Kneeling, she pulled her handkerchief forth before dabbing the corner of it on her mouth, wetting it. She rubbed away the blood, taking care to not disturb the array. There were several spots where she believed the lines could be thickened and renewed. She tucked that away in her mind for Rosline later.

After she finished, she went to the desk, pulling the small chest from beneath it and opening it. Her familiar sewing implements were there, and she tousled them a bit, making sure they seemed as though they were regularly used. She scattered them as she scoffed. Rosline had simply wrapped the book in several layers of cloth instead of replacing it within the false bottom.

Careless.

Eleanor pulled the tome to the desk. As she set it down, she placed her pendant over her head and neck. She opened the page, beckoning for the myriad of runes to her. They shifted, speaking to her, but she couldn't sort through them well enough as her mind teemed with wayward thoughts.

Sehren can't be dead.

She leafed through the pages, but just like the man speaking to her downstairs, she was only half paying attention, only half involved as she sat there. Leaning back in the chair, she glanced over to the door.

176

It would likely be better for Rosline to try and find what she was looking for.

She has the better sight anyways.

Eleanor shook her head as she shut the book. Rosline was indeed talented, but her limited knowledge of words made finding the correct information trying at times. She was eager, and very loyal, her first action to always report to Eleanor on any findings she would have. Eleanor rarely had to come to the study these days to find anything, as Rosline would be already here, working as she had stacks upon stacks of information.

Eleanor glanced over to the journals, smirking as she thought of just how much they had collected together. Their lives had been easy the past few years, and as Rosline had grown into her confidence, Eleanor had grown into her wealth.

She tucked the book back into the chest, opting to simply wrap it within. When she had lived with Sehren, she had constantly been worried that someone would stumble upon it if she had left it so open, but not because she was afraid of explaining. No, Eleanor feared that someone like Rosline would be under Sehren's employ and upon seeing the book, would steal it away with its tempting knowledge.

However, after Rosline had entered her service, Eleanor had taken measures to make sure that they scoped out any new people hired, together. While Rosline hadn't truly learned exactly what Eleanor meant, together with her sight, all that came to Eleanor's home for employ could not dabble in their world. She had made sure of that.

A knock on the door pulled Eleanor from her musing. She stood up, wondering who had come to call. Creaking the door open, she saw Railand standing on the opposite side of the hall, following his orders she had given him when she hired him.

Never, on any occasion, look into my study.

Eleanor shut the door behind her, locking it before clearing her throat. "Railand. I wasn't expecting you."

"I was told you were done with your appointments today," he said, turning around. He had a braid in the tangles of his hair this day, while he wore his normal garb. His eyes searched her. "The steward mentioned that you were feeling unwell."

"I told him as much, yes."

"Something amiss?"

Eleanor pursed her lips as she thought, "Just a strange morning. I found myself not as engaged as I should have been, and instead of risking insult, I thought it best to postpone further meetings."

"A sound choice," said Railand.

"I admit, I was not expecting you to come look for me."

"If you're not dealing with merchants in your study, then it's my job to be at your side, remember?" said Railand, quoting another part of his contract.

"You remember all of it then."

"Of course I do. Else, I would constantly be asking you what to do next, and that does not bode well for a guard."

Eleanor smirked, "It does not."

As Eleanor started walking off, Railand fell in step behind her to her left. "Railand, a question."

"Certainly."

"What do Nacinimans say of dreams?"

Railand snorted, "An odd question. Why do you believe I would know?"

"You are worldly."

"Doesn't mean I know the world's traditions."

"Be that as it may, are you saying you don't know, then?"

Railand snorted again, "Of course I'm not."

"Well?"

"Nacinimans are not just all one people, as I'm sure you are aware. Like Candramans, different peoples of the lands have their own beliefs and traditions," replied Railand. "To know them all would be exhausting. Were I to have a people there, I would find myself knowing less useful things."

Eleanor nodded, "But if you were to have a people there that had such traditions, what would they say?"

"They would say that dreams are a mirror, but one that does not show the truth of your world but rather a reflection of the world as is," he explained.

"I don't understand."

"Nor do I. It's why I don't hold much stock in it."

Eleanor frowned, "I see."

"Anything else?"

"Have you ever wed, Railand?"

"Once."

Eleanor looked surprised, "What became of her?"

"Illness took her," he said shortly.

Eleanor felt disbelief at the way he said it, "Are you lying to me?"

"Never. There would be no point. If you can't trust me, then what point is there in our contract?"

"You've never spoken of her before is all."

"Why would I? It doesn't help me with my job."

Eleanor walked down the stairs with Railand behind her.

"Did you have a dream of your husband, Eleanor?"

Eleanor stopped, turning her head towards him.

"I didn't. I wondered if that meant something was wrong."

"It is because he is doing fine. If you dream too much of someone, it's because they are gone."

Eleanor contemplated that for moment, "Is that what you believe?"

"No, but I dream often of my wife," he said. "And if you don't see him, it's because he is too busy living."

He has to be. Rosline just had an errant dream.

"Thank you for your insight, Railand."

He bowed his head to her as he followed her. Eleanor paused a moment, before saying, "Would you accompany me to the cemetery by the Cathedral, Railand?"

"Of course."

She smiled at him before heading out the door, her mind still buzzing.

KARJA.

The ground seemed to be shifting beneath him, but he didn't move of his own accord. The sun shone on his face, but he couldn't find the strength to open his eyes. He felt the breeze against his skin, but the prickling in his arms and legs stole their gentle caress.

A small spout was put in his mouth, causing him to sputter when a stream of cool water streamed into his throat. He swallowed hungrily, before he remembered, before his eyes fluttered open, and he spat the rest out in defiance.

"You are not dead," said Astoria, looking over him with a blank face. "Good. I would hate dragging you around for nothing."

Karja reflexively pulled his arms, feeling a searing pain in his elbows and wrists as he did. He tried to move his legs, but more pain shot through him.

"If you fight the bindings you will fall. I will make you crawl," she said as she replaced the waterskin on her back.

Hatred coursed through him, multiplying when he spied the blades of his friends and his chief slung over her shoulder.

If I could get one…

Astoria adjusted her pack, maneuvering the straps before checking the ones on Karja's wrists. Nodding to herself, she lifted the litter onto her shoulders before dragging him along.

"You are lucky to be alive, Karja," said Astoria in between breaths as he dragged him along. "I thought you had bled out."

Karja shifted, not responding. He felt tight, sore spots on his body. Glancing down, he was shocked to see several of his wounds had been stitched up. Wounds that Sehren had given him.

"Why?" he said, the word painful on his throat.

"Why what?" replied Astoria.

"Why am I alive?"

"Because I want answers," she said. She started dragging him faster.

"I will never answer you."

"Sure, for now," said Astoria. "But if you think you will heal up before I get back to your people, then you are a fool."

"They will kill you on sight."

"That is what you are for."

The tone of her voice stole his response, filled with such anger and hate that Karja would not have associated with the woman. He tried to turn his head, but she had tied his arms up and his locked biceps prevented him from turning far. There were two black wounds on his arms, the skin around them burned. They stung every time the litter was jostled.

"You are a fool," he said to her, coughing. "They will never listen to a southerner."

"No but they will listen to you," she replied.

"And what makes you think I will speak?"

"Your life."

Astoria's responses were monotone, almost automatic, as if she had rehearsed them. Karja tried to adjust himself on the litter, but his body was weak and in pain. He attempted to pull himself up with his wrists but searing pain shot through both of his arms. He tried to adjust his legs but pain in his thighs and ankles stole his strength.

"You are a fool," he said again.

Astoria didn't reply, instead continuing her steady march. The sun went high into the sky, and she stopped, eating a small packed meal. After she finished, she put some food before him, close enough for him to eat if he wanted. His stomach growled, but he turned his nose up at it, refusing. She shrugged before tossing it to the ground. She drank from a waterskin before forcing the spout into his mouth and forcing water into his throat.

I could drown myself.

No. They won't listen to her. She is not us.

Karja sputtered and coughed, spitting out whatever water failed to stream down his throat. Astoria picked the litter back up again, continuing her steady march. They marched well into the night, Astoria only stopping when the night was so dark it was too precarious to continue.

She trussed him up, tying his wrists to his ankles before tying his mouth with a length of cloth. Her movements were rough, and whenever he struggled, she redoubled her efforts, tightening his bonds to make sure he couldn't move. She wrapped herself in a blanket and slept upon a bedroll, the weapons she had stolen tucked beneath her.

Karja tried shifting around, but every movement he made sent waves of pain through him, threatening to cause him to black out. He breathed, trying to find a way to escape, but Astoria had placed him away from anything. He scoured the ground, trying to find a stick or rock to use to break his bindings when he heard her soft cry.

He froze, turning his head as much as he could. She was speaking in the other tongue, the tongue of the southerners, but he could tell by her tone and pitch that she was crying. A singular word stood out.

"Sehren..."

Karja listened to her cry for a while, her cries broken by his name. A weight settled in his heart, but he steeled it, knowing he had made the right choice. Sehren had drawn on them, believing that they would tell everyone where he lived. He had forced the issue, instead of simply abandoning her. Sehren had turned his back on his people, their people, in lieu of this woman.

He'd made his choice.

Still, Astoria's cries did little to affirm his decision.

As the sky lightened, it seemed that Astoria was already awake. She rose from her bedroll, packed up her things and belted her blade to her side. She released Karja's binds only to tie him to the litter. Karja watched her eat another meal, his stomach aching as she finished it and brushed her hands off. She drank from the waterskin before once more forcing him to drink. He fought, but when she pulled it away instead of forcing him to drink, panic ran through him.

Astoria lifted him from the ground and started marching off. Karja tried to see if he could shift his weight, but he was weaker than yesterday, his arms shaking from holding him up and his legs aching.

"I thirst," he said after the sun cleared the horizon, his lips cracking as the words left his lips.

"Good," she said. "Why did you attack Sehren?"

Karja shook his head, and Astoria fell silent, continuing to carry him. Karja thought she would stop for lunch, but she continued trekking on. As the darkness fell and she stopped to eat, she once again put the remainder of her food before him. He grudgingly ate the scraps before she gave him water, his aching throat soothed as it washed down his throat. As she set them down for the night, Karja saw that the woods of his people were close. They would be there within the next day.

They will stop her.

Karja knew it.

He heard her cry once more as she laid upon her bed. Astoria had curled up, her back to him, but he could hear her cries in the night, could feel her shuddering in the night air. Her grief was palpable, but Karja once more steeled his heart, resolved that he had made the right choice.

184

He heard her move. Fear accompanied her footsteps. There was a slither of steel in the night. Roughly, she rolled him onto his back. It was hard to see in the night, but the moon illuminated her face enough to show him the sheer anger within.

"Why did you attack him?" she whispered. "We never harmed you. We took care of you."

Karja turned his eyes away from her, but she picked him up, holding him close to her face. He could see the streaks of tears still shining on her face, the desperation in her blue eyes as she shook him.

"Answer me," she said, her voice filled with anguish and anger. When Karja remained silent, she threw him to the ground as she reached for the blade. A blade, Karja realized, that was black as the night.

His fear turned to dread as she swung wildly at him. He shut his eyes, waiting for his life to end only to hear the blade cut deep into the earth. Peeking through his eyelids, he saw that she had cut within inches of his head, her shoulders shaking as she held the blade. She pulled the sword from the earth before replacing it in the scabbard. Returning to her bedroll, she draped the blanket over her shoulders. Karja heard her whispering to herself during the night, eventually stopping as she fell asleep. The morning came quickly after that though, and Astoria once again packed everything up before she ate. She gave Karja water, the soothing relief working its way down his throat before she lifted the litter onto her shoulders and started walking. It was around midday when Astoria reached the edges of their woods.

"They will find you once you cross."

"Good."

ASTORIA.

Astoria dragged the litter through the forests of Senkaman. The sunlight was muted by the thick canopy above, but that did little to slow her pace. Sehren had told her that as long as she continued to the west, she would eventually be found if someone was paying attention.

"I doubt they would show themselves though. They may even strike without warning."

That's what he's for.

Astoria looked over her shoulder, watching Karja. The man's lips were cracked, his face pallid, and his breathing harsh. That didn't stir her heart though. She felt he deserved the pain he suffered, and had it not been for her plan, she would have let him die like the others.

There was hollowness in her chest though, one that threatened to consume her whole, but she kept the feelings at bay by her desire to know. Her yearning to know. It was everything to her now. Sehren had never stepped into their lands uninvited, so she knew that it wasn't because he had trespassed. He hadn't ever attacked any of their people either, the only other visitors that they had in their lands being Nyeth and that large man. Nothing stood out in her mind that would have provoked them, nothing that would have led them to the vicious battle that had taken place.

And yet, here she was, trudging through the woods with Karja resting on her back, a fire in her that threatened to consume her. But she needed to know. Only then would she be able to sort this out.

Astoria continued marching, the refrain of '*Why?*' within her mind pushing her to each step. Karja coughed harshly, and she drew to a stop, drawing a skin of water from her pack and placing the spout of it into his mouth. She squeezed it, and Karja drank this time, sputtering for a moment after she withdrew it from him. Replacing the skin in her pack, she crouched down to lift the litter when she felt a tingle on the back of her neck and a thrum in the stone on her chest. The same one she felt when she thought Sehren was coming home.

Hope flared in her heart for a moment before she shook her head, tears already clouding her vision as she thought about him. He would never appear before her again, never stir her sensibilities. Even as she thought it though, a defiance burned within her, her mind refusing to listen.

She stood back up and waited as calmly as she could, despite the beading of sweat on her brow and down her back. She waited for them to show themselves, hoping that seeing one of their own in such a state would tempt them to step out instead of strike. She was just a southerner after all; what threat could she pose to them?

A rustle from her right pulled her gaze, her hand dropping to the sword on her side which she immediately released when she saw a towering man she recognized.

Ghorun gave her a severe look before looking at the litter and becoming confused. "What got him?"

"I did." She replied simply.

Ghorun frowned. His gaze traced around the scene. "Where is Sehren?"

The words caught in her throat as the tears spilled down her cheeks, gritting her teeth. She stared with venom towards Karja. "Him," was all she could muster before she fought the compulsion coming again.

Ghorun, seeing the pain and anguish in her face, looked aghast. He approached, his own blade in hand and drew back when he saw Karja. "He is maimed."

"He deserved worse," said Astoria, her voice filled with venom.

"She speaks lies," said Karja weakly.

A wave of anger welled within her. She wanted nothing more than to cut Karja's tongue out. With a shake of her head, she swallowed it, "He and two others came and attacked Sehren."

Ghorun seemed startled at Astoria's proclamation. He glanced at Karja, who tried to shake his head but was restrained by his arms. Ghorun was clearly unsure of what to make of the situation.

"I know you want to believe him," said Astoria, drawing the large man's gaze, "but he and his companions came to our lands. They were fighting with Sehren when I got there, and he used this," Astoria pulled the black blade that Karja had been wielding from her shoulder, drawing it slowly to not threaten Ghorun. "He brought this to bear against him."

Ghorun immediately frowned, approaching her and beckoning for the blade. She passed it to him, glad to be rid of it. He pulled it fully from its sheath, inspecting it. There was still dried blood on it. He muttered to himself before replacing it in its sheath.

"Do not move," he said to Astoria. Astoria nodded, sitting on the ground as he walked off before she watched the gloom of the woods swallow him. She listened to the sounds of the forest, but it was eerily silent: no insects chirping, no birds singing or making their calls. It seemed as though ages passed before Astoria felt more tingling on her neck. She rose, swaying slightly as the exhaustion hit her. She steadied herself though, anticipation tingling through her limbs and dispelling the fatigue.

Dark gloom coalesced near Astoria, thickening into a morass before Nyeth stepped from it. Ghorun followed to her left while Korrenth appeared to her right, both armed. As they took a moment to take in their surroundings, Nyeth locked her gaze upon Astoria, her piercing gaze upon her immediately. Astoria didn't falter, standing tall and firm before the woman as she fought the mistiness in her eyes.

Nyeth eventually broke her gaze before scanning their surroundings, her face softening as she said, "He really is gone?"

Astoria nodded, not trusting her voice to respond. Nyeth trailed her gaze to Karja, who shrinked before her scrutiny. She knelt beside him, talking in low tones as Korrenth approached Astoria.

"I understand your loss," she said soothingly. Astoria met her solicitous gaze before stiffly nodding as Ghorun joined her side. "I cannot believe what occurred."

"Nor can I," admitted Astoria. "If I had not seen it, if I had not crossed blades with Karja I still would deny it."

Korrenth turned her gaze upon Nyeth, who rose with a distressed look on her face. She called Ghorun. "Carry him."

"Yes, chief," he said without hesitation. He walked over to the man, untied him from the litter, and lifted him into his arms before marching off into the woods. Nyeth watched him until he faded away from sight.

"Astoria," she started tentatively. "Karja has told me many things."

Anger welled in her throat, but she pushed it back down, sealing hard as she said, "Like what?"

"It is much to sort through. We will be taking him to a nearby village where his wounds will be tended as his chief is called."

He is going to live.

"Why his chief?"

"Karja is a *krusho*," said Nyeth expectantly. The word held no meaning to Astoria so she beckoned for more. "He is a sworn warrior to his chief. Something of a brother and guard."

"Then why was he in our lands? Should he not have been at his chief's side?" Astoria didn't understand and the frustration was building in her.

"As I said, there is much to discuss about that. He said, however, that Sehren drew first upon him, telling him that he could not leave."

190

Astoria's head swam, "That makes no sense. We treated him before. He came to our camp after he was attacked by the *eiravuks*."

Nyeth and Korrenth exchanged confused glances as Astori's breath shortened. As she considered Nyeth, the woman said, "That cannot be true."

"What do you mean?"

"He was attacked around the borders of his people by the beasts," said Korrenth. "People have been talking of his survival of encountering them."

Astoria denied viciously, "No. He is lying. Sehren saved him when he came weeks ago to our lands alone. He brought Karja to our camp and we treated his wounds," her voice broke as angry tears streamed down her cheeks, "we fed him, gave him a place to rest, and when he started off back home, Sehren watched him every step of the way to make sure he was safe."

Nyeth and Korrenth shared a surprised look at Astoria's retelling, bordering one bewilderment. They whispered to one another as Astoria clutched her hands to her hair. "Did he say why he came to attack Sehren?"

"He spoke of his reasons, but we will not know more until Haljn speaks with him. He is weak."

"He should be dead," spat Astoria.

"Did you kill Beluk and Sejun?" asked Nyeth suddenly.

"If those are the names of the other two that were with him, then yes. They were also engaged with him, and I thought only of helping Sehren."

Nyeth and Korrenth traded glances. Nyeth said, "Astoria. I cannot begin to understand what happened fully here, but I have my suspicions."

"That is more than I have," said Astoria. "I want answers. I need them, Nyeth."

The woman nodded, "It may be a few days before we can get those for you. However, I do not know if I can have you within our lands, especially once his clan learns what you have done."

"I cannot go back," said Astoria firmly. "Karja knows of where we lived and had been inside our home. He could simply tell them where I was and this would happen again. I cannot. Even if there was something to go back to… "

She could hear the sound of the spine severing, her stomach turning as she thought of the brutal manner that she had killed them. She shook her head, trying to wrest away the sights, but they were waiting for her every time she shut her eyes.

Nyeth startled her by setting her hand upon her shoulder. Astoria immediately went to unsheathe the sword at her side, an action mirrored by Korrenth.

"Stop!" said Nyeth harshly to Korrenth before calming, "Astoria— will you be able to continue marching?"

"Yes," she said simply. "Sehren trained me to survive. I can march out of here if need be."

Nyeth shook her head, "No. I mean long enough to follow me to a nearby village. If you stay with me while we are there, that should provide safety for you until we can get this solved."

"Why would you do that? You are not fond of me," asked Astoria.

"Because I was fond of Sehren, and if you are right about what happened, then Karja committed a grievous and heinous act within our people. This will be my way of trying to set it right."

Astoria bit her tongue, swallowing her retort. She knew Nyeth was giving her the most respect that anyone from the kingdom would get, and yet, it all seemed hollow and pointless.

"Fine."

Astoria followed behind them, her shoulders bowed as she had nothing to distract her. She heard the soft voices of Nyeth and Korrenth speaking, both of them occasionally glancing back at her as they walked. It didn't bother her. As they continued walking through the woods, Astoria saw that the path they traveled became more and more beaten and eventually through the trees she saw the village: several closely packed wooden cabins and huts separated into several different quadrants. There were people walking hurriedly towards a tall man encircled by some of the villagers. As Nyeth approached, they parted before her like water before the prow of a boat, while many of them let out sounds of discontent and anger when they spotted Astoria.

She hardly heard them, her blood running cold as she saw several people tending to Karja's wounds and providing him water. He whispered to several of them in between drinks as his gaze landed upon her. Eyes snapped to her, several of the people leaving his side to approach her, their intent clear.

Astoria dropped her hand to the pommel of her blade, but Nyeth instead drew Korrenth's blade from her side, the slithering sound clear in the air.

"She is not to be touched. There is much to learn, and she is required for that," she declared in a stern voice. Discontent sounded out, several people incensed by her proclamation.

"Another mistake," said Astoria under her breath. She felt that Nyeth erred by bringing her there, and even as she quelled more of the rising voices, a man drew up before her.

"You make such a demand for someone so vile to do this to a *krusho*?" he asked, his eyes filled with violent disbelief.

"That man crossed into another chief's territory and attacked him," explained Korrenth quietly. "If he was justified in his actions, then we will expel her from the north as always. However, there are two stories to sort out and as such, we need to hear them both to get the real answer."

"She will speak lies, as they all do."

"Did Sehren speak lies?" asked Astoria, pushing past Korrenth. She felt a violent grab on her shoulder, but she didn't relent, breaking away from it as she moved forward, "No. He came before you all and complied with whatever you asked of him. He sat with you, shared meals with you, and you all welcomed him into your people. Then, you sent that man to kill him. For what? A grudge?"

"She lies," retorted Karja.

"*Enough!*" yelled Nyeth, silencing the retorts and shouts. She pulled Astoria back roughly, "We will find the answer to this all in the morning. For now," her gaze landed on one of the people, "lodgings for us."

One of the men shook his head, grumbling as he led Nyeth, Korrenth, and Astoria to a cabin on the far side of the village. It was sparsely decorated, looking to be for temporary use rather than a long stay.

"Take the bed," said Korrenth as she took a seat at the small table.

Nyeth mirrored her, looking at Astoria. "You are weary, Astoria. Take a rest."

"Why? Why are we waiting?"

"The people will not hear your cries of protest while they are still irate and surprised," said Nyeth.

"You do not welcome me here either," said Astoria flatly. "So, why wait any longer than need be?"

"If he did kill Sehren—"

"He did."

Korrenth's eyes flashed dangerously at her, but Nyeth held up her hand and said softly, "Think if it had been me." She settled back in her chair, still frowning at Astoria. Nyeth continued, "if he did, then he has to answer for it from our people. It is a serious thing to attack a chief, let alone invade their lands with two others and kill them."

"But he did," said Astoria as her emotions broke through the dam she had erected. She couldn't sit still, she couldn't stop and wait for the grief that she knew was waiting for her to come rearing up. "He and Sejun and Beluk came into our lands, *our home*, and they attacked him."

"You were there?"

"I saw Sehren fighting against all three of them! It was not hard to figure out what happened then."

"They came with murderous intent then?"

Astoria paused, "I do not know. What I do know is that it was Sehren's land, his sovereign land, and he told me after the ceremony what that meant for us."

Nyeth's face tightened. "I see."

"Am I wrong?"

She shook her head, letting out a deep sigh. "However, unless we can prove from Karja that is what happened, your word will mean little."

"Because I am from the south."

"Exactly because you are from the south."

Astoria felt bile catch in her chest as tears welled up in her eyes. She sat roughly on the bed, trying to catch her breath as they streamed down her cheeks. "Why? *Why?! We didn't do anything to you!*" She screamed at Nyeth. The woman was taken aback as Astoria clutched her knees to her chest, sobbing into her knees.

She heard the scratching of the chairs and the door open and shut as Astoria continued sobbing. There was weight that settled beside her on the bed, and Astoria jerked, seeing Nyeth seated beside her.

"You are right," said Nyeth calmly. She curled her fists into her legs as she spoke, "You and Sehren had not done anything to us. In fact, you showed us respect and honor that we did not know your people possessed."

Astoria wiped her eyes, sniffing as she listened to Nyeth.

"But your people before, they did indeed do things to us. They harmed us, burned our villages, and hunted our people down like animals as they fled. They fought without honor or remorse, because they believed that they were the righteous ones during those dark times."

Nyeth shook, her anger clear in her voice, "I remember them, to this day. In the nights when I feel all is peaceful, I remember the flickering fires in the dark, the screams that tore through the air, and the feeling of needing to run somewhere, anywhere safe. Safe from those demons called men, safe from those knights and their soldiers. And I am not the only one, Astoria. Most of my people my age are survivors of that time. We witnessed it all, and only by hiding on the edge of our lands, with little to sustain us, did we survive."

Astoria trembled as she saw Nyeth staring into the middle distance, her silver eyes filled with hate.

"It is not something easily forgotten, no matter how many years we spend healing, nor should it be forgotten lest we allow it to happen again. You and Sehren reminded us all of those days. Even if you never laid a hand upon us, even if you never set foot into our lands, you stirred those thoughts. Even now, all you have done by maiming Karja was remind us of the savagery of your people."

"And that meant Karja was right in attacking Sehren? That nothing mattered because of others?" asked Astoria, her heart hurting.

Nyeth shook her head, the difficulty of which was not lost on Astoria. She said, through gritted teeth, "We chose to bring Sehren into the clans again. We together as a people brought him in, and even when confronted about you, he said he would give it all up if it meant keeping you safe."

Astoria felt a pang of warmth in her heart, "He said that?"

"He did, and everyone who was there knew him to be sincere. Sehren would not do anything to risk you. Even telling others your name was too much and was a favor that I did for him out of the respect I held for him." Nyeth unclasped her hands, clearly agitated, "I know what you desire, Astoria. If it is true what Karja did, then he committed a grievous crime. But only his chief will be able to sort that out."

"But I saw him! I was there."

"It matters little in the eyes of our people. Karja was an esteemed man, one of the most honorable of his clan, and above most in all of our people. If his chief believes him, then there is nothing that can be followed upon that."

"He will go free?"

Nyeth nodded. "And if he does, I ask you not to act in anger or deceit. I will not protect you if you do."

Cold clutched her heart as Nyeth rose from the bed. The woman gave her one more glance before stepping outside with Korrenth.

196

NYETH.

There was a hush over the village as Nyeth waited outside the cabin the next morning. No one, not even the early hunters, had risen or left early to go about their business. She knew they were all waiting for Haljn, waiting for the chieftain of Karja to come and absolve him of his actions against Sehren, and hopefully, bring justice to Astoria.

Nyeth felt sick as she considered it.

She never thought that Sehren would find himself pit against someone like Karja. No one, not even the most indignant of her people, had shown themselves to be violent towards the man. He was peaceful, contemplative, genuine, and honorable.

And yesterday, Nyeth had learned he was slain at the hands of one of the most honorable people she knew.

Karja had survived as she had, had fought the biting cold and frigid nights with little to warm them save for the small fires they made below ground to keep the light dim. He had risen through his people as they had grown, had become an exemplary fighter and man, and had sworn himself to clan Chuyara in ways that few would.

So why did he fight Sehren so?

Nyeth had to believe that he had a sound reason. A reason he hadn't told anyone. When Ghorun had come to tell her of his findings, he had said only that he was thirsty, hungry, and waiting for Haljn. Ghorun had prodded, but Karja had remained resolute, asking only for nourishment. He hadn't even asked for something to dull the pain, something that many respected from such a tough individual, but felt out of place to Nyeth. She thought he was perhaps trying to garner favor as a survivor, or to depreciate Astoria's actions against him. Another part of her believed that he was suffering for his guilt, but even if she could place the guilt of his actions upon him, only Haljn could determine his fate.

Nyeth took a moment to dispel the drowsiness from her. She had told herself that she was keeping an eye out for people that would try and come to harm Astoria, but in truth, she thought the woman would be vengeful after being informed that they may not get her answers. Nyeth had waited in case the window broke or the door opened so that she could usher her back inside, but the woman had simply curled onto the bed and laid there. Whether she slept or not was unknown to Nyeth, but based upon the times she would hear her crying, she believed that Astoria found little rest in her waiting.

As the sun rose, she heard movement from within, stirring Nyeth to open the door and check. Astoria was up, belting her blade to her waist and pulling her leather coat over top. One, Nyeth realized, that she had given Sehren many months ago. Astoria's gaze snapped onto her as she immediately tensed. They traded glances for a moment. With a stiff nod, she shut the door, trying to still the beating of her heart.

She is like Sehren.

Even telling herself that, Nyeth found it hard to quench the hatred within her. Astoria was right though: she had never harmed Nyeth personally, had never done anything that would bring danger to their lands or otherwise disrespected them in the time she had been with Sehren, and yet, Nyeth still couldn't quell the feelings of loathing that churned within her at the sight of Astoria. Feelings that she knew were mirrored in the hearts of everyone that lived in the village.

Nyeth pushed herself from the door as she heard Astoria approaching. When the door opened, she sent her a questioning glance.

"I want food," said Astoria. "And something to drink."

"And you were going to hunt, I would guess?"

"I cannot just sit here waiting. It is driving me insane."

Nyeth nodded, letting the woman step from the cabin. "Follow me then. I cannot let you be out and about alone."

"Because someone will try to kill me?" asked Astoria.

"Yes," replied Nyeth simply. They walked together, Nyeth guiding Astoria away from the outskirts of the village. Astoria moved with a hunter's gait, almost identical to Nyeth's as they traveled together. The woman made little noise as they crossed through the underbrush of the trees, until they came to a fast flowing stream that cut through the silence of the woods.

Nyeth crouched to it, cupping water in her hand before pulling it up to her lips and drinking deeply. With an appreciative sigh, she said, "It is clean."

Astoria knelt at the stream, setting her hands in it and shuddering when the cool water washed over her. She cleaned her hands a moment before cupping some of the water within them and bringing it to her lips. She took several large mouthfuls before she coughed, drawing Nyeth's gaze.

"We had a stream like this that ran through our camp," said Astoria thickly. "Sehren widened and deepened it over the course of several seasons so that it would flow more freely. We never found where it came from, but it always had a bite to it whenever you would drink from it, no matter what season or time of day you drank from it."

Nyeth remained silent, not sure how to respond.

"When will I get my answers?" asked Astoria.

"When Haljn arrives with his people. It should be around midday, but it could be later if the messenger was held up during their run at night."

"Can they not simply travel as you and Sehren do? Just close distances in a matter of moments?"

Nyeth frowned, not sure to what extent Astoria knew of the *kymbra*. Her distrust of the woman was screaming at her, but it seemed more a musing question than that of any true knowledge. She remained quiet again.

Astoria washed her hands again before sliding the blade from her side and setting it upon her knees. It was snow white, with a fuller of black steel, and an almost translucent edge. Astoria took some of the water from the stream and ran it over the blade before wiping it clean. She took several moments to stare at the sword until Nyeth broke the silence.

"That is the Ombroj blade," she said, glancing over it. "It is old."

"It was Sehren's," said Astoria. "When I started hunting more, he thought it would be best if I had a blade that we both knew could handle the rigors that would come with constantly cutting and felling beasts. To this day, I have never failed to fell a creature with his blade in hand."

Astoria shook a moment as Nyeth saw her face cloud a moment.

"He gave you the blade."

"He said it was better for him that it be in my hands in case I find danger," said Astoria as she laid the blade across her knees. "And in truth, I felt proud. Sehren took to wearing an old blade we found on our way up here, but the confidence he had in me drove me to learn to care for his sword and to keep it in as pristine a condition as he had given it to me."

"He never told you anything else about it, did he?"

"Should he have?" asked Astoria.

Nyeth eyed white steel, the dark fuller drawing memories of stories from when she was a young girl. "My father spoke of the Ombroj a lot, namely of the one who wielded that blade. We have an art for crafting weapons, and every clan has their own preference for which they decide to use. Swords were not common, not for a long time, as many of the conflicts that arose in our lands stemmed from fighting savage beasts, and it is much better to fight a beast with a long weapon than to carry a short blade."

"Sehren told me that when I first started hunting," said Astoria, her face brightening slightly, "he said to use a sword against a bear or wolf would be a folly, and that hunting deer was a task meant for spears and arrows. I thought it odd, but over time, he was right. I learned to draw the bow more than I learned to fight beasts with the blade, but I came to find comfort in its lightness and ease of cutting."

Nyeth gave her an appraising look as she heard the small, uplifted tone in her voice. It was evident that Astoria cherished Sehren's lessons and praise. "Once our people grew larger though, things became contested between them."

"Nyeth," started Astoria, her voice dimming once more as she considered the white steel. "I find that I do not care."

Nyeth blinked, the disrespect flaring anger through her. She saw Astoria's blank eyes as she stared into the sword, and a sadness muddled the rising indignation. "Right."

They sat beside one another for a while, the only sound the flowing stream before Nyeth rose with Astoria following behind her. They walked to the village in silence, only the sound of grumbling voices and protests following in Astoria's wake.

"I cannot let you hunt," said Nyeth as they returned to the cabin. "However, I shall grab you something from the morning meal if you remain here."

"Fine."

"Do not leave, Astoria. It would be unwise for you to travel with everything that is happening."

"Right."

Nyeth sighed as Astoria stepped into the cabin, the woman immediately heading to the bed and sitting upon it. She pulled the blade once more from her side and laid it across her knees, her gaze trapped upon the white steel as though she could see nothing else.

Nyeth shut the door, looking around to see what was made for the morning. Upon greeting several of the cooks, they gave her a bowl of stew, asking her questions in hushed tones about Astoria. Nyeth shook her head before holding her hand out for another bowl, and grudgingly, they gave her another one before she turned away from their pointed questions.

Why was Karja there?

Nyeth couldn't piece it together in her mind, and to her, that meant someone was either leaving something out or lying. Astoria had been pretty forthwith and the details she provided were plausible to Nyeth, even if not entirely believable. She walked back to the cabin, responding to passing calls she heard, and opened the door, expecting to find Astoria still staring at the steel. She was instead seated with her back against the wall, the sheathed blade resting against her shoulder with her gaze on the door.

"Eat," said Nyeth as she set the bowl down at the table, taking a seat beside it. She spooned a bit of it into her mouth, cocking her head when she saw Astoria hadn't moved. "I thought you were hungry."

"I was," she said simply. "I found my hunger has disappeared."

Nyeth continued eating, as Astoria rested against the wall. Every now and then, she pushed the pommel to reveal about an inch of the white steel before letting the blade rest once more in its sheath. Eventually, Astoria reached beneath the collar of her shirt, pulling out a chain with a small, iridescent stone attached to it. She stared at that too, her eyes glassy as she considered it. She let it rest against her chest before she met Nyeth's gaze.

"I know you hate me," she said calmly. There was no accusation, no blame, just resigned acceptance.

"Not you personally," replied Nyeth as she took another bite, "just your people."

"Aye. I understand it now." Astoria sat her head back against the wall again. "Even as I wait here knowing you are trying to do me a favor, I find myself angry simply at the thought of you. And of Haljn, even though I have never met the man. The idea that he will name Karja innocent solely because of the distrust and hatred of people like me, completely disregarding my own words, fills me with disgust."

Nyeth frowned.

"Did you know that Sehren never had peace?" asked Astoria. Nyeth paused, unsure. She continued, "His wife was kidnapped, tortured, and raped. They cut off her hand and left it in his home as a message to him. Before that, he was constantly fighting alongside trade caravans as a guard, with murderous people targeting him. Did you know that?"

202

"I did not."

"It was because he was north-blooded. A north-blooded savage, they used to call him," said Astoria with venom. "I remember when he would stay at the tavern, and people would spit at him behind his back, or mutter slurs and insults under their breath. He told me many times that it did not bother him. In time, I came to believe him. But he still came north, trying to get away from all the deceit and knives in the dark solely because of who he was."

Astoria hiccoughed, "And then we met you. And your people. And you hated him because he was southern-blooded." She let out a short bark of a laugh, "The irony of which I only learned after the years, after hearing him tell me about the other times, when his peaceful tone would turn back into his regular voice. One that accepted who he was and what people thought of him."

Astoria pulled herself to the edge of the bed, her hands shaking as they clutched the sheath in their grasp. "And then when we found a place where we could have peace, he lost his oldest friend. He had to take care of me, and the peace we could have had was lost in my own childishness, my own temper tantrums, and my resentment. But still, he worked, until we had peace, Nyeth. True peace."

She choked up, tears falling from her eyes as she said, "And that man took that away from us. He came into our peace, without invitation or remorse, and took that from us. From me. While I wait for his kin, his people, to tell him he was right so that they can have their peace. Your peace."

Astoria's breath had grown short and choppy as she stifled her hiccoughs, "And you expect me to accept that?"

"You think you could do otherwise?" asked Nyeth.

"I could kill him. And his chief, and you if I needed to," said Astoria in a savage voice. "But I think about it, I think about all the blood I would have to spill to try and gain my peace, and it *destroys* me."

Nyeth felt a pang in her heart at her anguish. Astoria cried in full. She pulled her knees to her chest and rested her head against them as she cried.

"You just want to know why," said Nyeth quietly, rising from her chair. Astoria nodded, coughing as she cried.

Nyeth watched her for a moment, her belly filled with a hot meal but there was a coldness in her chest that wouldn't go away.

Astoria tried to stifle her sobs but her voice broke as she said, "All we wanted—" she hiccoughed again.

"Was peace," Nyeth finished, letting out a sigh. Astoria wiped her eyes, coughing as she nodded. "I cannot promise you that. I cannot promise you anything, Astoria, other than no matter what is determined from this, you will leave in peace. None will draw against you, and I will guide you from here myself if need be."

Astoria sniffed. She clutched her legs, "Sehren told me it was time to go home... I did not know what he meant. I thought he meant the camp, but when I returned there it was so crushing that I could not believe that is what he desired."

"Did you bury him?"

"I set our camp ablaze with his body in the pyre," said Astoria in a strained voice. "I did not want animals coming to find him or to dig him up. I wanted him to at last be at peace."

Nyeth rose from her seat, true indecision within her. Astoria was everything Sehren had hinted her to be: strong, willful, and loyal. She was kind as well, and Nyeth knew in the depths of her heart that only Karja's actions had driven the woman so close to destruction.

"Try and rest, Astoria. Haljn and his will be here soon."

"Will you wake me?"

Nyeth, firm in her voice, said, "I will."

ASTORIA.

Astoria's dreams were hazy, fragmented, and filled with unease and unsteadiness that offered no rest. She saw small tendrils of darkness that marred each image, before being swept away by another cast before her mind's eye. A soft voice was calling to her though, stirring her from the tangled dreams, before she opened her eyes with a fright, her heart racing as she felt someone, something over her. She reached for the pommel of her blade, stopping when the soft voice became loud enough for her to discern as female. As her vision cleared, she saw Nyeth and Korrenth, the latter ready to strike her in case of violence, standing beside the bed. Astoria sat up and rubbed her eyes, forcing the grogginess from her with several large breaths of air.

"They are here?" she asked as she looked at Nyeth.

"They are here."

A jolt ran through her which drove the last vestiges of her sleepiness from her. The images that had initially taken up residence in her mind were replaced with a searing desire for knowledge, for the truth, and as her stomach turned, for revenge. She nodded before searching for her blade, taking time to belt it on her side as they waited for her. Once she was ready, she followed Nyeth out, with Korrenth close behind her.

A large gathering was present within the center of the town. Karja was being carried by another before being set in a seat. He winced from pain with the movement but gave a thankful nod to the man before he took stock of those around him. When he spotted Astoria, his face stiffened, and he pointedly looked away. Hatred bubbled in her chest, but bit the inside of her lip, trying to distract herself from the ruinous thoughts within her mind.

A large procession was marching towards Karja, and at its head was a man that Astoria could only believe was Haljn. The deference afforded to him was second only to what was given to Nyeth when she passed. He spoke slowly with several people before drawing up to Karja, his face filled with concern and anger.

Astoria watched as Karja slowly spoke into his ear. His gaze trailed over through the people, stopping on Nyeth for only a moment before it settled upon Astoria. There was a visceral disdain within his piercing gaze, but Astoria merely matched it with her own.

Come then. I'll show you firsthand.

Her hand rested on the hilt of her blade as a trickle ran down her spine, but suddenly, his line of sight was broken. Not by Nyeth or Korrenth though, but by Ghorun, the man's bulk interposing himself between Astoria and Haljn. He crossed arms over his chest and Astoria heard Nyeth give him small thanks for it.

Astoria peeked around Ghorun, watching as Haljn's face grew steadily more somber with each word. His eyes flashed dangerously, and when Karja paused for water, he straightened and started walking before Nyeth.

Her heartbeat quickened as the hairs on her neck rose, but neither Nyeth nor Ghorun moved when he approached.

"Where is my blade?" asked Haljn.

"I have it," said Ghorun. "Until the matter is done."

"That is inappropriate. Do you forget where you stand, Ghorun? These are my lands."

"As they were Sehren's," said Nyeth, stealing Astoria's retort. "Do not forget who Ghorun stands beside, Haljn."

206

"You would believe the word of the southerner? A group of people prone to lies and deceit solely for the purpose of putting us in the ground?" retorted Haljn, incensed.

"He did," said Astoria, drawing Korrenth's gaze and a sharp noise from her. Blood thundered in her head though, and she cared little for appearances.

"You dare address me?" spat Haljn, looking past Ghorun. Astoria pushed past the large man, shrugging off Korrenth's grasp and ignoring Nyeth's sound of protest to stand before him.

He quite a bit taller than Astoria and seemed older than even Nyeth. He eyed her with open loathing, but Astoria merely clenched her teeth as she said, "I do. You heard his words, now you hear mine."

"I will not suffer the lies. Karja's word is beyond reproach."

"Is that why he took your blade to kill *eiravuks* that had already been slain weeks before?" countered Astoria. "Beasts that inflicted wounds upon him that *we* treated? Beasts that would have torn him to pieces if not for Sehren's intervention? Or did he forget that part of his story?"

Haljn's lip curled at her impudence, but Astoria saw a small flicker of doubt in his eyes. She pressed on. "Go on then: Peel away his shirt, and you will find small dotted marks around the site of his wound. Techniques of triage that I doubt you or yours use. Go then, and see who is lying."

"You stand to lecture me about lies and deceit when you have not even told them who you are?"

Astoria felt a chill through her as she narrowed her eyes.

Haljn gnashed his teeth, "That is right. Come then, tell them all who you are and why you came so far north."

Astoria gripped the hilt of her sword painfully, about to answer when movement from her side drew her gaze. Haljn drew away suddenly as Ghorun moved to Karja. He picked the man up by the front of his shirt, lifting him from his seated position and drawing protests from everyone around.

"Is it true that she treated you?" he asked calmly.

207

Karja tried to reach up for Ghorun's hands, but hissed in pain as he bent his arms. "She lies."

"I do not think she does," said Ghorun. "Now, either tell us or I shall check myself."

"Unhand him, Ghorun! And Nyeth, control your hound!" shouted Haljn, looking to the others that had accompanied him.

"I would like to hear his answer myself," said Nyeth calmly. "If not, Ghorun lift his shirt."

Once again Karja tried to fight Ghorun's grip but shuddered from the pain as he reached up. Ghorun lifted the hem of the man's shirt, bringing it up to a recently healed wound, dotted around the edges with small pin marks.

"Sehren sewed his flesh together using a bone needle and sinew," explained Astoria. "There should be another similar wound on his back that I tended to."

Ghorun turned the man in his grasp, his eyes flickering between her and him, "So she speaks the truth. You were attacked in their lands and helped by them."

Karja said nothing, his face defiant as he stared at Ghorun.

"You lied," said Nyeth simply. "You took Haljn's blade and lied about your intentions with it. Is that not right?"

"I merely told him I needed it to fight a beast," said Karja as Ghorun set him down roughly in his seat.

"Is that true?" asked Nyeth, turning her gaze to Haljn. When the man seemed hesitant, Nyeth barked, "Answer me."

"That is true. He made no mention of what beast. By the looks of him, it seems that he did indeed put down a savage beast."

"I did that to him," commented Astoria. "I cut the tendons in his arms and cut his hamstrings so he could not flee while I went to Sehren's side. Before he…" Tears stung her eyes but she shook her head, willing them away.

Not here. Not now.

"*You* savaged him so?" asked Haljn, his face red with anger.

Astoria straightened as she met his murderous gaze, "I trussed him up like a deer and carried him to your people, right Karja? After you murdered Sehren for your own twisted reasons?" she shouted at him, trying to step forward but Nyeth's hand on her shoulder held a tight grip upon her.

Haljn spat, "You showed such disrespect to a *krusho*?"

"He deserved worse," retorted Astoria.

"Enough," intervened Nyeth, glaring at Astoria. He focused on Haljrn, "Karja has told you what happened. We have heard her words."

"You have not heard her reason," said Haljn. "That woman, that blight upon our lands, shares the blood of the king that left our people to bleed."

The procession grew intensely quiet. Haljn looked at Astoria, "Is that not right?"

"Who told you that?" asked Nyeth, truly confused as she looked between Astoria and Haljn.

"Karja."

"And who told him?"

"A knight from their lands, who told him that great ruin would come once again to our people if we did not find a way to bring her back to her kingdom." Muttering broke out from the procession, with several severe glaces going to Astoria. "The king seeks his heir, it seems, an impetuous child who fled from her duty."

"You take the words of a man from the south and then tell me that all of us speak nothing but lies?" asked Astoria quietly. "Or rather, do you take his words because they justify your hate?"

Haljn looked affronted.

"All I have heard from every one of you is that we lie," continued Astoria, her voice shaking with anger. "That we lie and deceive. But when the first lie you hear makes your truth sweeter to your ears, you believe it. You use it to justify coming into our lands to disrupt our peace. Peace that we fought for. That we earned."

She looked pointedly at Karja, who once again broke her gaze.

"Are you proud to call yourself honorable for that? Are you glad to know that you killed a man that only sought a reprieve from the world?"

"I never said I was glad," replied Karja, his voice turning all eyes to him. "I did what I did for my people. I asked him to have you leave peacefully. He drew his blade in response."

"You came to force me to leave *our* lands," shouted Astoria, "and then you bit off more than you could chew with Sehren."

"He is the one who is dead."

"Because I let you live, you piece of shit!" Astoria screamed at him. "Because I hesitated when I saw it was you attacking us. And once again I kept you alive. I fed you and watered you while I carried your limp and useless body back to your people and now you feed them lies!"

Her voice broke with anger, her vision going red as she stared at the man. Tears clouded it though as the rage abated, "We did nothing to any of you, and that is how you repay us. And then you call us evil." Tears fell down her cheeks. She watched Karja look away with guilt.

Nyeth stepped before Haljn, "Karja slew a chief in their own lands of his own volition. Do you deny that?"

"No. But I believe his belief in the nature of the threat. He was protecting our people."

"Karja," said Ghorun, "that woman has proven to me time and time again to be an exception to her people. Sehren proved to us all that even those bearing their blood can be honorable."

"I am a *krusho*, as are you Ghorun. Would you not do anything you could to protect the people?" asked Karja.

"If I felt they were in danger, yes. But nothing in the years I have known them would indicate that kind of threat."

Karja shook his head, "You do not remember then. He defeated Nyeth, did he not?"

The procession grew quiet once more.

"Is that not how he secured passage through the lands, chief?" he continued. "He said as much before we fought. You lost to him in a *kruparu,* and he forced you to let him through."

Nyeth hesitated in her answer, drawing some muttering from the crowd when Astoria said, "It was a draw."

They all focused on her. She steadied her voice, "Sehren forced a draw with her because I was in danger. There was no winner or loser. It was my life for hers."

Nyeth's silver eyes flashed, knowing that Astoria was lying. She didn't care.

Haljn said, "You drew danger to our chief?"

"Nyeth drew first, without regard. Sehren did what he could as he did then. We traded lives solely for passage and peace."

Astoria knew then that she would find no solace from this, nothing that would ease the pain in her heart. Shaking, she gave Karja a glance before looking over Haljn and saying, "We wanted somewhere away from everyone, away from the lies, the danger, and the need to kill other people. Karja brought that to our door, and you expected us to roll over. We did not. I know you will not take his life, and I know you will never see that as wrong."

Astoria mustered all the anger and hate she could as she uttered, "You support a man that murdered peace. I will never forget that. Ever." She gave one final glare to Karja before looking at Nyeth expectantly.

She set her gaze upon Haljn, "Does he walk free?"

"I will not punish him for his belief in our safety."

Nyeth gave a stiff nod, "Very well then. Ghorun, leave the man be."

As Ghorun let out a sigh, he walked by Haljn before stopping and saying, "You may have forgiven him, but it is as the girl said: I will not forget that you let one of your sworn walk into another chief's land with your blade to kill them."

Haljn stood defiantly, "And why is that?"

211

"Because that proves you will allow yours to endanger our people, on their whim, while feeding you lies. Do not expect welcome in our lands, Haljn. And if I should find that you have indeed come into our lands, then know I will exercise the same faith that you bestowed upon Sehren. I will remove any threat without hesitation, and I will not return them to you as she had."

Haljn looked stricken, "You would turn against your kin?"

"You already have. You allowed him to walk free. We will not forget."

Astoria looked at Ghorun as he returned to Nyeth's side, the massive man giving her a nod of solidarity. Haljn looked murderous but remained silent as he bowed his head to Nyeth.

Nyeth glanced at Astoria, with a look she already knew was coming.

It's time to go home.

NYETH.

"This is where we part ways, Astoria," said Nyeth as led the woman to the edge of their woods. She could see the sprawling lands of the kingdom beyond, and it did little to steady the beating in her heart as she regarded it. Astoria had been silent after Karja had been absolved, but Nyeth heard her soft cries in the night when they broke for camp. She warred with two emotions within her: the sympathy of a companion so close lost to an injustice and the bitterness of having someone who could potentially bring destruction and ruin to their people. Nyeth tried to steady the hate within her in the wake of the news that she had dismissed so readily.

Sehren was dead.

It was unsettling to her. Sehren had proven almost as indomitable as the land he had inhabited, the man never bowed or bent by the savageness of the world he lived in. Time and time again Nyeth had challenged him to reassert herself, initially to prove to herself that she was truly his better, while later on she wished simply to learn what he had learned in his time in the wilds. He had refused, however, stating that he had nothing to gain by throwing away his life, had no desire to try and take hers, and the absence of both had stolen any true desire for him to fight her. Nyeth found it strange at first, but understood that Sehren in his core fought solely for purpose. Every time he drew his blade, there was a solid reason in his mind that he had done so.

And now he was gone.

Astoria nodded at the woman, a pack laden with goods on her back. She adjusted the straps as she glanced out over the region, her blue eyes filled with a solemness that quelled Nyeth's budding disdain. Astoria had distorted Nyeth's expectation. Even in her grief, she proved to be helpful and kind, if not a bit stiff about it. She knew that the woman was trying not to lay blame upon her shoulders, but Nyeth saw her own hate quite clearly when she met the woman's gaze.

"I wish you well in the future," said Astoria quietly.

Nyeth wanted to say something to her, but Astoria quickly turned on her heel and marched off, her pace quickening as she broke away from the edge of the forest into the kingdom.

"It is odd," said Ghorun, his arms over his chest.

"What is?"

"They are getting their heir back, but because of Karja's actions, should she take the throne, she may march back anyways for revenge," he said with a frown.

"Possible," Nyeth watched her for a bit longer before turning around herself, "but I doubt she will."

"Me too."

Nyeth had noticed that Ghorun seemed partial to the woman, as much as he could be towards anyone of southern descent. Even when he had continued their trade while Nyeth had been with child, Ghorun had never spoken positively about Sehren, and yet when they shared watch during their march to escort Astoria, Ghorun had lamented her loss, and even used his hulking stature to secure accommodations for them as they trekked from village to village. Few found themselves brave in the shadow of Ghorun, a fact that he had played on for years. Nyeth knew he would meet that expectation as well if someone stepped before them, and while he never indulged in the savagery of battle, he was no stranger to it.

Nyeth turned away from the trail that Astoria took, wondering if the woman would ever come to terms with her grief. She knew that Karja and his kin had stolen from her the peace that she had come to

214

know, and Nyeth truly wished that the woman found something else to help placate grief that had nestled in her heart.

"The Chuyara will be resolute in their anger until the blade is returned to them," said Nyeth to Ghorun as they walked.

"Let them be. Better for them to lose that than for Haljn to lose his head."

"You don't believe for an instant that he did not know of Karja's actions, do you?"

"Not at all. That would be like you being unaware of what Korrenth would do in your absence. None of this makes sense, and even if it is resolved, there will be strife."

Nyeth chewed on her cheek, "Our people will have to remain neutral for all the tribes' sake. We cannot move against the Chuyara after Haljn absolved Karja, nor can we place stringent measures on them otherwise."

"You cannot. However, my people, my clan, can and will. The days of chiefs killing one another cannot return, for if that were to occur once more, then our people would not have to worry about the kingdom. We would be extinct before Astoria or the king could march to war."

Nyeth bit through the side of her cheek, tasting blood as she remembered. Long before *Javeaf,* their people had been much more apt to infighting with one another, as tribes saw themselves as wholly different people from one another. Territory was fought and lost and battle was common among one another over slights. However, the worst casualties were the children of chieftains, as they tended to challenge other chieftains for control of their people. Upstarts and challengers had come and gone and eventually the once vast number of tribes had become the seven that lived in this age.

"It would be a folly indeed. We can ill afford to disrupt our people's restoration, but I know this will stir up old grudges and rivalries that could sever bonds between the people," said Nyeth.

"If you wish for me to return the blade, chief, I will," said Ghorun with no hesitation.

Nyeth shook her head, "We must stand firm in that decision. I would not wish to alienate your clan because of my own misgivings. The more solidarity we share with this, the better off we will be. I will need to speak to Aida though, once she arrives. I fear she will be the more tumultuous about this."

"Because of her intentions for Sehren?"

"Because she is the youngest chieftain," explained Nyeth. "I know she will fear reprisal if she openly supports your decisions, or will feel like she will lose my support if she joins the Chuyara cause. I wish to tell her to go with her own decision, but that I will always try to work towards solidarity."

"She has a sound head on her shoulders," said Ghorun. "I feel that with some explanation, she will come to the right choice."

Nyeth nodded, her gaze sweeping before her as they continued walking back to the village. She took a glance over her shoulder, hoping that Astoria would heed her warning and follow the road home.

Nyeth returned back to the village with Ghorun trailing behind. Their trek was a silent one, with both of them using the *kymbra* to lessen the distance home. Even though she felt fatigued, she was filled with an anxious energy as she considered what she had left to do.

"Ghorun, when the others get here, make sure they talk with me first."

"Of course, chief," he replied. "I imagine many, if not all, of the Chuyara have left."

"With supporters of their own."

Ghorun let out a gruff laugh, "Of that, I doubt. Their actions, both Haljn's and his *krusho's,* broke our traditions."

"Even still, despite my intentions there was still ill-will towards Sehren and his ward. You saw how the people glowered at her when she was there."

"I did. And did you see how they cowered when she stood defiant before them?" Ghorun got a glimmer of amusement in his eyes, "Her mere words and presence caused fear to run through them."

Nyeth shook her head again, "Karja proclaimed that she killed two other *krusho*. I am certain they believed her to be almost akin to a dangerous animal, especially with her outbursts."

"Outbursts which I noticed, you did not interrupt or stop."

Nyeth set a gaze upon him, "I share her sentiment, even if I could not see eye to eye with her."

"You think the other tribes will see Sehren's death as a boon?"

"It is too early to say." Nyeth felt a tightness in her chest as her head buzzed with the thoughts. "I know there was animosity to my decision, and those that held it within them will see this as both a victory for them and a slight against my will."

Ghorun shook his head before he stroked his chin in thought. With a bow of his head, he walked off into the village. Nyeth trailed his path for a moment before diverging and making her way to her cabin. She heard murmurs from people she passed, the dissonance heavy in the air. Her decision to condemn Haljn's decision had set a tenseness through her people. Nyeth knew it would pass, but it would be an arduous time until then. She stepped inside the cabin and took a seat on the bed as she took a deep breath.

This cannot happen again.

She shook with frustration and anger as she took another breath. Her people killing one another was never supposed to be the case, ever again. Nyeth remembered the days when she had to spill the blood of her kin, remembered every young upstart that dared to step to her. There was never pleasure or cruelty in her victories. Rather, they were carried out with the simplicity that her father and grandmother instilled in her: let her strength show through. But now, with Karja's attack on Sehren, it changed the relative peace that her people had shared for the better part of three decades. Furthermore, it undermined her rule of the people, for if others thought that Sehren was not worthy of being afforded the same rights and privileges of the other chiefs, then it meant her word was worth less than they had led her to believe.

Not again. I will not let this happen again.

Nyeth let out the breath she had been holding, her gaze traveling to the window of the cabin. She allowed herself this moment, but only this moment, to doubt. With the other chieftains coming, she needed to be steady, composed, and succinct. She rose from the bed and crossed the room to the door. She took a glance, a moment to remember that Astoria had just sat on that same bed, her mind teeming with anxious energy. A wry smile crossed her face as she left.

Nyeth walked amongst her people, taking stock of their demeanor while she spoke with them. Some possessed the same anxious energy that had built inside of her, but she needed to be the stone for her people to hold to, the pillar they could rest their worries upon. She allayed their fears as best as she could, firmly but graciously, until Korrenth called for her as the sun began to wane.

"They are here."

Nyeth nodded, signaling with her head back to her cabin. Korrenth went to the approaching entourages, the members of the Varjund and Kabrea marching determinedly. They broke ranks once they reached the village center, and Nyeth watched as Aida, garbed in leathers with her hair banded from her face, strode over to her.

"*Cesogez*," she said, bowing respectfully. Her voice dropped, filling with a disquieted tone. "Is it true?"

"It is," said Nyeth stiffly. "By Karja's own admission, he slew the Ombroj chieftain."

Aida spat on the ground, "And he still walks?!"

"Haljn absolved him of his actions."

"Since when did his word override all of us?" Aida shook her head. "I was under the impression that Nyeth, not Haljn, led the people."

"It is a complicated matter, Aida," said Nyeth, her patience wearing with the younger woman. "When Olwynn arrives I will discuss it in detail with you both."

Aida gave a stiff nod. Her eyes still held obvious contempt for the subject at hand. She scanned the people closest to them before Nyeth said, "The Chuyara left many days ago."

"Of course. Guilty minds make anxious feet."

"Or perhaps they wished to avoid unnecessary conflict."

Aida gave her a wry smile before she wandered off for a moment, talking to her own people as they waited.

Olwynn arrived with his people a few moments later. He bowed his head respectfully towards Nyeth before giving a courteous nod to Aida. "*Cesogez.*"

"I apologize for the hasty nature of my request," said Nyeth. "I would not have called for you though if it was not serious."

"I have heard," said Olwynn, drawing a nod from Aida as she crossed her arms over her chest. "The Chuyara have made a grave error. Did the *krusho* make mention of his thoughts up to the act?"

"What difference does that make?" protested Aida, stealing Nyeth's answer. "He acted against the will of the people. Our collective will and our choice."

"He had his reasons," said Nyeth. "Ones I think might warrant review."

"And did he voice his reasons to his chief, or to you? Did he call us together to try and remedy this as a people?" Aida let out a huff, "He stole away with his own thoughts and attacked a chieftain."

"His reasons were because of the potential threat of a southern invasion." Nyeth's curt tone stole Aida's bluster. "He acted in accordance with his memory and the doctrine I have enforced for so many years."

"A southern invasion?" asked Aida incredulity. "A threat like that and he conferred with whom, exactly? Was Haljn aware of the threat before he marched off?"

"I am not inclined to believe he was, but regardless, Haljn has supported his actions based upon his trust in Karja. As is his right with his kin."

"And what of our kin?" asked Aida. "What if this loose, raving dog decides that the Thunzi, or Kabrea, or the Varjud are a threat? Are we to stand aside and let them walk through the villages killing our babes because of some 'southern threat'? Conversely, what if I feel that their actions threaten our people? Should I send my kin out to alleviate the threat and then beg forgiveness afterwards?"

"Aida. Enough." Olwynn's voice was ill-tempered. Aida recoiled but still sported a scowl. "Haljn exercised his right as a chief, just as you or I could."

"He whispers into the ears of a blind chief that in turn soothed his actions. And you and Nyeth both believe that to be fair, even if the outcome is not what you agree with." Aida huffed, "If we are not here to discuss the consequences of Haljn's folly, then why summon us?"

"Because I do not want this action splintering the tribes," said Nyeth. "Our solidarity has given us the ability to grow and rebuild. It is strength and temperance we need now."

"We showed strength during the remembrance, when all of us sat with the Ombroj and made him one of our own," said Aida. "We showed temperance when we set aside our grudges and hate to bring him into our villages, with our children, and taught him the ways of our people. Those are not what we need now for Haljn and his people. By our ways, the Ombroj was our flesh and blood."

Nyeth refrained from sighing, the weight on her growing in the wake of Aida's words, "Yes. He was. Haljn and Karja, and all of the Chuyara are our flesh and blood as well."

"A notion they do not have an understanding of."

"What would you do, Aida?" asked Olwynn. "Would you go and slay Haljn and corral his people as a tyrant?"

"I have no use for the Chuyara. It is obvious they share none of the principles me and mine hold true, and I have no interest in reforming them." Aida met Olwynn's accusing gaze with a determined one, "Survival kept us together. Then it was Nyeth's steady hand. It seems they hold neither in high regard anymore."

"You would go to war, Aida?"

"Never. I do not hunger for blood or vengeance, Olwynn. I demand only from other chieftains what has been expected of me since I took lead of my own." Aida became serious, calming as she spoke, "Our lands have tasted the blood of our people far too often for my liking. However, the Kabrea will remember this, and I am certain others will as well. The Chuyara will find no respite in our lands, and that is a sentiment that I believe will be shared among others."

"You would incite the people?" Olwynn's disapproving glare broke against Aida's retort.

"No. I have no need to. I will simply tell them the truth, and those that share my devotion to our people and ways will be incited on their own."

"You claim to put much stock into our traditions, Aida," said Nyeth. "If I demanded that you grant the Chuyara pardon for this for the solidarity of our people, would you contest?"

"Are you?"

"Am I what?"

"Demanding it?"

Nyeth repressed a smile for the woman as she saw her eyes sparkling with insight and understanding. "I am no longer the tyrant upholding our ways."

"Then I leave myself to consider your words for the future, but I will maintain my stance."

"As is your right. And as is Haljn's right."

Aida got a shrewd look on her face. She looked at Olwynn, "And what will the Varjud do?"

"We follow the *cesogez*," he stated firmly. "Our people are stronger together. It would be poor to let our people suffer as a whole. We will watch and be aware, but we will keep the lines open."

Nyeth nodded her approval, "Aida. I am not going to tell you what to do. I simply will tell you that our people are stronger together."

"They are, but those that feel outside the fold are going to feel endangered more now than ever." Aida gave Nyeth a bow before saying, "My people will provide for the meal this evening. I am sure you and Olwynn will have more to discuss."

"You feel it is unimportant to you?" asked Nyeth.

"I feel that my focus is not on the same goals that you wish to have at the moment," clarified Aida. "When I find that, I will return."

Aida bowed once more with a respectful nod to Olwynn before leaving.

"She is still learning."

"She has every right to." Nyeth stretched her neck before saying, "It will become more complicated next season, Olwynn."

"We will hold," he said confidently, "even with the disruption this will cause, our people hold you in high regard. They will look to you and defer to your decisions."

Nyeth nodded, but she couldn't help the small tinge of frustration as she thought of how her decision beforehand had brought them to this point.

ASTORIA.

While the road had become different, the path worn in a different manner over the years, there was a sense of familiarity in Astoria's mind as she tread it. The small, worn path that Termesa had carried them upon. The creaking of the wagon filled her mind as she remembered lying upon their goods, everything that Sehren had been able to get them. All of the comforts and supplies they needed for the road ahead. She felt a gripping grief, a lingering shade that fell upon her as she took each step towards the kingdom.

Towards home.

Astoria hated the notion. She hadn't wanted to consider the kingdom home and hadn't ever intended on returning even with her noble claim. She and Sehren had made their home as far as she had been concerned. While she had once held thoughts of what life would've been like growing up at the Friar's Reprieve and had spent long nights thinking of Rosline and Celeste and all the others that had worked alongside her, her wistfulness had been dispelled by the soft breathing of Sehren beside her.

No, the kingdom had never been her goal. She believed that over time, the other people of the north would come to accept her, with Sehren making great strides in building rapport with the other tribes. She dreamed of the days when she could walk underneath the canopies of the vast lands of Senkama, learning of the different people that lived within.

It had been a child's dream. A fanciful tale that had shown Astoria just how much more she had to learn. They would have never accepted her, even if she had come to bear Sehren's children. They would have never allowed her to meet with the others, to hear the chittering of the children that Sehren told her ran rampant through the villages, or to learn at the side of Nyeth for what would be expected from her.

Karja had shown her in stark relief what the northern people thought of her, and in her grief and anger, that hate was reflected in her soul. Even walking alongside Nyeth, who had so calmly accepted that Karja would live, had proven more of an ordeal than she had believed, with every night she spent in her presence a reminder that the woman detested her. She had supported her not because she liked Astoria, but because she had believed in Sehren. She nursed resentment towards Astoria solely because her heart beat with the blood of the south, and now Astoria understood that caustic hatred.

Each step along the well-traveled path brought Astoria closer to the final town they had visited before leaving the kingdom's influence. She recalled it being named Harthglen, the small village a haven for trappers and loggers. With a sigh, she stopped and pulled the pack from her back. She dug through it, looking for the threadbare coin purse. While Sehren had spent as much of his coin as possible before they left the kingdom, he still had quite a bit left as they had left late in the season, with little to spend it on with the restrictive stock. Her tally left her at twenty-seven of the gold pieces, with a little over twice that amount in silver. Tying the purse to her belt, she picked up her pack before making sure the hilt of Sehren's blade was within reach.

My blade now, I would guess...

She choked up at the thought. With a shaking grip, she drew the sword from its scabbard with barely a whisper, the white steel catching the sunlight. The edge was as fine as it had always been, and she ran her thumb along the deep, black fuller. Astoria stared into the steel, seeing the hint of her reflection in it. She wondered how long she would keep it. It was a remnant of Sehren, one of his belongings, but she also knew that it had belonged to his mother and from what she had learned, his people before that.

I'll bury it at the farm. I didn't want to leave it in the north with them. I know that Sehren regarded the farm as his true home in the kingdom.

She rubbed her eyes, willing the tears not to fall, before she slid the steel back into the scabbard. Determined, she followed the path, and as the sun began to set along the horizon, she saw the town on the edge of the horizon.

Astoria kept pushing, even after the night fell in full, the comfort of the moonlight guiding her steps. She passed into the town, being halted by a militiaman as she approached.

"Oi, you're lookin' like the rough sort," he said, brandishing his spear in her direction as he cocked his head. "You don't look familiar."

"Just passing through," she said. The rough Candraman sparked images of drunk patrons and dancing people in the city. Astoria shook her head to dispel the flood of images in her mind, "I'm hopin' I can find a place to stay for a day or two and then be on my way."

"Aye, and to where are you headin'?"

Astoria hesitated a moment, before saying, "Orinth."

"That's a long walk," he said.

"Don't I know it. Please, I would just like a place to stay for the evenin' and perhaps a bath."

The militiaman gave her another once over, before nodding curtly, "Look for the Badger's Nest, in the middle o' the town. They should have a few rooms available."

She fished a silver piece from her coin purse and tossed it to the guard. "Thank you." He stumbled a bit to catch it, smiling appreciatively at her as she passed him.

Astoria followed the beaten path, the memories flooding back to her. She didn't recall there being militia before, but it had been a long time since she had come to the town. Perhaps there were brigands in the area and the increased presence was to protect the town. Shrugging, she continued walking before she came upon a large two-storied building, with an entrance surrounded by a brick staircase that led to a basement. The sounds of drunken laughter, although muffled, emanated from within. Astoria felt her heartstrings tugged as she approached the door. She pushed it open, her eyes scanning the scene before her.

She saw almost a dozen round tables with a smattering of people drinking and eating, with a heavy-set woman at the bar tucked away in the corner. Five of the twelve stools were occupied and they talked in loud tones. There was a strained feeling in the air, and she noticed that wary glances made their way to her before returning to their cups.

"Welcome to the Badger's Nest," called a voice beside her. She faced the man, a taller, slim man with smiling brown eyes and a genial smile. A rough shadow of hair ran down his cheeks and chin, "The name's Otto. Are you going to be needing a room?" His eyes scanned the laden pack on Astoria's pack and a glimmer of familiarity twinkled in his eyes.

Astoria nodded, "For two, maybe three nights."

"Aye then," he replied, scrunching his brow as he looked over her face. He grabbed a small lamp from beside him and beckoned with his head towards the staircase tucked away against the left of the common room. "This way then. We'll get you sorted out."

Astoria followed behind, marking well the men that were watching her. She didn't feel animosity from them and believed that they were simply taking in her odd appearance.

"You a hunter?" he asked as he led her.

"Why'd you think that?"

He grinned, "Been doing this a while. You got a thick pack, hunting leathers, and while it's not rare to see a woman so outfitted, few carry so many weapons." He gave her an appreciative smile, "It's a compliment: Hunters keep the lands 'round the town safe and that helps everyone." His voice was kind, and Astoria couldn't help but smile at his consideration of the townsfolk.

"I do hunt every now and then," she said with a proud tone, "but just travelin' through at the moment."

226

"Shame. The town could use more people like you," he stopped before a door, pulling an iron keyring from his belt and sorting through it. He found the key and inserted it, turning it in the lock as he pushed the door open. With a small clank, he set the lamp down on a small table against the wall before he lifted the glass. Using a small timber, he lit the candle that sat upon the table. A single bed with a chest at the foot of it took up much of the room, and there was a curtained window opposite of the table. Shaking out the burning timber, he smiled and looked to them, "Will this be okay?"

"Sure will. What's the price?" said Astoria, trying to shake away the burning feeling in her eyes, "and you guys have tubs for bathing right?"

Otto tilted his head before looking her up and down with a nod, "Aye, we do."

"The guard told me on the way in."

"Ah, right! Gotta get around to thanking them. They always send whoever asks for a room." He smiled again, "'Fraid dinner's already been long and done, but if you're hankering for something, I can see if I can rustle something up for you."

"No, that's okay. Thank you, Otto."

"Of course. If you're wanting I can get you settled for the room, and if you're still looking for that bath, I can get that set up for you as well."

Astoria nodded as he grinned again before ducking his head and leaving the room. Astoria set her stuff down beside the chest at the foot of the bed before walking to the window and feeling the crushing nostalgia hit her.

We could've stayed here if it wasn't for the Knights, Sehren. We would've been happy.

She clutched the curtains as tears streamed down her face. Fighting the urge to rip the curtains from the wall, she settled herself before wiping away the tears and heading to the door. A small key was set on the table, and Astoria pocketed it, using it to lock the door before heading downstairs. She felt gazes upon her as she walked over to Otto, who was writing in a ledger. She ignored them though, her hand resting on the hilt of her sword.

Otto looked her over, his eyes landing on her sword, before nodding, "So then, the two nights? Or three?"

"Three," she said. Now that she had stopped in a familiar place, the urging to keep marching forward had subsided. She started examining what options she did have to her, not sure if making back to the city of Isle would be the best decision. She fished the coins from the purse on her belt before scattering them upon the counter.

"Right! Everything will be in order, just need a name to set the room under," he said cheerily.

Astoria hesitated, "Is it okay if I go without, for now?"

Otto looked curious, cocking his head thoughtfully.

"Is that okay?'

"It's not the first time I've been asked it, but usually it's from more unsavory looking folk," he said, looking her up and down. "But I've been chewed out enough in my lifetime so 'fraid I can't do that, as much as I understand it."

"You do?"

"Aye. I don't ask a lot of questions, but I can see someone that's fretting about something serious when they pass by. Not sure what ails you, but I know that sometimes, you just want to be somewhere it won't bother you none," he said easily. He sorted through the ledger, "Tell you what: how's about you join me for a drink later, after most the folk are gone, and I'll put you under another name?"

Astoria felt a tinge of embarrassment, remembering that Sehren had done the same thing long before. "Sure, that'll be fine."

Otto grinned with a nod, "How's 'Leanne' then?"

Astoria froze a moment, before slowly nodding. "Right. About that bath then."

"Aye, I'll get one of the tubs filled up in the basement, and I'll fetch you when it's ready. Sound good?"

"Aye, that's fine." She hoped her face hadn't betrayed her, but Otto continued smiling at her. With a wave, Astoria returned to her room, locking the door behind her and taking a deep breath as she laid on the bed.

I'm here now, but should I stop here? I could keep going, find another place like this and just... what?

Astoria felt a wildness in her heart, one that had burned since she had accepted that Sehren and her were going to live in the untamed lands of the north. It raged on, now fueled by an anger that she knew couldn't be quelled by a simple life in the town.

Do I go back then, to Isle and what? Find this Ricard? Even then, what would I even do? What could I ever do?

Astoria ground her teeth, the strain causing her jaw to lock slightly as she did. She could find him and accuse him. She could attempt to kill him, but what would that do for her? Would she even be happy? She'd become a fugitive and would have to flee the kingdom, just as they had to years ago. Was she ready for that again? This time, she'd be alone.

I'm tired of running.

She knew that the wildness within her was driving her, mixed with her own fear and anger.

You never prepared me for this Sehren.

She was surprised by the resentment, by the unfairness that stung her. Sehren had never talked of coming back to the kingdom, and while she had entertained the idea, she had always believed that it was a dream. Sehren had never fostered the idea of returning, but even if he had, what would they have done? If what Karja had said was true, then her identity would be known in the city. She could very well be walking into a trap.

Or maybe, I am walking to my fate. Maybe Isle is the best answer after all.

She thought of Aruhn, the barkeep probably having taken a backseat at his tavern. She thought of Rosline, wondering if she still worked at the tavern, and of Celeste, who was probably running its day to day while Aruhn went back to brewing. She thought of the others that met frequently with the barkeep, contemplating whether or not Celeste would be dealing with them as well. She thought of Jaks, and a spark came into her mind.

If he's still there... he had known. He and that woman. He would be able to help me with what I want.

Astoria could make out the man's peculiar attire and face in her mind's eye, and suddenly, there was a goal. She could go to Isle, and in turn, she could learn more about what was going on. He had known many things, and by Sehren's admittance, had even known where that clandestine guild had kept his wife. If anyone could help her find a path, a goal, Jaks would be the one, even if he hadn't seen her in years. Maybe the wily man would be able to get her somewhere safe in the south, away from the reach of the city.

She was pulled from her thoughts by a soft knock. Astoria rose from the bed before walking over to the door and creaking it open. Otto stood outside by the opposite wall, giving her space as she opened it.

"The tub's prepared," he said simply. "Just head to the basement and you'll find it waiting. I wouldn't wait too long though. Don't want it to get too cool." He gave her a bow before heading down the hall. Astoria followed behind him, locking the door as she made her way to the basement. Otto waved at her as she left the common room, and she followed her memory to the basement where she saw the wooden tubs. They were banded with metal, each surrounded by a low-hanging curtain that hung from an iron ring on the ceiling. She saw a wooden step nailed into the side of it, along with a roughspun towel settled beside it on the floor.

Pulling the curtain shut, she unbuckled her belt and set it beside the towel. She divested herself of her clothing, piling it beside her belt before climbing into the tub and dipping into the water. It was warm and soothing, and as soon as it enveloped her, the grime of the road melted away as relief rushed through her. Her mind, once buzzing with anxious thoughts, calmed, letting her enjoy the warm water. She found that she had a harder time getting comfortable than when she was last there but rested against the side of the tub either way. Her gaze went to the ceiling.

We could have been here the whole time.

A surge of anger and frustration coursed through her. They had already sorted out where they were going to stay, and Astoria remembered that she had been offered a job there at the tavern. Sehren would have still decided to live out in the hunting cottage he had found, but together, they would've been part of the town.

How different would it have been?

Astoria knew foremost that she would not have been able to help Sehren in combat if they had stayed. Not in the way she had now. She would have been softer likely, her body more attuned to the life of a barmaid rather than a huntress. Her skin would have been dotted and lined with less scars, and she knew that the taut, lean muscle she had gained over the years wouldn't be as familiar. The weight of the sword on her side would've been foreign rather than comforting, and perhaps, they would have had peace. She probably wouldn't know the Senkaman tongue, and after a certain amount of time, maybe even Sehren would have stopped training.

No. He would do his dance every day, as he always had, and probably gone hunting alongside Termesa.

Her heart hurt as she realized that Termesa would be alive. She would be with Sehren at the cabin, likely drawing the wagon whenever they came to town to trade. He would be a grizzled hunter, but the town would've come to know him as a capable, honest man.

All while they lived a life with different names and different backgrounds.

Could I have lived that way? Lying to everyone?

Astoria sank into the water, letting the surface of it just sit below her nose.

That's what I'll have to do if I go back.

Astoria settled in the water, letting her thoughts run rampant.

After she finished drying off and dressing, Astoria made her way back into the common room, where she saw several people still carousing. They spoke in bawdy voices, their words slurred from the drink. It brought a smile to her face as she saw the once familiar scene after all the years.

"Have a good soak?" asked Otto as she walked by.

"I did. Thank you."

He smiled, "Not a problem. Nothing like a nice bath after a long time on the road. You still up for that drink or you looking to rest for the night?"

Astoria was slightly confused, "I thought that was for the favor?"

"Aye, but you're gonna be here another day or so. I imagine the road was long, so I wouldn't be insulted if you wanted to turn in."

She gave him a once over before nodding and saying, "I think I will turn in tonight, just to rest. Tomorrow then?"

"Aye. Have a good night then," he bowed his head as he leafed through the ledger before him. Astoria waved before heading back to her room. After setting everything down, she took a glance out the window once more before shutting it and laying upon the bed.

She draped her arm over her eyes, trying to stymie her racing thoughts as she considered her next step. Try as she might though, she kept remembering the small trip they had taken to the small pond outside the village, and Astoria found her tiredness accompanied by tears.

We could have been so happy

ROSLINE.

Rosline removed the cloth from her eyes, feeling exhausted after a long day. Lately, when she had taken to her sight, she found herself distracted as she worked. More often than not she wanted to look north, to see Astoria again, but try as she might, she found she was unable to see the woman again in the pitched gloom. Eleanor hadn't made mention of her lacking work at the time, but Rosline could feel her disappointment with her work. At mealtimes, when Rosline and Eleanor made plans about what they should do, Rosline had been ill-prepared to answer her questions, a fact that Eleanor, while understanding, did not appreciate from her pupil.

Rosline stared into the basin, wondering where this obsession with Astoria was coming from. It had been years since she had even actively thought of the woman, and it hadn't been uncommon for stretches of months to pass without her gracing her thoughts once. And yet, that poignant dream was burned so vividly in her mind that she couldn't help but wonder what had happened to her, and by extension, to Sehren.

No, her curiosity over Astoria's fate hadn't abated, and Rosline felt that until she had a tangible answer, she would find herself distracted in her work and life.

As she rinsed her hands in the basin, Rosline paused, listening to the scuffling noises of the servants walking through the halls. It was late; everything was winding down for the coming days of the festival, and Rosline knew that Eleanor would spend much time there spreading her influence and meeting with more potential allies for them. There was talk of her meeting with suitors as well, but Rosline repressed a smirk about the rumor. Eleanor had explicitly told Rosline that unless she found herself blessed with a suitor that would allow her to continue running her own business and household without becoming subservient to them, then she would remain without a spouse.

She couldn't blame her. When Rosline had accompanied Eleanor to calls to the manors of other lords, she had been dismayed to see the obvious expectations put upon not only her but upon Eleanor. It was expected, and when Eleanor had only delivered kind courtesy instead of what was expected, the hospitality of their host had dropped considerably. Eleanor hadn't minded though; more often than not, it was simply a courtesy call rather than anything that Eleanor had considered fully, not wishing to insult anyone in any circle of the lords. With everything finally returning to normal after the upheaval of the lords and the trials of the Knights, the aristocrats had gone back to their self-serving ways, and Eleanor had quickly shown Rosline just how little the gilded words of the elite class meant when they perceived an insult against them.

Rosline, while appreciative of the life that Eleanor had given her, disliked the constant dance of the aristocrats. As a barmaid, she had only really dealt with lords bored with their wives, or young lords looking to experience more of what the world had to offer before their nuptials had been established. In most instances, Rosline had profited from their dalliances, letting Aruhn know the names of the lords. In turn, the tavern had profited overall and life had been simple. With the requirements of her station, however, Rosline had learn how to rub elbows, so to speak, with the lords and ladies of Isle, and while the dinners and other accommodations made for her due to her relationship to Eleanor had proved exciting at first, eventually it had lost its luster, instead replaced with a feeling of unease as she noticed the condescension associated with it.

Rosline left her washroom, stepping back into her room and sitting at her desk. She grabbed the brush and began working through the tangle that had developed through the day, her eyes drawn to the door when she heard hasty footsteps followed by heeled-boots. It creaked open. Her daughter's wide grin greeted her followed by Jaks and his customary smirk. Rosline set down the brush as she rose. Her smile widened as she threw her arms around him and placed a kiss upon his cheek.

"How was she today?"

"As usual, rambunctious and utterly stunning to the other children around her. You'd think people would learn to not duel wits with a daughter of my loins, but they do, leaving them to their dismay and confused amusement."

Rosline smiled, looking at Kyrah with pride. She indeed had astounded most with her wit and mindfulness, harboring the kindness of her mother with the inner fire of her father. She was quickly removing her outerwear, tangling herself for only a moment in her trousers before stumbling to the floor and removing her boots.

"And everything else?"

Jaks' eyes glittered, "The city's quiet and has been for years now. I doubt that will change until the succession of the new royal line. With that, there will be a scattering of the people, and depending on who it is, there may be a shift within the city itself."

Rosline frowned, thinking of her daughter. "You think you are in danger?"

"I'm always in danger, and I would prefer to keep it that way. Life becomes precarious when you're not on edge," said Jaks with a smirk. Rosline felt uneasy. "Fret not, unlike many others Rosline, should there be an upheaval of my people in the wake of a new king, we will be safe."

"How can you be sure?"

"You have the security of a prominent lady of the city," said Jaks, "while I have my own contingencies."

Rosline met his gaze, the cool confidence within his segmented eyes allaying her concerns. In all her years knowing the roguish man, she had never heard of anyone bold enough to take a shot at him, noble or not. But her gaze trailed over to her daughter, and her worry returned tenfold, thinking of the people that would harm her simply to do harm to Jaks.

"I told you, it will be a terrible day indeed should someone wish to bring her harm," said Jaks confidently.

"You can't be everywhere, Jaks. And eventually she'll get older, wanting her own life. What then?"

Jaks smirked, his face filled with cunning as he said, "Rosline, my life's goals have been to let my competitors know that I am indeed everywhere. I promise you, things will be fine for her."

Rosline sighed, before leaning against Jaks. She felt a tug at the hem of her dress. Kyrah said, "Mama! You should have seen the others. They were so surprised."

"Were they now?" asked Rosline, kneeling down and picking up Kyrah. The girl nodded with bright enthusiasm.

"They asked me many times to name what they drew, and I only missed two!"

"Really? That's so good."

"Papa says that I'm gonna be very talented."

"Because you are, dear," Rosline beamed at her daughter who smiled back and clutched onto her. Rosline set her down onto the bed, tucking the blanket around her before looking back to Jaks, who was still standing in the doorway. Rosline went to him.

"Things are still quiet," he said to her as he cleaned his pipe.

"And you haven't heard anything about the north?"

He shook his head, "Not anything you were looking for." He eyed her, "You know, your dream could've been just that."

"You know how these things are, Jaks. They're never so cut and dry." Rosline bit the tip of her thumb, a habit she'd gotten over the years. "I thought you were everywhere."

"Everywhere that matters," he countered. "The north has never intrigued me outside of the Kris family, and I find that they hardly warrant the resources I expend on keeping tabs on them."

"I'm sorry," she said, "I know there are more important things that you have to keep tally of, and me wasting your time on this... I know you don't expect anything."

"Sweet Rosline, one of the most precious things to me is knowing the comfort of your mind," said Jaks with a grin. "It is but a small task for me to learn what you wish, and reaps the benefits of so much more."

Rosline's face flushed as she smiled at him. "You have other things to do, don't you?"

"I am afraid so," said Jaks, "much to my own dismay when considering that glimmer in your eye."

She laughed, resting her head on his shoulder a moment before saying, "Well, perhaps you can make your way back soon."

"I will be out of town in the coming week or so," said Jaks. Rosline looked up. "Business I need to settle for an associate of mine."

"Oh, right," she said.

"Fret not dear Rosline. I find that the thought of your waiting arms, among other things, stirs me to return much quicker than I usually find myself."

She laughed again before heading back into her room. Jaks caught her by the waist, turning her about and giving her a deep kiss before releasing her.

Rosline shook her head, trying to dispel the heady feeling within as she heard his heeled boots walking down the hallway, his cheery voice calling to the servants as he passed by. Rosline closed her door, latching it shut as she contemplated.

Jaks had not heard anything of Astoria's travel through the north. She thought the woman would be coming back in the wake of what she had witnessed, but everything, including her own sight, told her nothing of the sort.

Maybe it was just a dream.

Rosline let out a sigh as she climbed into her bed beside her daughter, who had already dozed off. She tucked the hair hanging in her face behind her ear before placing a kiss upon her brow.

I should be focusing on her and home. There's so much that I should be doing to make sure everything works smoothly here.

Rosline couldn't shake the feeling though, and couldn't shake the sight of the small shadow sprites dancing around in her mind's eye.

ELEANOR.

"Must we truly be here for the entirety of the festival?" asked Railand as his petulant gaze scoured the surrounding crowds, wary of danger.

Eleanor chuckled, "Not necessarily, but there are opportunities to be had here, and I expect that anything that arises would take a lengthy amount of time to complete."

The festival of midsummer took place within the grand square before the cathedral. Members of the clergy walked about the procession, calling out in the faith of the Lady. All aspects of the citizenry of Isle was present, from the lowly laborers and workers to the aristocratic merchant class. Even the king had been present for a moment to commemorate the season as well as to congratulate the clergy for preparing the festival, in hopes that the people would be able to find pleasure in the respite. Much of the city came to celebrate, and with the rumors abounding about the shifting of the families, the distraction was welcome.

Eleanor greeted several of the others jovially, taking the time to foster goodwill. While normally, she would have considered the festival just another opportunity to build her connections, she found herself in high spirits this day. Rosline had stepped up in her wavering work, and with everything she had learned from her, Eleanor was in a bright mood. As she walked among the crowd, she felt secure with the presence of Railand at her side. She was drawn to conversation with several people that she held in good faith, opting to listen as they spoke to her about the upcoming season. Eleanor saw no need to push her advantages today: for her, it seemed better to let the other merchants lull themselves into the festivities and expound upon their own upcoming feats rather than to try and needle them for details. As the conversations grew long though, Eleanor spotted a friend of hers that she would have preferred talking to, and excused herself as politely as she could before making her way over to them.

"Gavin," she said politely, smiling at the man. He was finishing speaking with an acolyte who eagerly ran off once done.

Gavin graced Eleanor with a smile, "Lady Eleanor. Sir Railand." He bowed his head.

"Just Railand," corrected the man as he tipped his head towards the priest.

"Of course. I take it you are both enjoying the festival?"

Eleanor nodded, "It's a nice commemoration of the season. I'm glad to see so much went well. I know you had your concerns before."

"Aye, the king had wished to utilize the Knights of Isle, but I was able to convince them to let those feeling more charitable do the work, in exchange for the saving on the expense."

"The church has to stay financed somehow," said Railand shrewdly.

Gavin chuckled, "Yes, and while today should prove good for that, the other expenses went to paying the volunteers for their time instead of lining the coffers."

"Intriguing." Railand cocked his eyebrow. "An actual man of the cloth."

"I appreciate the compliment," replied Gavin with a bow of his head. "I know as of late it seems the church hasn't been so involved with the people, but with the right people taking charge, we can hope to have a good season and hopefully ride out the year with everyone safe, fed, and warm."

Railand looked over the priest, before giving him a nod, "I expect that will be."

Gavin smiled before looking up at Eleanor, "You seem in fine spirits today, milady. It seems the summer sun has filled you with vigor."

Eleanor beamed, "It feels good to be out and not necessarily working. Don't get me wrong, I do so enjoy my work, but some days it would be nice to have the freedoms I once had before."

"As both the head of the house and head of your business, I imagine days of respite are few and far between."

Eleanor nodded, "As I bet they are for a high priest."

Gavin chuckled, "Aye, and I do apologize for not being able to share meals with you as we once had. I did enjoy our talks that we shared."

"As did I, but our responsibilities have grown," replied Eleanor. "More people are relying upon us these days. Perhaps though, we can schedule a time to enjoy a meal together as we once had?"

"I believe that could be arranged," said Gavin. "However, I do have other things to attend to today, milady. If you'll excuse me."

"Of course. Hopefully we can speak later," Eleanor bowed as Gavin headed off, his voice sounding and calling acolytes to his side.

"A goodly priest," commented Railand. "They do exist."

"Yes they do," said Eleanor fondly. "Gavin is one of the people that actually gives me hope for the clergy. He's gotten much reform done with its members, and even though he bristles some of the more established members of the church, I don't believe there is another man with so much support."

"An enviable position," said Railand.

"Yes, but unlike in the world I work in, he will find few people that will want him dead for it."

Railand laughed, "Milady, the people that would see you dead would just as readily hop into bed with you. You have such a prominence for a woman within the city, it's not a wonder as to why."

Eleanor smirked, "You are right on that account, but those same folk are not bold enough for either, I would wager."

"Few would find themselves that bold. In my time here, I've not met a more timid folk than the aristocrats of Isle. It is rather sad, to harbor so much wealth and influence and be trapped within the confines of their own fears."

"People who have gained power don't wish to lose it, Railand."

"Yes but letting it sit and rot until time comes for you anyways is no way to spend life," countered Railand. "With all the opportunities afforded by such a lofty position, I'd expect people to be more bold. Such as yourself, milady."

Eleanor met his gaze for a moment before her hand ran along the stump of her wrist. "Sometimes, the price for such boldness is far too high for its payout."

"That may be, but if it's never broached, then no one will truly ever know their worth."

Eleanor flushed. She straightened her dress before saying, "We should try and meet with as many as I can bear today. I would hate to waste such a good day on mercantile pleasantries, but it must be done."

"Lead the way, milady," said Railand.

As Railand escorted Eleanor home, she felt quite exhausted from the day. Gavin had been true in his estimation that Eleanor had not had the luxury to spend a day in simple reprieve from her duties. There was too much to manage and if Eleanor found the time to actually take a breath, she usually filled it with something else to help push her own goals. It kept her busy, and when she was busy, she didn't have time to wonder about the things that Railand so often brought up.

Eleanor's mind started teeming once more, her mind becoming clouded with all the spiraling outcomes that her dealings would bring in the future. She already had several new people for Rosline to begin looking into, with hopes that her findings would put them in a favorable light rather than the normal disappointment that she found from the discoveries. Regardless of the outcome, Eleanor was sure that things would be well underway when autumn rolled around, and if the year went well, she could see herself set for a rather long time.

As they continued walking through the avenues of the city, Eleanor let her mind wander, just following alongside Railand. However, he stopped her after a moment, raising his arm before her as his other hand fell to the blade at his back.

"Railand?"

"Something's amiss," he said quietly. Eleanor glanced around, her hand instinctively going to her necklace. A tendril of dismay writhed in her when she remembered that Rosline wore it these days.

"What do you see?" she whispered, drawing close to his side. It had grown late, the sun having set already, but Eleanor hadn't thought the route they took to be particularly dangerous. Railand cocked his head, listening, his breath almost silent as he waited. Eleanor felt the tension then, the uncertainty of the unknown around them manifesting images of figures in the dark looming around them.

The silence was broken with the sharp sound of Railand drawing his blade. "I know you're there. Come now, show yourself."

Nothing stepped forth from the gloom. Railand took measured steps with Eleanor at his side, his eyes scanning as he waited. Eleanor let him guide her along, wishing she could see what he had noticed.

"There will be a rush," he said calmly. "A distraction will ring out, followed up by an attempt on you. Do not leave my reach."

"Okay," She continued to follow him as they tried to break for a more open part of the avenue. She glanced around, wondering if she could spot any of the city militia or perhaps a Knight of Isle. It was eerie for her to find that neither were present, that the area around them seemed quiet and lacking of any activity.

A setup.

Her nerves began to fray as they moved, and she winced when Railand swept his blade across her, the clanging steel snapping her eyes open as a dagger fell to the ground. She stepped towards him as the expected rush came from her side, and with another strike of steel, Railand intercepted the attack. Eleanor glanced at the assailant, a lithe and limber person shrouded in dark cloth and leathers. They bore a

243

short blade seemingly burned black while their other hand reached for a dagger at their side to break the lock Railand had them in.

She fought the urge to run. Railand told her specifically to stay within reach, so she mustered her courage. No matter how the assailant mustered his attack, Railand always interposed himself between him and Eleanor, parrying the strikes with calculation. They traded blows, Railand's expert flowing movements placing the assailant off-balance before a swift cut across their chest drew a line of blood. They staggered back, running their hand against the wound, before considering Railand.

Railand readied his blade before him. He seemed an entirely different person than the man she had been walking with, his face telling that in no uncertain terms would he relent. There was a promise of death in his eyes, and Eleanor felt the comfort of security in his imposing presence.

Two more figures joined the first, circling around the pair of them as Eleanor shifted closer to Railand.

"Who are they?"

"Hired blades, it would seem," he said, eyeing them.

"Three though? Will we be okay?"

"Of course, milady. That's what you pay me for," he said with confidence. He was steady, his tone confident but not arrogant. Eleanor saw as a sheen had come over his eyes as he regarded the three of them and noticed subtle changes in his stance. "All I ask is that you don't fight the flow."

"Flow?" asked Eleanor.

"Yes. The flow of combat."

Railand tensed, waiting for them with his blade before him. The assailants seemed to consider for a moment, one drawing forth a dagger from their side as the other took stock of their surroundings. The dagger was loosed towards Eleanor, but Railand batted it from the air with hardly a thought, his focus still upon the figures. They came at them in a sword rush, and Eleanor tensed, wincing as she heard them approached.

Railand snapped, his thrust surging out blindingly fast, catching one of the men beneath their collarbone. Eleanor was exposed as she tried to turn with him, but Railand's grip upon her dress pulled her alongside his rushing stride as he pulled his sword from the man. She was once more moved behind Railand, the expected blow cutting naught but air. Eleanor noticed that Railand seemed to throw the man upon the ground as he spun, his momentum spinning him around and placing her behind him once more as his blade slid free. He caught the short sword in a parry, before kicking the assailant away and spinning his blade to reverse his grip. The other assailant had already lunged towards Eleanor, who was swiftly retreating from him, but Railand interposed himself between them. The blade skidded along the edge of his sword, sliding up towards his shoulder before they broke apart, with the assailant trying to cut at his head. Railand leaned away from it, the tip of the blade within inches of his brow, before running his own edge against the side of the man's wrist. Blood spurted free and the assailant howled as he drew back, clutching his hand to stem the flow of blood.

The first man rose from upon the floor, but Railand sent a snap kick to his face, stunning him before flickering steel sank into his throat. He clawed at it, sputtering blood from his mouth as he fought to pull the blade free. Railand turned the blade with a sickening crunch, stemming the heaving and sputtering. However, the one he had kicked had already recovered, thrusting forth and sinking the tip of his blade into Railand's side. Eleanor screamed, but Railand spun away from the man, another kick spinning up towards his face and cracking against his jaw to send him spiraling to the ground.

"Railand?" said Eleanor, solicitously checking his side, "are you okay?"

"Fine. That's what the armor's for," he said before pushing away her hands and drawing his blade from the sputtering man's throat. The kicked man staggered to his feet, stumbling away from Railand as he approached. Eleanor made to follow, but Railand held his hand up behind him. "The battle's over. You don't need to witness this."

Eleanor looked to the other man, who was vainly trying to stem the flowing blood from his wrist, his movements erratic and jerking.

He's bleeding out…

She shuddered, closing her eyes at the scene as terrible memories flooded through her mind. Mocking laughter and searing pain flashed through her. She fell to her knees.

"No... no no no..." she shook her head, clutching her hair in her grasp. She heard the slither of steel through flesh, and her stomach turned. She heaved as she retched, wiping her mouth and turning away from the scene before her. Still though, the tormenting images surged through her mind, and she fought, trying to will them away.

"There's a lotus upon the wrist of one of them," said Railand, his voice seeming to be miles away. Eleanor felt her stomach turn again.

Remnants of Madrid? After all this time?

She shook her head once more, trying not to look upon the fallen men, but her gaze was drawn to them, and all of them were lying in their own blood, their bodies strewn upon the avenue like marionettes with cut strings.

"We have to leave now, milady," said Railand. He lifted her to her feet, but seeing that she had shaking legs, tucked his arm beneath her leg and swept her up, carrying her from the scene. Eleanor wrapped her arms around his neck as she tucked her head into his shoulder, the sensation bringing back memories she had long thought buried.

Blood and lotuses. Pain... so much pain.

She breathed heavily, trying to focus on something, anything other than the terrible memories. Railand's steady breath soothed her, but the smell of blood was on him, and it sent her back.

Sehren...

"I'm sorry," she let out in a hoarse whisper.

"Don't worry, Eleanor. It's what you pay me for."

ROSLINE.

Rosline waited at Eleanor's beside, her emotions a mangled mess. She could hear Railand's steady voice from outside the chamber door, speaking slowly as if the person he was talking to was touched in the head. Eleanor was tucked beneath her blankets, disheveled and unfocused. Rosline sat, waiting for her to speak whenever she was ready.

She had been fetched by a courier late in the night, having taken the chance to stay with Jaks this evening. When she had been told of what had occurred, she immediately grew concerned for her safety. The attack had failed though, and Railand was sorting everything out for her while she waited in her room. However, Eleanor had specifically requested Rosline by name, and also to bring Jaks along if he was with her.

So together they walked the streets at night, accompanied by the courier until they returned to her manor, and after exchanging details with Railand, they both wound their way up to Eleanor's room. She wouldn't see Rosline with Jaks though, and the Duhoviman had placed himself outside her chamber door, waiting for what would be asked of him.

Rosline held Eleanor's hand, but she simply waited, listening to Railand through the door.

"It'll be okay," said Rosline to Eleanor, rubbing the top of her hand.

Eleanor's eyes flickered, scanning over her from. She nodded.

"Do you know who would have done this?" asked Rosline as calmly as she could.

"I have some suspicions," replied Eleanor quietly, "but we will discuss them once the Knights leave."

Rosline nodded, holding onto Eleanor's hand tightly as she waited. Eleanor gripped her tightly as well, "Thank you for coming so late."

"Of course, milady. You know that if you ever need me, it is simply a word and I'll be at your side."

Eleanor's green eyes looked Rosline up and down before nodding. They sat in silence until Railand's voice quieted. Several loud footsteps echoed down the hall and the door opened, revealing Railand and Jaks as they stepped in. The roguish man shut the door behind them before latching it. He tucked away his pipe, wafting away the clinging smoke as he did.

"They were the right old sort, weren't they," said Railand.

Jaks considered him, "What do you mean?"

"Stiff, pompous, and uncaring. It seemed more of an inconvenience for them to have to look into the matter. You would think they would care for the attack on one of their own. And then to threaten me with irons for acting in accord with my contract?" he shook his head. "They are just upjumped soldiers."

"You killed the men," said Jaks simply. "Even if they could investigate, as far as I know, corpses don't speak."

Railand frowned, distaste on his face, "*Knights...*" he said in a derisive tone.

Jaks smirked, before looking over Eleanor, "They're gone, Eleanor. With what you wanted them to know."

She nodded, "I don't want a repeat of before..."

"Aye I know," said Jaks. Railand looked concerned for a moment before he continued, "this isn't the first time the Knights have come calling to her home."

"I don't wish to discuss that either," she said sharply, clutching Rosline's hand.

"Right," said Jaks, appropriately shamed.

Railand looked confused. "Milady?"

"It was before you were hired," she said shortly.

"If it will give us insight to who might've done this, wouldn't it help?"

Eleanor clenched Rosline's hand painfully as she said, "I don't want to discuss that."

"It was a horrible time, Railand," said Jaks.

Rosline looked between each of them before asking Eleanor, "What would you have us do?"

"Railand, organize the guard to make sure we have everything covered."

He frowned, "If I'm to abide by my contract, I should remain at your side."

"I would feel safer knowing that you had my guards sorted out. I feel you would be more competent for this matter."

Railand paused a moment before bowing, "As you wish. I'll return once I have the patrols properly set up though." He departed with haste.

"He's a dedicated one," commented Jaks as he approached the bed.

"Jaks... I need to know."

"Aye, and I think you already suspect us," said Jaks, looking at Rosline.

Her surprise was immediately followed by hurt, "Milady? Do you believe we did this?"

"Someone had to, and few people knew that I would be alone with Railand today."

"Much to their displeasure," commented Jaks

Rosline gripped Eleanor's hand, "Why would— I would never do anything like that, milady. You've given me so much..." Her eyes stung as dismay clutched onto her.

Eleanor regarded her for a moment, before squeezing her hand, "I'm sorry, Rosline. I just— ours is a duplicitous world. You are one of the few that would know. And I didn't see you at all today."

"You gave me leave to be with Jaks and Kyrah for the festival," she explained. "I wished to stay with him tonight. I never would do anything of the sort."

Eleanor looked up at Jaks, her gaze unfaltering as she asked, "And you?"

Jaks let out a hollow laugh, "Milady, if I had orchestrated something so crass against you, you'd know. Namely, I doubt the outcome would have been in your favor."

She narrowed her eyes as Rosline said, "Jaks!"

"I'm not saying I would," said Jaks. "But to assume that you or I would wish Eleanor dead is speculative and insulting, if I'm being honest."

Eleanor let out a sigh before nodding, "I'm sorry... it's much for me to take in."

"Of course. And for the record, I've already started trying to sort out who would do this."

"The assassins had lotuses on them," said Eleanor.

Jaks looked puzzled, "Interesting."

Rosline released Eleanor's hand, her head swimming, "I don't understand any of this."

Eleanor and Jaks shared a look before Eleanor said, "Jaks, would you know of anyone still affiliated?"

"Aye, of course I do."

250

Eleanor rested her gaze on Rosline, "Very well. Rosline, take him to the study and let him help you find those people."

Rosline was taken aback. "Milady… are you sure?"

"I am," she shook a moment before saying to Jaks. "I am trusting you with one of my house's oldest secrets."

"Are you sure that's wise?" asked Jaks, his smirk coming on his face, "moments ago, you believed me to be the one that orchestrated all of this."

"I believed that Railand himself had considered it as well, Jaks. It was not pleasant, but I trust you. You've never given me reason not to."

"Aside from who I am, that is," replied Jaks, his smirk going wide.

"And despite that, you came when I beckoned."

Jaks gave her a bow, "Of course. I find that of all the aristocrats I have to deal with, you are among the fairest, Eleanor."

Rosline trembled slightly but nodded as she rose from the bed, "Is this what you want?"

"It is. I know I told you not to share your work with anyone, but I wish to know, and if this will help Jaks sort this out, then so be it."

Jaks looked between the two of them, "This is turning out to be a tense deal. I imagine it's just a chronicling of all who you do business with."

"In a manner of speaking. Rosline, take him. If Railand is back before you all, keep what you do to yourself."

"Yes, Lady Eleanor." Rosline bowed before beckoning Jaks to follow her. He followed behind her, walking with her as she went to her room.

"My, my Rosline, is this the time for this?" he said with a sly tone.

Rosline let out a short laugh, "I need to get the key to the study." As they reached her room, she stepped inside and went to her bureau, opening it. She slid the hanging dresses along until she found the key hanging on a peg behind. Grabbing it, she shut the bureau and returned to Jaks.

"Kyrah is with the steward?"

Jaks nodded, "Aye, still sound asleep as well."

Rosline started walking off, each step bringing with her a nervousness she had never known before. As they stood before the study, Rosline took a breath.

"Jaks, what you are about to learn here can never be spoken to anyone else."

"That's a phrase I never expected to hear from you," he said with an amused tone. When Rosline didn't smile at him, he grew concerned. "What is it that I'm going to learn here, Rosline?"

"What I really do for Lady Eleanor."

She pushed open the door, revealing the darkened study to Jaks. Grabbing a lamp upon the desk, she used one of the candles in the hallway to light it before setting it down. Jaks walked in, his eyes darting around from the stacks of journals on the desk to the heavily curtained windows, before settling on the array affixed on the floor.

"Interesting..." he said as he knelt. "I'd heard rumors of thaumaturgy within the kingdom. People capable of great feats with little more than their own will." He reached the tip of his finger out to the edge of the array.

"Don't do that," called Rosline. "Else I will have to fix it."

"And that would be bad?"

"That would slow our task immensely," she said. Rosline felt trepidation as she took a breath, hoping for the best, "I work with Lady Eleanor to do research on interested parties."

Jaks nodded, "Like what I do."

She shook her head, before getting one of the journals and offering it to him. He took it, leafing through it, his eyes scanning the pages quickly. "This is quite the compiling."

"That is from one week of work," she said. Jaks snapped his head, surprised.

"Really?"

"Really. My job is to observe those that Lady Eleanor does business with and find any information regarding them that may assist her."

Jaks' eyes glittered, "And you've been doing this the whole time?"

"I have," she rustled through the pages, "she discovered my talent years ago when I mentioned the small shadow sprites to her. My learning of my talent came soon after that."

"When you lost your eyes," he reasoned with a frown.

"Yes. She swore me to secrecy, because what we do here is not in the Lady's favor, Jaks. She told me if someone were to find out, we could all be in danger. Before, it didn't seem much different than listening in on things with Aruhn, but after a while, she tasked me with learning more and more. Delving deeper into their lives."

"Who can you see?"

"Whoever I want."

Jaks' smile went wide, his eyes flashing as the opportunities abounded in his mind. He turned back to the array, "And this is the source of it all?"

"That's a gateway, so to speak.

He swept over to Rosline, taking her into a dip and planting a kiss upon her lips. A deep, yearning one. Rosline felt her face flush but eventually righted herself. Jaks said, "Rosline, you grow more beautiful by the day. Who would've known that something so simple as shadow sprites would unveil such a glorious talent?"

Rosline felt an icy chill in her as she thought about that statement. About who Jaks really was, "Did you know?"

"Know what?"

"Jaks, I need you to be plain with me." They had a child together. Their lives were intertwined in such a complicated way. Before it had seemed fanciful, like a fable she would have heard in Aruhn's tavern, but with everything so suddenly being revealed, she needed to know. "Did you know what me meeting with Eleanor would do?"

Jaks eyes flickered in the low light, before his gaze upon her softened, "When I brought you to meet Eleanor, it was because you mentioned seeing her husband, Sehren. You had that dream about him, one so stark and biting that I thought it prudent to involve the only other person in the city that would care."

"Eleanor."

"Eleanor. Has she ever told you how she lost her left hand?"

Rosline shook her head. She had been curious about it, but when Rosline first commented about it, saying she could help her more if needed, the woman had lashed out at her with much anger.

"See, your lady was indeed in love with the knight, but unlike many of the lordly ladies in the city, she was not idle. She ran his household, managed their finances, and together they were a great and happy couple. After the divestment of his knighthood, Eleanor was given a chance few ladies in the city get: a chance to branch away from her father to make a name all her own."

Jaks pulled the pipe from his belt, before reconsidering it and stowing it back away, "She became very prominent very quickly, and there were whispers about her dealings. Other merchants grew envious, and before long, Eleanor's name was spoken with both a mix of admiration and fear. She tread too far, stepped on the tail of a viper, and in spectacular fashion her household was slain. She was abducted and subjected to horrors that I believe still haunt her to this day."

Rosline cleared her throat as she pushed away the encroaching tears, "And you knew?"

Jaks shook his head, "I knew she was taken and where she was taken. I told her husband where to find her, and in similarly spectacular fashion, he not only rescued her, but slew the leader of their insidious organization, as well as over a score of men. And he returned her to her father, before leaving her in the city alone."

"Why did he leave? What— how could he have been so callous?"

"There's answers that I don't know, Rosline. But I know for a fact that there was little more that Sehren loved more than his wife, his steed, and his home."

Jaks looked over to the array, "I've spent the better part of five years dismantling the Lotus' power within the city and abound, but like vermin they keep crawling back from the dark. And it seems that they are taking their vengeance out on Eleanor, a woman that has already suffered so much at their hands."

Rosline felt a fiery vengeance within her. She grabbed the pendant from the desk beside the journals and walked towards the center of the array. As she passed Jaks, she grabbed his hand, "Do you know the names of the people who might have done this?"

"I have my suspicions," said Jaks, his tone becoming excited as he regarded Rosline.

"Good. We will start there."

Rosline untied the cloth around her brow, tying it to her arm as she beckoned her sight forth.

ARUHN.

The Friar's Reprieve was empty this evening, with the festival having gone long. Aruhn had already dismissed most of his maids to free evenings of their own, knowing that the few patrons he might have would be easily tended to by himself. Diyane had opted to stay as well, taking her customary seat at the bar, as she said that she didn't feel she understood the nature of the festival enough to appreciate it. Aruhn had laughed: Normally she would have gone to gather more information for Jaks, or to keep tabs on members of the Lotus, but he believed that when she learned he had no intention of going himself, she decided to keep him company.

Aruhn knew she would never admit it though. The woman much preferred her own company instead of Aruhn's but the promise of free wine plus a place free from prying eyes for a moment would give them both the respite they needed.

That respite found Aruhn in the small, hidden cubby behind his bar, the trapdoor opened for the first time in many months. Diyane was keeping an eye out for anyone to make sure that they didn't stumble upon him within, and as she already knew of the place's location, Aruhn knew that he could trust her enough to do so. He leafed through all the things he'd accumulated through the years, his tired eyes scanning over the myriad of documents stored within. He sighed though when he recalled that he'd long ago given the ledger of Astoria away to her.

She's in better hands now, she is.

Aruhn pushed at his lower back, trying to get the soreness from it as he walked to the ladder and climbed from the small storeroom. He shut it before sliding the barrels back over it. Afterwards, he grabbed a broom and swept around the bottoms of the barrels, making sure that none of the scattered dust looked too out of place or disturbed.

"A keen eye will find the trapdoor," called Diyane's voice.

Aruhn smirked, "Aye, but they'd have to be lookin' for it first. I reckon that it's normal to have some dust in the back. Too clean, and yeh'd wonder why."

Diyane conceded his point, pouring another glass of wine from the pitcher before offering it to Aruhn. "Everything is closed up, and I highly doubt any wayward souls will find their way here. You should take a drink, if only to remember why you sell it."

Aruhn chuckled, taking the offered cup, "Aye, I reckon you're right. Gotta have some moments to ourselves, right?"

"Precisely." She took a long drink from her cup before setting it down. Aruhn offered her the pitcher after he poured his, but she shook her head. "I think I've had enough."

"I've never seen yeh drunk before. We're takin' a night off. Why don't you unwind?"

"Because I don't ever take a night off, Aruhn," she said with a smirk. She shrugged off her overcoat, revealing the sleeveless vest she wore so often before. With the summer in full, Aruhn reckoned she would be wearing that more often. His eye caught the lotus on her shoulder.

"You still wear it?"

"Of course. It was a nuisance to obtain. It seems foolish to discard it," said Diyane as she leaned against the bar.

"Our friends with the red haven't been stirred up much lately." Aruhn poured himself another glass and took a sip, letting the wine coat his tongue before swallowing it down. "A good vintage."

258

"You know how to pick them," said Diyane. "And no, they haven't."

"Times change then, eh? I remember when seein' one of you was a weekly expectation."

"Business," she said simply. "Tabs have to be kept on people, and you have a good knack of keeping eyes where they were wanted."

Aruhn let out an exasperated chuckle, "Aye, and it paid off more than not. Still, I admit not havin' them knock on my door so often has been relaxin' change of pace."

Diyane simply shrugged as Aruhn poured himself another cup. Soothing warmth flowed through him. He regarded the woman a moment before asking, "Yeh think she's safe?"

"The wife or the daughter?"

Aruhn shook his head with mirth, "The daughter."

"I doubt it. Safety is something that is cultivated through the comforts of society. You could argue that she would have been safe here. Constantly watched, with peers around her? She would have wanted for little and few would have stepped so boldly as we did."

"But they still could've."

"That's true regardless of where she decided to reside. But at least here, she would've had more to watch her back than a grieved knight."

Aruhn sipped steadily, "I miss her. A lot. Been thinkin' if we made the right choice all those years ago."

"Probably." Aruhn raised his eyebrow at her, prompting her to continue, "You asked if I thought she was safe. In the wildlands of wherever she is, she only has the one set of eyes on her back. There may be less to fear from nature, but that still doesn't mean she's safe."

"Right."

"Her flight from here was a calculated risk. One I believe was correct. With the growing turmoil amidst the whispers, any mention of the crown's succession would be sure to place a mark on any bastard child of the king. She is away from that now, and if her longevity is all that you measure in terms of the value of her life, then she should find it well, provided the wilds don't have other plans for that."

"Do yeh feel the wilds are place for a woman?"

"Why not? They are no more perilous than living in the small hamlets that rim the cities of the kingdom. Women are born, live well, and die peacefully in those lands."

"And some are taken into places and worlds they'd never wish for."

"Aye, by people. I find comfort that if I was ever cornered by a savage beast, that it wouldn't draw out my death should I fall. Only people are concerned with elongating the suffering of others."

Aruhn rubbed the back of his neck, "Aye, yeh're not wrong." His face felt incredibly warm, but he attributed that to the lack of drink he'd partaken in over the past few months. "Still, some places just aren't suitable for women."

Diyan smirked, "Your chivalrous ideals are amusing, Aruhn. Tell me then, if you find the wilds so inappropriate for a woman, what do you think of the den of the Crimson Lotus?"

He stammered a moment, "I'd think them unfit as well…"

"Why? Because killing is a man's sport?" she asked, her eyes glittering. "Or perhaps I'd have served better as a broker, such as yourself. Not truly dipping into the murkiness of the underworld, but neither being clean."

Aruhn shook his head, "I didn't mean it like that…"

"Your ideals of where women belong solely comes from your notion that destiny is decided by what is between your legs," she said with a laugh. Aruhn flushed. "I recall my first job, when Marson congratulated me on my success. He told me that he was surprised to see such a clean job done."

Diyane turned to face Aruhn, resting her head upon her hand as she met his gaze, "He too sputtered when I told him that steel stops a heart regardless of whether or not the wielder bears a cock. Even in our world, there are tasks that are considered too much for a woman, as if our sensibilities are less than that of yours."

260

Diyane tilted her head, "You seek to protect Astoria as if she wasn't capable of doing it herself. And yet, by your admittance, she is the blood of the king and filled with boundless potential."

"Aye, but to have that potential sullied by the roughness of the lands or dealings with wild men. She don't deserve that. No one really does."

"So it is not her capability that you fear for, but rather whether or not she deserves that kind of life?"

Aruhn nodded which drew another smirk from Diyane. "It's not... look I'd known the lass for years. I'd watched her grow, and in another life, I'd've given her the tavern once she was ready."

"So a high strung tavern for a bastard princess," said Diyane in a mocking tone, "what a fulfilling life for someone with so much potential."

Aruhn shook his head, "I'd rather her be alive and safe, Diyane."

"Of course you would. You, who had a hand in raising her, protecting her, and grooming her, would've wanted to see that investment pay off. Just like all of your work, Aruhn."

Aruhn was indignant, "Aye now, that's crossin' it. I wanted more for the lass, always did from the moment I saw her shinin' blue eyes. But I couldn't give her more—"

"More than a tainted tavern? What a commendable gift."

"I didn't want for her what I'd been through," retorted Aruhn with a growl.

Diyane cocked her head, "Ah yes, the fabled debt of Aruhn."

He growled at her, which turned to a cough. He cleared his throat before downing the rest of his wine. "I did what I could with what I had."

"That's what everyone tells themselves, Aruhn," said Diyane in a bored tone. "The number of times I've been told, *'I've done everything I can!'* only for it to be a farce. No, you simply did as anyone else would at the time."

"Yeh say that like yeh're not self-serving."

"Everything I do is self-serving, Aruhn. That's the dance we do. Each move is made in accordance with our own goals and desires."

Aruhn shook his head, "Some days, I forget how cruel yeh actually are Diyane."

"I am as cruel as I need to be, Aruhn. The world wasn't built upon promises made with smiles, but debts forged in blood. And when people forget that they make mistakes. They bring attention to things that they shouldn't."

Aruhn was surprised at her tonal shift, the once condescending tone taking an almost sympathetic quality to it. "What do you mean?"

"Who did you speak to about the wife, Aruhn?" asked Diyane calmly.

Puzzled, Aruhn said, "The wife? Yeh mean Eleanor, right?"

"The one and the same."

"I haven't mentioned her to anyone outside of us," he said.

"Yet you brought her up today, as if she was also on your mind."

"Aye. I didn't do her right, especially after how I got along with her husband." Aruhn truly felt guilty for how that turned out, but he shook his head. "You act like you did any better."

"I did. I spared her life by taking her hand instead of cutting off her head like Madrid had instructed," replied Diyane calmly. "I didn't offer anything else to her though. What happened afterwards was solely from his anger."

"And that makes it better?"

"No, not at all. But I made a choice and now she lives."

Aruhn tugged at the collar of his shirt as he coughed again, his head swimming. He hadn't been this drunk in a while, and it was taking its toll on him. "I didn't talk to no one."

Diyane's eyes flickered as she took a deep breath, "You once believed we were cut from the same cloth, Aruhn."

"Aye."

"Maybe we were once. Disseminating the right amount of information to the correct sources is no easy feat. I am impressed you weathered as long as you have."

Aruhn still felt hot in his face, and his vision was swimming.

"Aye…" he tried to lean away from the counter, but stumbled to the ground. Diyane walked over to him, calmly standing over him. He rubbed his eyes, startled for a moment as his heart hurt.

She looked like his late wife Nira.

"Who did you tell Aruhn?" her voice was soothing, beckoning him. He shook his head again.

"I didn't talk to anyone."

"Jaks doesn't think so."

"I— what?" He rubbed his eyes again. Nira was staring back at him as she knelt.

"Jaks. Remember? He trusted you. And you're the only other person that knew who Eleanor was."

"What…" he coughed, "Yeh know. He knows. Hell, even Marson knows."

"Marson is dead, Aruhn. He has been for quite a while," Nira smiled at him, "That's why the Lotus is in disarray. And why you've had peace. But you told someone, Aruhn, and I need to know who."

Aruhn felt a searing pain in his throat as he tried to speak, "I— didn't…"

"I overestimated your constitution, it seems," said Nira as she rose up. She let out a long sigh, "It's been entertaining working alongside you, Aruhn, but I know what I need to know moving forward, and even if you don't know who you told, someone will."

Aruhn tried to push himself up, but his arms were weak, weaker than they had ever been. "I don't… why?" he coughed.

Diyane looked at him, as if the answer was obvious, "Times change, Aruhn. And with them, the faces in the game."

He clutched at his chest as Nira flickered before him once more, her soothing voice in his ear.

Sleep now. It's easier this way.

His eyes shut as the pain left his body.

ASTORIA.

Astoria's eyes snapped open as she heard a scratching at the door, her mind immediately thinking of lurking beasts in the dark. As her eyes adjusted though, she realized it was someone setting something down beside the door, before their footsteps carried them down the hall and down the stairs.

Astoria rose from the bed and rubbed the sleep from her eyes, trying to dispel the grogginess as she approached the door. She unlocked it, cracking it open a bit before glancing down at the frame. A smile made its way across her face as she saw a tray with food laying there with a tankard of mead beside it. She picked it up, took it into her room, and set it on the desk. After locking the door, she set herself down before the meal, which consisted of a stew with a hunk of bread. She spooned some of it into her mouth, feeling the warmth trickle down her throat as she savored the spices. She oddly had an appetite today and consumed the rest of the meal rather quickly before sitting back and sipping on the mead. She rose with the tankard in hand and made her way to the window. Pushing the curtain aside, she watched the industrious people of Harthglen at work as mules pulled laden wagons through the town.

It brought comfort to Astoria. The days they had spent in the town before were coming back to her. She remembered when she would listen to the trappers and loggers that came in from a hard day's work during the evening while she recovered during the morning. Her hand dipped beneath the collar of her shirt, feeling the scar that laid beneath her collarbone. It had become less prominent over the years, but compared to the other scars she bore, it was still the largest upon her by far. She lifted her hand and held it before her, eyeing the calluses and small scars that dotted the sides of her fingers. She didn't believe that anyone would recognize her after all the years and all that she went through, and yet she believed that Otto had remembered her.

Leanne might also just be a name he remembers of that young lass he met so long ago.

Astoria looked out the window once more as she considered it. It wouldn't be odd. She had remembered plenty of people's faces when she worked as a barmaid, but names were things she only remembered about people that interested her.

Jaks. Rosline. Sehren.

Her heart skipped a beat as a wave of sadness hit her. She looked back at the bed, thinking how much smaller it felt to her now that she was taller, but also that it felt emptier, lonelier, and she choked a bit as she thought about how a similar bed had held her and Sehren so easily before.

She willed away the feelings threatening to overcome her, shutting the curtain as she set the empty tankard on the desk. She pulled on her overcoat and belted on Sehren's sword, pulling it slightly from its sheath to make sure it would draw freely. Confident that she was ready, she grabbed the tray and tankard, left her room, and headed downstairs.

It was later than she had first thought, and the common room was rather empty considering. She saw Otto wiping down the tables, and he gave her a wide smile as she saw her approaching.

"Figured you were still havin' a lie in so I thought I'd grab you somethin' before we cleaned up," he said as he took the tray from her.

"Thank you."

"It's no problem. Room comes with meals included, though extra's gonna be a bit more," he laughed as he set down the tray and continued wiping. He eyed the blade on her side for a moment before saying, "You off on a hunt today then?"

"No, it's just somethin' I carry with me," she said easily.

"Oh, I figured you might be. There's some folks gettin' together to deal with this ravenous beast that's been hitting some of the sheep."

"Oh?"

He became grim-faced, "Aye. There's been some kind of beast lurkin' 'round the outskirts of the town. Taken down almost a dozen sheep, and no one's been able to find where it's lairin'. A couple of the guys went to try and trap it, but they say it outsmarted them and scampered off." Otto paused, wiping a moment as he continued, "Took one of their legs clean off though and scarred up another fella that tried to stop it. Now, seems like they're trying to get more people involved to deal with it. Some folks are saying they'll get the Knights of Isle involved if it keeps going on."

Astoria felt a chill through her as she thought of the Knights, namely the one that had issued the ultimatum all those years ago, "Would they come?"

"Probably if they thought it was worth it. They're pretty good to us since we feed them when they go on northern patrols and such. If we were losing too many sheep, they'd see it as fair value to come."

"Right. When are the people gatherin'? Do they let women go along with them?"

Otto considered her for a moment before nodding, "Aye they'll see you've got a fair bit of experience on you. I heard they were meetin' at the well around midday to try and get somethin' sorted."

Astoria nodded, "Thank you, Otto."

"Hopefully you all get the beast. It's always a pity when the hunters come back bloodied."

Astoria gave him a wave before she took her leave, letting the door shut behind her as she left the tavern. The town had grown since she had last walked through it, with more of the buildings huddled together in more clusters. As she walked through the town, she noticed that there were more militiamen patrolling the streets. She attributed that to attacks from the beast, but she also noticed a tenseness in the air that she couldn't quite place. The people spoke in strained voices to one another, quieting when she would walk past. They greeted her cordially, as she remembered them doing before, but Astoria could see a glimmer of wariness in their eyes.

She stopped one of the passing guards, "Pardon me, but I heard that people were gatherin' to deal with a ravenous beast?"

He eyed for a moment, "Aye. You a hunter?"

"I am. I think I might know what it is as well. Do you know anyone that can describe it for me?"

He raised his hand to his chin, "I think one of the hunters that came back from before is leadin' it. Last I heard, he was gatherin' people 'round midday. Stick around the well and you'll be sure to find him."

"What was his name?"

"Amar. Got torn up pretty bad by the sound of things last time, so he's vying for revenge."

Astoria nodded, "Thank you."

"O' course. If you help us, the whole of Harthglen will be thankful," he said with a genial smile.

Astoria watched him walk off, smiling in the wake of the sincerity of the people. No one seemed to care who she was, nor did they think less of her for traveling alone. They seemed to be concerned with what was best for their kin, a sentiment that Astoria could appreciate immensely.

There wasn't time to be fussing about things that didn't really matter up north. It was me and Sehren, and we had to sort everything out so we'd make it to the next season. It's the same here.

Astoria waited by the well, her eyes going skyward as she took measure of the sun. As she waited, she saw more and more people coming to mill about, all with different kinds of gear. They spoke to one another with familiarity but again she could sense the tension. Every now and then, a curious gaze landed upon her, but she simply smiled as she waited for Amar.

268

A burly man with tanned skin and a mess of black hair upon his head walked towards the well. His skin had an almost leathery appearance from his time in the sun, and he walked with a limping stride. As he got closer, Astoria saw a smattering of scars along his arms and along the bottom of his neck that dipped beneath his shirt.

He looked over the group, his voice calling out, "Less than I'd thought, but should be enough." He continued scanning the people, nodding at familiar faces, before he stopped on Astoria, his expression becoming puzzled. "I don't reckon I know you?"

"I'm Leanne," she said confidently, "A hunter, much like yourself. I was staying at the Badger's Nest, and the owner there told me about troubles you were havin' with a beast. Figured I could lend a hand."

He took measure of her, "Hunting leathers, a longbow, but a sword for hunting? That's a little personal to be using."

"It is a little different, but I know what I'm doing. I had a few questions though about the beast, if you didn't mind? One of the guards said you'd be able to describe it?"

Amar's face became grim, "Aye. It's a large wolf-like beast, with dark, shaggy fur and teeth almost as long as daggers. It's larger than most, but the most distinct thing I remember was the anger and malevolence in its eyes."

"Sounds like an *eiravuk,*" said Astoria.

Amar cocked his head, "A what?"

"*Eiravuk.* That's what I was told it was named anyways. Somethin' like a tundra wolf. The beasts are ferocious and incredibly smart, capable of luring their prey as we would. It's no wonder it's been givin' you grief."

"You've hunted these kinds of beasts before?"

Astoria gave him a short nod, "I have. But you're most likely dealing with a pack rather than a single beast. They're rare, but they can cause the most experienced of people, myself included, grief."

Amar frowned, "What do you think we should do?"

"I would hear your plan first. From what I've heard, you tried to corral the beast before?"

"Aye. We went out with half a dozen men, not all hunters, mind you, but trained enough. The beast crippled us one by one once we got close to where we thought it would be. I figured, more men this time means more eyes watching and less of a chance of any one of us getting ambushed."

"That'll work," said Astoria as she looked around, "but if it is a pack, they most likely won't strike at once. It'll be tryin' to push us around and keep us separated. I'm thinking though, with the numbers we have here, that four to a group should do, giving us a good steady four pack."

"Aye. Anything else we might need to know?"

"If it's not a pack of *eiravuks*, then it might be a few wolves working with it. They are almost kin, so it's not unusual to have them workin' together."

Amar shook his head, "They're just beasts."

"They are, but just like everything in the north, they've learned how to survive."

Grumbling emanated around from the group, but Amar quieted them before saying, "Aye. We'll do it that way then."

"If the beast is spotted, let me deal with it," said Astoria.

"You thinkin' you can handle it yourself?"

"I'm thinkin' it'll increase our odds."

Amar looked unconvinced. He shrugged, "Fine. If you manage it, I'll buy you a drink once we get back. And you can keep its pelt."

Astoria smirked, "Sounds like a deal to me."

Astoria led them through the trees where the townsfolk said the beast was laired up. She could hear the short breaths of the men following behind her, and could hear their scratching steps as they walked through the underbrush. Astoria had her hood and mask upon her, with her longbow in hand as she led the group. Amar was close

270

behind her with a pike, but the man's limping gait couldn't easily keep up with her smooth flowing stride.

She kept her senses tensed though, waiting for the sound of the nearest scratch against the earth, or a low timbre growl of warning. She eyed the torn earth around the trees, as well as the myriad of claw marks in the bases of the trunks.

"You think it's around here?" asked Amar in a quiet voice as he drew up to her.

"Aye. Those marks there aren't normally made by wolves," she pointed at the tree. "Normally, bears will do that to clear their claws or release tension, but those are too shallow for that. There's an *eiravuk* here. We just have to keep an eye out for it."

Astoria continued walking, waiting for the beast to show itself. She knew that with so many, it would most likely circle around for the group that seemed the most afraid. However, with her in the point position, she hoped that it would instead be drawn to her at the front.

A shout from behind her left pulled her attention, and she heard scuffling as the men put their arms to bear. Two wolves, shaggy grey, had approached from the dark, their jowls raised as they circled. More growls emanated from the surroundings. Astoria saw as a pack of wolves came circling around them. Still, even with the pack the beasts were outnumbered, so Astoria nocked an arrow and waited.

Where are you?

The men started shouting to rouse one another, brandishing their spears towards the beasts, and getting confident when they saw them draw away. Some of the men followed after, shouting at the wolves.

"No, they have to keep together!" Astoria shouted as she saw one of the men go rushing off. Amar shouted out, but his call was muffled by a screaming as the wolves pounced upon the man and dragged him into the underbrush as he clawed futilely against the ground.

Astoria loosed an arrow at the beast dragging him, causing it to release him with a pained yelp, but another one leapt upon him and continued dragging him off.

Damn it, where is it?!

The men wanted to break to rescue their friend, but the chorus of growls quelled their attempts. They tucked beside one another as they raised their spears. Astoria listened, trying to hear the pitch she was looking for, when she spotted a figure looming in the trees. She drew a bead as shifted through the brush, and let loose her arrow, the quarrel finding its mark as a baleful howl sounded. Several of the men looked fearful, with Amar getting a worrying look upon his face as he met Astoria's gaze. She took several more shots, trying to trace the running beast through the trees. With another baleful howl, it broke free and stood before them.

It was taller at the shoulder than the other wolves, with dark fur. Sharp teeth protruded from its mouth as it growled, and Amar had described, its eyes shone with a malevolent intelligence absent in the other beasts.

Astoria dropped her bow to the ground as she drew her blade, the sheen of white steel bolstering her own confidence.

Just like before.

She rushed towards the creature, her blade ready to swing should the beast lunge at her. It bayed and howled, and the other wolves around it turned their attention towards Astoria, drawing her to a stop.

She looked towards Amar, who was moving as quickly as he could with his limping gait, but he wouldn't reach her in time. The other men were tangled with more beasts, but stalking towards her were four of them, including the beast.

Just like before, she told herself again. She tightened her grip upon her blade, waiting with anticipation for the beasts to strike. She paced their movements, trying not to get surrounded. One of them lunged forward, a tempting target, but Astoria quickly saw that if she had taken the strike her side would have been exposed. She waited, wanting to be able to strike two of them in succession so that if the other pair attacked, she would only have to fend off two sets of fangs.

One of the wolves took a strike at her, rushing towards her side, and from the angle, Astoria knew she was exposed, but she couldn't let it simply score a hit on her. She rounded about, sweeping her blade before her, catching it in the face as its maw lunged for her. It yelped,

272

battered to the side before it crouched and paced away. Astoria was already following it, feeling the tearing at the air behind her. Her intuition proved sound, hearing the clamp of jaws behind her as she rushed forward. She spun about, her blade leading, battering aside the wolf before kicking it away and trying to scamper away.

You're being reactive. Force them to act, not the other way around.

Her heartbeat sounded in her ears, but she remembered. She had hunted these beasts before without difficulty. The terrain was different, but the battle was the same. Composing herself, she held her blade before her as the wolves worked her sides with snaps. With a surprising lunge of her own, she caught one of the wolves as they snapped forth, her blade shearing it at the shoulder. Swiftly drawing away, she reversed her swing, setting her sword in line as the other beast lunged at her, letting it impale itself upon her blade. Using her foot, she slid the beast off her blade as the *eiravuk* struck. Her edge was in line, however, which fended off the beast. The first wolf she injured snapped at her side, and while its wound stole the strength of its bite, the fact that it had snuck around her guard alarmed her. She moved with the hit, letting the momentum carry her away from the *eiravuk* before slamming the hilt against its skull to dissuade a follow up. She ran her hand along her side; the leathers were ripped but her flesh beneath was still fine.

Astoria heard a rush and slid back, almost tripping on a root before she caught herself and sprang up. The *eiravuk* had thought to attack her as she slid back, imbalanced, but she had already swung mightily before her, and the tip of her blade caught against its chest, cutting deep and drawing blood. It staggered away, but Astoria chased after it, leaving her side vulnerable to take down the beast.

Once it's down the others will be easier.

She felt a tear at her leg, stealing the speed of her rush. Cursing, she swung at it, frustrated as the *eiravuk* stalked away. Her blade caught into the wolf's neck, snapping through its spine, and she pulled her leg free as she chased after the *eiravuk*. She could hear the other wolves loping behind her, but the *eiravuk* wasn't too far, and Astoria knew she could catch it.

It turned, growling at her before lunging forward, and Astoria knew she couldn't raise her blade in time. She instead dove forward, rolling underneath it, before standing and charging after it. She planted her sword in its spine, drawing another long, pained howl, before pulling it free and stabbing again. The beast limped and tried to turn, but Astoria unleashed her frustration upon it, striking it again and again until it moved no more. She heard the rushing wolves coming towards her, but pain yelps drew her attention as they were skewered in their sides with spears. Astoria saw that most of the wolves began to flee after the *eiravuk* was slain. As the adrenaline flowed through her, she let out a long breath to slow her heart. She felt a tugging pain in her leg, and when she reached down, the warmth and wetness of her blood awaited her. She knelt, seeing that the wound was wide but shallow, and with a wince, tied it with a bandage from a pouch on her belt.

"You did it," said Amar as he approached her, his spear bloodied. He knelt beside her, looking at her leg.

"It'll be fine with a few days of rest. It wasn't very deep," she said.

"Aye, but still, you did it," he looked at the mangled mess of the *eiravuk* and shook his head. "That thing was savage and brutal, but you had a handle on it."

"Would've gone better if it hadn't roused its kin," admitted Astoria. "But with it dead, that should keep the sheep safer. I'd recommend taller fences if you can manage them. That should keep the other wolves away."

Amar reached out his hand to her, which Astoria took as he helped her up. She could walk, but even with the binding there was much pain. She would clean the wound once she got back to her room, and hopefully with a little rest she would be okay.

"You're staying at the Badger's Nest?" asked Amar.

"Aye, that's right."

"Consider your stay covered," he said to her. "I'll let Otto know."

"Oh, I hadn't planned on staying long. Maybe instead, could you help me with some supplies for the road?" she asked, looking at Amar.

He raised his eyebrow, looking at her leg, "You gonna be fine travelin' on that?"

She smiled, "Help me find a good horse, and I'll be fine."

He laughed, lending his shoulder as they walked back to the village.

CONTACT.

It was a morass of black and grey. Blotted shadows flitted in and out of existence, some over the course of what felt to be forever, while others were in the blink of an eye. There was a resonance between them, a tenuous link that guided and maneuvered the specters together in a myriad of shapes and forms that coalesced into existence before their time was fluttered out. Order was enmeshed within the shifting variance, lending itself to a mockery of the forms that shifted into being only to melt away into nothingness.

Yet the shades moved with will, with purpose and determination undecipherable. Some would flicker into existence, only to meld with another and take the form of a more familiar object. These too would become extinguished, fading away into the morass as part of the whole.

Some forms existed longer than others, forming scenes of familiarity.

A lone deer walked through the shadowed boughs of the trees, each step it made oblivious to the danger that laid therein. It seemed obvious, but the deer pranced on, each leap and stride filled with tenacity and resolve. It leapt through the underbrush, its hooves smashing through obstacles with ease. It cared not for the whistling of

277

the quarrel in the air that sunk into the trunk of a nearby tree. As the deer bounded off, the scene faded away, becoming once more a pit of darkness and shadow.

Familiarity. That scene was familiar, as if seen before. As if experienced before. But the world shifted, stealing the moment away in a breath.

A breath. A moment of being, more than just existing. That too was stolen away in the swift current of the lightless world.

A baying hound erupted from the dark, circling around a fallen deer, the deer from before. Teeth bared, darker than its form, gnashing out against the backdrop before it tugged upon the carcass, dragging it away. The scene faded.

That too, was familiar, but as the moment passed, the familiarity was stolen away, replaced with nothing but the sinking of the void.

Void. Empty.

An absence filled the scene, stark in the gloom.

No, there was more. Thoughts teeming with more. Scenes flickered in and out of existence, resisting the temptation of being swept away, yet fatigue sapped away the will. The will fought against the roiling tide but still the scenes faded away. It was easier to combat, to not have will, to be washed away. Yet more scenes, lightened skies dotted with small flames that dispelled the gloom. Beams slipped between the canopies of trees, sending dizzying light throughout.

All of this had been experienced before. Fighting against the void however, made them fleeting. They slipped away, leaving nothingness around.

Yet the will remained. Clinging to the only constant that it could identify.

Fatigue.

With the fatigue came the allure of release. Yearning and beckoning. Fading into the void and combining with it. But the fatigue also anchored it. The promise of peace was tempting, but the fatigue broke the yearning for it.

278

A singular phrase, warbled and incoherent, as the tenebrous clutches of the abyss distorted it, echoed throughout. Its call was fleeting but so tempting, so much more than the promise of peace.

The scenes returned, gliding before the will, each commonplace and recognizable, and yet they shimmered away into nothing. What was it that brought them so? There was nothing before, and that was peace and now the peace was warped by the flashes of others.

Nothing? No, always something, always the cool, tempting respite, the comforting grip of the shadows bringing serenity. But never did they fade away as others. Instead they persisted, more than nothing, and now the nothing filled with flashes of corporeal. Trees? Animals? Recognizable in the gloom but having no meaning here.

Yet as it fluctuated, more and more, there was permanence, something in the gloom residing there regardless of the sweeping tide. Permanency within was unfathomable, an anathema to the realm within, and yet there stood a constant, one that overwhelmed the tenebrous and flowing change of the void.

That phrase. Sounds. Words. A singular sentence. It grew more clear with each passing moment.

More scenes played out. Verdant fields with tall grasses. Long troughs of earth. Swaying strands of grass in meadows. Trees surround the vale. Open sky, azure with alabaster clouds.

Alabaster, like steel.

No, steel is silver. Steel is grey. But the blade is alabaster.

The moments passed, but the will remained. Burned into it. Focused onto that.

The blade is alabaster.

Alabaster steel stained red.

Steel is grey.

The blade is alabaster.

A lightness in the blade, a soothing dance. Dance? Flowing, step by step. Black is the steel-center, black like the hair of the dancer.

A soft voice. The phrase broke through.

279

"Welcome home."

Danika stared down, her smile kind. Her eyes, grey like steel, yet almost glowing in the gloom, watched with such pride and happiness. Her voice, almost distant, rang out. "Welcome home."

Home? Home is comfort.

The tents and fences. No. That is something else.

Home is the solitude of the vale. The sweeping grasses. The empty sky above, the sun shining down.

Home is not here.

"Can you stand?"

Stand? Nothing stands alone. Yet Danika stood, on two legs, with a dress of flowing black that seemed to mesh with her hair. Her flesh was pale, stark against the grey backdrop. With an extended hand she reached out, her palm inviting. "You are home. Can you stand?"

No. There is nothing to stand on.

"Reach for it. Will it."

The will is tired, fatigued. The tempting peace calls. The hand retracts.

"Then sleep. Wake when you are ready."

Ready for what? There is a pulse. A beat. Then another. Then another. There is a steady rhythm within.

Danika smiled, "That's right. Come then, can you stand?"

Stand? There is nothing to stand on.

"Stand on your own, or take my hand," Danika offered her hand once more. "You simply must reach for it."

There is nothing to grip. Nothing to reach out with.

"It's okay. You can do it."

The yearning overcomes the wish for sleep, the trials of fatigue. Steadily, a pale hand reaches out.

My hand?

280

Danika smiled, "There you go, Sehren. Welcome home."

Sehren?

Grey eyes opened in the gloom.

ROSLINE.

She walked into the tavern with Jaks at her side, the melancholic air immediately hitting her as she crossed the threshold. She saw Celeste standing at the bar, Aruhn's customary spot, before pausing a moment. Jaks walked past her and approached Celeste with hushed tones. The woman seemed to be on the verge of tears but fervently spoke with Jaks. Rosline walked around, the familiar common room bringing waves of nostalgia over her. As she approached the hearth, she saw the familiar cast iron grate. It was cold now, the morning not cold enough to warrant an open fire with the ovens working, so she ran her hand along it, admiring the soot that coated her fingers as she did.

Did we do this?

Rosline trailed back to Jaks, who sported a solicitous face. Not his fake one that he placed as an act of condescension, but his true one, his eyes not sporting their normal mischievous gleam. As he finished talking with Celeste, he approached Rosline, his eyes scanning the common room.

"They said they found him cold on the ground behind the bar the next morning. It seemed he had drunk himself to death. There wasn't anything missing, and the doors were locked."

"And the maids?"

"Aruhn had sent everyone home early in the evening, not expecting people to be coming to the tavern after the festival. Everything points to him seemingly having had enough." Jaks' face softened, "I'm sorry. I know he was your previous boss for a long time, and possibly even your friend."

"He was a kind old man, which in my line of work, were three words you could rarely mix together," she replied, looking back at the grate. "He was thoughtful, sometimes gruffly so, but enough to be enjoyable to work for."

"At least he chose a better way than most to go," said Jaks. "He probably didn't even realize when he had gone too far. Just slipped away in a drunken cloud."

Rosline nodded, sniffing as she felt sadness flow through her, "I can't believe he's gone..."

"He's been around longer than most," said Jaks, "like a fixture in the city. I suspect the details are already traveling around. There will probably be many people coming to pay their visits and their respects."

"Will there be a funeral?"

"Celeste knows there will be a burial. Not so much a ceremony after that. Seems he didn't really plan much for his passing," Jaks took out his pipe, packing it with his favorite blend before lighting it with a strike of his flint. "Was there anyone else you wanted to see?"

Rosline looked at Celeste, who was dabbing her eyes with a cloth. She glanced around the familiar tavern, but the realization that she hadn't set foot inside of it for the better part of five years bowed her shoulders as she shook her head, "No. We should go."

Jaks offered his arm to her, which Rosline took. She gave a fleeting look at the tavern as they stepped over the threshold, and she sighed.

"Jaks?"

"Yes?"

"Why is it that you don't call Eleanor 'Lady' unless you're being snide?"

284

He let out a laugh, "Because I've known her for a while. And in a more personal capacity than most I deal with. My lack of using titles is not a slight against her, but rather an endearment to her. Eleanor knows this, and while she expects courtesy from anyone who would come across her, she prefers my genuineness more."

"You don't think she deserves the title of Lady?"

"I feel there are few in the city more deserving of the title than her, Rosline," said Jaks confidently. "The things she has survived, the obstacles and endeavors she has overcome, Eleanor has earned more than life has seemed fit to give her."

Rosline furrowed her brow. "Do you think more people will come for her?"

"Most likely. But with Railand at her side, I believe anyone that does will find themselves hard-pressed indeed to harm her. The man possesses a certain zeal about him, reminiscent of another that I knew."

Rosline gave him a scandalized look, prompting a laugh from him. "People are comfortable with what they are familiar with, my dear."

"I know, but that's not a favorable thing to say."

"When have I ever been about being favorable, Rosline?"

Rosline started speaking, before catching herself. He was a scoundrel, and in some cases, people enjoyed his cavalier-attitude and manners. Rosline certainly did, and she knew that when Eleanor spoke to the man, she held annoyance towards him, but she could also see the begruding fondness for him beneath.

"I really hope Kyrah doesn't end up taking to your personality when she grows up."

"I would be affronted if she did."

Rosline laughed.

Jaks led her to a nearby park, where Diyane was waiting for them. She was lulling amongst the park, turning her head slightly as Jaks pulled himself from Rosline and began speaking with her in her own tongue. Rosline let her gaze wander around, watching as others took walks throughout. They spoke for a long time, Diyane giving long expositions to Jaks who simply nodded in return. Jaks finished up, dismissing Diyane before he turned back to Rosline.

"Sorry my dear, business and all," said Jaks. "Diyane said when she left Aruhn he had been drinking but not to any real extent. They had shared a glass before she went on her way for another job."

"I thought she watched over him."

"She did, after a spell. Diyane performs many tasks for me within the city, and she believed that with everyone alerted by the festival, Aruhn would be safe. Turns out, neither he nor Eleanor would find their festival night unscathed."

He bit the tip of his thumb, thinking, "The last of the Crimson Lotus attacked Eleanor, and that's something I would have never predicted coming. I thought Sehren had murdered all that had been involved, but I guess the mouse gets bold as the lion goes missing. Diyane assures me that Aruhn was in good, if reminiscent spirits when she left, and the man is not known for drinking too heavily. He did seem to mention Astoria though."

A spike of nostalgia pierced Rosline, "What about her?"

"Just wondering how she was doing, and if we made the right choice all the years ago to send her away."

"You said it was the crown seeking her, right?"

Jaks' eyes flashed as he looked around, "Yes, in a manner of speaking. Her safety would have always been in question if she had decided to stay within the walls of this fine city. Her accompanying Sehren seemed the most reasonable option for her."

"I'm sure he just missed her. She was the obvious choice to take over the tavern when he felt it was time to move on. Everyone who worked there saw it. I reckon it was why Celeste gave her such a hard time."

Jaks smirked, "Yes, and now she does seem like she's bitten off quite a bit more than she can chew. However, I've found a remedy for that, at least in the interim."

"Oh?"

Jaks nodded, "But that's not our concern right now. The Friar's Reprieve won't fall overnight. For everything that's happened, it seems that the vipers that came for Eleanor will indeed be skulking away to either lick their wounds or contemplate their next step."

Rosline hesitated before asking, "Do you think I could find them?"

"I think you would be quite capable of finding them," conceded Jaks. "But, do you feel that would be wise?"

Rosline cocked her head, "Why not?"

"You'd be stepping into my world, Rosline. And while I'm sure you've heard and seen some things that would make your skin crawl, the world I live in is a markedly different place than you've been."

"I want to help Lady Eleanor, Jaks. I don't care what I have to see," she said emphatically. "If it helps her, I'll do it."

Jaks pondered for a moment, "It's not something you'll forget."

"Is that why you do it?" she asked him. "Because you can't forget?"

"Because all of this," he said with a wave of his hand, signaling the city, "causes all of that."

His voice had gained an edge that Rosline had only seldom heard before.

"I thought you liked the game."

"I do Rosline. It's part of who I am." Jaks regained his smirk, his eyes glittering as he regarded her. "But I fear that you may get addicted to it as well."

"Really?"

He nodded, "And then perhaps, I will have found a competitor that I could never match."

The way he said it, the anticipation in his voice, sent a chill through her followed by a shudder.

AMOS.

Amos stepped off the cruising boat, waving away the chants of "Lord Commander" as he walked up the steps to the fort. Waves crashed against the coast, the roiling tide giving the landscape an oppressive and onerous demeanor. As Amos walked along the dock, he let his gaze trail along the edifice, his mood becoming somber as he entered.

The Prison of Isle.

It was a hard place, with comforts few and far between for the prisoners. Even the knights who were stationed there tended to harden during their time at the prison. Amos walked staunchly with his escort, acknowledging the respectful nods and bows he received when he passed. A visit from the Lord Commander was rare, but over the past few years, Amos had come to call more often in the aftermath of the witch hunt.

Good men, left to rot.

He shook his head and pushed away the thoughts before they became too heavy. Try as he might, he couldn't do as much as he wished for the men sentenced there. After the mass defection, Amos found that his protests against the witch hunt fell on deaf ears, and more men found themselves locked away within the high walls of the prison. Worse was that in the time since the last indictment, there had been a relative peace within the kingdom, and while Amos attributed it to circumstance, many believed it was because the corruption had finally been stymied.

People will see what they want to.

"We are here, Lord Commander," said his escort, bowing his head as they reached a small visiting room, "I'll bring the prisoner here in a moment."

"Thank you," Amos took a seat. He tapped his foot upon the stone as he waited, turning when he heard the door open once more. A man with disheveled blonde hair and dilapidated clothes was ushered in, his wrists bound with manacles. He heavily sat across from Amos, his gaze focused on the table before them as he sat back. A coarse beard was spread across his chin and cheeks.

"It's been a while, Aeir," said Amos, sitting forward.

"What do you want?" called his hoarse voice. He turned his gaze upwards, his eyes hollow and filled with derision.

"That's still your Lord Commander," called the guard. "Pay your respect."

"Kindly wait outside," said Amos, cutting across Aeir's retort.

"Sir?" The guard looked confused.

"I wish to have this conversation alone."

"Is that wise?"

Aeir let out a wry laugh, "That's your Lord Commander. Best pay your respect."

The guard became red-faced, but Amos gave him a stern look. With a nod of his head, he said, "I'll be outside, sir. If you need me."

"Very good," Amos returned his gaze to Aeir. The door shut, the sound echoing in the chamber.

"To what do I owe the pleasure of the Lord Commander's presence?" The last three words dripped with sarcasm.

"A check on your well-being," started Amos.

"Well-being? No one has cared about that for years. Tell me what you want so I can go back to my cell."

Amos recoiled slightly, "Aeir, I have spent the years trying to absolve you of your crimes. I've fought for your release, among others."

"And what's come from it?" He tilted his head up before looking pointedly around the room, "Nothing but more charges and accusations. I had peace before I sided with you, Greyfield. After that, I've had nothing. Nothing, except more men demanding more testimonies, saying 'this will help you' or 'this will lessen your stay.'" Aeir's derision turned to hostility, "So what is it now that you're offering? Another false promise for more men to be driven here like chattel?"

"I come because the men are being investigated again," said Amos. "I am doing what I can to mitigate it as much as possible."

"Mitigate it? You call this mitigation?" Aeir growled.

"Better than execution, is it not?"

"I once considered that when my sentence first started, when I thought I had two years within these walls. Eight seasons." Aeir growled again, "It's been almost twenty three seasons. I've watched them pass while working in the quarry, watched them fall from my cell window. And all I've thought about is how perhaps things would have been better without witnessing them at all."

"You speak as though you are a defeated man, Aeir."

"It is best to recognize your own limits, isn't it? Isn't that what we're taught when becoming knights, to understand and recognize when enough has passed?"

Amos frowned. "You are willful enough to wake each morning and do what is required of you. You continue to eat and drink and engage in whatever you need to continue on. You're not defeated, Aeir, yet you hang yourself like you are."

"I do not hang myself," barked Aeir. "I was left here to rot, Greyfield. Visits only came when self-serving men like yourself found a need to either find an advantage or to absolve your guilt. The number of times I've been drawn into this very room for meetings— why, I would need more fingers than I have hands to recount. It is tiring, and pointless, and if I'm just to be used for gain, then I'd rather not be used at all." Aeir sat back, the rattle of his chains sharp in the room.

"And yet, still defiant. As I would expect for someone who served with Sehren."

"Do not utter that name in my presence," spat Aeir, the venom of his words so caustic they clung to his statement, burning. His eyes, once hollowed, were filled with such rage that Amos almost felt scorched by his gaze.

Amos cleared his throat, "I am sorry for what has happened to you Aeir. I believed that we had taken the best course of action. I thought that I could turn the opinions and secure your clemency," Amos let out a breath. "I could not foresee the rampant blame that would be laid upon you and the others. I could not predict Clyde taking his men and fleeing, levying even harsher punishments on those already condemned. But I never stopped working. I never ceased in trying to rid the brotherhood of its rot and trying to bring you freedom."

"And that may help you sleep at night," replied Aeir, "but it does nothing for me. So either ask what you will or get out of my sight. Leave me with the follies of my trust."

Amos stopped then. With a nod he rose, wanting to say something that might soothe the festering hate. He knew though that Aeir was set, and nothing he could say would provide a balm for the injustice and anger in his soul. Amos departed the room with his escort after Aeir was escorted out by a guard.

"Are things well here?" asked Amos.

"We get the job done with what we have, Lord Commander," replied the guard in a determined tone. "No one here signs up because it's easy."

"And you have the means and are provided the supplies to maintain the people?"

The guard nodded, "It's been a bit more delayed recently, but we've attributed that to the shifting season and less men in the city."

"How would you consider the welfare of the prisoners?"

292

The guard gave him a measured response, "Except for the ones that are clearly dangerous, most are treated well enough. Do they do hard labor? Of course, for that is their penance, but it is within reasonable amounts. Few are openly mistreated and even the most dangerous ones are given well enough respect. Defectors, however…" he trailed off, clearing his throat, "It's a divisive topic, sir."

"It shouldn't be."

"Serving at the prison puts those assigned here, myself included, in a much different mindset than those in the open forts, sir. We rarely leave the island and when we do, the city feels so much further away. Our quarters and such are fine; I doubt there's a keep in the kingdom that eats as well or is as regularly supplied, but the men that serve here find their former brothers either detestable or pitiable."

Amos frowned. "They are still within the order."

"Except for the ones that are not, milord. Many renounce their allegiance after their first few weeks or months, and there is little pity for the forsworn here."

Amos gave him a severe look, listening to the matter-of-factness of the guard's tone. Serving at the prison was a demanding job, but it also gave a pedigree to the knights that volunteered for the position that was on par with active warfare. Even though the city was only a boat ride away, many men opted to stay stationed at the prison, and there were fewer places in the kingdom that would foster a bond as deep and strong as working in the prison.

Additionally, knights that sought captainship would apply for the prison, but only those that possessed a cool head and absence of prejudice would make their bones there. Amos understood, however, that seeing other men of the order shackled and chained alongside the other corrupted influences would be alarming, and in some cases, despicable. It could wear on them, and that in and of itself could inflame grudges.

"Thank you for your honesty," said Amos, drawing a nod from the guard. "If there is something you find missing within the keep or things that need to be done, send a courier with word."

"Milord?"

"Yes?"

"There have been rumors that the king is abdicating the throne. Is it true?"

Amos weighed his words carefully as his temper bristled, "The king is not leaving anytime soon. Those are the rumors of people believing that another families' rule would bring better fortune for their own personal gains."

"If the king does change, what will become of the people locked beneath their chains at his word?"

"They would likely be reviewed by the new sovereign. Put it from your mind, however. I am certain King Saiho will live out the remainder of his reign rather than stepping from his throne."

"Yes, milord."

"Where, perchance, did you come to hear this from?"

"One of the newer prisoners mentioned it," said the guard. "He was shouting that the king held no interest in who was being imprisoned but rather, that someone else did. It was rambling, but it is all we have to listen to at times."

The guard gave him a deep bow before returning back up the steps of the prison. As Amos climbed aboard the boat, he contemplated the rumors, his gaze trailing up the high walls. Other men like Aeir were imprisoned within, and he had a fleeting thought of whether or not his hand in everything was beneficial after all.

ELEANOR.

Eleanor sat at the desk in her conference room, waiting for Rosline's return. Her household was on high alert, with Railand maneuvering the guards and scheduling their patrols so that there was little time for break. When he wasn't conferring with the guards, he was at Eleanor's side, his practiced gaze taking stock of her and of whatever surroundings she had been around. He stayed beside her with a calm confidence that steadied her nerves. The attempt on her life had shaken her to her core, and with that, had unearthed deep-seated fears that she had thought long laid to rest. Even still, when the night fell, she found herself trembling in the comforts of her bed, the familiar feeling of dread returning to her after almost half a decade.

She hated it. Seeing the slain men had flashed the images of Tillinghaust and Claire, and all the others that had once served her and Sehren. She could hear the jeering voices of the men, once packed away in the recesses of her mind, now present in the waking dreams and nightmares that she had. She was exhausted, bags marring the pristine green of her eyes, but she fought defiantly against the crashing wave of terror until her rage played itself out and she found herself tired and alone beneath the blankets of her bed.

Railand seldomly left her side, his armor still damaged from the strike against him. When Eleanor had asked him about it, he simply stated that a minor bruise would not deter him from performing what he was paid to do. He took to staying in Eleanor's room when she would try to sleep, with a promise that he would remain awake regardless of his own mounting fatigue. She had asked him if he did ever sleep, and he stated that he rested when he found the time to, usually between guard shifts, but if he even felt the fatigue of his duties, he never showed it.

Eleanor estimated that he slept when she would find respite in the hours before dawn, the rare moments when her mind would be silent and at last she could shut her eyes without being subjected to the horrors of the past. Unable and, secretly fearful, to leave her home, Eleanor had tasked Rosline with meeting with her appointments, if only to inform them that Eleanor had taken ill and would have to meet them again in the future. Normally, this would be fine, but paranoia had caused Eleanor to believe that someone would try to strike at her home if they learned she was ill, and as such she had asked Railand to maintain a full watch with the guard at all times.

She shook her leg as she waited in the conference room, Railand seated beside her. He calmly braided his hair, his eyes scanning around before returning to Eleanor to take measure of her. A bowl of fruit sat before her, hardly touched. His eyes flickered to it and back to her.

"You should eat," he stated.

"I find that I lack an appetite."

"I understand that, however, if you fail to nourish your body, then your waning spirit will soon be mirrored with it. I can protect you from blades in the night, Eleanor, but I cannot protect you from your own actions," he reached out and pushed the bowl closer to her. "Eat."

Eleanor took some of the melon from the bowl, eyeing it before biting into it, "Most servants don't speak to their benefactors in such a way."

"Most servants aren't paid as handsomely as I am to ensure their benefactor's well-being," he retorted with a smirk, "You asked me to do a job. I'm doing it the best I can."

"I know," she took another piece of melon, trying to coax the first piece down her dry throat. "I worry for Rosline."

296

"Jaks is with her, and her daughter remains within the manor under steady watch," said Railand. "Worry for yourself. It does no one well for you to be so out of sorts."

Eleanor scoffed, "I am not out of sorts."

"Addled. Distracted. Pick whichever word feels best to you, but either way the end result is the same." He touched his side, hissing lightly as he pressed against it.

"Are you well?"

"Enough for this. The blade destroyed several of the overlapping scales and dented them inwards. It seemed he tried very hard to kill me." He let out a wry laugh as he drew his hand away. He continued his braid with a knock on the door drawing his gaze. A guard poked his head into the room as Railand rose, his hand on his blade.

"Milady, there's a man here to see you. A priest from the Cathedral."

Gavin?

"Send him in," said Eleanor, straightening her dress and hair as she waited. She took another piece of fruit as Railand watched the door, waiting. "I doubt they would send a priest I knew to attack me."

"Your disbelief is what rouses my suspicion," he replied simply. As the door opened and they both saw Gavin, he looked from Railand to Eleanor with a wary look on his face.

"I see you're taking quite the precautions," he said with a laugh, holding his hands up non-threateningly.

"Just doing my job," replied Railand.

"With what has happened, I would have to say that's a good job you're doing then," he sized up Railand before giving the man an approving nod. He indicated a chair close to Eleanor before asking, "May I?"

"Certainly." Railand took his seat again as Gavin did. The priest immediately gave a solicitous look to Eleanor, reaching out his hand towards her.

"I heard about the attack from the Knights. Are you doing well?"

"I am. They didn't lay a hand on me, thanks to Railand," she said with a warm smile to the man.

Gavin frowned as he regarded her, "I understand that but I mean… are you well?"

Eleanor considered her answer for a moment before her eyes darted over to Railand, "I'm— as well as can be expected. We are taking measures to keep me safe, and that's all I can really do right now for me."

A solicitous gleam filled Gavin's eyes as he said, "Truly I wish that this had not occurred to you. When I heard what had happened, I wanted to come check on you, but as I once mentioned before, my duties are not to be lightly discarded. I spoke with Amos though, telling him I wished to check on you after what I learned. He gave me leave to come and check upon you, with the condition that I let him know. I hadn't realized you both had become so distant in the past years."

Eleanor gave a wry smile, "There's little time for the ex-wife of a Knight to have the Lord Commander call without causing rumors and such to abound. I thought it better to distance myself."

"As I understand," Gavin steepled his hands before him, before lacing them together, "He still worries for you though. Even in the passing years. I find myself grateful, though, that you are in the hands of such a good protector."

"Thank you," said Railand with a smirk.

"Will there be reprisal?" asked Eleanor.

"As far as I've heard, there is no action being taken on behalf of the fallen men. The knights are conducting the best investigation that they can but so far, nothing has turned up save for the fact that the men were dregs of society. Hopefully, they found rest."

"You wish them rest?" asked Railan with a frown.

Gavin nodded, "My duty isn't to punish those that perform wicked deeds. It's to help those that might have lost their way. The Lady will distribute the appropriate judgement upon them in the afterlife."

"You would sit idly by and let them do as they wished?"

Gavin shook his head, "Do not mistake me: I have no qualms of using the means bestowed upon me to bring resolution to conflict. I have just seen enough suffering and violence in my years to find it an unsettling and undesirable meal."

Railand gave the priest a long gaze, and Gavin stared right back, undaunted. "You think me a fool."

"I think you are a holy man that actually believes in his faith," replied Railand.

"Is that such an oddity?" asked Gavin.

"In my line of work, yes. I've protected priests, bishops, clergymen, you name it. You'd never think a man in the service of a deity would require someone like me to protect them, but then again, you've most likely never met a priest that would need them. I have seen the church capable of great things, Gavin, but also too have I seen the other nature nestled within. Be it royalty, faith, or wealth, men in power tend to share commonalities."

Gavin smiled, "Yes, that is something to consider. All I can hope is that perhaps I can help you see past your jaded view of the church."

Eleanor laughed, drawing the men's gazes, "I've found the Lady fickle in the past few years. But Gavin, I believe that if more men like you found their way into her service, then all could benefit from it."

"Thank you, Lady Eleanor." Gavin bowed his head. "I do apologize for this brief visit. I wished to make sure nothing had befallen you, and that you were in high spirits." He smiled. "You've grown strong, milady. Truly so. Your father would be proud of the woman you've become, and I know Sehren would as well."

Eleanor felt her face flush slightly as she said, "Thank you."

Railand cocked his head, "You knew Sehren?"

"Aye," said Gavin with a nod. "He was a good man. His heart was always on his duty and his lady, even when it seemed to falter in other regards. The men he led were cut from a similar cloth, and I truly wish for the days that the Knights of Isle can have that spirit within them again."

Railand raised his eyebrow, but didn't respond.

Eleanor cleared her throat, "Gavin, if you do find some time free, I would like to pay you a visit after all this has passed."

"Of course. Just send word, and I'll do what I can. You'll always find a friend in me, milady." Gavin rose from his seat, before bowing courteously, "I do have to take my leave now, but thank you for having me. Railand, it's been a pleasure to become more acquainted with you. I see why Lady Eleanor trusts you so."

"And I am swiftly learning why she had made mention of you before. You are a testament to your faith, Gavin." Railand gave the man a bow of his head as Eleanor rose from her seat. She walked over to Gavin before curtsying. He bowed one more time to her before leaving.

"He's a fair man," said Railand. "I sense a calmness within him tempered from a rough life."

"You'd be correct," said Eleanor as she returned to her seat.

"Do you think he had a hand in this?"

She froze at Railand's inquisitive tone, "I had not considered it. Do you believe he could have?"

"I told you, I've met with many men in powerful positions, and a commonality between them is their tendency to overreach and overreact. I don't believe that to be the case for Gavin. He seems sincere and for such a man to come and meet whenever he was able to is rather telling of his nature. But, his mention of the Lord Commander has me concerned."

Eleanor considered his words, "I don't believe Amos would have anything to do with this. Nor Gavin."

Railand nodded, "I didn't mean to insult them. I'm just considering the possibilities."

"Of course."

Eleanor sat at the table, pensive, before a steady knock on the door and creak revealed Rosline. She bowed to Eleanor before seating at her side, with the clacking boots of Jaks echoing within.

"A long day indeed, Eleanor, and unfortunately, I have little to tell you about what occurred." Jaks sat several seats down from

Eleanor. He untied his hair, shaking it free as he said, "The only confirmation is that it was indeed the Lotus, or rather, what remained of them. I wasn't able to learn anything else beyond that."

Rosline nodded in accord with Jaks' words. She let out a sigh, before looking expectantly to Railand. He excused himself, walking to the door and shutting it behind him.

"How was the notice of delays received?" asked Eleanor.

"Well enough. Most didn't ask too many questions, and I expect everything will be ready for you when you are ready, milady," replied Rosline.

"You are certain then?" asked Eleanor, pointedly towards Jaks.

"As much as I can be," said Jaks.

"Though not as certain as I can be," added Rosline. "However, without knowing where to look, I wouldn't be able to search for them."

Eleanor looked confused, "What is preventing you from knowing?"

"Me," interjected Jaks. "While this profound discovery is likely remarkable for you both, I believe that dealing with this through my contacts will be the most prudent."

"Why's that?"

"Rosline has expressed to me her desire to do what is needed to find a solution to this all," said Jaks, "however, what if you find that the solution is more than you can handle? Will you be content with the knowledge of who may have orchestrated the attack against you, only to find that you lack the ability to move forward? Or worse, would you endanger Rosline again for your gain?"

Eleanor's mouth thinned to a line.

"You know I'm right, Eleanor. I shall get you an answer, and it will take some time for that. However, I will do it through my means."

"Are you afraid of that which you don't understand?" she asked Jaks.

"No. I understand quite clearly what it is Rosline can do," he said. "I, however, also have considered what happens if someone else not inside this room learns it as well. My suspicion is that this may have played a factor into that, and while I respect you, Eleanor, gambling on Rosline's well-being is not something I'm keen on."

Eleanor let out a sigh, "Very well. Keep at it then, if you could for me Jaks. I just… I want to feel safe again. I forgot this feeling, and I really wish I hadn't had to experience it again."

"Understandable, Eleanor." Jaks rose from his seat, walking around the end of the table to give Rosline a kiss. He left, his clacking boots echoing down the halls.

"Is there anything else I can help you with, milady?" asked Rosline.

Eleanor considered her for a moment, "Yes. There are a few people I wish for you to look into for me."

Rosline nodded, "Of course. Just tell me who."

ASTORIA.

She unwrapped her leg, smiling as she saw the puckered flesh on the mend. With Amar's offer and no viable horse around, Astoria had stayed within the town to heal. She kept an eye on her leg though, making sure that the bite didn't fester. Astoria checked over it, making sure it wasn't warmer than usual and while it stung as she palpated it, it was less painful than the day before. As she rinsed it with water, she hissed as it stung. Dabbing it lightly with a length of cloth, she tied it once more before testing her weight on it.

I should have stitched it like Sehren would have.

Astoria took a quick look at the small kit resting on the table, still open from when she had helped the other hunters that had gone with her. The bone needles had been cleaned as Sehren had shown her before, and she still had plenty of sinew left to quickly sew up the bite she had received. However, she merely walked over to it, closed it, and put it away into her pack.

She rested her hand on it a moment, considering. She'd stayed longer in Harthglen than she had anticipated. Many members of the town had come to thank her after the hunt, and Amar had wasted no time regaling people with her prowess in the battle. Astoria had simply accepted the people's thanks, intending to leave as soon as she found a good enough steed that could carry her back to Isle. However, the next morning, she had found her leg much more sore than she had anticipated, and at the request of Amar, stayed a few days with her lodgings covered by the grateful hunter.

She shared meals with several people, opting to stay quiet as they asked about her background and where she learned to fight the beasts. Many of the questions seemed innocuous enough, but Astoria was always wary, answering as vaguely and humbly as she could so as to not rouse suspicion. Otto's eyes were constantly on her though, and Astoria swore she saw flashes of familiarity in them now and again. He said nothing though, instead simply sitting with the others when his duties would allow, and taking meals to her room when she didn't come down.

Astoria pulled on her boots, once more testing her leg. She smiled when she didn't feel any hint of pain or strain. She walked easily to the door, and with another test, left her room, locking it behind before she swept down the hallway to the staircase. Otto was once more at the bar, setting up plates, but the rest of the common room was rather empty this morning. As Astoria approached him, he gave her a smile, pushing the plate towards her as he filled a flagon with ale.

"Amar's covered it. I was about to take it up to you, figurin' you'd want a lie in."

Astoria thanked him, taking a seat at the bar before grabbing at a fork and cutting into the meal. She nodded appreciatively as Otto pushed the flagon beside her plate.

"You've riled up a lot of the men," said Otto, cleaning several plates and taking them to the back. Astoria wiped her mouth with the back of her hand as she gave him an inquisitive look, "Most ain't ever seen a woman as good as you were. I'd reckon you'll have several men lookin' to scoop you up before you head out of here."

She gave a strained laugh, the idea sending a pang through her. "I doubt it."

"Why's that? You're capable, an easy talker, and from the sounds of it a much better hunter than most. Add onto that your beauty, and you could have anyone in the town."

Astoria tried to give him a look of thanks, but it must have come out awkward as he furrowed his brow before asking, "You don't think so?"

"I think that's a little overestimation of me. Yeah, it was a good hunt, but without everyone there, it would've been a hard one either way." Astoria scooped more of her meal into her mouth before she washed it down with some ale. Coughing she said, "It's not uncommon for women to be hunters 'round here anyways."

"True, but most ain't proper ones like you. The way you walk and move, even the way you eat meals, shows a ruggedness and ease with the wild life. I'd estimate you've been hunting most of your life?"

Astoria nodded, unsure of where he was going with this.

"Just sayin', men ain't used to that. I mean, most of our women know their way around a spear, and they're proper tough, me ma included," he let out a laugh, "but you're different, Leanne. You're confident, and I have to say it's a bit intimidatin' and intriguin' all together."

"Is that so?" she finished the flagon of ale, before saying, "Well I appreciate that, but I imagine that's more a reason for me to be headin' back down south. Don't want any folks here thinkin' I'm tryin' to make off with their man."

Otto laughed, "Aye, I can see that being good. It'll be dimmer here without you though, but I imagine that whatever's waitin' for you back home's eagerly doing so." He picked up her plate and flagon before heading to wash it out as she took a moment to think.

What do I have waitin' for me, anyways?

Astoria thought of Aruhn, but as she tried to think of the Friar's Reprieve, the faces she had once known so intimately were hazed, as if she couldn't truly make them out. She frowned, thinking harder, but she could barely remember what Aruhn's face looked like, let alone any of the other maids.

She palmed the stone on her necklace, looking down at it as Jaks' face swam in her memory. She could remember him, his distinct eyes, tan skin, and long hair all taking her back to the years where he would sing and play in the tavern, his bawdy songs tunes that she would hum to herself over the following days. Try as she might though, she couldn't remember those either.

She thought of the farm, the place she planned to lay Sehren's blade to rest, and even that felt unfamiliar. She could only remember the firepit and the well, as their tent had been nestled beside the both of them, but the land itself was clouded in her memory.

"You all right there?"

"Huh? Oh," she shook her head, "yeah, just thinkin' of the road ahead."

"A familiar trek, I imagine," Otto said with a smile.

"Yeah, somethin' of the sort."

"Think you'd ever find your way back up here?"

Astoria shrugged, "Not sure. I think it'd be better to keep travelin' around."

"That must be a life. Just the wild road, and the skies and trails beyond," he gave her an appraising look, "Like I said, you're pretty intriguin'."

"Thanks," she rose from the bar, adjusting her belt, "there's a provisioner in the town, right?'

"Aye, three buildings south of here," Otto's face saddened a bit, "You gettin' ready to leave?"

"Aye," said Astoria, trying to avoid his gaze, "I think I've healed enough for the road. Don't wanna be spending too long or I might end up staying."

Otto laughed, "I reckon that wouldn't be a terrible thing though."

Astoria was going to answer when the inn door opened and she heard heavy footsteps walk in. Her gaze was drawn to two men in plated mail, with tabards draped down their torsos that held the sigil of the sun and moon intertwined with wings holding them aloft.

They spotted Otto and with a cheerful call, made their way over to the bar. Astoria watched them carefully, noting the one closest to her was doing the same.

306

"Oi, Otto. Who's the gal?" asked one of them as he dropped some silver coins on the counter as Otto filled flagons for them.

"That's Leanne," said Otto as he scooped up the coins with a smile. "A travelin' hunter, believe it or not."

"Aye, really?" He looked her up and down, clearly impressed as he took a drink. "You look the sort, but I say you're a pretty one. Leanne, was it?"

"It was." She shifted her hand to rest easily along her pommel while brushing her hair out of her face with the other.

"Name's Trenten." He smiled at her as introduced himself. "And that fine fellow there is Jonas."

"Pleasure to meet you both," she looked back at Otto before saying, "three buildings south, then?"

"What? Oh, right. Yeah you can't miss it. Crates stacked outside the front."

Astoria thanked him before walking out of the Badger's Nest. She turned her head up and down the avenue, before spying a building with crates out front. She walked into it, speaking lightly with the merchants before getting the most provisions she could afford. As she considered a tent, she sighed, wishing she had a horse to help carry it all. With a frustrated sigh, she lugged it all back to the tavern, stopping for a moment to adjust some of the supplies before heading in.

Both knights were still at the bar, their faces turning to meet her as she crossed the threshold. She gave them a short nod before taking the stairs up to her room. Once inside her room, she emptied her pack upon the table, sorting the things she still had with the things she had purchased. Trying to remember how Sehren had tied their tent to the back of Termesa, Astoria tried to bundle the tent together in a similar fashion before lashing it with several straps of leather. It took a majority of space within, and she was sorting the rest of her belongings when a knock on the door drew her attention.

"Who is it?" she asked cautiously.

"Otto. Mind if we talk?"

Astoria released her grip on her blade, before walking to the door and unlocking it. Otto stood outside with two mugs of mead, "Got a bit?"

"Sure," she invited him in, watching him as he set the mugs on the table.

He looked over her strewn belongings before saying, "You were serious about leavin' then."

"Of course. Why wouldn't I be?" she returned to combing through her stuff. She heard Otto take a drink. "Did you leave the knights at the bar alone?"

"Ma's got it," he replied. He cleared his throat, "You mind if I ask you somethin'?"

"What?"

"Why do you use a fake name?" he asked. He became sheepish, before making sure no one was in the hallway before continuing, "I mean, these people are never gonna know who truly helped them, and I just think— I think that'd be sad."

"Sometimes, it's better to try and forget," said Astoria.

"Right, and I get that, but I mean to come and help with such a tryin' problem, even getting maimed during it just to leave thankless."

"I've received thanks," said Astoria. "Meals, this room. Even the hunters came by to thank me."

"And you helped them even more with that curious needle of yours," he said, taking another drink.

"I like helping people," explained Astoria. "Is that so hard to believe?"

"Not at all. I admit I was more curious about the name mostly," he considered for a moment, "There was a lass I knew, a few years back. Maybe three or four, bright lass with hair like yours. She was talented too, and her name was Leanne. When I saw you, it all kind of came back to me. That's why I thought of it."

Astoria nodded slowly, watching him carefully. He was staring into his mug though.

"I had almost gotten her and her pa to stay in the town. And while I might not think about her a lot, I wonder what would've been sometimes if she had stayed."

"What happened to her?"

"Dunno. She and her pa left the town suddenly without a word. Just a horse, a wagon, and a somberness about them both that told me they weren't comin' back."

Astoria continued packing, "They probably left because it was their time to move on."

"Right, and I get that. I just wonder, y'know, being here my whole life. I'm not even a good hunter or nothin', so I'm not goin' around with Amar and the others. Then someone like you comes 'round the inn, and for a few days it's like livin' another life." He took another drink.

"You want somethin' more than this, Otto?"

"I'd think there's more to life than simply pourin' drinks for hunters and loggers," he admitted.

"Tell me, do you have peace?" She met his gaze, which was filled with confusion.

He looked puzzled at the question, "Aye, plenty of that."

"Then don't wish for anything more," replied Astoria, her voice getting an edge to it as she felt a burn in her eyes. "Peace is more than anything you could want. The road, the wilds, there's no peace to be had there. Nothin' waits but a slip up and an early grave."

Astoria tightened another bundle before packing it into her pack, "I'd wager that's what happened with the other lass. Just disappeared into another part of the world." She closed the pack, lifting it up with some effort before strapping it to her back and adjusting the straps. Seeing that it would be comfortable and the weight wouldn't bother her leg much, she nodded to herself, satisfied. She took the pack from her back as she looked over at Otto, seeing the man pensive. Grabbing the mug from the table, she took a cursory sip before drinking deeply of it.

"You wouldn't want peace?" he asked quietly.

Astoria sputtered a bit as she drank, wiping her face as she asked, "Who wouldn't?"

"You could stay here then. No wilds that I don't think you couldn't handle, and there'd be plenty of others that'd want to help you out. You'd make a good livin' here hunting, and I'd wager our beds are better than sleepin' on a bedroll in the wild."

"I've thought of that now and again," admitted Astoria. Otto looked up at her brightly.

"And?"

"It's not my peace," she said simply. Otto looked puzzled. "This place, everything in it. You've had a hand in it. Your ma, Amar, everyone here has had a hand in it." She shook her head, "I'd never find my peace here, and the sooner I realized that, the better."

"Right," said Otto, his face becoming crestfallen. "Still, you've made an impact. People will be talkin' about you for months to come."

"I hope not," she said in a teasing tone, before becoming serious. "Thanks again, Otto. For the meals and food and stuff."

"Like I said, it's not often we get someone so interestin'. I always try to make them stay."

Astoria laughed, "Has that worked yet?"

He gave a wry smile, "Nah, it hasn't. Makes me more inclined to leave though, but then I realize, I know nothin' about what's beyond the town."

Astoria knew the feeling. She reached for the pack, "I think it's time I left."

Otto looked sad, "I understand. Mind if I walk you out?"

Astoria pulled the key from her pocket, shaking her head as she said, "I don't see why not."

They walked down the hallway, Astoria glad her leg could manage the weight well without having to worry too much. As they got to the common room, she saw the knights looking her way again, the one named Trenten rising from his seat and making his way over.

"Aye, so Otto's right then. You are heading out."

"I am."

"A pity. A woman like you is a rare find."

Astoria raised her eyebrow, "I'm sure a Knight of Isle could find a better woman to wed."

He laughed, "Better's subjective. There's a fire about you, and it's more than your hair. I can see it in your eyes."

"I'm surprised there's anything inside them, if I'm being honest," she replied.

He smiled at her, "If you can delay a bit, me and Jonas can travel with you a bit 'til you get where you're heading. Otto said south."

"Did he now?" She gave Otto a withering look before clearing her throat, "I don't want to have to wait on others, or be bothered by their own things. I'm sure you have other things you need to tend to as a knight."

"You'd be surprised. With everything happening with the king, and people getting worried about a split, there's much to do. Still, accompanying a maiden safely along the road is something no one can fault us for."

She cocked her head, "What was that about the king?"

"Hadn't heard?" he gave her a grin. "If you share a drink with me, I'll let you know more."

"We share a drink, but I leave alone," she countered.

He stroked his chin, thinking, "Fine, fine. Can't resist a charming woman."

She gave him a simpering smile before sitting at the bar with him, setting her pack down beside her. Otto returned back behind the bar, smiling before he regarded Astoria's face.

"So, what's happening with the king?" asked Astoria as she scooped up her mug. She pretended to drink, watching Trenten carefully as she set her mug down.

"King's done it seems," he said in full voice, drawing a shush from Jonas. "What else would you call it? The man's defeated, but he's not realizing it's time to abdicate."

"I'm not sure what you mean," said Astoria.

Trenten grinned again, "He's got no heir, and he's grown old and weary with the crown atop his brow. His wife died a few years back giving birth to their child, and the child didn't make it either." He took a deep drink, "Nothing left of the Mistletain line it seems, and while the other families have been pushing for a change, he's not given up that easily."

"Sometimes, people don't know when to quit."

"Aye, a sentiment shared by the other families, I can tell you. The Kris family is wondering if he's gonna talk with them about inheriting the line, but seems like the king isn't keen on meeting with anyone. Figures as much."

"You're really loud, Trent," said Jonas, looking around.

"No one else's around, and even if they were, they'd know I'm speaking the truth," replied Trenten. "King Saiho should take what he has left and head back to the west with his forebears. Leave the throne to someone that wants to do something with it."

Astoria considered it for a moment, "Aye, he should."

"If it weren't for his queen being so harsh, he could've found a bastard and claimed them," continued Trenten. "Not an uncommon thing, though I know that would've ruffled a few feathers."

He and Jonas shared a laugh.

Astoria simply nodded, pretending to drink, "I didn't realize things had gotten that way. And Isle?"

"Oh the city's fine. Between the Lord Commander and the clergy, they're doing just fine all tucked away in their southern homes," he replied with a tinge of annoyance in his voice. "They leave the honest work to the frontier holds and cities."

"Here, here," said Otto, before blushing as Astoria regarded him.

"You heading there?" asked Trenten.

"No, but I was just seeing if I needed to make adjustments to my travel," Astoria set her mug down before grabbing her pack, "Thank you for that, I appreciate the information. Say, either of you have a horse you'd been willing to part with?"

Both of them shook their heads, with Trenten saying, "My horse sits two pretty well, if you're rethinking leaving alone."

"I'm not," said Astoria. "Again, thank you for the information. And the drink." Astoria tightened her straps before leaving the inn.

She heard footsteps following her, and annoyed, she turned, only to find Otto behind her. He paused for a moment, seeing her severe face, before saying, "I just wanted to say, I hope you don't get lost in one of those corners of the world. Really."

Astoria gave him a smile, "I won't."

He hesitated, "Would you mind if I know your name?"

Astoria looked at his face, filled with honest curiosity, before looking over his shoulder to the knights at the bar. She said, "If I find myself back here, I'll let you know then. Deal?"

He beamed, "Aye, I can agree to that."

Astoria left, feeling his gaze on her back. She walked back towards the outskirts of the city, nodding her head at one of the guards that had gone with her hunting. As she considered the road before her, she took a steadying breath before slightly drawing her blade from its sheath. The pearly white steel shone in the light.

Back to the farm. I can decide what I do then.

CONTACT.

*F*lowing grey grasses swayed in the unfelt, silent wind, dancing in the dark. With each moment they swayed faster. Danika danced with them, the only true specter in the umbral gloom, her dress black, like her black flowing hair trailing down her form. With kind eyes, she peered back, her smile wide.

"You stood before, stand again."

A shake, filled with resignation. There is nothing to stand on.

"There is always something to stand on." She cut a swath through the grass, a shimmering length of steel in hand.

The blade is alabaster.

Sehren.

Sehren?

Another shake brought her gaze back, with bounding steps bringing her near. She smiled before resting the blade in the grass. "Reach for it, stand. And then again. And again."

A pale hand reached out.

Pale in the shrouding gloom, pale against the backdrop of the umbral grip lurking below.

Pale like the steel.

Danika nodded, "Good. You see? You can reach for it. You can stand."

Why?

Suddenly a sensation bloomed, searing and hot. It was distracting, itching, burning, tearing, and suddenly all-encompassing.

Danika watched, her head tilted, "Is that all it is then?"

It is everything. It does not stop.

"It always stops. Will it."

Will it? It is all there is. Nothing else exists.

"There is always more. Stand through it."

Stand. Stand once more. Stand against the tide.

Danika smiled, "You understand now. Reach for me, and stand, Sehren."

Sehren?

Pain seared forth, with tugging and pulling, clawing the words back down. Danika frowned, shaking her head, "You can do it."

"I-" More pain. Viscous and choking, thick in the throat.

Danika reached her hand out once more, "Almost. Again."

Again. The refrain. Again.

Red hair flickers in sight.

No, there is nothing here. "I-" More viscous pain.

Danika shook her head, "Again."

Again.

"Again." The pain pushed, but it was not choking, not clinging to. Danika's eyes widened. "Good! Again."

"Again."

She stood, reaching out once more, "Stand again, Sehren."

"I cannot." More pain, but a growl holds it at bay.

"You can. Stand again."

Shaking, with a rush of fatigue, but all dispelled by a growl. Her encouragement rang out, "You're almost there."

A hand reached out, clasping hers. There is no warmth, no support. Her hand slipped through like sand in the wind.

The grasses flowed, but there they stood, Danika walking through.

"Where?" The pain returned, clinging to each syllable like a caustic plague.

"Here. Home," she said.

Home is a vale. Nestled between the trees. Home is tall grasses, ready for harvest.

Harvest? A farm.

Home is a farm.

The grasses fade. A cottage rests in the gloom now, with a well before it. A firepit flickers with darkness as a wild field ranges beyond it.

"Home." Danika nodded, walking towards the cottage. She looked expectantly back. "Are you home?"

A nod, followed by another rush. Nostalgia?

Danika smiled, "Come then, we are home."

White steel flowed from her grip as she stepped into the field. She danced, the steel a part of her with each flowing step. She wove with each movement, the practiced dance beautiful to behold. Artistry.

No, not artistry. It is a blade.

Blades are meant for death.

"That's right," she said quietly. "It is beauty. It is art. But the art is to kill."

She smiled sadly, "You know the art."

Do I?

She nodded, *"I taught you the dance."* She started once more, and she was right. Each step was already known, plotted and planned, but the dance was fluid. One step can replace another. She nodded again, *"No dance is set. It is planned but improvised, with each step weighed. You know all the steps."*

I do.

Danika smiled, "You do." She halted the dance, looking to the barn in the distance. *"The art is to kill. But killing need not be evil."*

To protect?

"That which is valued."

Valued?

"Cherished. Wanted. Needed."

That's right. Dance to protect. Learn the art to fend off.

Shades pranced on the edge of the farm, baying and howling. Familiar, their growling grows. White teeth, harsh against the backdrop, stalk forward.

Danika watched them calmly. White steel in hand, she walked towards them.

Danger.

No, she knows.

I know.

The dance flowed, the shades dispersed, and Danika smiled. She looked back.

"You know this."

Do I?

"You do."

I do.

"It is home."

Discordance. Pain built once more.

She smiled, "This is home."

"Is it?"

More choking pain, but with a cough and growl, the throat is cleared.

Danika looked concerned, "It's okay, my sweet little dove. You've grown so fast."

Familiar. The words are familiar.

Danika's eyes turn bright, "You are learning."

"Am I home?"

Danika smiled, "Are you?"

Yes?

No.

Home is a forest with blustery winds. A wide fence around. Thick tents with fires nestled within. Home is red hair, dancing in the breeze with blue eyes bright with life.

Pain clung against the throat once more, stealing away the answer.

"Take me home," said Danika, beckoning him.

He looked over the scene, the farmland with the cottage. He looked to the sky, now dotted with pale, grey spots. Familiar spots.

Through the pain, through the choking spittle tinged dark, he said, "North."

"Then lead the way. Stand against it."

"I can't."

"You can. Take a step."

The pain grew, pushing against progress. The yearning to sleep returned, but Danika shook her head, "No. Not now."

"I am tired."

"So? Push through."

"I cannot." A shake, "I cannot."

"You can. You already have."

She's right. This too is familiar. Faces flashed, each one a searing beacon in the gloom, but they cannot be discerned.

"Pain is nothing, Sehren. You know this."

I do. Pain is an empty stomach from failure. Pain is the eyes of the crestfallen, watching on. Pain is the cries of loneliness.

Pain is not the arrow in the shoulder, the steel in the gut. No, those can be overcome. Pain is doubt. Pain is uncertainty.

"Exactly. It is nothing. Take the step."

It clung on, unrelenting. Sleep is easier.

Sleep is not home.

Take the step.

A growl and shout echo in the empty gloom, and suddenly, the pain was gone.

AMOS.

Amos waited inside the small meeting chamber. The Cathedral of the Lady was calm this time of day, with most afternoon services completed and only those with appointments with a priest lurking about. Several people meandered through the halls and pews of the Cathedral, but most who were there stood or sat in silent prayer before the mantle of the Lady, hoping for respite or grace to soothe their ails.

Amos had walked by them all, wanting to remain inconspicuous. He was tired; the last fortnight had been spent fighting with the tempestuous king. One day, he urged Amos to look into seeking a meeting with the other royal families to determine the next ruling line only to recant his decision the next and become surly as Amos scrambled to come to a solution for the king. The man was wavering, and Amos could see it, but he also knew that the proud king wanted to go on his own terms rather than backed into a corner by the other families.

All of the families saving the Zweihanz family had sent missives to the king, stating their right to claim the grand throne, and while Amos had read over their letters, he doubted that King Saiho had even managed a cursory glance over them.

The crown weighs heavy upon a man with crumbling shoulders.

Amos heard the door open, and Gavin stepped inside, smiling at the Lord Commander.

"Welcome, Lord Greyfield," he sat across from him, his eyes crinkling with kindness, "It's good to see you in good health."

"The feeling is mutual, Gavin. The church seems quite active after the festival, though with everything coming around for you, I can only begin to imagine the headache."

He let out a chuckle before saying, "Aye, it's quite a task indeed. But once we get the duties sorted out for the season everything should roll along smoothly."

Amos nodded, "Aye, as it will. You've come a long way from when I first met you, Gavin. It's always heartening to see someone climb so high with their dedication."

"Devotion is more the word. There are many that see the faith as a rich man's salve, but I've always desired to make that a rumor rather than fact. And through that, I've been granted the means to make it so." He adjusted himself in his seat before fixing the sleeves of his robe. "To what do I owe the pleasure today, Amos?"

"The stresses of the responsibility are ever-reaching," said Amos sitting back. "Combine that with a surly king and it drives down even the most steadfast."

"There is much to consider. Talk of the throne changing hands has brought many people to call, worried about the fate of the kingdom to the fate of their children," Gavin shook his head. "It is worrisome, but in the end, I believe that with your guidance, and the king's determination, you will come to a solution that will keep the peace that we have achieved over the years."

"That may be, but at what cost? The past years found good men jailed for indiscretions they had nothing to do with. Guilt by association ran rampant until it seemed that the accusations fell upon deaf ears."

Gavin gave a grim nod, "That I do remember, and it was not the best thing in the history of our order. But, those men that have returned show renewed faith and an understanding that I feel will push the order further."

"Even in the wake of change coursing through the city?"

322

"All of the most difficult things bear the best fruit, Amos. It will take time, but that is the nature of the kingdom and the Lady."

"And with you walking alongside it, it may very well come to be a better time."

Gavin gave him a nod of his head, "My service isn't done yet, nor do I feel it will end anytime soon."

"I wish I felt the same some days. I find the idea of stepping down more and more enticing with each new conundrum the king lays upon my shoulders."

"It will be a sad day when you step down Amos, but I know that the decisions you have made over the decades in the king's service have helped mold it into the realm it is today."

Amos gave the man a smile, before becoming downcast, "I take it you heard about Eleanor."

"Aye. Terrible thing to happen to her. I paid her a visit, to make sure she was well, and I was glad to see she was unharmed." He paused for a moment, "But the incident stirred something within her again. I can see it, deep in her eyes when she speaks. Even though she says she will be well, I can tell that something is askew inside of her, and I'm afraid her pride will prevent her from asking for help, perhaps until it is too late."

Amos was stricken, "Perhaps I should pay her a visit."

"She mentioned you hadn't."

"Aye. I didn't think it proper. Without Sehren, the Lord Commander paying a visit to a lady is scandalous and draws unwanted attention to both parties."

"Is that all she was to you?" asked Gavin. There was no judgment in his tone and his eyes shone with a desire to understand. After a moment, he said, "Ah, I understand."

"What?"

"Do you blame yourself for what has happened to her?"

Amos started shaking his head, the feeling coarse.

"I would understand if you did Amos. Truly. You were a fixture in her husband's life, first his knight, and then his mentor. I'm sure you paid them many visits when he still lived with her. But then, everything happened, and before anyone could take a breath, their lives became so complicatedly fractured."

"You are perceptive, Gavin."

He smiled at Amos, "I am. But I also understand what ails the soul, and guilt for what befalls others you are invested with is a dangerous ailment to be had. Sehren was the logical choice to succeed you in the order, and his departure from the brotherhood would have weighed heavily on both you and Eleanor."

"It seemed more than just him was afflicted by my presence, Gavin. Men that I walked alongside, and that walked alongside Sehren faced condemnation. And it was an odd thing to witness, as men with spectacular records within the order were clasped in irons and taken prisoner." He sighed, his age catching up to him. "Eleanor had already suffered so much, I thought it unwise to be a reminder of the life she once had."

"Or perhaps, a reminder of the friend she once made," said Gavin sagely. "In truth, men, especially righteous ones, would rather shoulder the blame themselves than let it afflict those they hold dear. It is the flaw of those that believe they should be strong enough to lift up their peers." He shifted in his seat, "If you feel you made a better choice by not going to Eleanor and perhaps bringing more misfortune, then believe it wholeheartedly. But if you find within yourself guilt about her well-being despite it, perhaps another choice is needed."

Amos smiled warmly at the priest, "You've grown wise, my old friend."

"I have the experience of many that come to me, Amos. I simply spread it to those who need it most."

As Amos left the Cathedral of the Lady, he wrinkled his nose as a sour pungent smell wafted through the air. He glanced around, trying to find a source, when he came upon a flamboyantly dressed man seated along the steps. As he turned to face Amos, a flicker of recognition went through his odd gold-yellow eyes as he stood up and dusted himself off.

"Lord Commander, is it not?" He said through the pipe he held in his mouth.

"And you might be?"

"Don't remember me?"

Amos shook his head, "I'm afraid I don't"

"Truly, it is a testament to your character that you are unfamiliar with me." He gave Amos a wide smile. "We met many years ago, in the presence of a mutual party. Perhaps you recall our meeting with Lady Eleanor DeVille?"

Amos took a moment, trying to think of the time. He shook his head again, "I can't say that I recall."

"Unfortunate. It was a trying time for us both," he blew out some more sour smelling smoke, trying his best to keep it away from Amos but the breeze carried it to him.

"Is there something you needed?"

"Oh, no, not necessarily. Rather, I believe I had something you might enjoy." He smirked, "The name's Jaks. I solve problems, even those that you might not realize you have yet."

Amos frowned at him. "I see. And what problem might that be?"

"Straight to the point. I figured you might be," Jaks took another drag of his pipe before blowing it out, "you're in danger, Lord Commander. Or rather, your family is."

"Excuse me?"

Jaks nodded, "I know, I know, a strange fellow coming after your attending of chapel to tell you that you're in danger. Unbelievable and partly suspicious. But it's not me that has their sights set on the Greyfield family."

He drew more smoke in before saying, "Greyfield. An old name, isn't it? Almost as old as, say, the Mistletain name. You were commoners before, peasants in the service of a lord."

Amos eyed him suspiciously.

"Farmers I think," he blew out the smoke, tapping his pipe against the side of his boot, "resigned to sow in the sodden fields of the Wyrmcrest mountains to the west. The kings of the west!" He smiled. "Then, suddenly, you were drafted to the king's call, as were most back in those days. To fight alongside the king in his war, against his squabbles, until at last you were able to return home a hero. And from that, you took the name Greyfield, where there was none and walked alongside the Mistletain family for generations."

"You've done your research. Is this supposed to impress me? Knowledge of things that I know? That anyone might go and learn of?"

"Not at all," replied Jaks. "But you admit that you don't recall who I am, where many who bear proud names in these times would shudder to learn I've come to pay them a visit. Mercantile pigs that have sown their paths in the misfortune and exploitation of those they seem less suitable than themselves."

"A scoundrel then," surmised Amos, his eyes narrowing.

"Among other things. And a mantle I wear proudly." He gave a mocking bow. "I told you: I solve problems. And yours is most pressing, Amos Greyfield."

"You speak of danger yet what could you possibly come across?"

Jaks grinned again, "Odd then, for both your sons to die so young."

Amos felt his blood chill, "What did you say?"

Jaks lost his grin, his face taking a solicitous look, "I know what is to have lost family so young. Especially such bright sons that would have carried the Greyfield name. One taken, barely a man, and another well into his knighthood. I am sorry, Amos, that you have suffered such in your life."

Amos continued to narrow his eyes at the man, his voice rough as he said, "You said you solve problems and yet all you've done is speak rot."

"Your brother, too, found his way to an early grave," said Jaks. "although his story is a noble one, saving those that also bore the crest of this great nation. He rests well though, knowing that you carried on the torch it would seem.

"And then, for your nephew to almost fall in similar regard," continued Jaks, his voice softening. "A tragedy that left him with no other option but to flee the lands of his birth, never again to find peace amidst the wondrous City of Isle."

His voice almost caught in his throat, "How did you know that?"

"I am Jaks," he said simply. "I made it my life's work to discover the things laid so plain that they're hidden. And this I can tell you is the truth. I bore these to you with no regard, no other intention solely to show you my capabilities."

"To gain your trust?"

"Oh, heavens no. I would expect you to distrust me as a person, for I am indeed a scoundrel and a rogue. Rather, I expect that you will trust my words when I say you and yours are in danger. Elaine, was it?"

Amos wanted to throttle the man, his anger simmering in the face of his cool confidence. Jaks, however, simply packed more pipeweed into the pipe before lighting it.

"I am not the one that endangers you, Amos." He took a draw from his pipe, blowing away. "I find it deplorable to get so involved."

"And to bring up the pain of lost ones is more righteous."

"I never claimed to be righteous and to assume so is a folly," countered Jaks. "I bring up those moments in an attempt that the grief of their reminder will stir you to consider my own words."

Amos did consider them, "Tell me then, who endangers me?"

"The very same one that your nephew accused of trying to kill him," he stated simply.

Amos' head snapped to Jaks, scanning the man. He simply smoked though, his demeanor calm and unfazed.

"You learned of his accusations?"

"I've heard the rumors. I listen, Amos, and when you do that in a city so grand, so filled with people trying to impress one another, you find nuggets of truth within the offal. Armor breakers are not common in the armaments of simple brigands, and yet without them you knights are rather hard to kill."

Amos glanced around, trying to spot other things about this, but Jaks continued to smoke unperturbed.

"If I were to arrive at the time you were to be attacked, I would hardly be good at my job."

"What do you want?"

"What I want is immaterial to all of this. It's so simple that you wouldn't believe me even if I told you. However, I'll settle for you simply owing me a favor."

Amos frowned, "And what might that entail?"

"You act like I'm the only one that plays this game, Amos. You may have managed to get by without it, but I assure you there are far less honorable people in positions just as lofty as yours, and I assure you they do not care for morals."

He blew out some smoke, "In fact, Eleanor believes that you might have been responsible for the recent attempt on her life."

Amos was stunned, "She what?"

"I know, a strange notion indeed, especially after meeting with you. You don't play this game, Amos, at least not in the way we do." Jaks' eyes glittered as he regarded him, "And that's why I am here. You wouldn't have seen it coming otherwise."

"You think that the same person Sehren thought tried to kill him is coming after me?"

"The king is a defeated old man in a position he doesn't wish to leave. And yet, he makes no efforts to strengthen his position." Jaks cocked his head. "You, however, are not defeated."

"I would attribute that to the soldier in me. There's too much to do for the people to be caught up in other things."

"Precisely. A soldier. A man of war and action. The king finds his crown heavy and the people within the city are already aligning themselves to the new reign, even if men such as yourself will not. It's easier then, to start fresh rather than to try and bring everyone on board."

Amos drew back from the man, "And what do you care what happens to our king?"

"The king. Not my king," corrected Jaks. "While I may love this fair city that your kingdom has built, my heart and blood are solely of the southern lands of my home. Things here just happen to me more fun than there."

Amos was truly at a loss of what to make of this man. "King Mistletain rules."

"With the Greyfield family at his side. And yet, both lines will end. No heirs, no future, nothing except two old men trying to hang on to a bygone era."

Amos bristled. "What would you advise then, if you have a solution."

"Simple. Return to the lands west. Let the others throw themselves upon the burning brazier of the kingdom, to flicker out in the coming years as everything strikes. What does it matter to you?"

"It is the lives of the people. The citizenry that looks to the crown for support and protection."

Jaks laughed, "One king fits just as well as another. Release your ego, Amos, or you may find that you won't live well at all."

Jaks tapped his pipe against his boot once more, the ash spilling onto the step before he swept it away with his foot. Amos watched him for a moment before saying, "Does Eleanor truly believe I would orchestrate a plan to hurt her?"

"Go and ask her yourself. I would've thought that a barren woman would have been beyond the reach of such things. It turns out, however, that you Candramans are far more evil than I could've anticipated." Jaks meandered off, his boots clicking loudly against the stones of the path.

Amos took a deep breath, resolved to first find the truth, if any, to his words and second to find the resolve to fix the problem if he did.

ELEANOR.

Eleanor visited the grave of her father, standing before it in the family plot that rested in the shadowed vale. The Cathedral loomed behind her, its grand marble walls shining in the sunlight. She could feel the late summer breeze wafting through the meadows that surrounded the different family plots. Stray hairs tickled her face and neck as they were rustled by the wind.

She stood solemnly, reading over the epitaph that she had chosen for her father. She recalled watching the words carved into the stone, making sure that each line was finely traced before the stonemason's chisel went to work. Cut into the white stone, they were filled with a dark ink to highlight the words, and the ink remained unfaded to this day. Eleanor knew that she had chosen well with the words on the headstone, but even still, she felt they didn't reach to her own core as she reviewed them.

Loving Father.

The first and most foremost to her that had stood out when she thought of him. He had given her more than she could've asked for as a girl. Whenever she had an interest, he indulged it to the best of his ability, nurturing her growth with it. And if her interest waned, he riddled her not with guilt, but with a sense of wonder for what may lay next for her, spurring her to follow the whims of her heart. As she grew, he found her the finest tailors and maids he could reasonably afford her, wanting nothing more than to dress her in the finest garbs that she enjoyed. And even as a budding young woman, where most lordly fathers would sell their daughters off to the highest bidder, he had paired her with a man that she had come to love more than anything in the world.

A coil of resentment slithered through her though, recalling that while he may have given her the best he could bring, his desire to do, in his mind, the best for her brought her the ache and sorrow that afflicted her. She knew he thought nothing more than trying to save the name of their family, her family, and yet she could still recall when he informed her that he had severed her marriage to Sehren. He had seemed proud then, as if the choice had been the most logical and correct choice to take. However, he had acted without consulting her, without taking stock of how truly it would impact her. With a simple word, he had taken from her what she had come to love for over a decade.

Dedicated Husband.

He had been that as well. Eleanor's mother Soleah had been a bright woman, filled with her own peculiarities that had drawn her father to her. Upon their marriage, Allyn had found not just a woman to lay beside and bear his kin, but a partner that could manage well on her own alongside him. He had been filled with wonder at her inquiring mind, and slowly, so slowly, she had taken down the limiting walls instilled within him by his forefathers. He embraced his wife as the thoughtful, insightful woman that she was. He had learned what it meant to be a partner to her, and together, they had grown the DeVille name further.

But Eleanor knew too that the lessons her father didn't know, the ones that he would fail to understand, would have cast him away and called for heresy and resentment. Soleah had been as gifted, if not more, than her daughter, teaching her the ways of that other world effortlessly. She had shown Eleanor the power that truly laid within their blood. She gave her the confidence to walk along the other members of the aristocracy not bowed and muted but proud. However, when she grew ill, her lessons ended, and it was all Allyn and Eleanor could do to bring some form of peace to Soleah as she slowly withered away. He had spent the coin on exotic doctors, had tried to beseech the

332

Lady for her mercy or grace, and had even thought of turning to anyone else that might have been able to save his ailing wife, but in the end, his efforts had not been enough.

Proud Merchant.

This was, in Eleanor's opinion, the meanest of his achievements but one nonetheless. He was a frugal businessman with a sound mind for both finance and calculated risk. In a society where his name had meant little, Allyn had fought and forged a path for them against the tide. He had stepped on those that got in his way and had befriended those that would cooperate with him, all while building the nest egg that his family had come to rely on. Eager and proud, he had given the DeVille name a reason to be heard within the higher echelons of society and through his efforts had cemented their place with the other families of Isle.

His triumphs were not without aid, however. He never knew of the true influence his wife, and subsequently, his daughter had upon his trade. While Eleanor knew he would have never accepted the truth, she also knew that their family's rise would have fallen short if not for their actions. Proof need not be shown; when she was Sehren's wife and wholly devoted to the man, she focused her efforts upon her knight husband rather than her lord father. And while Allyn hadn't ran himself into the ground, there were several years where he confessed to her that the competition was stiff and growing, and he wondered if he had simply lost his touch.

No Father, just your most valuable assets.

Eleanor knelt before the grave, hoping that even though he may have been sent there earlier than he would've wanted, that he had gone as an accomplished soul. She looked over to her mother's tombstone, faded by the years, before clearing away some of the dust that had settled in the crevices of the carvings. She breathed deeply, hoping her mother had grown proud of her.

"You are fortunate to have such a lovely place for your kin," said Railand, stirring Eleanor from her thoughts. "Many of the people here have to settle with unmarked plots or burning them away in a temple."

"Those who have fought for their place within the city earn it, even in death," said Eleanor calmly as she rose. She faced Railand, who watched the path carefully before he met her gaze.

"Fought or bought?" he asked cynically.

Eleanor laughed, "In my family's case, both."

"Better than others, I would presume."

"Most people in these plots have had to work at some point in their families' history, and some even today."

Railand raised his eyebrow, "And what would happen if you stopped?"

"Why would I do that?"

"Sometimes, a person gets so focused on the fight that they forget what they're fighting for," he replied. "Eventually it is the fight that consumes them, and without it, their endeavors are pointless."

"Are you saying that is what's become of me?" asked Eleanor with a frown.

"Not at all. You have a goal, though one I cannot seem to ascertain. However, I spend little of my time figuring that out, as that is not what you pay me for."

Eleanor smiled, "Railand, in our years together, is your contract all you care for?"

"It's to me what dealing in leathers, furs, and goods is to you," he responded. "It gives me a reason to hone my skills past what they are, further than needed to simply guard someone."

"If not me, then another," reasoned Eleanor.

"Precisely. You came upon me at a time where I sought a contract worth keeping."

"I thought you never broke a contract."

"If that were the case, milady, you would never have been able to hire me," he replied. "However, before this, I was akin to a sellsword. My contracts were brief and bloody, just the way I preferred things."

"What made you want to change and work for stuffy merchants in their gilded homes?"

"In truth, nothing. But finding that I have both a place to rest my head and eat delicious food quells the need to constantly spill blood." He took a moment to look her over, and Eleanor saw the truth in his eyes.

"I never asked after your interview, Railand, but why here? Why this city?"

Railan's smile grew indulgent, "I was once told that places such as these, so filled with splendor and wealth, harbor some of the most vile of people. But even with that warning, even being told that my skills were better off in service to a brigade of sellswords or mercenaries, I found that I wanted to see for myself if the tales were true."

"And were they?"

"Are you asking me if I find you corrupt and vile, Eleanor?" he asked with amusement in his eyes.

"I'd like your opinion on the matter," she replied with a smirk.

"You harbor something within you," he answered easily. "I could see it from when we met. You are not all that you seem, and whatever you have within you is dangerous."

Eleanor raised her eyebrow, "Dangerous."

"Aye. But not the dangerous that comes when a hound crosses your path, foam dripping from its jowls as raw flesh sits beneath matted fur. Nor is it the danger that can be found when darkened steel is drawn in the depths of night, with glittering eyes filled with malice. It's the danger of a survivor; someone who knows what they are capable of overcoming and will not allow anything else to drive them past that."

He signaled himself, "Hence, hiring me."

Eleanor's gaze dropped to her hand before returning to him.

"It is subtle, milady. Almost hidden beneath the glimmer of your verdant eyes. And no, it is not the stump that tells me of such a harrowed path, but the way you carry yourself, the aura of confidence that you exude from you when you speak, and walk, and even sup. You are clear where your line is drawn, and you protect yourself to make sure that line is never crossed again."

Railand smiled, "I respect that. That is why I am in your service."

"Because I wish to stay safe?"

"Because I know you have no qualms with me taking a life to prevent that line from being crossed. And because I know that someone so controlled as you will constantly have that battle ahead of them."

Eleanor saw the gleam in Railand's eyes, his steady voice giving way to tinges of passion. He would fight, would want to fight, until he crossed an enemy that he knew he couldn't defeat. And even then, that wouldn't dissuade him. He would fight, solely because that was what mattered to him.

"In our time together, you've hardly had to draw your blade," she said. "Most of the time, it was in warning. But you say you wish to stay contracted to me because of the fights that lay ahead?"

"I stay contracted to you because having a reason to hone my skills is better than growing bored with the thought of battle."

Eleanor shook her head, "I don't seem to understand."

"That's because Railand possesses a rare zeal about him. One that urges him to push the boundaries of perfection in hopes of finding it," called a voice, turning both their gazes to the path. Jaks stood there, respectfully waiting as they considered him. "Am I not welcome here?"

"Are you always eavesdropping?" asked Railand, frowning.

"It's only eavesdropping if the conversation was attempted to be kept secret," countered Jaks. "You were both speaking with such spirited voices, I also thought to knock before interrupting."

Eleanor's mouth thinned to a line, "Some indicator of your presence would have been appreciated."

"I thought it rude to interrupt," replied Jaks nonchalantly. "I sought you out at your home, milady, but they told me you were out at the cemetery."

"To what end?"

336

"To give you the news you desire to hear." Jaks smirked, waiting patiently at the edge of the plot. Eleanor pardoned herself from Railand's side as she walked over to Jaks.

She dropped her voice low, "You were able to learn the truth?"

"That's a tricky thing," said Jaks. "What is the truth one day could become unraveled the next. However, I have been able to root out what might remain, and with Rosline's help, that will be taken care of in a matter of days."

Eleanor felt a rush of relief, "And the other matter we discussed?"

"Taken care of, it seems," replied Jaks. "I have my people in place. Your secret is kept with me."

"Unless someone else buys it from you," frowned Eleanor.

Jaks faked a hurt look, a mocking smile spreading across his face, "Come now, Eleanor. I'm not easily bought. Coin is easy to come across. No, I'd much rather have a friend that owes me a favor."

"What kind of favor?"

"One that will eventually require you to put me in contact with someone in the higher echelons of the aristocracy," explained Jaks. "I won't bore you with the details now, but I will eventually need an introduction to someone that would be able to nestle among the servants of higher nobility."

"I see…" Eleanor paused a moment, "I believe I have a sparing few that I can contact with that. However, their cooperation will be hesitant, especially with an unknown party."

"I find that unknown parties become bosom friends quite easily, especially when it comes to me," said Jaks with a smirk. "And if not, I'm certain that Rosline or you could find a remedy for that."

"You'd extort them?"

"Exort sounds so negative. I prefer the term 'coerce' or even 'convince'. People who get so far and climb so high tend to be very determined to remain there."

Eleanor narrowed her eyes, "And some may become dangerous."

"If they don't recognize the true enemy with me standing before them, Eleanor, then they didn't have much sense to begin with," replied Jaks. "Either way, that is my price, and I plan to collect when I need it."

Eleanor watched Jaks' face gain a conniving quality before returning back to his normal smirking visage. He glanced over her shoulder before dipping his head to Railand, the man giving him a curt nod in return. After he left, Railand drew up to Eleanor's side.

"He's a very odd one. I don't entirely trust him."

"You shouldn't," replied Eleanor. "But Jaks has proven to me over the years to be more reliable than the merchants and aristocrats I've come to know."

"That may be true, but even coiled vipers seem docile to some," countered Railand.

Eleanor smirked, "You are right. But today he's given me a great gift."

"And what might that be?"

"Railand, I didn't think you'd be so interested in my own affairs."

He laughed, "When they don't involve the carting of leathers and furs, I find them more attractive indeed."

Eleanor shared his laugh, "It seems he's taken care of whomever offered my name to those that attacked us before."

Railand furrowed his brow as he narrowed his eyes, "He is certain?"

"He feels certain of it."

"It seems like a tangled web, is all. I wonder if he already knew from the start."

Eleanor considered that for a moment, looking back to the path that Jaks had taken. She shook her head, "He needed Rosline for it. I believe he has his hunches, but acted only when he was sure."

"If you say so milady." Railand looked over the grave plot one more time before saying, "Are you finished this day?"

"For now, yes. I have another stop I wish to go to."

"Of course, milady. Lead the way."

ASTORIA.

She marched into the small trading post, running her hand over some of the supplies. Her back ached from the laden pack she had carried over the weeks of travel. She saw an older man moving several provisions around as a small girl followed behind, her young face bright with a smile. She turned her head to Astoria, her toothy grin widening as she said, "Papa! It is a buyer!"

"Aye, you mean 'customer' Ellie," said the man, turning a kind smile to Astoria. He looked her up and down a moment before saying, "Hunter eh? What can I getcha?"

"I was hoping you'd have enough stuff to last me until the city of Isle," replied Astoria, pulling out the small coin pouch. She counted out what coins she had left and hoped it would be enough to give her a few nights without needing to hunt.

After she passed the coins over to the man, who counted them carefully before saying, "If you stretch what you buy it'll last 'til the city, but I reckon you'll definitely have to stretch it."

Astoria sighed before nodding, "I'll take that then. Better than nothing."

He scooped up the coins, smiling at Astoria as he started sorting out supplies, "You coming in from up north?"

Astoria nodded again.

"How far? We don't get a lot of true northern folk, and you look the sort," he asked curiously. "Oh, pardon me. Name's Kenneth. Don't mind me too much, we get a lot of folk through here so I'm always wonderin'."

"It's all right," said Astoria. "I'm just feelin' the road a bit more than I was expectin', and I don't really find myself in the most talkative of moods."

She felt a small tug on her leg, drawing her gaze to a small girl holding out a cup filled with a dark liquid. She had a beaming smile as she said "Pa says to try and give people things when they come to visit."

Astoria took the offered cup, holding it in her hands as warmth emanated through it. "Thank you."

Ellie smiled before returning back behind the counter. Astoria brought the cup to her face and sniffed lightly. It smelled of tea and honey. She took a small sip, feeling warmth settle within her as she did.

Kenneth laughed, "Seems like she rememberin' some of the things. Tryin' to keep people comin' back."

"She's a kind one," said Astoria. She took another sip as Kenneth prepared a pack for her. After finishing the tea she set the cup down on the counter and sorted through the pack.

"Aye, she gets that from her ma. I'm tryin' teach her some wariness but it's hard when all you folk are so kind to her," he laughed. "O' course I think she's growin' up fine, and she'll eventually be runnin' the place if her ma gets her way."

Astoria felt a tinge of guilt in her heart as she nodded before scooping up the pack that Kenneth finished. "I appreciate it."

"You headin' straight there?"

"Why?"

"Just wonderin'. It's a long trek, and I know every now and again people stop by and look to travel together to the city. Safety in numbers and whatnot."

Astoria considered it for a moment, thinking it would be nice to sleep fully instead of with one eye open. However, sinister faces
342

flickered through her mind and probing questions she knew she'd have to dance around caused her to shake her head.

"That sounds good, but I'm in a bit of a rush. Thanks again."

Kenneth gave her a wave, talking with his daughter as Astoria left the post. She scanned the small town, remembering all the years ago when she came through it.

It's the same. It's all the same.

She took a moment to set her new belongings together, adjusting the straps on her pack to mitigate as much chafing as possible. Footsteps approached her. She reached for the pommel of her sword before looking up at the source of them.

An older woman, with brown hair streaked with grey, approached her tentatively. She had a question in her eyes and urgency in her step, but she hesitated as she grew closer.

"Do you need something?" asked Astoria.

"Are yeh a hunter?"

Astoria gave a shallow nod. "Why?"

"My son's been missin' for a few days, and I don't know what to do. Guards can't spare no one to go look for 'im, and I'm too scared to be doin' it alone."

Astoria gave the woman a once over, noting that she seemed to be trembling. "I'm sorry about your son, but I can't really afford to be lookin' for him."

"Please…" her eyes shone with tears, "I don't know anyone else here who could. There's not many folk like yeh."

Astoria let out a sigh, her heart heavy as she thought.

Sehren wouldn't have done it.

His lessons kept me safe. But…

She looked at the woman again, "I'm sorry… are you sure they can't spare anyone else?"

The woman shook her head dismally, "No, they can't be sparin' no one…" She sniffed, "I get it, yeh've got to be on yer way…" She bowed her head at Astoria, before turning and starting to shuffle off.

Astoria wrestled with her turmoil as she watched her walk away. She turned away from her, marching a few steps before she felt guilt creep up her spine. She spun around, her swift gait drawing her to the woman's side, "I can only spare the day to search. Afterwards I have to be leavin'."

The woman's eyes went so wide that Astoria thought they would fall from her head. "Oh thank yeh, thank yeh. Are yeh needin' somewhere to stay?"

Astoria nodded slowly before hitching her pack on her back, "Do you know where he might've gone?"

The woman became downcast, "He used to be goin' around berry pickin', bringin' back what he could in the bottom of his shirts. I told him to stop dirtyin' his clothes like that, but he always came back with more…"

There was another pang in her heart as she heard the pain in her voice from loss. She understood.

"Yer the first one to be takin' interest, and I thank yeh so much for it."

"I haven't done anything yet."

"Hope, dearie, yeh've given me hope," she turned her smile back onto Astoria, and she just gave a tentative smile in return. She followed the woman to a small cabin on the outskirts of the trading post. She ushered Astoria inside, revealing a small, homely space with a hearth within.

Astoria set down her belongings inside the door before digging through her pack and retrieving what she would need. "Do you know how far the patch is from here?"

"Oh not too far, perhaps an hour or so walkin'," said the woman with nervous excitement. "I really appreciate you helpin' me."

"Let me see what I find first before you thank me," said Astoria. She adjusted the quiver on her back before flinging her bow over her shoulder. "I'll try to be back before dark."

"Just bring him home if you could. Let him know ma's not angry."

"I'll let him know," Astoria drew up her hood and left.

She walked through the brush and trees, trying to find some clue of this missing boy. As she walked along though and crouched to the ground, she didn't see any evidence of recent passage of creatures, let alone people. The path seemed untouched for a while, and Astoria wondered if she was going the right way.

There aren't many other paths a child would have taken. At least, not ones I would've taken.

Astoria continued stalking along, glancing to the sky now and again to keep track of the passage of time.

Just one day of this. That's all you said. You do this, and whether or not you find him, you can leave without feeling guilty.

She continued trying to track the boy, searching for any sign of him, but became increasingly flustered when she found nothing to indicate his passage. As she took a break, she sat against a tree and drank from a waterskin, thinking. Her frustration mounted though, stealing away her thoughts and she rose, continuing her tracking.

Astoria found the patch of berries almost another hour of tracking later. Small critters and vermin scattered from the bushes as she approached, and she scouted around it, frowning as she once again couldn't find even a single small footprint of a child.

Maybe there's another patch somewhere?

Astoria did rest there, picking several of the berries as she drank deep of her waterskin. She listened to the critters picking their way around her to get to the patch. Every now and again she would cock her head, trying to listen to see if she could sort out footsteps or anything through the sounds of nature, but nothing stood out to her, her surroundings filled with naught but the sounds of the wilderness.

The quiet made her anxious, a feeling she was unused to. She had always been comfortable in the wilds, her hunts taking her days away from the encampment. It was peace and tranquility, accompanied by the edge of danger that told her to lapse too much could spell her demise. It kept her sharp though, always ready for whatever might loom from the dark.

Now, it grated against her, stealing away her peace, and once again, she rose, anxious energy filling her as she resolved to find something to tell the woman. She glanced at the sky and estimated that she had several more hours before the sun would set. With that in mind, Astoria tried to pick up the trail, each step filled with determined energy. As the sky darkened though, she started making her way back towards the woman's home, feeling dejected. She took another path home, hoping to find something she could tell the woman.

As she walked back, she spied a small crag covered in a thicket. Curious, she made her way over, before feeling glum. Crumpled there, into two pieces, was a small skeleton, picked clean by animals. Astoria approached it, hoping against hope it was something else. However, when she approached it, and saw the teeth marks against the bones, with the marrow pulled clean from within, she recoiled. A torn shirt with long, tearing marks hung from the torso, and Astoria spied the tell-tale stains around the hem of the shirt amidst the blood stains and mud. They were dark and blue, like the berries she had eaten hours ago.

Her breath coming short, Astoria pulled the shirt from the body, before looking around for a way to mark the spot for return. She mustered some stones around the top of the crag, trying to make it stand out, before she looked over the skeleton once more.

I didn't even get his name. Or hers.

There was a pit in Astoria's stomach as she stood before the boy with respect. Tears gathered in her eyes, but she wiped them away before folding the shirt and packing it away into her pack. She gave the crag one last look, before turning away and heading back to the trading post.

"Did yeh find him?" asked the woman after she opened the door. Astoria met her frantic, hopeful gaze with a solemn one.

Wordlessly, Astoria set down her pack and dug into it. She pulled forth the shirt, unfolding it as she stood up and holding out for the woman.

"He was…" she choked a bit, her throat dry, "I found him in a crag a short walk from here… I pulled this from what I found so you could have something from him."

The woman's eyes watered as she took the shirt with shaking hands, her voice becoming gravelly as she asked, "Was he…" She ran her fingers over the tears and stains, tears falling down her cheeks.

"I'm sorry," said Astoria. She thought about telling her about the animal marks on the bones, or the fact that he was in two, but hearing her pained cries stole the words from her throat.

"He's… not gonna come back, is he?"

Astoria shook her head, fighting the bile rising in her throat. "He isn't…"

The woman nodded, clutching the shirt close to her as she said, "Thank yeh for finding him."

"I marked it so you can find the site. It's south of here, if you want to see him."

"Tomorrow." She walked over to a small room, setting down the shirt on a table. Astoria felt as though the walls around her were pressing in and when the woman was out of sight, she gathered her things and left.

I never got her name. But at least I brought her peace.

Tired but filled with a buzzing tide, Astoria left the trading post, hoping to leave her grief behind her.

The road proved long for Astoria, but she pushed through her exhaustion, the skeleton of the boy still fresh in mind's eye. Whenever she would take a moment to rest or otherwise stop, the clawing visions of the burning pyre waited for her at the edge of her mind. Each time she saw them, she would rouse herself from her rest and push onwards, the only thought on her mind was the farmland.

She trekked through the night, the aching in her feet growing to a new height, but the pain distracted her from the mother's lamenting voice. It stole away the stinging in her eyes, forcing her solely to be focused on her breathing to push through every pained step. She shifted uncomfortably as the straps of her back wore against her skin, her chaffed shoulders raw from the constant march.

'Pain tells you your limits, Astoria.'

What about pain of the mind Sehren? What do I do for that?

Astoria bit through the inside of her cheek as she marched, the darkness around a comforting shroud. She knew there were many nocturnal beasts even this far south that could pose a threat to her, especially in her current beleaguered state. None came to bother her as she traveled, and before long, she could spy the tell-tale glow of the sun lightening the horizon.

How many days has it been now? I can't remember.

Astoria had a stark realization. All those years ago, when she couldn't fathom how Sehrne had mustered such a desperate march north without rest, when she couldn't understand why he never rested, Astoria had wondered what had driven him. She understood it now, the realization that to stop and do nothing was harder than simply putting one foot in front of the other and moving onwards, regardless of the pain she felt. His despair had allowed him to push beyond his own limits to act, just as Astoria's grief was allowing her to continue her path.

Until what? Until when?

Astoria continued putting one foot in front of the other. She saw no other course of action but took comfort in knowing that.

The path was unkempt and gnarled moving forward, but Astoria kept the rising sun on her left shoulder. The trees were far sparser than those in Senkama, but the ground had become more buckled and gnarled by comparison. There was no sense of familiarity as she walked, a sensation that unnerved Astoria at first, but fell away in the cloud of pain she carried. As she rested once more, she thought she could vaguely remember where she was, before she recalled that the trek through these lands were taken when she rested atop Termesa as

Sehren guided them. She could hardly recall those days astride the mighty warhorse, let alone the surroundings of their trip.

Astoria continued on, pushing through the tree and brush. Drowsiness pushed on the edge of her mind, but she dispelled it with a swift shake of her head.

It can't be that much further out. Just keep pushing.

Guided by that simple thought, Astoria pushed onwards.

The clearing had become almost unrecognizable after all the years. Brambles wove through the tall thicket, the clutching grasps of nature having overtaken all of the farmland. A ramshackle of a cottage lay in ruins, the roof collapsed inside in a tumble of splinters. The firepit crumbled aside, the stone surrounding it broken by years of neglect. Only the well still stood against the test of time. Astoria approached it, grateful that she could still draw a pail and toss it into the water below. She drew it up, relieved to see the clear water within before she took the time to refill her waterskin. As she finished, she drew the pail once more before taking it beside the decrepit fire pit and sitting against the rotted log that laid there.

Memories slowly floated back to her of her time here. Mornings filled with swordplay, afternoons filled with lessons of hunting. And somewhere between all that, there was time for rest and stories. That life seemed so far away from her now, so muddled and clouded that it was almost impossible to Astoria. She took off her boots, hissing as she felt some of the blisters she had accumulated over the hard march exposed to the air. Gingerly, she cupped water and washed her feet, letting out shrill hisses as her blisters stung. Eventually she washed her hands and face as well, before sitting back against the log and looking to the sky.

Sehren had told her long ago that staying there would have been a danger if someone had learned of its location from Eleanor. Astoria had asked him many times why they needed to go so far north, but he hadn't answered. In the quiet serenity of the farm, she understood now: Sehren had run north for the same reason that Astoria had run south. She wanted distance away from her grief, away from the memories that permeated her dreams at night. Her identity had only been another reason, another justification for their flight north. She considered the abandoned farm, and while the memories of before gave her small twinges of sadness, she believed she could've stayed there. It could become her home if she wanted, even if she needed to find a way to build a new home.

Sehren's last words to her weighed heavy on her mind.

Home. He said to go home.

This isn't home, but it could be.

Astoria bit the inside of her cheek. She was here now, her march ended, but sadly the only thing that remained present on her mind was the drive to do something. Anything. She attempted to stand, but found that her feet ached terribly and that her eyelids weighed heavy. She sat down, resting against the log, before the world darkened around her as she drifted off to sleep.

When next she woke, the lands around her were darkened, shrouded by an evening glow as the sun dipped beneath the horizon. She pushed herself up, feeling the vestiges of the long march aching through her. She continued rising though, standing up as she felt she should at least ready her tent for the evening. As she looked over her pack beside her though to the bundled tarp and poles, her gaze continued trailing to the dilapidated shack. She walked over to it, stepped over the ruined threshold, and peered inside. The roof had collapsed what remained of the floor, and there was rubble everywhere. She could barely spy the small stone that Sehren would kneel at from time to time through the mess. Moving some of the debris, she cleared the area around the stone and read the inscription. Her heart hurt for a moment. Sehren had never told her what had laid there and never mentioned it to her again. She knelt before it and cleared away the dirt that had gathered.

"I'm sorry," she said, her voice tight with emotion. "I tried my hardest, but it wasn't enough. Sehren— he would've made you proud. I was proud of him." She cleared her throat, trying to stymie the burning in her eyes. "I loved him. But I couldn't protect him like he protected us. Protected me." Tears ran down her cheeks, but she didn't wipe them away. "I hope he found peace. He was so tormented, and I hope that in everything that happened, he found his peace." She bowed her head, letting the grief fully fall from her shoulders as the tears streamed down her face. The sun dipped below the horizon, bathing her in darkness, but still she knelt. She eventually steadied herself, gazing at the worn stone once more. She looked around and found a length of board that wasn't rotted all the way through. Steadily, she gouged a line in the earth beside the stone, stopping only to measure it. She eventually dug it a few feet deep, leaving a long trench in the earth. She unbelted the sword on her side. Drawing it carefully, she stared into the pearly white steel, seeing her eye reflected in the moonlight that shone through the broken eaves.

This isn't my blade. It was his. And his mother's. It was their family's.

Astoria sheathed the blade, before leaving a moment to gather one of her shirts from her pack. She returned to the trench and wrapped the sheathed blade in her shirt before setting it in the trench.

She paused for a moment, letting the tears run down her cheeks. She unlatched the chain at her neck, staring at the white stone that hung from the end of it.

I love you. I love you so much.

Astoria unwrapped the blade before tying the chain around the hilt of the blade. She looked at it one final moment before wrapping it again. Slowly, methodically, she pushed the dirt over it, until it was fully buried once more.

Goodbye, Sehren.

CONTACT.

The world shifted constantly, ephemeral images coming into existence before flickering out in a myriad of darkening shades. Tall looming figures could be seen in between each scene, ever present and yet ever shifting. While they too melted away into the swirling lands, their presence could be felt even in their absence.

Danika was nowhere to be found, her once long strides and domineering presence vanished alongside everything else. Remaining fixed was an impossibility, and the temptation to simply wash away along the shades grew with every passing moment.

Focus.

Focus was only present with Danika. In her absence, focus meant nothing.

Cling on.

Onto what?

Onto home.

Home is gone, swept away by the tide just as everything else had. The fields, the barn, the well, all taken by the ceaseless passage of time.

No. That was not home. Merely a home.

353

Lost and found, only to be abandoned.

No. Not abandoned. Father was there.

As was mother. Mother was taken from there.

No. She left for us.

To abandon you.

To protect me.

Protect me?

The blade weighed heavy on his belt, but as he reached for it, it vanished.

Gone, as is she. It is nothing. Be nothing.

Be at peace.

"*Peace ain't what it's cut out for, is it?*"

A scene melded before him, a common room of a tavern. In the corner was a hearth, black now with no flame to light it. But still it was clear, a fixture in the spiraling gloom. At the bar were several stools, with an older man waiting with rag and tankard in hand.

"*Yeh should take a load off,*" *said Aruhn, his smile kind.*

He approached the bar, settling onto the stool as Aruhn continued cleaning, setting down one tankard to pick up another one.

"*Yeh've been gone a while, ain'tcha?*"

Has it been that long?

"*Aye it has. Barely recognize you.*"

Who am I?

"*Don't yeh know? Yeh're Sehren the Steadfast! Didn't think yeh'd be that daft.*" *He chortled, the sound so familiar but muted in the gloom.*

I am?

"*Aye, yeh are. Least, yeh were.*"

I was.

354

Another laugh, *"Yeh get hit hard on yehr head? Never thought yeh'd be the one for repeatin' things yeh already knew."* He slid a tankard before him, *"Go on then, take a drink."*

For what?

"For whatever yeh're wantin'. Celebration, relaxation, escape. Even peace."

Peace?

Peace was nice.

"Aye, always is. Funny how it's always gone in an instant though. Chasin' it seems to be all anyone thinks of, from farmhands to kings." He cleaned another tankard, *"There's only few places to find it though."*

Home?

"Aye, that's one. Nothin' like home to still the heart."

What else is there?

"Aye, there's home. Then there's peace in another's arms, though I think yeh know that one already." He laughed, *"The right person can make all the difference."*

Golden tangles on white sheets floated before his mind's eye, before being taken away in a fleeting moment.

Auhn gave a solicitous look, "Aye, but doesn't always last. Then there's peace in the doing."

Doing?

"Aye. Some call it duty, others call it a job. The satisfaction of doin' the work right." Aruhn set the tankard down, before resting along the bar top. *"Then there's the lastin' peace."*

Lasting?

Aruhn nodded, "The peace of simply movin' on. Takin' a rest, and lettin' the world move along."

His voice sounded content, accomplished, and sedate, as if the thought played well on his mind. So simple and yet, discordance rang out, as though it didn't fit correctly.

What of the tavern?

"It'll be here for whoever's next. Sometimes hangin' onto what we want is why peace can't be found. Just lettin' go can feel so well."

That doesn't seem right.

"Never does, but it's the truth. Let someone else handle it. Peace is so much better."

Peace is finality?

"Can be. Sometimes, reprieve can be all that's needed."

Rest does sound tempting.

"Always is. Take a breather, ain't yeh done enough?"

Yes.

No.

"No?"

There is more to do. Focus is all that's needed.

'That's right, just focus, Sehren.'

"Focus? I mean, yeh that can bring peace. But why?"

Why did you work for so long?

"Aye, my peace died long ago. And yeh took my other peace."

Took your peace?

Red hair, blue eyes, and a bright smile flashed in his mind's eyes.

"Aye yeh know it."

It was what was needed.

"Yeh think? Or did yeh not want to be alone?"

It was your idea.

"Aye, but yeh still accepted. And now what of it?"

She's out there.

"Aye, on her own."

356

Focus.

'That's right Sehren, focus.'

This isn't real.

Aruhn cocked his head. "O' course it is."

It is not here.

Aruhn smirked, "But somewhere else is?"

It is.

"Then why yeh wastin' time. It's not for peace."

Why am I here?

Why?

"I died," said Sehren, his voice ringing clear.

The tavern vanished, Aruhn standing before him in the swirling gloom.

"Figurin' that part out then. But yeh said yeh died."

He looked down, his own body clouded by shadow. He saw his arms, felt his chest, but no heartbeat. Unless…

"Aye, it is thrumming," said Aruhn, looking around.

"I died," repeated Sehren.

"Aye, and yet yeh didn't find peace."

"Peace in death is not what I sought."

"Yeh sure about that?"

"I am."

Aruhn smiled then, looking solemn as he gazed over the field of black. "Would be nice, considerin'."

"Considering what?"

"What's left out there I mean."

"There is much left out there."

"Aye, and all of it away from peace. Is that what yeh're wantin'?"

I don't know.

Focus. Focus on what counts.

"I died."

"Aye, yeh did." Aruhn gave him a sympathetic look, "Yeh fought hard."

"Not hard enough."

"Yeh didn't slip. She did."

Who?

"Yeh know who. She slipped and the blade caught."

"Not her blade."

"Nay, but a blade nonetheless. Yeh didn't slip."

Pain came at his side, a tearing, agonizing pain. He lurched to the side, fighting against the feeling. Images flooded back but amidst the torrent of pain, they were clouded, hazed, and muted.

Focus.

"It's okay to let go," said Aruhn, kneeling to look at him. "Yeh've fought enough."

"Not. Not enough." *The words were harsh in his throat, spilling forth warbled. He uprighted himself, focusing on the pain and pitting himself against it.*

As he had done before.

It is nothing. Nothing you've never dealt with before. And it will fade.

But you will not.

"Aye, the Steadfast," said Aruhn with a beaming smile, "I get it now."

Sehren pit himself against the pain, pushing it away even as it threatened to encompass him. He shut his eyes, forcing his will against it.

He opened them, alone once more. The pain steadily subsided as he looked around, the silence looming in as the plains swirled around him.

Clinking jewelry accompanied by heeled boots against cobbled stone sounded through the silence. A smirking visage with long hair tied in a bandana approached him.

"You've seen better days, haven't you?".

ROSLINE.

Rosline sat in the garden with Kyrah, seated in the shade to avoid the heat. She was waiting for Eleanor's return as her daughter watched the butterflies that were fluttering around the flowers. Rosline fanned herself gently and gave a smile to Kyrah whenever she pranced over with questions on her face.

"Mama?"

"Yes, my dove?"

"How come they float away?" she pointed towards the small smattering of them that were swept away by the breeze.

Rosline took a moment to appreciate the wind washing over her before she said, "They have other places to be."

"Like papa?"

"Like papa."

"So then, they will be back!" Kyrah watched them flutter away in the breeze, her eyes wide.

Rosline smiled kindly at her, her bright eyes filled with understanding and pride. She knew that Jaks would often leave the city, but Rosline had told her that he would always be back. And he hadn't proved them wrong, coming back each time with stories for Kyrah and adoration for Rosline. Rosline had thought that he would have been inattentive to his daughter, but on the contrary, when he was in the city, they were nigh inseparable save for when he had to work. And even then, regardless of his work, he always returned first to Kyrah, letting her smile and cry in joy when he would sit her on his shoulders.

As she thought of his current travel, to some town she'd never heard of, Rosline idly wondered if he had other children that he visited. It wouldn't surprise her; the man was a scoundrel after all, and before they had coupled, Jaks had told her that he found it hard for a single woman to sate his desire. There had been plenty of stories and rumors about the man, and Rosline had the pleasure of experiencing most of them firsthand. He was a common topic among the other maids at Aruhn's tavern, his graceful stride and exotic features evoking fantasies uncommon for the women. Rosline even remembered the first few times she had seen him when she started working at the tavern, with hushed giggles and flushed faces behind working hands.

She had never thought about it, not even when she had found out that she was with child, but seeing Kyrah laugh so easily and readily for her father gave her an odd sensation of familiarity. Jaks seemed practiced in the matter, which Rosline had attributed to his ability to inexplicably charm anyone he wished to.

And if he has other children, so what?

As she contemplated the idea, Rosline found that it didn't bother her as much as she thought it should. His other children would hopefully be older than Kyrah and much further along in their lives. If Jaks made it a point to visit them while he was doing his work, that only helped soothe her mind about Kyrah's future. Jak had proven, after all, that he could bring delight to her daughter, and in Rosline's mind, she felt comfort that at least she would know who her father was.

Well, perhaps not entirely. Or perhaps… maybe that is him?

Rosline smiled once more, her mind sifting through her thoughts as she watched her daughter. The sun beat down upon them both though, and Rosline grew uncomfortable as the day grew longer. While summer had proven to be tamer than usual this year, Rosline still found it stifling to be out for long periods. She had never been a fan of the heat, and while the City of Isle found reprieve from the heat with the breeze that wafted in from the docks, on days like this when the air laid still, it was a trying time indeed. Rosline continued fanning herself, wondering how Eleanor managed to wander through the day without finding herself disheveled by the heat. She tended to wear more elaborate dresses when she attended her appointments, much to the pleasure of the lords she visited, but Rosline could only imagine how stuffy the garment would become. Especially when she considered that Eleanor regularly walked to her appointments instead of taking a carriage.

Her thoughts were stirred when the gate clamored open. Rosline quickly beckoned her daughter over and took her by the hand. She walked to the front, happy to see Eleanor and Railand returned. Eleanor held a parasol upon her left shoulder, shading her from the beating sun, and when she saw Rosline, gave her a soft smile. Kyrah slipped her hand from Rosline as she made a beeline for Railand, who simply grinned at her before looking to Rosline. She nodded, and he cocked his head, letting the small girl dart off as he followed behind.

"Did everything go well?" asked Rosline.

Eleanor had followed the retreating pair with her gaze for a moment before returning it to Rosline. "Yes, things are settled. The preparations for autumn are set, and if everything goes as expected, then this winter should be an easy one."

"That's fantastic."

"It is," Eleanor continued walking towards her home, "but let's continue discussing this inside. I've found I have grown tired of the heat."

Rosline fell in step beside Eleanor as she offered to take the parasol from her. Eleanor simply acquiesced as they crossed the threshold, one of the guards holding the door open for the pair of them. Eleanor led her to the conference room, where she took a seat by entrance. Rosline took a spot beside her, sweeping her dress beneath her legs. Rosline beckoned for a servant to bring them a drink before taking a deep sigh.

"Were you able to discern anything new about what we discussed?"

Rosline shook her head as her cheeks tinged with shame, "Nothing as far as I can tell. I peered for a while as well, trying to see if there were any patterns or routines, but even that was still as expected."

Eleanor tilted her head, "And I sense you were a bit distracted."

Rosline bit the inside of her lip before nodding, "I was. It's been a tremendously hot day, and I found the study a bit uncomfortable, even when I was focused. I'm sorry."

"It's quite all right. It has been a stifling day. Even I found myself beleaguered by the heat while at my appointments." The servant returned a carafe coated in condensation and poured them two glasses before leaving them to be with a bow. Eleanor took an appreciative sip before locking her gaze on Rosline. "Rosline, I have something I've wondered for a while."

"Yes, milady."

"What is it that you aspire to?"

Surprised, Rosline asked, "Milady?"

"Yes," said Eleanor with a smile, "what is it you desire in life? What do you see yourself aspiring to?"

"I'm not sure," admitted Rosline. "Before, I never really thought of havin' more than I did."

"When you were younger?"

"Aye. It was kinda just one day, I was a kid, running through the streets with the other kids, and then another day, I was working. Before I knew it, I was hopping from tavern to tavern, wherever I could find work, before I met Aruhn and he gave me a proper job."

An icy sliver went through her heart as she thought about him.

"He was your first true job?"

"Aye, paid me proper, gave me the stuff I needed to work, and set expectations for me. From then, I thought I had what I wanted."

"And did you?"

"I did, until I met you milady," said Rosline. "Then you showed me more of what I could be, and I just wanted to do that as best as I could."

364

"And you don't want for more?"

"What more could I want, milady?" asked Rosline sincerely. She looked around the very room they were in, still after all the years not able to appreciate the wealth that was present around them. "You've given me a room in a wonderful home, beautiful clothes to wear, a job that is fulfilling and pushes me more every day. My daughter has never known hunger and has a teacher that I could only imagine a child of mine having. You found me Geneve, and she has made life so much different than I have known. Milady, I don't know what else I could want."

Eleanor gave her a genial smile, her green eyes filled with understanding, "Your life has taken a charmed turn since you came into my employ, Rosline. And you've become instrumental to me in my daily work that sometimes I wonder if I rely on you too much or have set my expectations too high."

"Never, Lady Eleanor," replied Rosline earnestly. "I feel like there's so much more I can do for you."

"That is good," said Eleanor. "I would be incredibly sad if I found one day you wished to leave my service, but I would also be proud if it was in service to someone more established, or even to strike out on your own and make a name for yourself."

Rosline felt heat in her face as she said, "Thank you, milady. But I don't see myself wishing to work for another. And as I mentioned, I don't see myself wanting more for myself."

"What about for your daughter?" asked Eleanor curiously. "Would you not want something for her future?"

Rosline did consider and hesitate then, before saying, "I had thought she would eventually come into your service, as I did."

"And she can if that's what she desires, but what of her own talents and desires? Railand has told me that she possesses a sharp mind, even for a lass of her age. He says that there is budding wanderlust in her too, a yearning to see more and learn more."

"Then I think Jaks could help her with that," conceded Rosline, though an uneasy undercurrent ran through her.

"Perhaps," conceded Eleanor, "but I just wondered if you had considered more for her, like marriage to a lord or something."

"That's a long ways off," laughed Rosline. "She's just a small girl."

"Small girls don't stay small for long," replied Eleanor. "I only bring this up because if there was something you wanted, some plan or other idea of how you wanted her to be, I could try and start now to help you with that."

"You would do that?"

"Of course Rosline. And of course, I would try and convince her that being in my service would be the best decision as well," she laughed before taking another sip, "I may be willing to help her, but I admit I have my own desires as well."

Rosline sat up straighter, "What are those?"

"Oh no, Rosline, it is partially a joke. As you said earlier, Kyrah should have as much time as she can as a child, before the matters of her future plague her as they did me."

Rosline nodded in agreement but still she pushed, "I want to help, milady."

Eleanor swirled her drink, before locking her gaze with Rosline, "Very well then. If you would do anything, please try and keep an eye out for if she sees the shadow sprites. You mentioned you saw them at a young age, and if she does, then I would be very interested in keeping her in my employ."

Rosline's unease grew immensely, "The shadow sprites?"

"I know, I know," said Eleanor, sensing her emotions, "but we've learned so much together, that I think we could find a much safer way of blossoming her talent if she possessed it."

Rosline nodded, agreeing that they had spent many nights learning together. But she also remembered the vivid blackness that had taken her eyes all those years ago and hoped her daughter would never have to experience that grief. "I just worry for her, milady."

"As a mother should. But we do know more now than we did all those years ago. If anything I would test to see if she can read first,

366

before doing any serious study. It is just something I would look for in her."

Rosline gave a tentative nod. "Milady, may I ask you a question?"

"Of course."

"Why is it that you and your husband never had any children of your own? From what you've told me, and from what I've learned, any of your children would have been remarkable."

Eleanor gave her a sad smile, "I was stricken with barrenness at a young age. An unfortunate turn of fate for us, but at the time I didn't think it so terrible. However, I have recently come to wonder what our children would have looked like, and I admit, it would have been nice to have something to remind me of him in these years."

Rosline heard the traces of longing and sadness in her voice. "I am sorry, milady."

"I came to terms with it many years ago, before I met you. As I mentioned it is only recently that I've come to appreciate the potential of."

Rosline nodded in understanding before asking, "Is there anything you wish to achieve in the coming years?"

"There are many things I wish I could do for the future, but mainly I desire to keep my family name going for as long as I can, while just keeping all who work for me paid well and comfortably."

"But after you, won't it eventually—" Rosline grew quiet, her face flaming with embarrassment.

"It will," conceded Eleanor, "but some families are known for generations to come, and it is my desire for that legacy to remain for as long as possible."

"I can carry that legacy for you," said Rosline earnestly.

Eleanor cocked her head, "Why?"

"Because I feel like I am part of it, milady. I know that we are not of blood, but I feel a closeness to you that I once shared with another maid I worked with before. It's like being sisters, or something close to that."

367

"I appreciate the sentiment," said Eleanor before taking another drink.

"I just want to help, milady."

Eleanor simply nodded again, leaving them in silence and Rosline with her thoughts. Aside from working, she didn't know what she wanted for herself, but she knew that regardless of what happened, she would always push as hard as she could for both Eleanor and her daughter.

ASTORIA.

When Astoria woke, she found herself riddled with aches in her shoulders and legs. The dull throbs broke her from her slumber. As she laid atop the bedroll, teeming thoughts raced through her mind, stealing away the serenity that she had found in sleep. Agitated, she rose, throwing off the blanket before instinctively reaching at her side for the blade that she vaguely remembered burying.

Repressing the twinge in her heart, Astoria went to her bundled pack and pulled one of the blades she had taken from the men before. It was light, solidly-made, and Astoria saw no burr or nick in the edge of the steel.

This is one of the blades that killed Sehren.

Revulsion coursed through her veins as she gripped the pommel. She wanted to throw it into the dirt, to throw it aside so that it could never be found again, but in the wakes of her tiredness, she simply stared into the steel as her bluster ran out. She knew she would need a weapon for protection as she continued on.

Continue onto what?

Try as she might, Astoria could not envision this as becoming her home. She could spend the time and effort to rebuild something for herself but deep down she knew it wouldn't provide for her what she

369

wanted. Belting the blade on her side, she stepped outside of the tent. Her gaze trailed over the thickets of grasses that spread over the field. Memories trickled back into her mind, each one a glimmer into a gilded life she wished they could have kept.

Why didn't we stay, Sehren? Why did we go so far?

Astoria ran her fingertips beneath the collar of her shirt, feeling the scar that ran beneath her collarbone. She may have never felt the spear pierce her flesh if they had stayed here. Sehren had insisted that they left because of their lack of supplies, but that could have been remedied with runs with Termesa to the trading post. Her building anger played itself out though, understanding his grief. It had been too much, too many things that would have had to be done to keep them both safe. Their flight north had proven that. Even so far away, beyond the lands of Senkama, they had found them.

Why? Why then, after everything? And how?

Her questions beckoned as her anger simmered. How had the king come to learn of her flight? How had Ricard, that man that Sehren had sparingly spoken of to her, learned just how far she had traveled past the northern lands? And how had he spun a tale so believable that those who wouldn't believe that she never meant them harm would march to the threat of an army?

Lies. Deceit and lies and fear.

Astoria felt bile rise in her throat as her anger swelled. It wasn't fair. Sehren and Astoria had spent years cultivating a tenuous peace with the Senkaman people, and it had been tossed aside once it was more convenient for them to try and get rid of her. Sehren had told her that they only tolerated him and despised her, but she had believed once they had begun regularly trading that Nyeth had finally looked past her hate. And perhaps the woman had, but Astoria had hoped that her confidence in Sehren would have spread through the xenophobic people. She believed that it was only a matter of time before she and Sehren would finally be welcome to wander their lands and to see the villages that Sehren had told her about.

I was a fool.

When she saw Karja's hate etched in his face, even as he was bleeding to death upon the ground, she knew the folly of her dreams.

370

Nyeth may have come to accept Sehren, may have even pushed forward for him to become the chieftain of his line again, but nothing would convince the others to see past Astoria's blood. She would always be a cursed southerner, and Astoria knew that Sehren didn't speak more of the ceremony not because he didn't want to make her lament being unable to go, but rather because he knew she would never be able to do so.

Her stomach turned with both hunger and anger, but Astoria simply threw the pail into the well before pulling forth more water and drinking deeply of it. She cataloged what she still had remaining left in her mind and realized she would need to hunt soon if she wished to not go hungry in the coming days. Her gaze trailed off to the path she came, knowing that it would only be a few more days of travel to get to the City of Isle. With no coin or other things, she didn't know what she would do from there, as even the lowest of taverns would require coppers that she no longer had.

Maybe Aruhn could help me for a bit, just to get settled. I could work as a barmaid again.

The thought sent a tendril of hope through her, but it also sparked her imagination. She recalled that fateful night when he stood against those that had come for her. He'd shown more grit than she'd ever seen from the man, and even when Marson threatened to kill him, he accepted it with a resigned understanding of the world they both walked in. Then Jaks' had shown up and everything Astoria had known had been flipped. There were still some nights where she would stare into the stone of her necklace, not believing that she was noble-blooded. She had the proof though, and that along with the two old certificates that Sehren had brought along with him, were the only real treasured things they had. Sehren had shut them away in a small pouch, coiled around one another and hidden away with their things.

What did he tell me to do with them so long ago?

Astoria wracked her mind, trying to remember, but it was lost in a haze of everything else she had learned through the years. She returned to her pack and sifted through her belongings, pulling out the pouch. She untied it carefully. The pouch had grown stiff over the years, as she and Sehren rarely opened it more than once or twice a season. After untying it, she carefully pulled the yellowed parchment out of it, rolling it over her knee.

She read it slowly, the Candraman lettering having become unfamiliar to her over the years. The ink had faded as well, but it was still clear enough for her to make out.

Caine Greyfield?

As she read, she remembered the name on the stone and an icy chill ran through her.

His father. He never told me.

She continued reading, wincing as she read the details of his apparent demise.

She read over the other piece of parchment, her mood growing more somber as she read the details. Even in the faded ink, she could see many different hands had scrawled across the parchment. A trembled ran through her hands as she read through the underlined list:

Katski, Chuyara, Itzalak, Ombroj, Varjud, Thunzi, Kabrea.

Ombroj.

His name?

Astoria flipped the page over, the last one another certificate like the one of his father, with the name Danika Ombroj penned at the top. Except there were no honors or laurels here. Written in plain detail was the method of her death. The method of her execution. Dismay accompanied stinging in her eyes as she read the name again.

Danika Ombroj

His mother… They killed his mother… The kingdom killed his mother.

Astoria gently coiled them back up, rolling them together before she stowed them away. She wiped her eyes as indignation flowed through her veins. The kingdom had interrogated his mother and when they were done, had killed her. Her stomach turned and she rose quickly, steadying herself as it roiled. She was breathing hard as everything fell into place.

Sehren hadn't just run away for her sake and because of what had happened to his wife. He had run from this, wanting to get away from it. All the nights he told her stories during his knighthood with his voice edged with resentment came into clarity for her. To her, they had been fanciful tales, but to him, they had been a reminder of all he had given for the kingdom, just to learn what that had meant.

I was a fool.

Sehren had never let her read the coiled parchments, but some nights, Astoria would wake and find him reading over them in the lantern's fading light. She thought they were letters from Eleanor, something he had brought with him as a memento. Those nights, she would call to him to let him know she was there, but never had she gone to him. It felt like infringing on something too personal, and Astoria had learned to respect those moments. The following morning he would not mention it and life had moved on.

Why? Why this?

The small ledger that Aruhn had given her was still out, and she picked it up, opening it to see the miniature portrait within. Her name was written in curly writing at the top, and the portrait was of her as a young girl. It was a simple thing, and she recalled that when she first beheld it, her world took a twist she would have never expected.

Aruhn had known all along who I was. Was that why he was so keen on me? Was he hoping one day I'd lift him out of his world?

She tucked the ledger away into the pouch and tied it off carefully. After stowing it away inside of her belongings, Astoria considered what lay ahead. There was a pit in her stomach, the wrongness of everything hitting her. She and Sehren could have been happy, but it seemed so many people didn't want that. She tried to steady her breathing, but she couldn't get a handle on it. Her gaze trailed over the farm, now almost completely unrecognizable from all the years ago. Sehren had told her that he grew up here, and had learned from his parents all the lessons he had shared with her. He told her of the long frost alone, and she had thought it odd, but never dwelled on it as he had already accepted it. She knew now he had also lost both of them here.

I was a fool.

She couldn't stay here. This wasn't her place. It hadn't been before, when they were trying to find somewhere to hide, and it couldn't be now. There was nothing here for her, nothing that would quell the rage she nestled in her heart.

We just wanted peace.

It was time to go home.

AMOS.

Amos waited for his guest to arrive as he sat at the table. Now and again he would shift uncomfortably in his chair, his mind teeming with questions. He heard steps approaching the door and rose from his chair to greet them as warmly as he could. As the door opened, a woman with golden hair stepped through followed by another woman with a wrapped cloth around her eyes. They were led by one of Amos' servants as he led them to the table. Amos smiled upon seeing the first woman's face, greeting her cordially.

"Eleanor, it's been too long."

"Lord Amos," chimed Eleanor with a smile and a bow, before the smile became a smirk, "I admit, I thought you had forgotten where I lived after a while."

He chuckled, "It's been a trying few years, milady, and that has given me less time to pay calls as more and more things have developed around me. I apologize for that, but I am glad you accepted my invitation for this evening."

"Of course." She walked to one of the seats before the servant drew it out for her and settled in with a mild thanks towards them. The action was repeated for the other woman, and Amos sat down across from them with a curious look towards her.

"This is my handmaiden, Rosline. These past years, while good to me with my own efforts, have been made easier by having her at my side. I hope it was okay for me to bring her along."

"Of course. I merely was curious about her as I don't recall having met her."

Rosline bowed her head politely, "We have not had the fortune to meet before, Lord Greyfield, but it is an honor to make your acquaintance. I've heard many things about you from Lady Eleanor."

"Good things, I would hope," he said with a laugh.

"I've told her many things about how you encouraged some of my husband's antics," she said with a sly smile.

Amos felt a tinge of guilt, but the amusement in her face led him to smirk as well. "Only sometimes."

"Is it true that you were her husband's mentor?" asked Rosline.

"Aye, I taught him much of what he knew about the knights and the kingdom. He was a fine man."

"That he was," said Eleanor in a clipped voice, "but hopefully you didn't simply invite me out to talk about him."

"Not at all. I wish to speak with you, to learn about how you have been faring."

Eleanor was about to reply but her attention was drawn when the door opened and several servants carried in the portions of their meal. Amos nodded as they set it down before lifting his goblet and taking a sip. He gave another reassuring nod and they started eating, the conversation remaining light and pleasant. As they trailed along topics, Amos cleared his throat and said, "I heard about the attack on you a few weeks ago. Were you harmed?"

Eleanor looked stricken for a moment before she simply shook her head, "Thankfully I came out unscatched. I have my bodyguard to thank for that."

"I am glad to hear that. Gavin mentioned he went to see you and said you seemed in good spirits, but still I worried about it."

Eleanor gave a stiff smile, "I treasure the thought that my well-being was on your mind. I imagine you must have been entwined in other matters if you could not find the means to pay a visit yourself."

Amos felt slighted but understood from her tone that she didn't fully blame him. "I apologize for that, Eleanor. I rarely find that I have the time to tend to my own wellness, but I feel that is a poor excuse for keeping myself apprised of those I've grown to care about."

He took a drink of his goblet, "The years have seemed to sap much of my time, and as I grow older I find myself trying to utilize as much as I can despite it being so little. And amidst all the tangling with courtly endeavors and dabbling with aristocrats and the brotherhood, finding time to visit you slipped my mind more than I care to admit."

"You share a heavy burden with the king," said Eleanor with a nod.

"One that I do as my duty."

"Even still, I'm sure you have faced much adversity over the years. Me being a lapse in your mind is something understandable, and in some cases, expected."

Amos regarded Eleanor with a smile, recalling why he had sought her for Sehren's hand. Even with everything that happened to her, she had an even disposition towards the realities of life, all while having a spirit undiminished by aristocratic expectations of her birth. He had believed that her temperament would mesh well with his and give him the prod he needed to achieve great things in his life.

And together they did. Even now, from all accounts, Eleanor is a remarkable woman.

"That, perhaps, is to be expected, but not so much the source of the quandary that stifles me so."

Her eyes shone with comprehension as she quietly asked, "It's true then. About the king?"

Amos released a deep sigh, "Each day saps more of his will as the crown sits heavy on his brow. It's not an easy task, for the lives of many rest upon shoulders, but to become so irascible and despondent to things is not ideal. Especially when it is these times when rumors abound that the people need guidance and a pillar to rely upon."

Eleanor sampled some of the meal before her, dabbing her lips with her napkin as she said, "I've heard tales that the Estocri family calls to sit upon the throne."

Amos nodded grimly, "They and the Kris family both lay claim to the seat."

"The Kris family?"

"The Blightwinter was unkind to the northern province. They have barely started to recoup the tremendous losses they sustained. Their claim to the seat is as recompense for their sacrifice."

"And I imagine the Estocri family has a similar claim."

"Yes. And the loss of one of their beloved heirs would hold truer than that of the people."

"Which I imagine the Kris family is not taking well."

"No, they are not," confirmed Amos, "and there was contention between the two families before this. Unfortunately, there have also been rumors that the Klins province may pull away from the kingdom in the wake of all this, no doubt stirred up by the royal family."

Eleanor shared a glance with Rosline, her face darkening as she said, "I hadn't realized that it had grown that poor."

"Indeed, and I would appreciate your confidence in it."

Eleanor smiled, "Of course, Amos."

"You're right about the people being concerned," said Rosline. "But wouldn't something such as a province breaking away cause more turmoil for the people?"

"The nobles of Candrama have a history of placing the wellness of the citizenry below their aims," said Eleanor.

"You are not wrong," affirmed Amos, "but in times like these, it falls more to the men in the council of the kings to point out the folly of their actions."

"Men that are not being listened to," surmised Eleanor.

"That and other men elevated to such positions that are only concerned with their own well-being. It has become a nest of vipers and sloths, with only a few left that remember their duty to the kingdom."

378

Eleanor looked pensive as she considered his words, "Perhaps the problem is that there are no voices of the people around the king."

"What do you mean?"

"The people that surround the king are those of privileged positions, either obtained through valor or through circumstance," observed Eleanor. "But, and I may be ignorant of this, there is no one of the people amongst the king. Even his servants are likely men and women of the aristocracy that cannot speak of the ills the people face. In turn, he has become oblivious or numb to the struggles of the people, especially if his grief is as thick as you mentioned."

"That is true," said Amos. "Over the years, through the efforts of several men of the council, the king has been increasingly surrounded by cousins and kin of their families, which is not uncommon, but they are woefully unaware of how disruptive the change could be."

Eleanor continued on, "Perhaps that's where it needs to start, with an addition of people that could impress upon the king when he is most lax. Men strung up in meetings with council and other prestigious members tend to be guarded and non-receptive. However, a statement made at meal time or when at rest, even a non-pointed one, can have a poignant effect."

Amos considered it for a moment, "Perhaps. I think you're on the right course, but exposing the king to the wrong individual could also prove caustic to the well-being of the kingdom."

"Yes, but sometimes risks have to be taken if we're to move ahead," replied Eleanor.

"I don't believe risks and gambits are what is needed right now," commented Amos brusquely.

"With or without risks, left as it is, the king will simply become more or less a figurehead," said Eleanor. "It is hard to believe that this is the same man that moved forth north during the Blightwinter."

"He has lost much, Eleanor."

"We all have, Amos," replied Eleanor in a sharp tone. She composed herself afterwards, "I apologize. That was imprudent."

Amos shook his head, "It was no offense to me. And I understand where it comes from. But to wager the well-being of the people on something like that while the situation is so unbalanced could spiral into disaster."

"It was merely a thought," said Eleanor. "I wouldn't have entirely bet it upon a person with unknown intentions."

"What do you mean?"

"Amos, I have no desire to complicate what you've told me. In truth, the kingdom shifting means little to me, but in the spirit of wanting to rebuild our relationship, I offer what I can to help you," Eleanor leaned back, "To that end, I doubt that tanned hides and leather accouterments will assist you, but I do have the pleasure of breaking bread with several prominent people in the city. If you thought it could help you, I could try to find someone similarly aligned with your aims to help the kingdom."

"You would spy upon your peers and colleagues?"

"That is a much more devious title to it than I would prefer," said Eleanor with a shaky laugh, "but I do admit it would likely be to that effect. But not to gather information. Rather, I'd seek someone to help lend us aid, if you feel that would be prudent."

Amos shook his head, "I understand how you believe that would help Eleanor, but to engage in such means would degrade you to those that I find deplorable in the city as it is. It would be remiss to have you act as my agent, especially given our relationship."

Eleanor pursed her lips, "I was under the impression that you were trying to find a way to remedy this, regardless of the cost."

"Aye, but not regardless of the cost. A victory won with duplicity and espionage is a spoiled one, with little to celebrate in the wake of the lives destroyed."

"Perhaps, but isn't a spoiled victory better than an honorable defeat?" asked Eleanor. "One of Sehren's firm beliefs was that you could win as many battles as you wished, but could only suffer one defeat."

Amos gave a grim laugh, "That was the mindset of a soldier constantly on the field of battle. This is—"

"A battle at home, with equally important consequences," countered Eleanor. "And I would say far more important."

Amos frowned but withheld his reply. Silence passed between them with Rosline sporting a shy look on her face, as if she felt she didn't belong.

Eleanor looked abashed for a moment before she continued, "I wasn't intending to clash our beliefs with one another, Amos. Perspective is a tricky thing. You mentioned to me your concerns, and I came with a solution from the kingdom I have dealt with. But that doesn't mean I'll apologize for the conclusion I came to, nor shall I take away my offer. Do not hesitate to request my aid if you believe it will better the welfare of the kingdom."

"I'll keep that in mind. Perhaps I've just witnessed how the meddling of others has brought us to this point within the kingdom. However, I won't let my own prejudices color my opinion of you."

"That is a feat that many men before have tried and failed at when it comes to me," said Eleanor with a sardonic smile. "I do believe though that you have proven better in that regard than the others."

"I try my best. Prejudice clouds judgment and in times of crisis that can prove to be fatal."

Eleanor bowed her head, "A fair assessment."

"Milady, I ask, what is your concern for the kingdom?"

Eleanor shared a look with Rosline before taking a sip of her wine and setting it down. She dabbed her mouth with a napkin before answering, "That is an answer I don't think you would find palatable, given our differing views."

"Still, I would like to hear it. I took measure of you when I sought someone for Sehren, and while the years may have grown us apart, I do believe I can understand your opinion."

"I'm certain you can. But for me, the kingdom is simply an edifice, built for those to achieve their ends. I once held all that was done in high regard, and being married to a Knight, believed them to be above reproach." She gave a nostalgic smile, "I was proud to attend chapel with the other lordly wives, and I thought my contributions to everything helped maintain the bastion I once believed in.

"Now, however, I see it built solely for those that wish to frolic in it, with little regard to legacy or contribution. There is a game at play here, and those willing to play it, much like myself, find themselves bestowed with the comforts and privileges that many others will not have the fortune to know."

"Does that bother you?"

"Me personally? No. Not anymore. I do what I can because I've grown accustomed to the life I live. But I still recall what happened all those years ago, when those who once broke bread with me and my husband turned their backs when it was most convenient to them. I can understand and in some ways, appreciate their actions, but I also despise them for it. And I despise that I contend with them to keep the life I so enjoy."

Eleanor took another drink, "My concern is purely personal, Amos, and has been for many years. I saw what happened when someone who gave everything was reduced to nothing. But you are part of that personal, for even in our lapse of connection, I know that you still would bleed for Sehren and myself if you thought it would help us both. That is why I wish to help you."

Amos was stunned by her pragmatism, "And our relationship? Is it a means to an end?"

"If I said yes, would that change anything? If I said no, would that allay your doubt?" She cocked her head, "I say that our relationship is convenient and profitable to me, as well as enjoyable for myself. Is that so terrible?"

Amos thought about it for a moment, "I would say likely not, solely because of your ability to admit it to me. I did seek you and your father out after all as means to an end, and truthfully didn't consider what a relationship with you would entail. Your talents and level-headedness as well as influence over Sehren made you a markedly better person than I could have expected, and in these times, I am grateful for such a relationship."

Eleanor beamed at him before they continued their meal, with Rosline asking sparing questions. Amos walked them from the room to the foyer, where a small retinue of Eleanor's guards were waiting. He spotted one of them that seemed much more aware and attentive than the others and met his gaze. Amos assumed that to be Eleanor's personal guard, and judging by the familiar way Eleanor spoke with him, he was correct. He nodded his head towards the man, and Amos watched as they left his abode.

ASTORIA.

Astoria walked carefully as she approached the North Gate of Isle. Many people were traveling through in large packs. Astoria could taste autumn in the air, and judging by the sun's rise and set, there was maybe a few days before it set in full.

I made it.

Fleeting memories crawled through her mind as she walked through the gates. The guards nodded at her with little more than a passing glance, but still Astoria tried to make herself look as inconspicuous as possible. She walked along a group of people, listening to their words. A brief wave of nostalgia washed through her as she listened, her mind sent back to the days at the tavern when she would listen to all the stories over the night.

That's where I should go.

Astoria veered off from the group, following along familiar paths and avenues. She stopped as she saw the park she once frequented.

Is that when this all started? When that man grabbed me in the night? No. No it had to be before that. I was just used to distract Sehren. He wouldn't have left me to burn if he had known.

Astoria turned her gaze away, continuing down the streets until she came to a familiar intersection. There was a lurch in her stomach as she regarded the tavern, especially as she saw the maids moving in the windows. Swallowing hard, she walked towards the door, raising her hand slowly before knocking. As she waited there, she turned and looked around the avenue, trying to recall familiar faces from before.

The door opened behind her. She was greeted by an unfamiliar maid who gave her a once over before saying, "Hello, are you needin' somethin?"

Astoria paused before asking, "Is Aruhn around?"

The maid recoiled before shaking her head solemnly, "No, he's not."

"Oh," Astoria frowned. Aruhn was always there before the tavern was open. "Will he be around later?"

"No, he's been gone a while now," said the maid, her face crestfallen. "He passed away a few months back."

Dread filled her veins, "He what?"

The maid looked clearly distressed. "They found him behind the bar. Seemed he drunk himself to death." She sniffed thinking about it.

That doesn't sound right.

"I'm sorry to hear that," said Astoria in a melancholic tone. "I— I used to be a regular here. Just came in." She took a hard swallow, thinking, "Is Rosline or Celeste here?"

"I'm not knowin' a Rosline, but Celeste is at the counter if you're wantin' to talk to her."

Astoria pondered for a moment before her paranoia set in and she shook her head, "No, that's fine. Again, I'm sorry about Aruhn." She choked for a moment, "He was a good man."

"Aye, he was." The maid nodded before shutting the door. Astoria saw her wipe her eyes as she passed the window, but she found it hard to catch her breath. She caught herself for a moment alongside an avenue as people walked by her with curious looks.

It doesn't make sense. Aruhn rarely drank and never that much before.

Astoria took several breaths to steady herself before she mustered what she could to move on. She thought about the documents that she had within her pack and panicked a moment when she contemplated someone learning of her lineage. She felt gazes on her as she straightened and walked off, before turning into the park she had passed by earlier. After she found a shadowed place beneath a tree, she settled there and took off her pack, her mind racing.

Aruhn is gone. He's just... gone. And I don't remember who Sehren told me to talk to before. I could try to find his wife, but then what do I tell her? If only... if only I could find Jaks. I think he'd know what to do.

She considered other avenues, but the absence of Aruhn had settled into a pit in her stomach. Unlike others, Astoria had expected that Aruhn would be around. He had been a pillar to her, and even as a lass, she had understood that he had found a place beyond his tavern in the rungs of society. But a coldness crept in that almost smothered the anger she still nursed. Her heart ached and beneath that her stomach soured. She recalled the times in the north lands when she felt a similar desolation, but she realized that her solution back then had been Sehren. Even when they hadn't spoken to one another for days, his presence had been a settling factor for her, and their reconciliation had always come quickly after that.

Without that, in a city that no longer felt familiar, Astoria was truly lost.

Maybe... maybe my ma's?

Guilt crawled through her as she realized she hadn't thought of her mother. She rose from the shade and grabbed her pack. With a fleeting glance to the park, she took measure of her surroundings before she made her way towards the only home she had once known.

Astoria came upon the small shacks that she had grown up among. It was almost unsettling; the avenues, rough and unkempt, hadn't changed over the years. Astoria knew that she could unerringly navigate through the neighborhood. Pulling on the strap of her pack, she walked along the streets before eventually arriving at the familiar home she had once known. She started to reach for the handle but paused, her heart pounding in her ears.

Would she still be here? Would he?

Astoria's hand shook as she raised it to knock. It was late in the afternoon, and she believed her mother would likely be working. She had come all this way though, and she felt she needed to do something. With a swift knock, she waited. Several moments passed before she knocked again, this time a little more firmly. Still, there was no response and Astoria, her frustration mounting, banged on the door. The wood shuddered beneath her fist, and she recoiled.

Calm down.

She heard movement. Shuffling steps approached the door, and it creaked open, revealing a woman's visage with bright blue eyes and reddish locks marred with grey.

"Can I help you?"

Her voice took Astoria back. Tears fell from her eyes without beckoning. There was a hitch in her voice as Astoria said, "Ma... it's me, ma."

The woman opened the door more, her eyes widening as she took in Astoria. "Astoria... my little princess, is that you?"

Astoria wrapped her arms around her mother, her tears flowing freely as she did. "Aye, ma. I'm back."

Her mother stroked her hair, laughing as she cried. "You've grown so much. You're so... you're different, my little dove."

"Can I come in?" asked Astoria.

"Of course, of course. I was just sleepin'. I have late work tonight, but come. Come in."

Astoria let her mother lead her inside the small home, a wave of images flooding through her mind as she stepped over the threshold. Her whole life before had been in this home. Astoria, though, felt odd, as though it couldn't encompass her anymore. She sat with her mother at the dilapidated table, noticing that more of their home seemed in disrepair.

388

"Is pa not doin' those anymore?" asked Astoria as her mother sat with her.

"Oh," said her mother, her voice holding anticipation, "he's gone. Been gone for almost two years now."

Astoria cocked her head, "And he didn't take you with him?"

"Couldn't, not where he was goin'. Some lady came by with Jaks, and they took him. I didn't ask where but Jaks said he wasn't gonna bother me no more."

"Jaks? He came by?"

Her mother nodded, "Aye. He comes by now and again, checkin' on me. Especially after your pa left."

Astoria thought that was a little odd, but seeing the state of her home, she didn't blame him.

"Tell me then, Astoria," said her mother. "Aruhn told me you'd been gone for a while learnin' so much. Is it true? Are you gonna follow in his footsteps then?"

Astoria's mouth went dry before she cleared her throat and replied, "I did learn a lot, but I think I learned too much. I'm not sure if the tavern's where I want to be anymore."

Undaunted, her mother smiled, "Aye, I'd hoped you learn more than bein' in this life. I can see it in your eyes. And you look so strong! You've grown so much, I'm just happy to see you back."

Astoria gave her a shaky smile, but her eyes darted away from her mother's, "Thanks, ma. Am I able to stay here while you're workin'?"

"Of course dear! If you're needin' anythin' before I go, let me know," she smiled at her before rising up.

Astoria felt a tightness in her chest and throat before she asked, "Ma?"

"Yes?"

"...Did—" *Did she know? Of course she knew. She had to.* "Did pa mention anythin' about me being gone?"

Her eyes got slightly sad as she said, "I don't reckon your pa minded very much. He never seemed to mention you after that."

"Oh." Astoria sat back in the chair, stirring when her mother walked over to her and cupped her face.

"I'm so glad you're okay," said her mother with shining eyes.

"Thanks, ma."

She kissed her on the forehead before heading to the small room in the back, where Astoria knew she must have slept alone. Restless energy started making its way through Astoria, and she got up, pacing about.

"Ma?"

"Yes, Astoria?"

"You mentioned Jaks comes 'round a bit, right?"

"Aye, he does."

"Do you think you could see if he would soon? I wanted to say hi to him, but I don't know where he goes these days."

Her mother walked back into the room, fixing up her hair as she said, "I think I can. I'm thinkin' he's been away for the city a bit, but I'll ask 'round to see."

"That's good, thanks." Astoria gave her mother a smile, and everytime her mother walked by her, she could help but beam. "Ma?"

"Yes, dear?"

"Is it okay if I sleep a bit 'til then?"

"Of course. Go on and relax. If you're wantin' somethin' to eat later, I still work at the same place. I can get you somethin'. Do you remember your way around here?"

Astoria nodded, "I think I can figure it out if I don't."

Her mother smiled again, "You are a bright lass, after all, though I reckon I can't really call you that anymore. You're a woman grown."

"I am."

"You'll always be my little princess though," said her mother as she finished getting ready, "no matter how old you get."

Astoria smiled at that, warmth flooding through her for the first time in weeks, "I reckon so."

Her mother kissed her on the cheek before heading out of her home, giving her one more glance before she shut the door.

Astoria crawled into her mother's bed, the mattress softer than anything she'd laid on in a while. She curled beneath the blanket as she laid her head down, hoping that Jaks could come around while trying not to wonder what she would do if he didn't.

ROSLINE.

Rosline sat in the study, penning down her observations for the day. She sat back and let out a deep sigh. The sun had barely lightened the horizon when she began her work and, judging by the light through the curtain, it was on its westward descent. She glanced around the room, her mind teeming with thoughts about her work.

Eleanor said it was important.

Rubbing her eyes, she continued penning what she could remember, making sure she noted each individual and their dispositions. She shut her eyes as she tried to recall the scenes, but as her eyes ached, she found herself distracted by the constant throbbing. As swiftly as she could, she wrote down what fleeting details she could manage before the throbbing overtook her and turned her stomach. Feeling sick, Rosline rose from her seat and carefully left the study. She greeted the servants as she wove by them before making her way to her quarters. She rushed into the washroom, steadying herself at the basin before washing her face.

Rosline wiped her face off with a cloth, the soothing water having taken the edge of sickness away from her. As she gazed into the mirror, she felt the throbbing abate from her eyes.

It's worse some days.

As the years had gone by, Rosline had experienced a shifting in the talents she possessed. Before, she only experienced discomfort in her eyes when she spent too long using her sight, or rather, when she pushed too far with it. It helped her learn her bounds, and for years she was able to steadily expand her sight while managing to keep the pains at bay. It was exhilarating for her, as Rosline was certain that Eleanor didn't possess the same talents she did, so there was a sense of freedom when she worked. As far as she knew, she was unique in this regard, even though Eleanor warned her that there might be others in the kingdom that would be as talented as she was. To Rosline, it was hers to muster and use, and she found distinct joy and pride in it.

Recently though, her work would leave her with a dull ache afterwards. Even if it was just a meager vision, she would find herself frayed and tired afterwards. Rosline compared the feeling to how she felt when she imbibed too much, or when she was kept up too late at night with Jaks. It would stay with her throughout the day, and it would only subside when she had taken time to calm or steady herself.

After she broke herself away from the mirror, Rosline returned to her room. Geneve had straightened up already, so there was little for Rosline to do, and as Eleanor was present in the manor, Rosline found her without anything else to placate her for the afternoon. Restless as she was, she departed her quarters and made her way down the staircase to the conference room. She saw two guards posted outside, with neither of them being Railand, and that told her that she was in a meeting with someone. With a nod to the guards, she took a seat outside the room, waiting for when she could speak to Eleanor. She heard the voices inside grow a bit louder, before they quieted. Hurried footsteps approached the door, and Rosline saw one of the merchants she had gleaned during her visions depart with haste. He gave her a once over before being followed out by what Rosline assumed to be his steward, and with another nod to the guards, Rosline made her way into the conference room.

Eleanor saw with Railand behind her left, the man sporting a blank face as Rosline entered. His blank face spread into a smile as he bowed his head, "Good afternoon, Rosline."

"To you as well, Railand," replied Rosline as she curtsied to him. Eleanor finished letting out a deep breath before her expectant gaze rested upon her.

394

"Are you finished for the day?"

"Partially. Just need to tidy up my notes. I had a throbbing headache during, and I took a break, thinking it would be better to sort them out when I wasn't distracted by it."

Eleanor's mouth thinned before she said, "Hopefully you can recall them by then."

Rosline felt a tinge of shame and embarrassment as she averted her gaze for a moment, "My apologies, milady."

Eleanor let out another sigh, "It is nothing to apologize for. I am just irate from my meeting and was expecting better news from you."

"It seems a poor day indeed," said Railand noncommittally.

Rosline met his gaze, "Bad discussion then?"

"Terrible. The man has a mule's ass where his mind ought to be."

Rosline chuckled before clearing her throat when she saw Eleanor just gave a sardonic smile.

"Yes well, that might be too kind, considering," said Eleanor as she sat back. Rosline sat at her right, scooting the chair closer to the table as Eleanor steepled her hands. "You have learned more about him, yes?"

"I have. And most of it is penned already. It is the other request that you had me working on that addled me."

"Right." Eleanor's visage softened as she regarded Rosline, "Your dedication is noted, Rosline."

"Thank you, milady."

"You mentioned your head was hurting," commented Eleanor.

"It was, yes. It's faded now."

"Are you well?"

Rosline considered her question, "Just a bit tired, milady. That's all."

Eleanor gave her a solicitous glance, "Let me know if you find that you need a rest from all of this. I know I set you on your project rather quickly and with urgency."

"I can manage. Really. I think I'm just worrying about other things related to it, and I think that they're causing me to lose focus."

Eleanor pursed her lips, "What worries you?"

"It's nothing, milady. Just some wanderin' thoughts."

Rosline felt Eleanor's gaze settle onto her, causing her to shift uncomfortably. She cleared her throat again before saying, "I was wonderin', about the dinner we had with Lord Amos."

"What about it?"

Rosline looked at Railand, who was still standing behind Eleanor. There was a spark of interest in his face but otherwise, he was content to listen.

"When I was thinkin' back on it before, I—" Rosline huffed, ashamed she felt so shy talking to Eleanor. "It's a foolish thing, really but were you plannin' on guiding the dinner as you had?"

Surprisingly, Eleanor smirked, "Planned how?"

"It feels more contrived to me than anything, and I think back on it and just wonder is all."

"Do you find that distasteful?"

Rosline shook her head, "No, I don't milady. But, something about it is just stickin' with me, and I can't seem to shake it."

Eleanor gave her a smile, "Are you concerned that perhaps I plan other things like that? Your employ, perhaps?"

Rosline's face flushed as she averted her gaze, meekly replying, "That's not to say... I'm not thinking..."

"Rosline, please look at me," called Eleanor, her voice filled with understanding.

Rosline managed to look Eleanor in her verdant eyes. There was no hint of deception or conniving in them. In fact, there was a deep caring in them, one that Rosline saw whenever Kyrah would stare into her eyes with an insight.

396

"I know that you've helped me with many things," started Eleanor. "And you've given me insight and information on those that I would otherwise suffer disadvantage with in my dealings. You have equalized that for me, to put me on level ground with them, and in some cases, elevated me beyond them. It is natural for you to believe that I would have done the same with you and my life."

Eleanor's voice took on a lamenting tone, "I often feel I should have, when I consider where things have taken me. But that is the lament of someone who has lived the experiences I have, and found that even though there is much to appreciate from how far I've come, I cannot replace the things that were taken from me."

Rosline nodded, "I am sorry, milady. It's why I want to help you best I can."

"I see that, and I appreciate that the most about you, Rosline. You have a geniality to you that is woven into the fiber of your character, and that coupled with your dedication has made me glad that I took you into my employ all those years ago. If you are concerned whether or not that was simply happenstance, then let me assure you that it was. Only Jaks' mention of you piqued my interest, and even then, I had a hard time seeing past my own prejudices."

Something seemed to settle into place in Eleanor's mind as she paused. With a cursory look to Railand, she continued, "I was a wretch when I came across you, Rosline. I was a shambling mess kept together only by the decorum expected from someone of my station. Jaks was likely aware of that, and in truth, I think the man had more lascivious plans for us. As that crumbled away, however, he had to settle with you simply becoming my apprentice."

Rosline heard Railand snort as she giggled nervously, "Thank you, milady."

"For what?"

"For being forthwith with me. I see now it was a silly concern."

"It was a concern nonetheless and by your own admission, one that conflicted with your work," corrected Eleanor. "I wish to help you whenever you may need, Rosline. You may be in my employ, but as I said before, I value you highly."

"And Lord Greyfield?"

"An old friend and an opportunity I took advantage of," replied Eleanor easily. "I saw a moment that could benefit the both of us and saw no reason not to mention it. In the end, it may amount to nothing save for rekindling an old friendship I once shared. One that I'm sure I distanced from to protect myself from how it made me feel."

Rosline felt foolish then, remembering the other part of the dinner. "I—"

"There is no apology needed, Rosline," said Eleanor with a firm nod. "You have the privilege to ask me when you feel you need clarity, and I would never take that away from you."

"Yes, milady."

Eleanor noticed her tone, "Another question?"

"Was your request of him truly for the people of the kingdom?" Rosline almost regretted asking it, but the nature of it, the idea of having someone in her service enter the king's service tingled her sensibilities. And perhaps, Eleanor already had her in mind.

"Partly," answered Eleanor. "I have a favor that I owe someone, and I do so loathe to fall behind on things."

Railand shared a laugh with her as Eleanor rose. "Now if you'll excuse me, I think I will take an early soak after all that ."

"Yes, milady," chimed Railand and Rosline together. Eleanor nodded at both of them before she gathered herself and meandered off.

Rosline rose as well, before she called out to Railand as he departed, "Railand, a word?"

"Certainly," he shut the door he had just opened and waited expectantly for her.

"What do you make of all of this?"

"All of what?"

Rosline made a general gesture of her hand before her eyes trailed back to the conference table. She sighed, "These dealings, these… plans. My work."

Railand shrugged, which made Rosline uneasy.

"You had nothing to say on it?"

"I'm not going to lie, I haven't an inkling of what it is you provide for Eleanor," said Railand. "I was under the impression that it was important for her work, and it seems to be."

"Wait, really?"

Railand nodded his head, "I have no need to know of the details, Rosline. My contract is to Eleanor, and it is simple: keep her safe and guarded. Escort her whenever she leaves, and tend to her when she is in the presence of those that are unfamiliar. It is simple but bestows me a goal to work towards."

"And she's never confided in you about our work?"

"Why would she?" asked Railand bluntly. "It doesn't aid my job and would be something else to deter my attention and focus. No, I quite prefer being left in the dark."

Rosline laughed, "I guess she does confide in me a bit more."

"It's the nature of your work, Rosline. You, from what I have heard, are instrumental to her process and to her dealings. She would likely think very highly of you and give you the privilege of her trust."

Rosline's face pinked, "Thank you."

"Of course. I do tend to Eleanor throughout the day, but our conversation rarely strays outside of the day's events and even rarely into the details of her work. I don't really care for the topic, and she knows it."

Railand noticed that Rosline still looked uneasy, "What?"

"I just— there are few people that Eleanor would owe a favor too."

"I admit, I found that peculiar. She is not one for owing anyone anything, which was a topic of concern for today's meeting." Railand adjusted the blade on his belt. "She is a prudent woman, and not inclined to take debts she can't readily repay."

"I agree. That's what bothered me the most, I think. I didn't know of the favor, and I worry about her because of it."

"Your worry for her is well-placed, Rosline, and even admirable, but it comes down to us trusting that Eleanor will not attempt to take on more than she can handle. At least, not without consulting us."

Rosline scrunched her brow, "You think so?"

"I do. I cannot protect her from things I don't know about, and you cannot effectively do your job without whatever she tells you. It would be in her best interest to keep us both apprised, and if there is anything I am sure about, it is that Eleanor always acts in her best interest."

Rosline chuckled, "Yes, I will agree with you on that."

"Other than that, we are here to help her, Rosline. Sometimes, that may feel more ambiguous than usual, and perhaps even sinister at times. But while we can ask her about it, who are we to decide her will?"

"The best we can do then, is what I did today," surmised Rosline.

"Indeed. And with more boldness next time. Eleanor reacts well to strength. Don't feel like you haven't earned yours."

Her face flushed as she thanked Railand. He bowed his head before leaving the room. Rosline ran her hand along the polished surface of the table, musing to herself.

Even still, I think there would be only one person that she'd willingly owe a debt to.

Frowning, Rosline brushed away some dust before leaving the conference room.

CONTACT.

Glittering, hueless eyes stared at Sehren expectantly. He wandered about, his boots clearly clacking in the gloom yet without sound.

There was a tugging within Sehren as he beheld the roguish man, accompanied by a nagging feeling.

Why is he here?

Why am I?

Where am I?

Jaks clicked his tongue, "Are you going to keep me waiting, then? What happened to your sense of urgency, Caineson?"

"What—" the shadow plains swirled around him, but there Jaks stook, a fixture against the ephemeral landscape.

"Urgency. You possessed it once, and it was a marvelous part of your character, alongside your devotion and repressed bloodlust."

"There was never bloodlust."

Jaks laughed, "Of course. Because a reasonable man kills over a score of men for a sound reason."

Sehren thought of the kingdom, but he caught the humored tone and the glimmer of amusement in his eyes, "You mean the Lotus."

"Perhaps, but truly I meant everyone. What is it that drove so many before the blade of Sehren Caineson?"

Duty was the initial answer, but it felt meek, fleeting. Command was the second, but even that felt meager in the face of the truth.

Bloodlust? No, there was rarely malice in his blade. And those that found it were well deserving of it.

Were they all? Or was it simply because they were the weaker?

No. That would be tyrannical.

"It was simply because you could."

Sehren glared at the specter, but something about his words, the simplicity and soundness in which he said them, made them hard to refute.

Jaks smirked, that damnable smirk he always had, "The truth is always a nuisance to behold."

"It is not that simple."

"Isn't it though? If not because you could, then why do it at all? Unless you harbor a penchant for dealing death, why bear the blade at all?"

"It was my livelihood."

"Something, I'm sure you found, that you could have done without. You possess many talents and skills, Caineson, but few of them matched your mastery with your blade and the depth of your tenacity. Almost like a wombat. Or no, perhaps a badger." He chuckled, the laugh distorted.

Jaks walked along, "Well come then, it's boring to stand around all the time."

"Where?"

"Wherever you wish, I find." Jaks stepped into the swirling plains, and Sehren tried to follow along, but the sensation was unfamiliar. There was an absence of self that stole away his step, and he felt something he had not experienced since viewing this place.

402

Frustration.

Jaks returned moments later, clicking his tongue again, "Come now, you can't tell me that you can't muster the will to move? You've done it before."

Had he?

"Yes, before." Jaks smirked and snickered, "When the grass tickled your feet with every step. When your feet ached against the soles of your boots while you marched to kill my people."

"They came into the kingdom," contested Sehren.

"As do many, and yet they were the ones seeming worthy of your ire."

"It was to protect the kingdom."

"One that you have found no worth protecting," countered Jaks. "My my, what has happened to you? You can muster retorts in the face of your actions but cannot muster to make new actions."

Anger simmered as Sehren pushed forward. Everything seemed to shift and swirl, disorienting Sehren, but he clenched his teeth and kept moving forward before reaching Jaks. Jaks smirked again.

"There it is."

"Even in death, you still vex me."

"Perhaps," Jaks shrugged, "but if anything, I proved that there is more than you considered."

"Anger."

"Conviction" corrected Jaks. "It is what separates lesser men from those that could change the world."

"I have no want to change the world."

"Even this world?" Jaks raised his eyebrow before he grimaced as he looked around. "Surely there could be more done to make this more hospitable."

Sehren stopped, confused.

"Come now, Caineson, you know that I know a great deal of many things."

"And what is it that you know of here?"

"Only the rumors and tales that I have thought to keep within my mind. And regarding this, few people know of it and even fewer speak it."

The world swirled again, threatening to stagger him.

Jaks laughed, "I thought you of better constitution."

"That has little to do with this."

"Does it then? Is it not your constitution that fuels your insurmountable will? The knowledge that you can muster on despite the odds? Or rather is one fueled by the other, in a cyclic dance until you expire?"

"You speak a lot."

"Because I have much to say. And most of it is interesting." *Jaks turned away from Sehren, once again meandering off.*

The world shifted again, but Sehren didn't fall into it. Flickering started emanating from within the gloom. It stirred Sehren as a reminder. The flickering lessened but continued on and Jaks returned once more.

"Figuring it out then?"

"What?"

Jaks looked towards the morass, now striated with the flickering, "This."

"I am dead."

"Figured that out, then."

"I had before you arrived."

"And yet, still you are here, disoriented and confused."

Sehren looked around.

"Where am I?"

"That is the question, isn't it? I can see where I am, but you appear to not have that luxury." *His tone held a mocking quality to it, as if he was privy to a joke that Sehren didn't know.*

There was a scintillation within the gloom which pulled at Sehren's gaze. Despite that, he couldn't fathom what lay beyond.

Where am I?

"Try and see."

"There is nothing."

"There's never 'nothing'. There's always something. Even here, where your senses are dulled and your mind is scattered."

Sehren growled, incensed by the mocking tone, but once more the gloom shifted, changing once more to an open tundra. A searing pain went through Sehren's side as he gazed over the field, and his sight threatened to fade away. He knelt, the sensation of his being threatened to be swept beneath the tide.

No.

No.

"That's the spirit," said Jaks. He walked before Sehren, kneeling down and extending a hand.

Sehren glanced at it, watching it as it seemed to melt away before it reappeared. "You are not here."

"I either am or am not."

"Is that your decision?"

Jaks laughed, "No. It is yours."

The searing pain encompassed his mind, but Sehren reached forward, not willing to submit. The shifting stopped, the suddenly churning of the abyss around him becoming eerily still.

"What is happening?"

"Truth," said Jaks, pulling Sehren upright onto his feet.

"I do not understand."

"That's the point. No one understands." Jaks looked around. "The more you do, the harder it is to comprehend. But it is there."

"What is?"

"Whatever you wish. Sometimes it's simply peace, for others revenge," he smirked, *"but for you, it seems like it can be what you so desire."*

Sehren glanced around, fragments of memories coming with the stillness. He recognized where he was, but he couldn't fully see it.

"Home."

"It can be," said Jaks with a nod. *"And perhaps it once was. But do you want it to be?"*

"Here?" The thought seemed nice, welcoming, and accompanied by the promise of rest.

There was nothing else though. No comforting breeze scented by the needles and leaves of the tree around. No cresting water as the creek swelled from the melt or rain. No scurrying of critters darting through the underbrush seeking refuge or sustenance.

It was dead here, no warmth of another. No feeling of sight upon him, no laughter of happiness. Quiet and peace, with nothing to stir.

"It is tempting to just drift away. I imagine it is most peaceful to become part of the whole." Jaks nodded to himself, *"But I myself find the idea a little too peaceful. Conviction, that is what seems most appealing."*

"And it is... my choice?"

"Now you're getting it." Jaks laughed, *"Do you remember what all was lost?"*

Sehren shook his head, *"I cannot. It is there, but I cannot see what it is."*

"Do you want to?"

"Why should I?"

Jaks snickered, as if the answer was obvious. *"Because it was yours. And was taken from you. Even if you cannot recall it, it still belonged to you."*

That resonated within him, but beneath that simmered pain. He remembered pain. It always taught him a lesson.

"What is the point of all this?"

"That's the answer," grinned Jaks. "There is no point. Not outside what you wish."

Sehren felt the world start to shift, but he growled again and forced it right.

"That's the conviction. That same lust for life you bore all the years."

"I am dead."

Jaks laughed, "Once. Have you heard how the world shifts? Light of the dawn moves over the lands, but still it is fleeting. The warmth of the day brings joy, but even that too fades, all coming to darkness. And yet, the world is speckled with life, teeming even, when the shadow falls over it all, and simply exists even without the light. Until it returns, that is."

"You are saying this is the same?"

"Me? You still haven't pieced that portion together. It is truth, Caineson, nothing more or less. A truth long forgotten. And in the end, it is what you do with it, what will that you muster, that matters."

Jaks started whistling, but instead of a warbled, muffled tone, Sehren heard the song he used to sing. Quiet, placating, but he remembered it.

'What more can I remember? Should I even?'

The lands around him were still, familiar and reminiscent, but so too was the pain.

ASTORIA.

Astoria woke to a darkened home, with scattering light coming through the simple windows from the abodes around. She could hear the chatter of people around her. It was dizzying, and she felt claustrophobic as she thought of all who were around her. Sitting up from the bed, she stretched before searching for her belongings, panicking slightly when she realized the sword she had taken was not beside her. After glancing around, she found it settled against the wall by the door. She belted it to her before grabbing her pack and slinging it over her shoulder. However, realizing she was in her mother's home, Astoria set the pack back down and dug through it to grab a few things she thought would be good to keep on her person. Most importantly of all, she grabbed the pouch containing the documents Sehren had taken and tucked it in the small of her back.

If I am stopped or corralled for any reason, these would be terrible to have.

Frowning, Astoria looked around her mother's home, trying to find a place she could hide them away when a knock on the door drew her attention. She waited. Thinking it might be someone else's home, she turned away but the knock came again, this time more urgently.

Jaks?

Astoria made her way to the door, her hand resting on the hilt of her blade before she cracked it open. A lone woman with auburn hair and curved blade at her waist stood there. She waited expectantly as Astoria opened the door more.

"You're looking for Jaks." It was a statement, not a question, and the woman's voice held an edge to it that raised the hair on the back of Astoria's neck.

"I am. Who are you?"

"Diyane." She cocked her head, ready to start walking off, before looking back at Astoria with an annoyed glare, "Hurry, then. It's a rather long walk."

Astoria shut the door behind her tightly before tucking away the pouch in her back as she had before. The woman's smooth gait had already carried her down the avenue and Astoria jogged to catch up with her.

Diyane looked over her shoulder as she heard Astoria reach her. She continued on.

"Are you taking me to Jaks?"

"I'm taking you to where you'll wait for him."

"He's not there?"

"He had other meetings before you." The woman's tone had a hint of agitation in it, and it was clear to Astoria she was trying to be brief.

"Do you... do you know who I am?"

"Of course I do. I was there when everything was revealed."

Astoria halted, the scene coming back to her. The woman that had been with Jaks the night Aruhn had been beaten for hiding her.

"Make haste. It is late and others are watching."

Astoria felt paranoia set in as she looked around but sped up considerably.

"Where are we going?"

"The Friar's Reprieve."

410

Astoria hitched, "I don't want to go there."

"You do if you wish to meet with Jaks." She continued walking, as though Astoria's protest was meager whining, but there was dread building in Astoria's chest as she considered the woman.

"Did you know Aruhn?"

"I did."

"How long?"

"Years. He was a persistent man, with a knack for getting in danger. But he also had his friends. Jaks was one of them."

"And you weren't?"

"No, in either instance. I wasn't his friend nor was he mine."

"Ah." They walked along the lamplit avenues, Diyane weaving around people with Astoria trailing behind. There was a cool breeze wafting between the buildings. Astoria's mind raced as the buildings became more familiar, until they reached the tavern.

It was bustling, with sounds of the bawdy patrons spilling out onto the cobblestones before it whenever the door would open. Diyane approached it steadily but stopped when she noticed that Astoria wasn't following.

"I don't know if this is the best idea. It's busy."

"And?"

"Someone will recognize me."

Diyane gave her an irritated glance before she turned to enter the tavern. Astoria waited outside for a moment before she gave in and walked inside.

Immediately, Astoria lurched as she was taken back years. She saw the numerous people seated at the tables, some of them with maids on their laps as they laughed. She heard the clinking of coins and cups upon the table tops and felt the gazes of the nearest patrons on her as she walked by. She spotted Diyane at the bar and took a seat across from her.

Diyane eyed her for a moment before she took notice of the bar.

411

"When will Jaks be here?"

"When he is finished. He had other things to tend to." Diyane's hawkish gaze scanned the crowd before she stepped away from the bar. Another maid took over while Astoria watched her walk towards the kitchen.

"Can I fetch ya something?" asked the maid.

"No, thank you. I'm not feelin' festive tonight."

"Right. If you're needin' anything, gimme a holler." The maid smiled at Astoria before she took to tending the others at the bar. Astoria rested her elbow on the countertop and placed her cheek against her hand as she looked around.

It looks the same, but it feels so different and wrong.

Aruhn's presence had always been palpable in the tavern. He sometimes had to act as a bouncer when folks got too belligerent or handsy with the maids. The regulars usually would stop by and talk with Aruhn for a while, but even that didn't distract from constant watch.

Astoria waited as the night went on, sparing a glance at Diyane now and again. Several patrons had approached her while she waited, but Astoria sent them away with a disinterested glance, coupled with a frown if she found they couldn't understand her message. The tavern dwindled down as the hours grew later, and eventually it was filled with only those that were too deep in their cups to manage themselves.

The door opened and clacking boots against the wooden floor filled the air. Astoria turned towards the door, a shock running through her as she saw the familiar man ambling towards her. He sat in the seat beside her, signaling to the maid with a wave of his hand.

"One for me. I feel this is going to be a long one," said Jaks with a wink to the maid. She quickly poured him a drink before sliding to him and scampering off, clearly recognizing who he was. Jaks nodded at Diyane, who started escorting those who didn't have rooms pointedly from the tavern.

"I thought your mother had gone crazy when she told me her little princess had returned," started Jaks as he took a sip. "And yet I sit here, and I swear it's like seeing a specter of the past."

412

Jaks' smile threatened to make Astoria break into tears. She turned her gaze and said, "I didn't think you'd still be around, given everything."

"And I never thought I would see you grace the Friar's again." He grinned at her, "Alas, I don't have the luxury of disappearing as many of my companions seem to do." Jaks took another sip, "Where, then, is the solemn one? Or perhaps that is now a mantle you see to wear instead of him, given your demeanor."

Astoria hitched again, choking up as she said, "You mean, Sehren?"

"Aye."

"He's gone."

Jaks, hearing the tone of her voice, placed a concerned gaze upon her, before promptly saying, "Ah. I see."

"Do you?"

"Now I do. It seems I had expected otherwise." Jaks raised his glass into the air, a salute, and took a deep drink.

"As had I," said Astoria with a pleading look to the bar.

Jaks sighed, "His age and a miscalculation of his own stock. He went in peace, from what I have learned, and without much regret."

"Much?"

"He missed you, lass. Dearly and wholeheartedly."

Astoria did tear up then, trying to remember his face. She could see him, almost blurry, in her mind's eye, but while she could see the outfit he wore and the streaks of grey in his hair, she could not truly make out his face.

"And the tavern?"

"Under Celeste, who thought it best to partner with me and mine. A paltry showing if I do say so myself, but it still harbors those of modest coin and employs some of the fairest maids I've had the pleasure to lay my eyes on within the city. Clothed, I mean." He snickered, but upon seeing Astoria only sniff, he stopped.

"Celeste is here… what of Rosline?"

413

"She is employed by a friend of mine and lives a much better life than she could have ever dreamed."

That brought a smile to Astoria's face, and she wiped her eyes. "You visit my ma?"

"Ever since Barnaby needed to leave, yes. She is a rather lonely person otherwise. I chat with her about the city, and she tells me of the times she dreams of you as a lass."

Astoria laughed, "Thank you."

"I enjoy the conversation. There is little need for thanks."

"No, I mean, for gettin' rid of him. She told me."

"Ah yes. Well that would be Diyane that you'd need to thank then. While most who know of me are rightly afraid of me coming to call, I do so loathe violence. She, however, has little in terms of qualms."

Jaks tapped the table, and the maid came back with a fresh drink, taking his cup away. Jaks offered it to Astoria.

"I don't think…"

"To their honor, Astoria. To the peace that both their beleaguered souls so deserved."

Astoria looked into the cup before taking it from him. She drank deep, the liquid burning her throat a moment. With a wince she finished the cup, setting it down with a large breath as she felt the warmth start coursing through her.

"Thank you…"

"A stiff drink can cure all that ails the mind. And when it can't, I find that another one will suffice."

"I reckon the one was enough," she replied. "I just… Jaks, I don't know what to do."

"That is indeed the question, isn't it."

"Sehren told me that if I came to the city to find someone to give these to," she said quietly, pulling the pouch from the small of her back. She handed it to Jaks who looked over it curiously before opening

414

it and unfurling the yellowed parchments. "He also told me to find his wife, and to tell her that his last request—"

She hitched again, but pushed through the pain, "That his last request was that she help me."

Jaks' glittering eyes read swiftly over the documents, his eyes widening as he read them all save for her ledger. "Perhaps she could." He coiled them back up and placed them within the pouch, "but perhaps, for now, you spend time with your mother. I have secured her a few days off, and I'm certain that she would love to reconnect with her daughter."

"What… what do I tell her?"

"That is the rub," conceded Jaks. "Telling her the truth would likely be the soundest advice I could give you, but it also threatens everything your flight stood for."

"I don't know if that's the right answer then."

"Indeed. I imagine you have many stories from your times, and on a night you are feeling better I would love to hear about them all. In a more… conservative setting, that is." He looked around to the curious maids cleaning up and to Diyane watching carefully.

"And then after that?"

"After that, I shall hopefully secure a meeting with Eleanor and together we can come up with a plan for you."

"Should I stay here?"

"Would you like to?"

Astoria hesitated, her anger bubbling up as she thought about it. "There's something wrong, Jaks. The man— the reason Sehren died was because a man here spoke lies to the people. Those lies crept up north and stole away everything we fought for."

"Odd. I was of the mind that most northerners wanted nothing to do with the gilded south."

"As was I. But they listened, and they came, with nothing but my dismissal on their minds. And Sehren fought them." She sniffed, "He lost…"

Jaks scrunched his brow, "I had believed that Sehren was a cut above most, if not all, that could stand to him."

"I messed up, Jaks," admitted Astoria, louder than she intended. Stinging permeated her eyes and she pushed away the tears, "He was counting on me, and I let him down."

"There's more to it than that, I would imagine."

"There isn't. It's my fault. I hesitated, and it cost him. It would have cost me but he threw himself in the way."

She was speaking louder now, which drew the maids attention. Jaks waved her down, "Astoria, truly I am sorry."

"Why? Why couldn't we be left alone?" asked Astoria. Her voice broke. "We didn't do anything to anyone."

Jaks set a sympathetic gaze on her then, "Your heart is so heavy with grief, Astoria. Give yourself leniency."

Astoria hiccoughed before she took a deep breath. "Sehren's gone…"

"And you lived. And if I knew the man as well as I believed, he would parade that fact around whatever afterlife he went to."

Astoria shook her head, "He's gone, and I'm here, and they… you read it. They took it all. The king. The kingdom." She clenched her teeth, her voice a deep growl, "What do I do?"

Jaks laughed, "Ah. There it is." He grinned, more conniving than sympathetic. "You are angry at more than just yourself."

"Can you help me?"

"To what end, Astoria? Things are changing. Little is the same as you remember."

"That's not what I asked."

"I know what you asked, Astoria." Jaks tapped the counter, another drink brought to him as he slid gold and the other cup across the counter. "And I don't have an answer."

Astoria deflated, "Neither do I."

416

"Spend time with your mother, Astoria. She has missed you so much. Give it a few days, and perhaps, I can give you an answer to your first question."

Astoria fidgeted, "And then?"

"And then we decide where you fit in this city."

ROSLINE.

Rosline walked with Jaks, her arm looped with his. It was a languid stroll, one that Rosline felt would be good for her. Recreation was coming fewer and fewer as the season's change came, and Rosline expected that it would be a rough, wet winter. As such, she and Eleanor were working harder to keep the season's bounties flowing into the coffers, and Rosline found that she hadn't taken time for herself in many weeks. Jaks came by and offered to take her on a stroll, and eagerly, Eleanor told Rosline to enjoy herself.

"It's good to see that your lady notices when the strain upon you has grown," said Jaks, stirring Rosline from her thoughts.

"She is attentive. Lady Eleanor makes sure that whatever I need is taken care of."

"Good." Jaks pulled her along, tilting his head as he passed a merchant stand. "I have plans for today, and I don't think it would be good if they were interrupted."

"Plans?"

"Yes. An old acquaintance of mine needed some help, and I thought it better to meet them with you rather than to spring it upon you later."

Rosline laughed, "Let me guess: female?"

"Of course. Do I tend to have many male associates?"

Rosline shook her head with mirth, before sighing, "Fine. But you owe me another day of leisure."

"I can give you a full night of that. Will that suffice?" He gave her a sly grin and a wink as she laughed.

"Perhaps. Let's meet your acquaintance before I decide."

Jaks looked aghast, "Consideration? I must have a discussion with Eleanor. You are learning far too much from her."

Rosline leaned her head against his arm with a smile as he snickered, "Need I remind you that you were the one to bring us together?"

"You don't. I do believe that our lives have been better because of it."

Rosline agreed. She walked alongside him, eventually coming to a park. Rosline spied a woman milling about, her gaze trailing to the fountain every now and again as if examining it. As they approached her, the woman turned to face them. Rosline's heart jumped.

She released Jaks and took several short steps towards her. She trembled as she looked over the woman, as if afraid. "A-Astoria?"

Astoria's face softened as she drew close to her, "It's me, Rosline." She wrapped her in a hug. "I go by 'Leanne' in public, though."

Rosline was unprepared for the wave of emotion that overcame her. She clutched her tight, laughing lightly as she said, "Jaks said it was an acquaintance of his. I didn't think— you're so different..." She held her at arm's length, taking in the weathered appearance of her hunting leathers, the casual way she wore the sword on her left, and the tan and freckles strewn across her cheeks.

"As are you. Are you workin' for a noble now? And why the eyecloth?" Astoria's voice was also the same, but was more emphatic, more nuanced than Rosline remembered. There were traces of an accent as well, not obviously apparent, but Rosline caught it enough in her words.

420

"I am. I'm a handmaiden and, well I guess stewardess is the best way to put it, for a merchant lady."

"You've come so far," commented Astoria, her voice softening.

"Thank you." Rosline smoothed out the dress she wore, "it's partly thanks to Jaks that I've managed so well."

"Only partly though," interrupted the man. He gave Astoria a grin, "I thought it would be good for you to meet with Rosline after you mentioned her."

"Thank you for that," said Astoria with a tip of her head.

"I'll give you both a moment," he said tactfully. He whistled as he meandered away from them, taking a stroll around the park as he did.

"You've changed so much," said Rosline. The more she looked at Astoria, the harder it was to believe the woman before her was the same lass she had worked alongside.

"Only just enough," replied Astoria. "Just enough that was needed." As the moment's excitement abated, Rosline noticed a melancholy undercurrent within her voice.

There was a strained silence between them as Rosline continued observing Astoria. She noticed that the woman seemed antsy, agitated even, with her gaze darting to the other people that walked by the park.

Rosline cleared her throat, "Where are you staying?"

"At my ma's," said Astoria, turning back to Rosline. "But likely not for long. That's what Jaks is helpin' me with."

Rosline cocked her head, looking towards the wily man. He smoked his pipe, his attention diverted away from them.

"I can't believe you're back."

"I have trouble believing it myself," said Astoria. "But I'm not back. I'm here, with everything else I learned while I was gone. And—" her voice hitched. She cleared it before continuing, "And I'm not certain how long that'll be, everything considered."

"Is it true then?" whispered Rosline to Astoria, looking around. Jaks stowed his pipe away as he walked back to them. "You went north to hide from the crown?"

Astoria placed a pointed gaze upon Jaks, who merely shrugged, "She was earnest in knowing how you were doing. She witnessed you being maimed in the north by a spear."

"How?" Astoria reached for her collarbone as she turned back to Rosline.

"There's a lot we need to catch up on," explained Rosline earnestly, "And quite a bit you may not believe."

"Rosline..." warned Jaks.

"If I can't tell her, then who can I tell? She's not going to bandy it about. Astoria was never a gossip before."

"And much less now," confirmed Astoria. Rosline beamed.

"It'll help explain everything."

"I still think you should ask your lady before that," pointed out Jaks. "You are in her employ, and it may affect her business."

Rosline conceded, "That's true. However, I'm sure Lady Eleanor will understand."

Astoria cocked her head, "Eleanor?"

"Mmhm. Lady Eleanor DeVille. She's the lady I work for."

Astoria placed a suspicious look upon Jaks, who merely grinned back at her. "Was she once married to a knight named Sehren?"

"Yes. He went north with you, correct?" asked Rosline quietly.

"I thought it was a secret."

"It was part of me telling her part of the truth," admitted Jaks.

"Part?" said Rosline, surprised.

"Yes, there happens to be another wrinkle to that story. One I don't think we should discuss so openly."

Astoria nodded. Jaks looked at Rosline, "Do you think Eleanor would mind terribly if we borrowed her conference room?"

Rosline paled, "I don't know if that's wise."

"Nor do I," said Astoria.

"Are you afraid of what questions she might ask of your dalliances? It has been a long time."

"No," said Astoria, becoming heated. "I just don't have the means in me to explain Sehren's passing to her."

Rosline felt cold, "He's... dead?"

Astoria grimly nodded, "He is."

"I am sorry."

"As am I."

Jaks cleared his throat, "There is little that can be done for what we cannot change. You asked for my help, and I am of the mind to believe that Eleanor is the perfect person for that. I understand there might be an unpleasantness to your meeting, but her and Rosline have the means to keep you in her abode without you succumbing to restlessness."

"I don't think it's a good idea," contested Astoria.

"Do you have a better one then?"

Astoria shook her head, "Not particularly, no. Why can't I stay in the tavern?"

"Because there are other things she can help you with, Astoria. Namely, the second question you had for me."

Rosline watched Astoria straighten, looking at Rosline. She almost didn't recognize her then, the severe look that came over her face stealing away all semblance of her girlish charm. Instead, it was replaced by indignation and a voracity that was unfamiliar on her face.

"Fine. Lead the way."

Rosline wanted to contest, but between Jaks' glittering eyes and Astoria's expectant gaze her resolve crumbled away.

They arrived at Eleanor's manor, with Rosline guiding them past the gate. Astoria looked around the gardens and said, "You've found quite the home for yourself, Rosline."

"Thank you." She guided them into the foyer with Astoria pausing now and again to take in the decorative tapestries that adorned the walls and watch the servants walk by.

"The conference room is this way," said Rosline, taking them to a chamber with a long table. As they entered, Rosline told the guards to fetch Eleanor.

"There is an important guest here for her," explained Rosline.

The guard nodded, leaving Rosline as she shut the door to the room.

Astoria hovered around the table, restlessly running along it.

She looks almost identical to the dream.

"Did you know about Aruhn?" asked Astoria, looking at Rosline.

An icy chill went through her, "I did. I attended his funeral. It's hard... thinking about him not being around anymore."

"Jaks told me he drunk himself to death," continued Astoria.

Rosline nodded, "That's what it seemed like."

"I think that's odd."

"Odd?"

Astoria nodded, "Never was that careless before, and I don't remember him drinkin' much before."

"People change in the years," commented Jaks. "Look at you for instance. You look more at home in the woodlands than back in the city."

"A thought I share," replied Astoria.

"From a barmaid to a huntress. If you can manage that, is it so peculiar that Aruhn would succumb to the alluring calling of the drink?"

424

"Perhaps not," conceded Astoria, "but I'm not sure the man would drink himself to death. He was also so careful."

"People change," shrugged Jaks. He sat at the table, next to where Rosline would usually sit. Astoria continued pacing until the door creaked open.

Rosline rushed to it to open it fully and bowed before saying, "Milady Eleanor, this is Astoria. Astoria, this is my lady and the head of the house, Eleanor."

Eleanor smiled at Rosline before her face sported an inquiring look. "I was told you were an important guest."

Astoria gave a slight nod, but Rosline saw she was uncertain how to approach the topic. "I don't know if you recall, but years ago, I was a friend of— of Sehren. I was a younger lass then."

Eleanor scrutinized her for a bit before she got a shrewd look on her face, "I recall something of the sort. Barmaid, yes?"

"I was."

"And now?"

"Astoria has spent many years out of the city," interrupted Jaks. "And is the last person to have had contact with Sehren."

Eleanor's eyes widened with exuberance, before she looked over the lass. "Is he well?"

"He is—" Astoria's voice cracked a bit before she said, "he's at peace."

"Why didn't he return with you?"

"Too many things," said Astoria, pulling a pouch from her back. "Namely, these things." She pulled out the two coiled parchments and handed them to Eleanor.

She read them silently, her face becoming more surprised as she did. When she finished, her eyes shone, and she said with a deep sigh, "And he won't return."

Astoria shook her head.

Eleanor looked at Jaks and Rosline. Rosline said, "From what I understand, he is unable to."

425

"Right." Eleanor almost crumpled the papers in her hand before she coiled them up and returned them to Astoria. "And you traveled all this way to share this with me for what reason, exactly?"

"Jaks told me you might have an answer to my quandary, and that is something I am very interested in finding."

"What quandary?" Eleanor took her seat at the head of the table before the door opened again and Railand stepped inside. He took post behind her to her left, his eyes scanning Astoria.

Rosline sat beside Eleanor, with Jaks at her side. "Come Astoria, sit."

"I'm fine standin', thanks," said Astoria in an agitated tone.

"Jaks may have misinformed you," started Eleanor. "I don't have anything I can truly offer you, even if you came to explain to me about my husband."

"I haven't asked my question," said Astoria. Rosline watched Eleanor's mouth thin to a line.

"Please forgive her, she's been out of the city for a while," said Rosline. "I don't think she meant to offend."

"I wasn't aware royalty could offend the masses," said Astoria curtly, drawing confused looks from all of them, except for Jaks who simply smirked.

"Royalty?"

Astoria nodded, "Royalty. I have royal blood in my veins."

Shock ran through Rosline as she watched the pair of them stare at one another. It was so quiet she felt she could have heard a pin drop.

"Preposterous," said Eleanor.

Astoria was about to answer when Jaks said, "It's true. It's why Sehren took her north. She was endangered by several different factions within the city, and the only course of action I thought prudent to protect her was to send her with one of the city's best knights."

"And you came back? For what reason?"

"Because the kingdom wouldn't let us live in peace," retorted Astoria.

426

It grew tense. Rosline felt uneasy as Eleanor rested her hand on her chin. She raised her eyebrow, "Well, go on."

Astoria took a breath, "We were at peace, and then something... something happened. The people of the north took the poisoned words of a man named Ricard and—" she clenched her teeth as she stopped at the table. "They came for me. And Sehren wouldn't let them."

"Ricard?" Eleanor sat back, her face becoming blank as she said, "Where is my husband?" her tone was dangerous, almost daring Astoria to answer.

"Milady?" asked Rosline with a solicitous look.

"He's... he's gone. Dead."

"I don't believe it," said Eleanor. Her voice was quiet, deathly so.

"I still don't some nights either," admitted Astoria. She brushed her face with the back of her hand. Rosline wanted to go and hug her, but Eleanor watched Astoria as though she had personally killed him. "But he is. Because of this," she pulled the pouch out again, this time pulling out a small ledger and sliding it across the table to Rosline. Rosline promptly passed it to Eleanor, who leafed it open before her eyes widened again.

"So it is true. You bear the king's blood." Eleanor's tone had changed. It was contemplative and conniving.

Rosline had heard it before. She swallowed hard as she looked back at Astoria, who was simply nodding.

"They came for me because they were afraid of the king coming for me," said Astoria. "And Sehren fought them. He would've won, but there were too many things we didn't know. Things—" she caught her breath, "Things I didn't do."

Astoria straightened, her voice tight, "The king's men did this, all of this."

"So what is it you want?"

"I want your help so that they can never do it again. I want to change it."

Rosline saw the zeal in Astoria's eyes as she uttered, "I want to make them pay for Sehren."

Eleanor smiled at her, her eyes sparkling as though she was seeing her for the first time. "Very well. I think I can help with that. Rosline?"

"Milady?" asked Rosline in a small voice.

"Send a courier to Lord Greyfield. Tell him I wish to have dinner with him." Eleanor scanned Astoria, who looked surprised. "Tell him I've found the person that can help us fix the kingdom from within."

Rosline nodded stiffly, looking at Astoria as though she didn't recognize the woman. So intent was her gaze that she didn't see the glittering eyes of Jaks beside her, his own smile wicked on his face.

ASTORIA.

Astoria sat on the balcony, her mind teeming as she watched the small figures ambling through the lanes. She was wrapped in a cloak as she watched, her eyes flickering through every small movement she noticed. A dragonfly landed on the banister, its wings lightly fluttering as it rested. Astoria watched it for several moments before returning her gaze to the people down below. Their voices echoed throughout the avenues, and occasionally, Astoria would hear a laugh or shout, the source unseen behind the high fences of Eleanor's estate.

Even despite her wariness, Astoria couldn't place a feeling of danger past her paranoia. And with each passing day and each moment she found herself in the city, that feeling lessened. She had first thought there would be many eyes on her, that her movements would be known after returning to the city. In times like these, however, when she was able to listen to the city and hear the people around her, she came to realize that it wasn't possible. And that discovery had jarred her, had put a disquiet within her that prodded and stoked a question in her mind.

Why did we have to leave?

The door beside her opened. Astoria reflexively reached for the blade tucked at her side before seeing the flickering wings of the dragonfly flutter by as it flew away from her.

"It's a nice evening, isn't it?" asked Rosline. She swept her dress beneath her legs as she took a seat in a chair. "The breeze is light, but you can taste the winter on it."

Astoria nodded, thinking that it was a bit too warm for autumn to be coming to a close. "It's loud."

"The breeze?" Rosline cocked her head, puzzled.

"The city," she replied, tucking her head on her arms. "It's awfully noisy."

"I imagine anything would sound noisy after living away from everyone for so long."

Astoria nodded "Aye, that's true."

Rosline gave her a small smile, "What was it like, Astoria?"

"What?"

"The north. The lands you lived in." She brushed her hair behind her ear, "The wilds. I only saw them seldomly, but they looked so enchanting."

Her face cracked into a smile, "They were. They had a beauty to them, wild as they were, but definitely beautiful."

"Do you miss them?"

"I don't know," stated Astoria plainly.

"And the people?"

"You mean the northerners or the Senkamans?" the last word stung Astoria's throat as she said it.

"Aren't both the same?"

"You'd start a fight saying that to either of 'em," replied Astoria. "They're not keen on one another."

Rosline looked contemplative for a moment, "Both, then."

Astoria heard the inquisitiveness in Rosline's voice, the familiarity of it another confusing wave from the past. She took a deep breath, "The northerners are honest, hard-working folk with a real no-nonsense look on things. They don't have time for much outside of what needs doing and plannin' for what needs to be done. It's different than here; they don't really care for much outside of each other and their homes, and it seemed like everyone loved workin' together to keep that going."

Astoria took another breath, "The Senkamans, they were a different sort. They're hard-working too, but in a different way, I think. And they're high-minded of themselves and not really having an understanding of others, especially southerners. There's a word for that…"

"Haughty?" offered Rosline.

Astoria shrugged, "I guess. They had their own things to worry about, but crossing over their lands having any kind of blood outside of theirs was almost a reason for war." Astoria grit her teeth, "They were supposedly warm and honorable, but I don't really know. Not from what I saw."

Rosline saw that she touched something there, Astoria's voice possessing a growl as she spoke. She cleared her throat, "I'm sorry, Astoria."

"For what?"

"That I brought it up. I'm feeling foolish, thinking back on it." Rosline wrung her hands for a few moments.

"You were curious."

"I should have been considerate."

Astoria cocked her head, "I get that. But you weren't trying to be mean. You were just trying to hear a story or two."

"Yeah. Like before, at the Friar's."

Silence crossed between them both as Astoria considered her words. Rosline also seemed put out as well at its mention but with another clearing of her throat, she said, "Like the days we used to just talk about things."

"Those days have passed for a while," said Astoria.

"That doesn't mean it can't be that way again."

"What happened to your eyes?" Rosline grew quiet as Astoria's gaze returned to the avenues. The silence grew long. Astoria smirked into her arms and said, "I told you they had passed."

"It's not something easy to talk about."

"I thought you wanted it to be."

"It—"

"Doesn't just affect her and you," called Jaks' voice as he stepped out onto the balcony. Astoria glanced up at him, not surprised to see him smirking at her as he closed the door behind him. "Rosline's service to Eleanor requires that she maintains a matter of confidence between the two of them. Even simple questions would have to be carefully considered, especially in the world they dabble in. And that was not what I would consider a simple question."

Astoria raised an eyebrow at him before glancing back at Rosline, "Neither is askin' about before."

"It does seem like you have indeed taken on the mantle of the glum one," said Jaks as he moved to the banister. He pulled out his pipe and, after a few moments, bathed his face in an orange glow as he took a deep pull of it. Blowing out the smoke behind him, he said, "You've been here but only a few moments, with a warm bed, delicious food, and familiar company, yet even that doesn't seem able to lift the smile on your face."

Astoria broke his gaze as she listened to the other voices out in the streets, "That's not a simple question."

"And yet, I pride myself on having answers for them." Jaks took another smoke, his glittering eyes set upon Astoria. When she looked back to him and saw the solicitous gleam in them, she caught her voice in her throat.

"It's exactly as you say," she started, pushing past the lump in her throat. "I've a warm bed here, with good food that I don't have to wonder about gettin'. There's a safe place to be and more all here, nestled away in this home and yet, there was the desperate flight. The rush of takin' me away from it, in hopes of findin' another place that's exactly like it." She clutched her arms tight around her legs, "So then why? Why did it have to end up this way? Why risk ourselves, everything we had, when we could've been here all along?"

Jaks tapped the pipe on the banister. He wiped away the ash, "You read why he couldn't stay, Astoria."

She shook her head into her arms again.

Jaks scanned her, "Ah. Guilt rests on you because you wonder why you yourself had to leave."

Astoria, through tear-filled eyes, looked up at him. Understanding crossed his face as Rosline looked as though she wanted to hug her.

"Your flight from this place, this kingdom, doesn't make sense when you can amble down to the garden and grab a peach for your delight. Or when you consider your ability to meander about the grounds, or rest in the study, or any other myriad of idyllic things that could so occupy your day."

"We fought so hard, Jaks. There were times we were so cold, so desperate, that I hated him." Her heart ached with her admission as more tears streamed down her face, "I thought constantly that there would be daggers everywhere, that any day I went out I'd be at risk. I convinced myself that the danger was here, that going to the north, to those blasted lands, was the best choice we had. So then why? Why can I sleep at night here, knowing nothing awaits me outside my chamber door? It doesn't…" she sniffed.

"The most mundane things don't seem to make sense, Astoria. Even if the answer is so apparent before you." Jaks sat beside her, taking care to leave distance between them. He blew more smoke out, wafting it away from her as he continued, "You think yourself selfish because you don't see what awaits you out in the avenues. You fail to grasp just what I've had to do to secure your lodgings, who I had to silence because their eyes were too watchful. You lack the understanding of who had to disappear just because they asked the wrong questions."

Astoria regarded him for a moment, dread in her stomach.

"You learned so much about the world away from here but even though you told me what the kingdom has done, what it did to rob you of your peace, you fail to see just how your presence here has stirred up the nest." He let out more smoke, "You've been here but a short time. And while your timing could not have been better, at least in terms of securing your lodgings, you don't understand what's happening around you. What, do you think Eleanor would have housed you when everything was first discovered? When the same vipers that sought her were the ones that cornered you?"

Astoria flinched in the tonal change of his voice, the condescension clear in the air. "I could've—"

"Fought? With what training?" Jaks raised his eyebrow, "And to what end? Were you to make enemies of everyone just to paint a target on a woman who was merely fulfilling her husband's parting wish?" He shook his head, chuckling, "No, no Astoria. It's simply not how this works. Even now I am making sure that people understand that Leanne and only Leanne has come to call. I admit, it's been a rather long time since I've had to work this much."

Astoria clenched her hands so tightly, she could feel the blood being squeezed from them. Rosline approached Astoria and knelt before her as she unwrapped the bandana from around her eyes. Astoria looked up, and saw that her eyes were different than she remembered. "I've felt your frustration, Astoria. I truly have. To say that I've just spent the years idly by in Lady Eleanor's home would be a lie." She paused before reaching out to Astoria. Astoria slid her hand down, grasping Rosline's hand. "I've seen what happens in the night, in the background. When everyone thinks no one is watching, I've witnessed what occurs in the dark. Jaks is right: there are things you don't know or understand, and that's not your fault. I— I still have trouble accepting it at times, but this is how things work. And Jaks has indeed spent many nights working on keeping things out of harm's way."

"The fact that you haven't seen anything is a testament to my efficacy, Astoria," said Jaks. "And I admit I find much pride in it."

"That means... I have to stay here then." She sighed. "You can't get me a job in the city for something, anything, that'll get my mind off things?"

Jaks gave her a sad smile as he shook his head, "Alas, Astoria, at this time and juncture, that simply wouldn't be a sound decision."

434

"But I thought that you had kept things under wraps."

"For the most part. There are still elements in the kingdom that I don't have the full means of mitigating or controlling." He let out a chuckle, "However, I do know that in time, that will be remedied too."

"What do you mean?"

"In time, Astoria. For now, take a few moments to consider where you are and consider how much you desire to follow through with your plan. If you still do, then we will have a talk again." Jaks rose, dumping the remnants of his pipe onto the floor of the balcony and brushing them away with his boot. "And try to be kinder to Rosline. Out of everyone here, she is the one who missed you the most."

He departed, but not before giving Rosline a kiss on the cheek. They could hear his heeled boots knocking against the floor as he walked down the hallway. Astoria sat back for a moment, regarding Rosline as she let out a sigh.

"Does this life work?" asked Astoria quietly.

"You get used to it," replied Rosline. "But know that we are both trying to help you the best we can."

"Do you think Eleanor hates me?"

Rosline shook her head, "No, I think you've just reminded her of another time, and she's still sorting what exactly to make of you."

Astoria traced her finger on the floor. It grew quiet, with the sounds of the people echoing through the streets.

"Would you like to meet my daughter, Astoria?" asked Rosline.

Astoria perked up lightly, "The little girl? I have."

"I meant, in a more familiar capacity. She's been curious about you but I told her to keep some distance as you got settled in."

Astoria glanced over the courtyard. "What are you plannin' on telling her?"

"That you're an old friend of mine who was out of the city for a while. She'll be curious though, so if you don't wish to have to answer too many questions, we can push it for another time."

Astoria stood up and dusted herself off. Resting her hand on the hilt of her sword she said, "No, that's fine. I should be gettin' used to it anyways."

Rosline smiled at her, "Thank you."

"What's her name?"

"Kyrah."

"And she belongs to you and Jaks, right?"

Rosline blushed slightly as she nodded, "Aye, she does."

Astoria let out a short laugh as she said, "All right. Let's meet her."

CONTACT.

A voice sounded through the silence, resonant and clear as the winter wind on a chiming bell. It was pointed and sharp, almost threatening to tear the silence asunder with its simple phrase.

"What are you doing?"

Sehren was staggered by the call, by the voice he'd almost forgotten in the decades. He turned to face the voice, and his surprise was palpable before him.

Caine stood, garbed in knightly regalia, the same regalia Sehren had donned for a decade. He walked dutifully, with purpose and conviction in every step. Drawing before Sehren, he watched him curiously, his face drawn as though to chastise a child.

Sehren met him, willing away from the aching within him. "Pa?"

"What are you doing, Sehren?"

He didn't know.

"Indecision?" Caine shook his head, "That's not a common thing for you."

"I am not indecisive. I am conflicted."

"Is there a difference? Hesitation stems from uncertainty. You know that." Caine moved to stand beside Sehren, gazing out over the field. He was roughly Sehren's height, and in his regalia Sehren could have mistaken him for a member of the order he'd once served with. "It's a strange thing, isn't it?"

"What?"

"This," he gestured before him, and Sehren's gaze was pulled, back from the farmlands, to the kingdom and lands beyond. Sehren felt dizzy as the expanses rolled around them, but Caine's gaze stood transfixed until everything settled.

"I am not sure what you mean."

"Sehren," he looked over his son, "you marched these lands. Do you not remember them?"

"I tried to forget them."

"Why?"

"What do you mean, 'why?'?" Sehren answered, incensed.

Caine smiled at his tone, "There's the boy I raised."

"That boy has been gone for a long time."

Caine laughed, "Has he?"

"Aye. He became something more."

Caine laughed again, "He is the same, then." His gaze trailed back over the lands, "You tried to forget them."

Annoyance, an odd emotion, rippled through Sehren as he looked out, "I wanted to."

"Yet you didn't." Caine reached down and touch the ground beneath them.

"I wasn't able to."

Caine scooped up some of the dirt, running it in his hands, "You are. You didn't want to. Your blood is in this soil, in the lands of the kingdom."

"I have wasted much of my blood upon the lands of the kingdom," said Sehren, anger filling his voice.

438

"And yet I am certain if you marched the lands again, you'd find them as familiar as they were when you were a boy."

"It is a hard thing to forget where you were maimed, injured, and pained."

"It is," he said. The scene shifted once more, the shadows stretching to an expanse of farmland. "Is there a reason to forget it?"

Caine rose, and Sehren saw he no longer wore the regalia of the knight, but instead the attire of the farmer. He walked through the fields, lush and overflowing with vegetation, his face set in a proud smile. "You didn't forget these lands."

"Why would I?"

"You lost much and suffered much here as well," he said. "We all did."

"It was home. Why would I forget it?"

"Home," said Caine, his voice shifting. "Yes. That is hard to forget. It was our home. The one we chose and made, not the one we were born in."

An unsteadiness flowed through Caine's voice as he spoke.

"Why did you let them take her?"

The scene shifted, becoming stark black again. Caine looked hollowed and worn, the same way he looked weeks before his death. "Take her?"

"Ma." Sehren felt seething anger seeping into him. His limbs burned as he felt lightning running through him.

"She left on her own." Caine met his accusing gaze, smiling sadly. He looked around the landscape, the farmlands overgrown and untended with their ashen quality giving them a withered look. "She chose to leave."

"Why? You could have fought."

"There was no point."

"There is always a point. Things could have been different. She could have fought against whomever came to our home."

"Like you did?"

Blood thundered in Sehren's head. He stepped to his father, staring him in his eyes. His dark eyes that were filled with neither accusation or guilt, but calm consideration. *"I did fight."*

"You died." It was calm, objective, with no emotion, nothing in it to hint disapproval or praise.

"You let her leave."

"Danika was of her own will, Sehren. From the way we were wed to the way you were to be raised. Nothing I could've done would've changed her mind."

"You were weak," he said, accusing his father. He recoiled, the rush of defiance and resentment for the man unfamiliar to him.

"There he is," said Caine, an empathic gleam in his eye. *"The boy I raised. You've been angry for years."*

"You gave up. You stopped fighting."

"You kept fighting. And in the end, we both died."

Sehren scowled, *"I fought as best as I could. I promised to protect her, and I did."*

"Aye. You did. Just as I promised to stand by Danika's decisions."

Sehren felt a moment of clarity. As he looked over his father, he saw in him the man he could've become. *"I was weak."*

Caine shook his head, his face becoming stern again, *"How many times do I have to tell you, Sehren? You are neither strong nor weak. Those are mantles that people give themselves to bolster their faltering skills or to excuse their lackluster dedication."* His gaze went over the lands again, *"No, you simply just are. You are strong of arm, sharp of mind. You possess foresight and boundless constitution. You are resolute and determined. You are also lacking of faith, and of poor courtesy. You are inwardly focused and unconcerned with the affairs of others."*

Caine drew up to his height as the hollowness of his features faded away. *"None of that makes you strong or weak."*

"I failed when it mattered most."

"Perhaps, but then, is everyone that fails weak? Is Astoria weak for faltering in her actions because of her consideration? Does your heart seethe at her?"

Sehren shook his head determinedly "No. Never. She did what she could muster."

"Aye, as did you. Why does that make you weak?"

Sehren flinched as memories flashed over his mind's eye. He recalled being a boy with tears in his eyes as his mother left off for her hunts. Ones that she never took him along on. He thought himself too weak or not helpful, but his father had reminded him.

He had been a boy.

"A boy, Sehren. Not weak. And a man whose strength didn't fail. You simply are."

"I could be more."

"More than what?" Caine crossed his arms over his chest, a disapproving look on his face. "You cling to this ideal of being something more than you are."

"The ideal you taught me."

"Do not confuse what you learned from others for what I taught you. I taught you better than that," Caine chastised. "You can choose to fight or you can choose to let go. Neither will change who you are, and the sooner you remember and accept that then the quicker you will learn to muster it. Have you forgotten?"

"I am not sure. I was a knight, I was a husband. I was... her protector." The words cut in his throat as he spoke them.

"You were also a son, a farm boy, an orphan..." said Caine. "And everything in between and after that. All of those are you. A life filled with many facets of the world. And yet, I would imagine there's far more to learn. However, If you don't wish to learn what else you are, then there's no more need to fight. You can let it go."

"And if I find that I cannot?"

Caine smiled, a wide smile filled with pride, "Then you are remembering who you are. You are remembering what fills you so. And if you cannot let that go, then don't."

EPILOGUE.

Far in the north, a ruined encampment laid nestled in a scorched grove of trees. Some of the trees were black with ash, burned and dead, while others had budded new branches from their burned sides. Remnants of a worked wood fence rimmed the grove, scorched and crumbling. Shoots and sprouts pushed their way through the soil, and the once worked dirt overflowed with long spiraling plants. Several large pieces of hide and leather, strung from tree to tree, were worn and weathered away, their edges coated with soot and ash. Overtop a flowing creek was a wooden-stand, with the remnants of a mesh net dangling in the rushing water. In the center of the clearing was a tangle of charred logs and sticks, with the grass beneath it burned away to the dirt. Even there, sprigs of short, stubby grass had slowly pushed its way through.

Nature had reclaimed the camp, with many thickets of tall grass scattered about. Trails of a variety of animals were woven through the encampment. The bounty of nature was full and fresh here. Birds sang in the trees as they watched the other animals wander into the clearing.

A pack of elk rested in the comfortable shade of the tree branches. They pulled the new shoots through the soil, munching away contentedly as the sun's rays slipped through the canopy. Several of them took long drinks from the creek, their eyes turned to and fro for any oncoming threats. The land was vast, untamed, and even the slightest lapse in attention for a moment could spell demise.

Not here though. There was no scent of a predator in the air, no hint of rumbling growls on the breeze. It was calm and peaceful. A place of respite. The wild growth beneath the trees had few tracks through them, and in the untamed land, it was a trove of sustenance and peace.

Suddenly, one of the deer cocked their head, sniffing the air. Their head turned left and right, as if trying to see something, but even as their nose wiggled and their ears twitched, it couldn't seem to find what had disturbed it. It cocked its head once more, but a shiver up its neck spurred it to sprint off, the rest of the herd following behind it with bounding leaps.

The darkened spot in the center in the camp seemed to grow darker, as if the shadow beneath the boughs of the tree was becoming thicker. It was imperceptible at first, almost as if the sun itself set and the horizon was darkening, but slowly it gathered as a thickening of the gloom filled the encampment. The gloom grew, shrouding the clearing in darkness. It continued to deepen, rising up from the ground almost as if being willed. It shifted and contorted for a long while, before suddenly becoming still.

From it, clinging with the shadow, clawed a form fighting against the clutching shades, as though the darkness was trying to drag it back in. It pulled against the ground as it broke free. The gloom cleared away almost as suddenly as it appeared. The form was breathing, each breath haggard and labored, accompanied by stinging coughs. As they cleared their lungs and took a deep breath, their eyes opened, revealing piercing grey. It sat up, looking incredulously at their arms and hands. He shook as he tried to stand, only to find himself stumbling back to the ground. Each movement was punctuated with stiffness, as if the actions were unfamiliar. Slowly, he found purchase upon the ground and sat up before rising once more. With a stretch and stagger he shook himself as if trying to clear the confines of his body.

His gaze peered around the encampment, slowly and methodically. Disbelief was evident in his demeanor. He reached down, cautiously at first, and scooped some of the earth into his hand. Fingers ran across the soft soil, uncertain. He spied the small bugs in the soil, teeming with life as they crawled through the dirt. His gaze trailed off, spying the shoots pushing through the earth and the budding on the trees.

With another clearing of his throat, he spit upon the ground, eyeing the darkened and scorched earth around him. Grey eyes looked over the ruined camp.

"She went home," said Sehren, clearing his throat once more. His voice was hoarse and heavy, but with another cough, he said, "It is time I did as well."

Glossary

There are several terms utilized by characters in the book which can be translated as below.

Senkaman

Domref: home

Davoarth: literally, ravenous bear. An ursine creature of immense might

Cesogez: chieftain; can refer to the united clan chieftain, or family head of a clan

Eiravuk: literally, winter wolf. A canid creature of cunning intellect.

Hyolih: literally many thanks

Javeaf: literally hellwinter; Senkaman term for the war with Candrama

Kruparu: blood challenge; blood means both in regards to heritage and deathmatch

Krusho: literally blood guard; members of the clan sworn to protect the successor

Ostwyn: literally, blade maiden; women who hold the combat traditions of their clan

Otedien: untamed; land that has never been settled

Svewyll: terror of the north; scourge

Tyljete: naive, or foolish child; equates to idiot

Tywaed: literally true-blooded; Senkamans with roots to the ancestral families.

Duhoviman

Talica: my child; my dear

Dorna zara a obilia: literally, good for the family.

AFTERWORD.

Greetings,

Nadir, much like Descrial before it, was completed only a few months after the release of my previous book. I had much of the groundwork prepared before I had released Descrial. However, with everything that happened during the pandemic, I found myself uninspired and severely under-motivated to complete it thoroughly.

I found my motivation in the place that had begun my foray into writing: bringing something to entertain others. It has been a hard couple of years for many of us, so I hope that in reading *Nadir*, you had a moment of respite and enjoyment.

The Rite of Kings is quickly coming to an end. I find it hard to believe that it has been five years since the release of *Tenebrous*, but with hopefully one more book remaining, I'll look back fondly on this adventure. And once more, I thank you for coming along this journey with Astoria, Sehren and myself.

Hyolih,

-Gabriel Renteria

www.ingramcontent.com/pod-product-compliance
Lightning Source LLC
Chambersburg PA
CBHW020459260626
47156CB00006B/1782